Memories of an Emerald World

Michael Bleriot

MacGregor Books, Inc
Washington DC MMXI

The following is a work of fiction.
Any resemblance to persons living or dead is coincidental

Cover art by Allison Mattice

ISBN: 0983375100
ISBN-13: 978-0983375104
Library of Congress Control Number: 2011929096

Printed in the United States of America

Memories of an Emerald World

Works by Michael Bleriot

Memories of an Emerald World

The Jungle Express

Flying Naked

To Frederick and Eleanor
who taught us to love books

Contents

Prologue ix
1. Welcome 3
2 Panama 39
3 Panama 2 47
4 The Problem with Panamanians 73
5 Peligro 81
6 A Cast of Many 93
7 Chuck 103
8 Imposible 119
9 Flight 143
10 Howard 155
11 Flight 2 163
12 Grandy 177
13 Flight 3 183
14 Checkride 197
15 Declan 241
16 Driving 249
17 Tamanaco 261
18 Isla San Telmo 281
19 Snakes 311
20 Flutie 321
21 Billie 359
22 Billie 2 367
23 The Importance of Being Ernest 393
24 Christmas 431

Prologue

THE OTHER JET knifed across the sky from our four o'clock, moving fast but slowing as it cut across our windscreen. When it stopped right in the center that meant we were on a collision course.

"One last time," my instructor said from the back seat. "You may never get another chance so do this right."

"This" was a rejoin, whereby I caught up to the other jet and parked myself next to his wing. By "right" he meant do it his way. The Air Force way to effect a rejoin of two fighter jets four miles apart was to draw near the other aircraft slowly and transition in a careful, controlled manner from my 500 mph speed to his 400 mph so that at the end of the maneuver we were flying together three feet apart. It wasn't easy. Imagine two Ferraris chasing each other down an interstate at a hundred and fifty miles per hour – then triple the speed and take away the interstate.

That was the Air Force way to do a rejoin. My instructor's method was less subtle. His nickname was Chumley, and Chumley's technique was to haul ass as close to the other plane as possible, then bank sharply and pull back on the stick until everything from our nose to tail shuddered from the braking action as though we were barreling over wake-up strips on the highway.

"You sure it'll work?" I asked, watching the beautiful lines of the white T-38 trainer ahead of me grow larger in the window. The T-38 had Coke bottle curves and a pointed nose that made it look graceful, even delicate, in flight. It was the aircraft equivalent of a deer: sleek, fast, and hard to catch.

"It will if you do it right," Chumley said. "If you do it wrong – well, just remember your ejection procedures."

We screamed toward our wingman with a hundred miles per hour of overtake. He was in a turn and so were we, enough that I had to peer over the bottom of the window just to see him. If we hit him it would be in the back of his aircraft, behind the wing and alongside one of the two engines that was streaming blow-torch heat. I hoped we wouldn't hit him.

When the picture grew too large for me to stand it any more I took a deep breath, banked farther, and pulled. Our nose came up and our wingman dropped from sight. G-forces pressed me into the seat. The whole plane shook like a paint mixer as the T-38 tried to stall. One-potato, two-potato, three-potato, four..., I counted.

I rolled back to the right and looked outside, half-expecting to see the other cockpit coming right at my face mask. But it wasn't. Our closure rate had dropped to nothing. We were twenty feet away, moving along now at 400 mph and with our vector parallel to his instead of right at him. With the slightest nudge on the stick I could slide us into position. Chumley's technique had worked.

"Told you," he said.

We cleared off from our wingman and proceeded solo to the south, high above the desert along the Arizona-Mexico border. It was my last flight in training: except for that final bit of formation practice Chumley decided to take it easy on me by flying a whirlwind tour of the state. We flew for a while in silence watching the brown, bone-dry ground below us slip by.

"That's good air," he said suddenly.

We were at 40,000 feet, setting up for a "boom ride" where we would light the afterburners to accelerate past the speed of sound. But while I was watching our Mach indicator Chumley was looking south. He knew that my orders would arrive within the week and that my first assignment out of training was to a base in South America, to a much slower aircraft that would never break the sound barrier and never perform rejoins as we had just done. Although as a true fighter pilot he believed there were no other planes worth mentioning, my assignment made him curious. He had never flown anything slow and he had never been south of the Rio Grande. Through the intercom and the oxygen mask I heard wistfulness in his voice.

"That's good air."

"What do you mean, sir?"

He sat behind me so when I looked in the mirror I could see only his face mask and a gloved hand that pointed to our right.

"There's a lot of nothing down there," he explained. "The First World stops here, right on this border below us. You go down there – it's open airspace. There are no controllers, no radars, no jet routes, no prohibited areas – hell, there are hardly any planes. It's the Wild West. You can do whatever you want down there."

I scanned the horizon, which at 40,000 feet was bigger than I'd ever noticed. To me, my new assignment seemed a mistake. For days I had considered asking the personnel folks to change it to something less exotic, something more in line with a "normal" Air Force career. "You think so?" I asked.

"I know so," he assured me. "You can be a pilot."

I dropped the nose and watched our airspeed climb past 500mph.

"Isn't that what I'm doing right now?"

"No," he said, gazing out over the Mexican desert to the horizon.

Our Mach indicator waffled near 1.0. Outside on our wings a shock wave built up, built higher, and then slipped away with a violence we didn't feel. Down on the ground, the few people within fifty miles heard the explosion.

I jiggled the controls which had suddenly become loose. They didn't work as well supersonic.

"What's wrong with the flying we're doing now?" I asked.

"Oh, nothing," Chumley sighed. "Except you're never alone. Don't get me wrong: flying upside down, pulling G's – this is good stuff. But up here you're never alone. You're always on someone's radar. You're always in formation. You're always being watched.

And you never go anywhere. You go up, pretend to fight bad guys or fly racetracks, then you land again where you took off. On a runway that's two miles long and on a big fat air force base."

"And down there?"

"Down there," he said, looking south, "you won't have anyone hold your hand. Look out there – look at that sky. And the ground below it is just as big. You're going to a whole continent where nobody will even know what you're doing. No radars, no controllers, and hardly anyone else in the sky. In the next few years you're going to find yourself in a lot of places where nobody is around to tell you what to do. Then you'll get to be a pilot."

I slowed the jet through the sound barrier again and turned us toward the field. The T-38 carried only an hour and a half of fuel. Our needle was pushing Empty so I drew a straight line toward home. Chumley was imagining me being lost on a continent – hell, I was nervous a hundred miles from the airport. I glanced back at the border.

"I'm not so sure about that," I told him. "I barely know what I'm doing right now."

"Get used to it," he said wryly. "It's a big world you're going to down there." He, too, looked back. "That's good air."

Caribbean Sea
HONDURAS
Tegucigalpa
NICARAGUA
Managua
San José
COSTA RICA
Panama
PANAMA
Isla de San Andrés (COLOMBIA)
Isla de Malpelo (COLOMBIA)
Martinique (FRANCE)
ST. LUCIA
BARBADOS
ST. VINCENT AND THE GRENADINES
GRENADA
Aruba (NETH.)
Netherlands Antilles (NETH.)
Barranquilla
Cartagena
Maracaibo
Caracas
Valencia
Barquisimeto
Port-of-Spain
TRINIDAD AND TOBAGO
Cúcuta
San Cristóbal
Ciudad Guayana
VENEZUELA
Georgetown
GUYANA
Paramaribo
SURINAME
French Guiana (FRANCE)
Medellín
Bogotá
COLOMBIA
Cali
ANDES
GUIANA HIGHLANDS
Boa Vista
Macapá
Quito
Equator
ECUADOR
Guayaquil
AMAZON
Manaus
Santarém
Iquitos
BASIN
Piura
Trujillo
Huánuco
Rio Branco
Pôrto Velho
BRAZIL
PERU
Lima
Cusco
Arequipa
La Paz
BOLIVIA
Trinidad
MATO GROSSO PLATEAU
Cuiabá
South Pacific
80
60
0

Memories of an Emerald World

1. Welcome

"GOOD PILOTS LIKE to fly low."

Walt said it as a matter of fact but I vowed to ponder his words later. We were skimming the jungle like a hungry pelican over a California beach and my eyes were too glued to the windscreen to think of anything else. The land passed in a green blur. We couldn't fly lower unless we wanted to drop the gear and taxi the plane across the Colombian border. There were things I wanted to say, most involving an increase in altitude, but didn't.

It was a year and a half after my flight with Chumley. I had finally gotten to South America and was now in a new plane with a new instructor, neither of which resembled the old. Far from being sleek and fast like the T-38, the C-27 was a squat cargo plane driven by two propellers. It maneuvered great but great for a cargo plane, not for a fighter. It was less like a deer and more like a baby seal. It even looked like a baby seal with a rounded black nose, wide-eyed cockpit windows, and a tubular body to store its pallets.

Walt was also a world away from the loud, lumbering Chumley. Sitting across the cockpit from me with an instrument panel between us, he was short and skinny and flew hunched over the controls like an old lady driving –an old lady driving and having a great time, but still an old lady. And where Chumley oozed nonchalance with every maneuver, determined to affect fighter pilot diffidence, Walt was the picture of enthusiasm. He greeted every new piece of airspace like a kid opening presents.

As I watched, he banked the plane hard left and pushed over to dive us into a ravine. Trees rushed up on both sides. *"Oh, Diegel!..."* he sang in a reckless falsetto. "Where *aaarrrrre* you, buddy? We know you're in here *some*where..."

My right hand moved to the controls and hovered, ready to grab them if he lost control and we plunged toward the ground. I didn't need this. Chumley had done crazy things, too, but at 20,000 feet. Now only a month after getting to Panama I had an instructor goofing off just a football field from the ground.

But Walt flew well. This was only our second flight together but it was clear he knew his way around a cockpit. More subtle than Chumley but just as confident, he finessed the aircraft when he could and forced it when he couldn't – and the plane always went where he told it to go. The bit of aviation philosophy came out more as a personal motto than a moral dictum. He was good.

What I didn't know was how smart he was.

"Look, a Tree of Cortez!"

He popped up fifty feet and banked sharply to the right so we could get a good look at the burst of gold foliage from the tree in question. Behind us the loadmaster tipped in his seat and cackled with delight. I looked out the side window. Our wingtip seemed to scrape its way through the forest the way one draws in the dirt with a stick. I looked straight down but couldn't see the jungle floor, so close together were the trees. They stood like blades of grass, so interwoven there was no way to distinguish one from the other. They were also two hundred feet tall which meant we were at most three hundred feet from the ground.

"You'll have to come right," I advised. My thumb pressed into the map on my knee both to mark our position and to keep my hand from trembling. "We're four miles left of course. We'll never find the airfield if we stay here."

"The course is a straight line, Mike. This is the scenic route." Walt smiled from the left seat. He made a point of turning his head to do it so I could see he was no longer looking out front. "Besides, you may have to find your way here by yourself next time."

He rolled level. We dipped into a depression and caromed out the other side. The jungle flattened out. A sea of unending green began.

We were leaving the foothills of the Andes. The Amazon stretched before us to the horizon and beyond. There was still terrain out there: valleys, canyons, cliffs, waterfalls, and rivers that cut through the jungle as thin as a wire or as wide as a city, but the foliage was so thick you would never see any of it until you were right overhead. From low altitude the jungle was as flat and infinite as if we lay on our stomachs in an alfalfa field and looked at the world from plant level. Finding our way over it looking for checkpoints was like navigating the Atlantic by watching for waves.

Behind me the loadmaster cackled again. A short, balding Puerto Rican with the shape of a torpedo, he had more hours in the air than some birds. Thus his nickname. Bird lived for new pilots. Not that I was new but I was new to this. My flying experience had thus far consisted of flying jet routes and taking off and landing at major airports. Looking for a dirt strip surrounded by hundreds of miles of jungle was a novelty for me. I was nervous.

And for good reason. A scraping sound from below made me stiffen. We had brushed the growth on a ridge that was invisible in the early morning shadows.

Walt shrugged as we soared past the ridge and into the canyon on the far side. "Sorry."

Bird slapped my arm.

"Hey, sir, you gotta relax! The captain knows what he's doing." He wasn't even looking outside. Maybe that was the way to do it. "At least I hope you do," he said to Walt, "'cause I'm not walking home through no stinking jungle. I'm not up for no Rambo stuff."

Walt was testing me, I knew. It was likely he flew this way whenever he had the chance but almost certainly the low altitude was for my benefit. Watching the trees race by so close I could pull petals off the dangling orchids, I heard reason argue that there was a fine line between exciting and stupid – and we seemed to be on the wrong side of the line.

But I reminded myself that I had signed on for the flying. My T-38 days were more than a year behind me. In the intervening time the Air Force had stuck me in a C-5, an aircraft so large that getting it to fly was like maneuvering the Queen Mary out of port and only half as interesting. In fact, the C-5 was heavy, slow, and boring. It had taken me twelve months to escape it which meant that it had been just as long since I had handled a real plane. My skills at yanking and banking had atrophied. Now I wondered if I was still up to the task.

"There should be a river coming up crossing left to right," I mumbled. "It's got a bend in it that's our turnpoint."

"Ah, yes, the bend-in-the-river turnpoint. Always a tactical lighthouse. Rivers are flat, the jungle's flat, you can't see either from low level... All rivers bend out here, you know, about a million times every couple of miles. And they're hidden until you're right overhead..."

"You see anything else? What was I supposed to use? This is your jungle, not mine."

The water appeared off the nose winding through the trees. Blocked by overcast and dour clouds, the sun's early rays couldn't reach it yet. Its metallic surface stood in contrast only to the heat-soaked green of the jungle that lined its banks. And as Walt warned it was hidden until we flew right up on it, which meant we were lucky to have been on course in the first place. But the river was there – a long, meandering ribbon of gray that narrowed into the distance until it disappeared – and nothing else.

"Uh, it's supposed to have a big loop in it somewhere," I apologized. "I don't see one."

"Nope, neither do I."

"Maybe this isn't the right river."

I pretended to stare at the map but watched Walt out of the corner of my eye, hoping to get an indication that he knew where we were.

He nodded, unconcerned. "It's the right one," he said.

"How do you know? Have you been here before?"

"Nope."

"Then how do you know it's the right one? There's no loop. There's a loop on the map but nothing outside."

"We're looking for a river," he countered. "This one isn't perfect but the timing is good and so's our heading. The map's probably wrong."

I raised the chart from my lap and looked at it more closely. "The map is wrong?" I repeated. "Maps aren't wrong. How can the map be wrong?"

He pointed outside. "Because it shows a loop and there's no loop, so clearly it's wrong. When the map and the terrain vary," he added before I could argue, "go with the terrain."

We overflew the river and offset from it a thousand yards. There Walt found his niche a hundred feet above the trees. We stayed there, boring a hole in the sky and following the river. Mist rose from the trees like steam. It condensed on our windows only to bead off immediately in thin rivulets that showed remarkably casual regard for the slipstream. From time to time Walt flipped on the wipers which was to me such an odd thing to do not only in an airplane but when it wasn't raining. I prayed like hell the weather wouldn't get worse, for where we were going there were no navigational aids and no runway lights. If we couldn't find it with the naked eye we weren't going to find it at all.

The weather flimsy was three hours old. I pulled it from behind the compass and read what our forecasters had given us. *SCT TSTMS ENROUTE. MSTLY CLR UNTIL 1400Z. CMULUS BLDUPS AFT MIDDAY.* The satellite photograph that accompanied it showed the continent of South America.

I looked back outside. The forecast was fine but the reality was different. Clouds were already low in the sky in an unbroken deck. And if we wanted to make it into our destination airfield, we would have to stay below them no matter how low they dropped.

The river bent and twisted through the jungle. The big loop finally appeared, several of them, so many that we hadn't a clue which if any claimed representation on the map. Like an earthbound sine wave the river now looped toward us and away at regular intervals taking the path of least resistance. It crafted such large oxbows that sometimes the water flowed past itself with only a dozen yards of separation, a tenuous arrangement that nature didn't stand for long. Occasionally we saw where momentum caused the flow to cut through such small embankments to hurry things along. The new path then created its own streamlined design and left the remains of the bow to fall by the wayside. The bow became a pond, then a puddle, then disappeared entirely in the trees.

What struck me about the river was that it had no banks. There was water and then there was jungle and that was all. No beach, no rocks, no shore. Where the two met, darkness loomed over the current.

Bird swiveled his seat around to hop down into the cargo compartment. "Anybody want anything from the back?"

"Yeah," Walt said. "Give me a paper towel. I've got a whistle up here somewhere."

Bird reached behind him through the sliding door of the latrine and grabbed a paper towel. The latrine was a stall the size of a phone booth just aft of the cockpit. It had a urinal and removable toilet but its primary function was storage. The outer wall consisted of an escape hatch over which hung a fire extinguisher, an emergency oxygen mask, and a first aid kit. Piled against the hatch were a hydraulic winch, a tool kit, the loadmaster's weight-and-balance pubs, and a dozen cans of hydraulic fluid. Keeping it looking like Fibber McGee's closet was part of our strategy to discourage people from using the latrine for what it was intended. It was a small plane, after all. Bouncing around the jungle was bad enough without smelling like a railroad station restroom.

Walt took the towel and folded it repeatedly until it was the size of a book of matches. Then he shoved it into the corner at the bottom of his side window, his knees squeezed against the control yoke to hold the plane steady. He listened a moment and then nodded, satisfied.

"Thank goodness. That thing was going to drive me crazy. Couldn't you hear it?"

"No."

He pursed his lips and made a whistling sound which he then grimaced at. Waving a hand to say it was gone now, he picked up a plastic bottle by his feet. The bottle had a straw and was encased in an enormous insulated cup with a picture of Bambi on the side.

"Is that water?" I asked.

He shook his head. "Coffee."

"You drink coffee through a straw?"

He sipped then held up a finger to make a point. "As a rule, the strength of the turbulence you encounter is directly proportional to the temperature of the coffee you're drinking. If you don't want to burn your lap, you drink through a straw."

That wouldn't be a problem since I didn't drink coffee. Even if I did, I couldn't imagine drinking it or anything else that was hot when it was already ninety degrees in the cockpit. Besides, who wanted to keep jumping out of the cockpit to pee? When I commented as much, Walt agreed.

"But," he added, "there's always something to worry about. The weather's always bad, the field is always farther than you thought – out here I would rather have a two-hour bladder and three hours of gas than vice-versa. Hey, Bird, let our pax know we're within half an hour."

"Will do. Don't kill me while I'm gone."

Bird disconnected the intercom cord from his headset and walked back to check the tie-down straps on the cargo. The two passengers were asleep, sprawled across fold-down troop seats on opposite sides of the cabin.

"The weather's always bad...so this is typical?" I asked, pointing outside.

Walt set his cup back on the floor. "No. It's the rainy season now so what's typical is what it says on that weather flimsy: clear and muggy in the morning with thunderstorms in the afternoon."

"How bad are the storms?"

"Bad enough that you won't want to get anywhere near them. We can't go over them and it's dumb to go under them so you have to go around them. Sometimes you'll deviate a long way. I had to go two hundred miles in the wrong direction once to get away from a bunch that had banded together. I had the gas to do that, though. Usually you don't. They're probably the biggest hazard down here, them and the mountains."

"And the druggies," I added.

"The mountains will get you first," he corrected me.

"So if this isn't normal why do we have a cloud deck at seven in the morning?"

"Do I look like a weather geek?" He shrugged. "I have no idea. It happens, though usually later in the day. But then the problem is the same: most of the places we go have no navaid so you have to see them to find them. If you fly over a strip and the inertial system says you're there but the only thing below you is an overcast layer, then you have to go searching."

"For somewhere else to land?"

"No, for a hole. *Never* land anywhere else unless you have to."

"What if there isn't one?

"One what?"

"A hole. What if you fly around and there's no hole to drop through?"

Walt descended to ram through a haystack-size cloud hanging just over the trees. The illusion of speed as we rushed up on it was disconcerting. The diaphanous mass grew large until for an instant it loomed impossibly close in the windscreen and I wanted to yank the controls and leap for safety. Then it burst around the nose. Instantly we were clear, the trees below looking suddenly far away.

"There's always a hole," he said, looking down out the left side as a rare clearing appeared and then just as quickly passed out of sight beneath us. "It may take a while to find it – which is why you always watch your gas – but it'll be there."

"Always?"

"Alright, not always, but then you use your imagination and figure out something else. You may have to go somewhere else – but you *never* want to do that – and in that case you still have to watch your gas because if you don't have it and you didn't prepare for the worst then you're going to be looking through an impenetrable cloud cover for a non-existent emergency field in the middle of a really nasty jungle. And you won't be happy."

The air outside got heavier with each mile we flew away from the mountains. Whether the moisture came up from the jungle or descended from the heavens, it didn't seem possible for the air to hold so much water without raining. Even in the cockpit it felt like a sauna. At what point did the skies just give up trying to hold back the flood and let loose with a good old-fashioned downpour?

"So," I summed up. "The weather is always better than this, except when it's not; there's always a hole, except when there isn't; and I have to make sure I always have enough gas, even though I won't know how much I'll need. And if I don't drink my coffee through a straw I'll burn myself. Is that about right?"

"Yup."

"How do I make sure I have enough gas?" I asked. "We haven't seen a road for hours."

"You don't. Always take as much as you can without going over the weight limits."

"But that means sometimes I'll have too much," I protested.

Walt guided us along a shallow hill and glanced over to watch the trees pass by.

"No," he mused. "The only time you have too much fuel is when you're on fire."

We approached the intersection with the second river.

"We coming up on our turnpoint?" Walt asked, sipping again from Bambi.

I pointed. "I hope that's it right there."

"Next heading 052?"

"Yes."

A smaller river appeared, meeting the larger at an acute angle. We flew down the middle of the Y.

We passed a widow-maker, a lone tree that stood up above its neighbors, then started the turn left. When the Y of the rivers was off the right wing I hacked the clock. Twelve minutes and fifteen seconds at two hundred knots should see us overhead the site we were looking for.

"Hack," I called. "Almost no wind out here so keep a straight line and we may find this place."

"That's not going to happen. The straight line, I mean. Look out front."

I looked. The ground rose and the clouds fell. On our previous heading we had paralleled the worst of the visibility. Now we turned right into it.

The thought of my first mission in-country aborting for weather caused a sinking feeling. There was no reason for it: the crates we were carrying had equipment that was important but not life-or-death material. Our passengers, too, could wait until another day. One was an Army colonel making his first trip to the jungle and the other guy was dressed in civvies and probably DEA. I hadn't asked and they hadn't talked since getting on the plane. So nothing we carried was critical. I just hated not being able to finish a job.

"Dude, this isn't going to work," I commented. "Cloud deck or no cloud deck we either have to turn around or go above this thing."

Walt got the look of an English teacher who has just heard the word *ain't.*

"Look at your map," he said patiently. "I told you the course is a straight line. The map tells us all we need to know about where we are, where we're going, and everything in between. All you have to do is keep track of our position. Know where we are all the time." He turned toward the new river. "Forget the clock. This river takes us in the direction we want to go. Start figuring how close we can get before we have to leave it."

"You're going to fly up the river?" I asked.

"Yeah."

"Have you ever flown up it before?"

"No."

"How do you know it doesn't just end?"

"You ever driven on Interstate 80?" Walt countered.

"Of course."

"How do you know it doesn't just end?" he inquired. "Say, in the middle of Kansas?"

I didn't think his analogy was a good one.

We angled toward the river. The weather followed us, funneling in from both sides, but near the water the clouds hung back as though unwilling to encroach upon its space. It was an illusion formed by the height of the trees but still it gave the impression of entering a tunnel. If we ever lost sight of the ground here we would have no choice but to make an immediate climb until we got above the clouds.

There was a click in the headset. Bird finished his walk-around and hooked back into the intercom.

"Cargo's good, pax are awake. Anything happen while I was gone? You guys lost yet?"

"We know exactly where we are," Walt told him. "But funny you should ask – we do have a problem."

We dropped down over the water and entered the tunnel. The trees were now on either side of the plane rather than below it, giving us three times the illusion of speed that we'd had before. Walt settled in at a hundred feet above the rapids. We were so close to the water that the radar altimeter barely registered. The radar altimeter shot a radar wave straight down and then caught the reflection – the calculation told us how high we were above something solid. Water wasn't solid, though, and when we were too close to it the two waves interfered with each other and generated random numbers in between the real answer. Thus 100 showed for a second or two, then 00000, then 12894, then 4, etc. It was as though the digits inside the instrument were arguing with themselves over what they should tell us to do.

Bird climbed into his seat and leaned forward over the center console. With his left hand he pointed at the pilot's airspeed indicator that was bouncing around at eighty knots. "We're way slow," he pointed out. "Push it up!"

"No, we're not." Walt's hand rested on the throttles. He flattened his palm across them to emphasize that he would move them if he thought they needed moving. "Co-pilot, what does your airspeed read?"

My airspeed indicator fluctuated around 130 knots. One look out the window told me that was wrong. We were doing at least two hundred miles an hour.

The two gauges read from a common pitot-static system which was fed by two ram-air tubes located on the bottom part of the nose-cone, beneath the pilot's and co-pilot's lower windows. There was no way to isolate one tube from the other so if either was blocked or damaged the altered pressure differential inside the tube would feed bad information to both gauges. I looked out the window but couldn't see either tube.

"We don't know our speed," I commented, thinking that that malfunction alone was enough to cancel the mission.

"The power hasn't changed and there's no wind," Walt commented. "We're flying fine, we've just lost a few instruments. Something's in the tubes."

"Ice?" suggested Bird.

"You kidding? You see any snowballs?"

In addition to the airspeed indicators, our barometric altimeters and vertical velocity indicators relied on pitot-static inputs. Their needles also now pointed in random directions.

"Our altitude, airspeed, and climb rate indications are all wrong now," I summarized carefully, hoping that by sounding disinterested I would also sound reasonable. "You don't think we should turn around and go home?"

Walt scoffed. Beyond him, out the left window, a backdrop of trees raced by with surreal speed.

"We've got groundspeed, the radar altimeter – such as it is – and the view outside," he explained. "Best of all, we've got you on the map. There's no reason to turn around."

"But we don't know our airspeed."

"Yes, we do," he insisted. "The engines tell us. I know that 600 on the torque gauge moves us along at around 180 knots. 700 give us about 210 knots. You just have to feel what the plane's doing."

"I don't have a clue what the plane's doing," I admitted.

"That's why you're *sooo* lucky to be on this trip. Think of all the experience you're getting."

A shout, muffled by the roar of the engines, reached our ears ear. Bird turned in his seat and looked back.

"Oh, dear," he said into the intercom. "One of the passengers looked out the window."

The florid face of the Army colonel appeared in the doorway behind Bird. He stood on the step to the cockpit and leaned over the loadmaster's shoulder. Bird's seat blocked his way so he couldn't come any further and Bird made no attempt to slide out of the way. Nevertheless, the colonel shoved his head and one shoulder into the available space and looked around. From the expression on his face, if what he'd seen out the side window had gotten him excited, looking out the front drove him into a panic.

"What the hell do you think you're doing?! Get this plane up into the air! You think this is some kind of fucking joyride? You're going to get us all killed! This isn't a fucking helicopter! You can't fly this f...."

From there he launched into an uninterrupted stream of expletives that, while not quite audible in the open cockpit, still found their way into the mouthpiece of Bird's headset and thereby into the intercom system. The colonel, thankfully, had no headset of his own and was limited to competing with the roar of the engines.

I had to admit feeling guilty, though of what I wasn't sure. I was a first lieutenant in the United States Air Force, this was a military plane, and we were on a military mission. So we were close to the ground. Okay, I conceded, looking outside, so we were very close to the ground.

That said, the guy was over-reacting. More importantly, he was violating the cardinal rule of aviation courtesy: never yell at pilots when they're flying. No matter who you are you don't tell a pilot what to do when you're riding on his aircraft. It's like telling a rancher how to manage his herd.

Walt felt his herd was in good shape. He let the colonel vent until he detected a break in the yelling. Then he interjected.

"Bird, tell the guy the weather's bad and we're staying low to avoid it."

He paused and waited while Bird pushed his own mouthpiece aside and shouted into the colonel's ear. The translation had barely finished when there was an explosion from the colonel as he launched into another expletive-strewn tirade. This one was about dangerous flyboy antics and who did we think we were and didn't we realize he was a colonel and did we think he was an idiot? He was taking down all our names and we would never see an airplane again much less fly one when we got back – if we got back...

Again Walt waited for the tide to abate. By that time I found a divot in the terrain. We had a photograph of the airfield we were going to that showed a dirt runway with some tents at one end and a deep wash at the other. The map showed what looked like a wash leading southeast off the river we were using as our ingress route. But the wash on the map faded out four miles short of the pencil marks I made to mark our destination. There was no guaranteeing the two ever met. For all I knew we would be flying up a closed canyon. I pointed out as much to Walt.

He nodded. "How far?"

"Six miles. You want to cut back on the ground speed?"

Another nod. "We'll slow to 180. No flaps yet."

Bird cleared his throat and interrupted, his voice calm.

"Um, sirs? The colonel said to tell you, uh, cocky motherfuckers that your worthless fucking careers are over and he wants us to get this fucking piece of shit into a climb immediately. He says..." He paused in his translation as the colonel shouted something else. "He says that's a goddamn order and he wants you to do it *now* -- excuse me, *fucking* now."

Bird's face was the picture of innocence. "Sirs," he added, "you realize of course that this is just a relay. I would never use such language with you sirs on my own."

It was clear from the colonel's face that what he really wanted was to reach out and throttle both the pilots. The only thing that stopped him was the view in the windscreen.

That view was getting worse. The river still skimmed below the nose. Visibility dropped to about ten city blocks. Every mile or so, trees rose out of the mist and raced toward us as the river bent: Walt would continue flying straight until we got close enough to have an idea of the sharpness of the turn. Then he would pull back gently on the controls and pop up and over the bend, dropping down to the new course of the river on the other side. It seemed easy.

"How are you not hitting anything?" I asked.

Walt didn't take his eyes off the view outside. "Basic flying rule: stay in the middle of the air."

"The what?"

"The middle of the air. Don't go near the edges of it."

"The edges of the air?"

"Yeah, you know, the ground, buildings, trees, interstellar space. It's hard to fly in those places. If you stay away from them you'll be alright."

I saw a fish jump in the river. We were close enough that if I knew anything about fish I could have identified it.

"Are you nervous being this low?" Walt asked.

"Yes."

"You want us to climb?"

I didn't. Not because I was afraid of looking weak but because I wanted us to get to the field.

"No," I said. "It just seems to me we're really close to one of those edges."

The colonel tried to look at my map but stayed so busy shouting I doubt he got much from it.

"Two miles. We should start to see something off the right side soon," I said.

"Roger," Walt replied. "The ground's still rising so I'm hoping for a break in that direction." He reached for the Bambi cup and sucked up the last of his coffee. "Where's the highest terrain?"

"Just as we make the turn into the wash." I pinpointed the spot on the map with my thumb and held it across the cockpit for him to see. "The MSA is 1600."

Anytime the minimum safe altitude was as low as 1600 feet you knew the terrain was mostly flat. It didn't mean you still couldn't hit the ground but it made you worry less about seeing mountain goats appear suddenly in a cloud.

"We gonna climb to make this guy happy?" Bird asked.

Walt shook his head.

"Well, he's going to pop a capillary soon."

"Tell him to stop looking out the window. Or if he's going to look out the window, tell him to make a game of it to take his mind off dying."

"A game, sir?"

"Yeah, tell him to look for Diegel."

"Who's Diegel?" I asked.

"Diegel Doone," Walt explained. "A pilot who went missing down here back in the thirties. We've got a guy in the squadron who thinks he's still down here somewhere."

"Who's that?"

"Skinny Steve. He's an odd duck."

"You don't agree?"

"About what?"

"About the guy still being down here?"

Walt smirked. "Sixty years later? Not hardly."

"Then why do you tell people to look for him?"

"Because it's funny. *Oh, Diegel!...*" he sang again in his squeaky voice, peering at the trees shooting past. "Where *aaarrrre* you?"

"Sir," Bird interrupted. "I don't think you should sing while the colonel's so mad. I mean, I don't want to tell you how to ruin your career but it's not helping. I'm also closer to him than you are and he'll probably kill me on his way up to get you."

"Alright, Load. Tell him we're going to be landing in ten minutes. In about thirty seconds we're going to start some heavy-duty maneuvering, too, so suggest he sit down and strap in. Tell him I appreciate his concern but don't have time to discuss it now. If he wants to complain he can do it after we're on the ground."

Bird nodded. "Very diplomatic. It won't work but it's diplomatic."

"If that doesn't work, shoot him."

"Roger."

"How's the other guy?"

"Sitting down. He looks bored."

"Okay, eight minutes to our window. Where's our wash, co-pilot?"

"Damned if I know." I peered outside. Everything was green and blended together. "Wait, I've got something. Right there!"

Walt looked cross-cockpit and saw the jungle on my side of the plane give way. The trees dropped back. In seconds a new path appeared under the clouds.

The wash had a stream, one so narrow you could step across it. Yellow bamboo grew along its banks. The walls of the wash weren't more than two hundred yards apart.

I looked up the main river. Visibility there was still over a mile. If anything the course of the water widened. To the north, however, the clouds began to rain. I counted three separate showers before the lowest clouds obscured my view. Walt was right. We wouldn't break into the clear up there. It was either this wash or give up right now.

"Looks good so far," he chirped.

If he had enjoyed the flying up to this point, he was in heaven now. He slid the plane as far over to the north side of the river as he could. We both hunched forward in our seats, trying to see around the turn. The opening approached fast.

"Clear right."

My heart stopped as we banked hard to the right, tilting all the way over to seventy degrees. For a moment all I could see ahead and out the roof window was trees. There was a *whump* and a crash behind me.

Then just as quickly we rolled left, back to level flight. The river was left behind.

"Dude, this is - "

"Oh, man, we're gonna be in trouble."

Bird cut me off. He swiveled in his seat, looking aft. The colonel was nowhere to be seen. "We done yanking and banking for the moment?"

"Yeah."

Taking advantage of our level flight, Bird unstrapped and hopped out of his seat. The DEA guy, or whoever he was, removed his seatbelt, too, and came up to help. I couldn't see what they were doing but Bird disappeared briefly into the latrine. The folding door, no longer on its hinges, was passed out to the DEA guy, who carefully set it aside. Then came several cans of hydraulic fluid. Next followed the fire extinguisher. Last came the colonel, half-carried by Bird. He was as limp as a politician's handshake.

"Somebody fall down?" Walt asked.

They laid the colonel on the fold-down seats by the crew entrance door. To keep him from rolling off they wound three seatbelts around his legs and waist. The DEA guy took some ice from the water cooler and wrapped it in a bandanna.

Bird came back up intercom.

"Is there anything else we want to do to get in trouble before we land?" he asked. "You know, maybe we could strafe an orphanage or buzz a heart clinic?"

"What happened?" asked Walt.

"The fuck-up fairy visited us again. What do you think happened? The colonel fell and knocked himself out."

"We kill him?"

"I don't know – sometimes it's hard to tell with these Army guys. It doesn't look like it but he won't be yelling for a while. He's breathing. Can't tell if anything's broken but he knocked the back of his head on the escape hatch. The only spot on the wall not padded but he found it."

Walt motioned for me to take the controls so he could look into the back. He took in the situation in the cargo compartment and shook his head. DEA Guy switched seats and belted in next to the colonel, holding the icepack under the injured man's head. The cargo hadn't shifted and nothing else was out of order but a colonel with a concussion was enough.

"You know," Walt said, "a good loadmaster would have made sure all the passengers were strapped in when the pilot told him to."

"Next time bring one with you," Bird shot back. He threw everything into the latrine and put the door back in its groove. "The other guy back here is cool. Doesn't say anything but moves quick when you need him. Why can't we have more pax like that?"

"Because we work with the Army," Walt replied.

Once in the middle of winter I flew a light plane through an ice storm into a small airport in central Illinois. That approach was terrifying. I was low on gas and high on stress and despite the freezing temperatures was sweating when I finally put the aircraft on the ground. Up to that point it had been the scariest situation I had ever encountered flying. Right now I wished I could go back and enjoy that approach again.

Walt watched me stress. It took all my focus to hold us in the middle of the wash.

"You ought to relax, you know," he commented. "The ground won't hit you if you don't hit it."

He spoke as he flipped through our maps, holding them up to eye level as he compared them with what he saw outside. Then he lay them on the center console and put his hands on the controls. "Alright, that's enough for you. I have the aircraft."

"Roger, you have the aircraft," I acknowledged. I sat back and wiped my brow.

"We're getting close. Let's run a checklist but stand by on the gear."

The clock was still running from our turn off the river: we had maybe six miles to go. Plenty of time so long as we could guess correctly when it was time to pull out of the wash. *If* we could pull out of the wash and still maneuver to the runway.

"The map's no good from here on," I announced. "All it did was get us into the wash. Now we're on our own. Load, you'd better tell them to put on a few more seatbelts because this isn't going to be fun."

"If you say so, sir." Bird shouted something to the DEA guy. Then he climbed back up to his seat and swiveled it around to face front. He still didn't look out the window but was content to stare at the instruments. He had flown with Walt before.

"Oh, you need to enjoy your work more, Mike," Walt observed. "If you go back to flying boring approaches into big wide runways you're going to miss this." He reached above him and shoved the curtain on his overhead window all the way open. "Bird, we need to find an opening up here. I'm going to be looking outside so let me know if the ground speed drops below 150."

"How? Your gauges are broke."

"You're an experienced loadmaster. Tell me when it *feels* like we're dropping below 150."

"Okay."

"And give the site a call. If we do find this place I don't want some idiot walking his dog on the runway making me go around."

"I'll make the call," I offered.

"No, no," Bird held up his hand. "Flying the airplane is more important than radioing your problems to some knucklehead on the ground who can't do anything about them."

He flipped his transmit switch to the FM radio.

"Rascal, this is Catfish. Rascal, this is Catfish."

There was silence in the cockpit while we waited for a reply. It occurred to me that I didn't even know who would answer.

"This is Rascal. Go."

"We're three minutes out. Your weather sucks. Clear the runway 'cause we only want to do this once."

"Roger."

Bird switched back to Intercom. "See, I told you. Helpful guy."

There was a reason this airstrip was so difficult to get to. Drug smugglers try to blend into the background. At the U.S. border there is a lot of background for them to work with. Commercial planes, cargo ships, vehicles: anything that moves they can stash drugs aboard to pick up on the other side. The sheer volume of traffic sways the odds in their favor.

In Central and South America, though, there was little background to blend into in 1990. In Colombia, for example, except for the stray missionary or chartered cargo hauler there was no general aviation community. Anything airborne belonged either to the government or to someone nominally at odds with the government. For anyone trying to fly illegally that was a challenge.

When pilots picked up their loads from labs hidden in the jungle it made sense to stay over the jungle as long as possible. Why not, since for a long time there was no one around for hundreds of miles to see and track their activities? From Bogotá south to Leticia on the Peruvian border is about the same distance as from Chicago to Jackson, Mississippi. An area larger than Texas with fewer roads than Key West, pilots flying for the cartels used the vast, sparsely-populated area the way moonshiners once used the mountains of Kentucky. They flew through the middle of nowhere. Until the mid-1980's they did so with impunity, the only risk being if a competing cartel tipped off the Colombian Air Force, the *Fuerza Aerea de Colombia,* to their flight. There was also the remote chance of an accidental encounter with a FAC fighter, though that was highly unlikely since the Colombians, due to maintenance and financial difficulties, had trouble keeping their Air Force in the air.

Then in 1983 the first U.S. radar site to be operated in Colombia began coverage of one of the busiest trafficking regions, along the Meta river near Villavicencio. In the next few years other sites popped up around the jungle. By 1990 there were six. Huge areas of the country were still uncovered but now the smugglers had to be more careful. Even if they weren't shot down by Colombian Super-Tweets or OV-10s, simply by being tracked from take-off to landing their whole operation could be compromised.

The pilots and their employers quickly learned where the sites were. They altered their routes, sabotaged the sites, or bribed local officials to pay no attention when the Americans reported hits on the radar screens.

Thus was born the strategy of the secret sites, mobile radar sites set up around the jungle with the cooperation of the U.S. Drug Enforcement Agency and a small cadre of Colombian, Ecuadorian, and Peruvian officials. By the time I arrived in Panama the operation had been underway for months and had already enjoyed enough success to justify the expense. The cartels were being blindsided. Someone was in the middle of nowhere with them.

Today we weren't in the middle of nowhere yet but we were getting close. Whoever picked the location for Site 2 knew something about being lost. The walls of the wash were tightening up. By the time Bird finished his radio call we were overshadowed on both sides by the high walls of a gorge. Waterfalls appeared between the trees, pouring into the ravine like leaks in a dike.

A feeling grew within me that at some point we would have to commit to the likeliest looking place along the west side of the ravine where the airstrip might be. Walt was thinking the same thing – he looked frequently at the ridge high up on his window.

"We've gotta be right on top of the place. Coming up."

He eased the plane level with the top of the wash so that once again we looked at jungle on both sides. The clouds hung just above the trees. If the ceiling was higher than fifty feet I would eat the weather flimsy.

"Come on, where are you?" Walt demanded, scanning the left wall.

"Your ground speed's 145," Bird advised in a neutral voice, adding "thereabouts." Walt looked inside, paused a moment to listen to the engines, then pushed the throttles up. "More like 148, but thanks," he said, then went back to looking outside.

"It's got to be up here," I said. "We couldn't have passed it yet."

"You want me to call 'em again?" Bird asked. "Tell them to build a fire or flash their lights or something?"

There was no response from the pilot's seat. So that Bird didn't feel ignored I glanced back and shrugged. The fire idea didn't sound half-bad.

"If it's that close," Walt said, "we probably won't get to --" He broke off, peering out his window at a spot on the ridge. Then his face broke into a broad grin. "There it is! THE MEADOW!!"

I didn't see anything that didn't look like everything else.

"Where?"

"Right there."

"Got it," Bird agreed. He pointed across the cockpit at a break in the trees a hundred yards away.

Even when I saw the runway I wasn't sure what I was looking at. I could just make out the burnt-yellow color of the soil where it began. The clearing it lay in was a good forty yards across but with the trees in the foreground blending into those in the background an optical illusion convinced the eyes it was smaller. The only obvious feature was a large rubber tree perched on the ledge by the far side of the strip. It leaned precariously over the ravine.

There was no way we could make the turn.

As we came abeam the strip we all looked left. In the brief glance there didn't seem to be a site at all. At the far end someone was running from one side of the clearing to the other but no buildings were visible. Two truck tires flanked the runway near the bluff, marking the touchdown zone. The strip extended two thousand feet into the jungle and then ended abruptly.

"Flaps 20. We'll do a right 270," said Walt quickly. "Clear right."

"Negative. Stop right!" I called. Out my window hulked the other side of the ravine with its trees covering the western ledge. The ledge on that side was higher than on the east and the overcast closed the intervening distance like a Pimlico favorite in the final stretch. "We'll go into the weather."

Walt swore. There was no room on the east side, either.

The site slipped by. In seconds it disappeared behind us.

We had painted ourselves into a corner.

"*Catfish, Rascal.*"

The FM transmission was garbled. Bird switched his radio button to FM but didn't answer, waiting for Walt.

"*Catfish, Rascal.*"

"What do you want me to tell him?" Bird asked, his finger on the transmit button.

Walt pursed his lips. An idea was working its way through his brain.

"Tell him,...tell him we'll be right back."

Bird considered that, making for him the unusual move of looking outside at the weather, but then he shrugged and keyed the mike. "*Rascal, Catfish, we're on our way back now.*"

"Negative. Weather is low and not getting better. Hold or divert."

"Everyone's a pilot today," Walt commented. "Don't even answer that, Bird."

"How are we going to go right back?" I wanted to know. "We're barely squeezing between the clouds and the trees. Trying to turn around would be the dumbest thing we could do."

"It wouldn't be dumb," Walt disagreed. "Bird, when do you know if a pilot is doing something dumb?"

"When he scares the crew."

"Exactly. And have you been scared yet today?"

"Not yet, sir."

"Alright, then. If Bird hasn't been scared then we're doing okay."

"How about me?" I asked. "You've scared me with all this mowing-the-jungle stuff."

"You're new. You don't count. How high would you say these clouds are?"

I looked at the overcast and let the argument slip past. The jungle rolled in waves on our left but lay like an open plain beyond the wash on my side of the cockpit. Nothing about the skies had changed.

"Fifty feet. Maybe less."

"And of course you know our wingspan?"

"Forty-seven feet, one inch."

"Sooo..."

"No."

"Sure we can. Right turn, crew. Keep me clear, co-pilot."

I took a deep breath and held it as we banked to the right. In a matter of seconds we were out of the wash for the first time in twenty minutes. Once more I looked down on trees the way an apartment dweller inspects a window box.

Walt's plan became obvious. That didn't mean it would work but if anything could get us pointed back toward the site this was it. By starting a gentle turn to the right to offset us from the wash and then reversing the bank to bring us back around to it we could alter our course 180 degrees. The only problem was this was going to be a *biiiig* turn with our left wing damn near in the trees. In banking to the right Walt could only go to just over ten degrees. We would need miles.

"How's clearance on the right?"

"What clearance?"

I couldn't even look at the right wingtip for more than a few seconds. The trees passing underneath were so close and moved so quickly I lost all perspective. Unless I looked forward I would never see an obstacle until it was too late. I was about to call stop-turn when Walt froze the bank angle on his own, the reason being that even at ten degrees our left wing disappeared in the overcast. It was a good thing no one had a problem with claustrophobia. We were a cat squeezing beneath a garage door.

"You know why there's a gap between the clouds and the trees here and not back at the site?" Walt asked.

"No."

"Neither do I."

We flew seven or eight miles west of the wash. Then Walt rolled back to the left, again to no more than ten degrees of bank.

This time the right wing probed into the deck above us. Clouds lunged down all the way to the wing root. Had anyone been there to see us he might have thought that half a plane was somehow carving a route above the jungle. But the maneuver worked. It was a long time before we got the wash in sight again but precise banking and a constant airspeed worked in our favor.

Walt rolled out over the wash, lined up with it, and descended once again between its walls.

"Co-pilot's controls."

"Co-pilot's controls," I repeated, and put my hands on the yoke and throttles.

He started bouncing in his seat, bobbing his head and flexing his shoulders like a boxer warming up in the ring. He cracked his knuckles and wiggled his fingers in the air. Maybe a boxer wasn't the right comparison – the doctor was about to perform surgery.

"This is what we're going to do," he announced. "Remember that rubber tree hanging over the edge? That'll tell us where the runway is. We'll pull up short of that, turn to final, and drop it onto the runway."

I waited for the details. None came.

"That's it? That's your plan?"

"That's the plan."

I looked at Bird in what I began to realize would always be a vain attempt to garner support. He held his hands up in front of him in a "don't get me involved" gesture. "I'm just glad this thing is a rental," was all he said.

"The survey says the strip is barely 2000 feet long," I pointed out.

"Then let's stop before that."

"Do you want me to figure landing data?"

"I already did," Walt answered.

"When?"

"Before we took off. Look, if it doesn't work we'll go around and get the hell out of there, because clouds or no clouds it's getting *hot* out."

He was right about that. Only seven-thirty in the morning, it was ninety degrees outside. With the windows all around us the cockpit was ten degrees hotter than that. Walt reached around the panel and directed all the air diffusers he could find toward his seat. The plane was an Italian design so the air conditioning only worked when it was cold outside, but the diffusers helped.

"Let's run through the checklist again," he ordered, taking back the controls. "Just hit the highlights but be ready with the gear and flaps. If I forget to say anything just go flaps full as soon as wings are level. Give them a two-minute call, Bird."

"Rascal, Catfish. Two minutes out."

Things began to look familiar in the wash. The bottom got shallower and the walls grew steeper. A waterfall I hadn't seen on the first run moved past my window. The water flowed out over the ledge in a smooth stream, curved through the air to leave maybe twenty feet between it and the wall, then disappeared into a pool halfway to the bottom of the ravine. The flow was so liquid, so seamless, that it joined the waiting waters with hardly a splash.

Walt added power.

Two minutes into the wash we spied the rubber tree. At our altitude it stood out against the clouds, a silhouette leaned crazily over the ledge. Making clucking noises with his tongue, Walt scanned down and up, mentally figuring the best spot to begin the roller coaster approach. With his right hand he pushed the props to max. They spun faster there, giving us more horsepower at low speeds. They also made a hell of a noise.

"Thirty seconds, Bird."

Bird made the call. I tried to imagine what the radio operator at the site must be thinking. We weren't a mile away, our engines had just leaped to full power, we were telling him we would be on the ground in thirty seconds and he still couldn't see a thing. He was probably standing in the door of his hut holding the microphone, looking off both ends of the runway and trying to figure out where the roar that echoed off the trees was coming from.

One quarter mile short of the leaning tree and two hundred feet below it, we began our approach.

Walt pulled both engines to idle and hauled back on the yoke. Fifty thousand pounds of aircraft, people, and cargo hesitated, then aerodynamics prevailed: the nose swung upward and we climbed like a homesick angel.

The press of g-forces built. The walls of the ravine shot by. The C-27, its three-bladed props leaving contrails in our wake from the humidity, burst out of the ravine a hundred yards short of the airstrip. Even before we cleared the trees Walt twisted the controls and stomped on the right rudder.

"Gear down! Flaps!"

I grabbed the gear handle and shoved it down. Then I went for the flaps. I hoped we were slow enough to drop them into the slipstream but really, if we oversped one or the other that was the least of our worries.

We banked ninety degrees to the right. Walt pulled back hard to bring us around the turn but the plane still descended. What the effort did mostly was kill the excess airspeed we carried over from the climb. We passed over the lip of the ravine in a hard bank and with the gear only partway down. There was no way we would hit the touchdown zone.

"Yeah, baby! *Work* with me here!" Walt shouted happily. We overshot the strip but he settled for it and came in on an angle.

"Gear's down!" Bird called as the indicators on the panel flipped from in-transit barber poles to little wheels.

Walt shoved the power back up and leveled the wings. The engines hesitated. Turbo-prop engines, which are just jet engines that drive a propeller, need a moment to spool and catch up with the position of the throttles. Ours were no exception but when they did catch up their response was powerful. The number one engine was faster and for a second we yawed right. Walt caught it and corrected.

We dropped through fifty feet as if pulled to the surface. I had no idea where Walt was holding an aimpoint or if he had one at all. Much of the short strip already lay behind us. We were halfway to the trees at the eastern end and hadn't touched down yet. My eyes caught the flap indicator hit the six o'clock position – flaps fully deployed. That was it. There was nothing left to help us slow down.

The main gear struck. All the potential energy stored in the descending aircraft turned kinetic in an instant as it transferred to the waiting ground. The nitrogen in the struts compressed until the gear hit the mechanical stop, sending a jolt through the airframe. The spotlight stored above my seat flew off its clip and struck me on the right shoulder. Out of sight above and behind us, the lift dumpers deployed over the wings, walls of aluminum that disrupted the airflow and destroyed any lift still there.

Walt's feet pressed hard on the toes of the rudder pedals even before we touched down so we landed with full brakes applied. The nose came down. Just before the nose gear touched he threw both engines into full reverse. A deep-throated howl filled the encampment as the pitch of the propeller blades changed immediately from full forward to 22 degrees in the opposite direction. The props were now literally trying to push us backward up the runway. Back in Panama Walt had bragged he could stop the plane in 700 feet. Here was the test.

The deceleration threw me against my shoulder harness. Dust billowed up in great clouds, blown by the props as they engaged in a furious battle of physics with our forward momentum. For a moment it hid the end of the strip and the trees that waited there but through a thin opening in the middle of the debris I saw them approach. There was nowhere to turn. Just staying in the middle of the strip was the only thing keeping our wings clear of the brush on either side. We hurtled down the clearing, the broken ground proving itself more uneven than it looked from the air. Bouncing in our seats, the dusty air seeping into the cabin and anything that hadn't been tied down flying around the cockpit, I could only hope that each bump would take away another knot of speed.

In the end technology, physics, and luck stayed on our side. We came to a skidding halt less than fifty feet from the end of the field. At the end was a small piece of plywood nailed to a tree that had one word painted on it by hand. *Bienvenidos,* it said.

Welcome, indeed.

Dust filled the cockpit. Outside the props still screamed in reverse. My headset lay crookedly over my right ear, making the din even louder. I adjusted it as Walt dropped the engines to idle. Once he did the noise died. Every gauge on the instrument panel swung toward zero. The shaking of the aircraft fell away and the clouds lunging outward from each wing stopped their climb.

For a moment all three of us remained against the harnesses, spent, reluctant to get up, catching our breath. In that moment it occurred to me that I had done the right thing.

In that split second it all made sense. It dawned on me why Chumley had been right and I had been wrong to worry about coming south and why almost being killed didn't give me a paroxysm of nerves; why we were there, why the two lunatics I was flying with had the jobs they did, and why that lunge in the harness wasn't a bad thing. In that fraction of a second I realized I had taken more risks that morning than most people saw in ten years; I realized that Walt had probably been 99% sure all the way down final that we would stop before hitting the trees – but not 100%; I realized that this wasn't going to be the first time I came close to dying in my new line of work but I also knew that risk wasn't the same as foolhardiness and that if I could manage the one and avoid the other then adrenalin would flow like a life-giving IV; I realized the jungle was the most beautiful and dangerous thing I had ever seen in my life; and I realized that I would grow to like this kind of flying. I would like it a lot.

"Did we land or were we shot down?" Bird asked, breaking the reverie.

"Ha-ha!" Walt slapped the dash. As much as he could while sitting down he did a dance of victory, bouncing in his seat and stomping on the floor. He grabbed his cup and sang to Bambi. "You're welcome," he told Bird. "Now shut up and get outside. Go do your loadmaster thing."

Bird clapped him on the shoulder and climbed down into the cabin.

"Nice job," I said, conscious of the fact that it would be a long time before I would have the skill, experience, and credibility to lend weight to the compliment. "Lucky, but nice."

Walt giggled in delight. Then, remembering that I was new and he was an instructor, he stopped dancing, slapped a stern expression on his face, and held up a lector's finger.

"Never trade luck for skill," he intoned. "Never trade luck for skill."

A crowd of people appeared as I climbed out of the aircraft, more than the three tents visible among the trees looked able to support. They gathered at the crew entrance door. Some hopped aboard and began to unstrap crates in the cargo hold.

Walt preceded me down the steps. In the back, Bird lowered the ramp so that two of the troops could help the still dazed colonel to the ground. They led him to a quad-runner parked in the grass and gave him an ice pack for his head. Others gathered around him, including the DEA guy.

I hesitated. I was the newbie – what did I know? But then I figured I should at least make the effort. Without waiting for Walt I walked toward the group. It was hard to decide how much concern I could show without looking apologetic. Either way I anticipated a hard response.

And got it.

A lieutenant colonel from the camp looked up as I approached. He started in on me before I'd had a chance to open my mouth. Then the colonel spoke up and his subordinate shut up.

"What is your name and rank?" he demanded. The tone was rock-hard.

"Lieutenant Mike Bleriot, sir," I said. "I - "

"What the hell do you call that landing, lieutenant?"

"Just our normal operational procedures, sir." That was Walt's voice, professional but friendly, right behind me. He had seen the crisis in the making as soon as I changed course.

The colonel switched his gaze to Walt. "Am I talking to you? I'm not talking to you so you keep your mouth shut."

Walt was shorter than average and light in build but he had worked with the Army before.

"Sorry, sir, but if you're going to talk to my crew you're going to talk to me. I'm the aircraft commander: I'm in charge of them, the aircraft, and everything on it so if there's a problem I'll take care of it. I'm sorry you injured yourself..."

"Injured myself? You insubordinate little shit." The colonel grabbed the arm of a soldier to haul himself to his feet. "You fucking Air Force puke. You think you're God's fucking gift to the fucking military but I guaran-fucking-tee you this was your last flight. In charge of the crew? You're not in charge of shit! You're a fucking accident waiting to happen! What do you call that bullshit getting in here? I ought to cut you in fucking half – you think I don't know that wasn't on purpose?"

The colonel took a step forward. He looked ready to eat us.

But before he could the other passenger moved into the picture. Mr. DEA was tall and thin, wearing of all things a white shirt that despite being soaked in sweat still looked neat.

"Alright, hold it." His face was as thin as the rest of him but his voice was deep. "If there's a problem this isn't the place to resolve it. Colonel, if you want to lodge a complaint against the pilots I'm sure there are proper channels for doing that but I recommend you go someplace and cool off first."

The colonel turned, ready to snap, but the civilian cut him off.

"I'm sure that wasn't a standard trip getting in here. I'm sure there are things the aircrew can work on," (not DEA, I thought – a politician?) "but don't forget I was on the plane, too. If you had kept your seatbelt on you never would have gotten hurt."

"*Goddammit,* I..."

"Go cool off, colonel," the tall man said, giving an order to a man who more often gave them himself. He turned to the camp officer. "Lt Col Haar, I was told you're the site commander. If you can spare the time I'd like to get a look around as soon as possible so I know where I'm going to spend the next couple of days. And I'm sure the aircrew wants to be on their way."

Now there's an idea, I thought.

The light colonel looked uncomfortable but whoever the tall guy was, nobody seemed to want to argue with him.

He and a sergeant led the colonel away, the latter looking like a pressure-cooker on full boil. The last we saw of him was his last look at Walt. It was hungry.

"You have a knack for pissing people off," I muttered.

Walt maintained a look of earnest professionalism until the colonel was out of sight, then he acknowledged my remark with a giggle.

The civilian overheard me and turned to offer his hand. "Peter Fromm," he said. With a glance to ensure no one was listening he leaned forward and added, "For my part I just want to say that was a hell of a ride. I just wish you had bigger windows in the back."

I shook his hand. "Glad to hear somebody had a good time. Who are you that you can tell colonels what to do?"

Fromm held his finger to his lips. "Shhh! Don't make my job harder than it is," he cautioned. "Congressional staffer, no more, no less. Okay, senior staffer...Armed Services Committee. But that's all. He might still kill you if you stick around."

Lieutenant Colonel Haar came back. He wasn't ready to be friendly just because the colonel was gone but with Fromm there he made an effort to mend fences.

"Sergeant Coleman says you brought all the right parts so whenever you're ready to go let us know and we'll make sure the strip is clear."

"Yes, sir," said Walt. The quickness of his response incited a sharp glance from the commander.

"And just so you know, Captain," Haar snapped, "I don't know how Colonel Tunbridge was hurt but it reflects poorly on you and your crew. You'll be hearing more from him. Also," he added quickly, before Walt could object, "the next time I tell you my site is closed due to weather you will obey that order."

"Understood, sir."

A yell from Bird caught our attention. He walked up holding what looked like a frayed telephone cable. On closer inspection it turned out to be a vine, four feet long and covered with leaves.

"Hey, sir, I fixed our airspeed problem."

He held out the vine to whoever wanted it. It drooped in his hand but not much, the broad leaves fastened to the vine as though with rivets. "It was wrapped around the pitot tube," he said to Walt. "Must've picked it up somewhere before the river."

Fromm's mouth dropped open. Haar thought Bird was joking until he saw Walt take the vine and nod as though he recognized his work.

"That...was caught...on a piece of the plane?"

Haar looked at Fromm for confirmation but the aide was fixated on the vine, thinking perhaps the windows were the right size after all. Bird took the vine back, regretting he'd brought it up.

"It happens," he said weakly.

"It happens?" Haar repeated, blowing up again. "It *happens*? You'll need a better explanation than that. You'd damn well better have another explanation!" He was speaking to Walt but Walt had a look that suggested the Army didn't deserve the first explanation, so the colonel turned to me. "Well? Lieutenant? What do you have to say, goddamn it? *What do you have to say?*"

Above us the cloud deck thinned and brightened, promising to let the sun shine through any minute. Some drops of rain ignored the warning and fell about us anyway. They pattered into the trees and perfumed the air with sweet scents of chlorophyll and something that was almost but not quite like pumpkin. Though the colonel was in my face, all I could think of as I breathed the air was how I never would have felt those drops and never would have seen those trees had I not sat by Walt as he flew that approach. My heart was still pounding but here in the middle of nowhere, four hundred miles from the nearest road, I was finally doing what I had become a pilot to do.

"Sir," I said, and then hesitated, struggling how to answer. Only one thing came to mind. "Good pilots like to fly low."

2. Panama

IN THE LATE summer of 1990, Howard Air Base was the most beautiful military base America had anywhere in the world. It sat just over the Bridge of the Americas from Panama City, on the west side of the Panama Canal and on a corner of land that overlooked the Pacific Ocean at Kobbe Beach. With Albrook Air Base five miles away, Howard was the gateway to Latin America for the United States military. It was the staging point for U.S. forces during Operation Just Cause and for decades had been the port of entry for anyone coming to the Canal Zone.

Its runway ran north-south; aircraft on final approach had a dramatic view of the Canal with the skyline of downtown Panama City as a backdrop. An open base, without a fence or wall around its perimeter, Howard was surrounded by jungle. It was an island of civilization carved out of the forests that grew unchecked on both sides of the Canal. Even during the long "dry" season from January to August everything on the base was green.

The effect of all that vegetation was striking. When I arrived at Howard for the first time late on a Friday night, the jet from California touched down in a stifling heat that we could feel through the walls of the plane. It was eighty-five degrees outside and the humidity pressed on everything like a warm, wet hand.

Worse, coming in on Friday night was a mistake. I had been so anxious to leave California and the dreaded C-5 that I had given no thought to my arrival until halfway to Panama. When I hopped off the jet on Howard's ramp it occurred to me that I had no idea where to go or where I would even spend the night. I was exhausted and just wanted to find a bed.

But after collecting my bags and showing my passport and ID to a sergeant inside the door of the terminal, I found someone was waiting for me after all.

Two dozen people stood outside the claim area behind a line marked "Passengers Only." I didn't recognize anyone, which was no surprise, but a young woman with bright eyes and a friendly face held a sign with my name drawn on it in crayon. She smiled and raised her eyebrows in a question.

"Mike?"

"Uh, is there money involved if I say yes?"

She was relieved not to have to keep standing there. "No, but you might get a ride to your hotel." She held out her hand. "I'm Laura. My husband is your sponsor. He's out of town but told me to pick you up. He had no idea what you looked like, so..." She waved the sign.

I shook her hand. Married or not, she was a nicer welcome than I had expected.

The parking lot was small and crowded. All of three cars clogged the arrival area and you would have thought a tailgate party was under way with all the commotion. Airmen in uniform mixed with civilians to welcome arrivals. Lights inside the small terminal cast shadows outside that jumped and danced as people hugged each other.

Behind the crowd was a wide lawn that faded into darkness, and in the distance several three-story buildings lit dimly by streetlights. The buildings were alike, an ocher-on-white colonial scheme with terra cotta roofs and extending beams. One had a pair of flagpoles in front of it: spotlights illuminated the American and Panamanian flags hanging side by side.

To the left of the terminal it was dark. Jungle.

"Friday night isn't the best time to get here," Laura apologized. "With the Freedom Bird it gets to be a zoo. My car's across the street. Can I carry anything?"

I gave her the daypack slung over my shoulder. "It's busier than I expected," I said. "I figured Friday night would be dead and I would have to find my own place to stay."

"You're right about finding your own place to stay but Fridays definitely aren't dead. It's an open base and that road,.." she pointed to a line of headlights in the distance "...is the only way for locals to get to Veracruz unless they go around the whole base, which would mean another twenty miles up the highway. You'll see it because we're going out that way. Most of the cars are women coming to the NCO Club," she added. She wrinkled her nose in distaste. "Or Chiva buses bringing them."

I had no idea what she was talking about so just nodded.

"Thanks for picking me up."

"Oh, you're welcome. If I hadn't, you would be wandering around right now thinking you had walked into a madhouse. My car's over there."

We maneuvered between waiting cars. She walked fast. Spotlights behind us lit up the aircraft parking ramp but on this side of the flight line fence it was dark. Once we moved from the terminal doors, anywhere headlights didn't shine was black.

"They let the locals on base?" I asked, picking up her thread of conversation.

"Oh, yes," said Laura, her tone telling all. "We're all *friends*, you know, invasion or no invasion, and we wouldn't want to *insult* them by restricting their access to where *we* live. Sorry, you've been here all of two minutes and already I'm whining. I should only tell you good things otherwise you'll wonder what you got yourself into. It's really a great place to be. Kevin and I have been here five months and we love it. Or rather, I like it and he loves it because he's got the flying. You probably didn't even know he was your sponsor, did you?"

"No. But things were pretty rushed once I got the job. If he sent anything it's probably still sitting in my mailbox in California."

A woman leaned against Laura's car, waiting for us.

"I found him," Laura called.

"He must've pushed everyone out of his way," the woman said. She was tall with a skeptical face. "If we hurry we can beat the crowd out of here. How can there be so many people on base I've never seen before?"

"Mike, this is another Laura. Laura Kerr. Her husband is Steve. He's the security police commander."

"Hi," Kerr said, offering her hand. "Steve is just the company commander, not the *commander* commander, so you don't have to be nice to me unless you want to."

"Whatever," the first Laura said. "He does all the work over there." She opened the trunk on the Tercel and moved things around, then motioned for me to throw in my bags. The larger bags fit but I couldn't find a place for the daypack.

"Hang onto it," Kerr advised. "Laura's a lousy driver so you may need an air bag. She got her third ticket the other day."

"That was my *second* ticket," her friend insisted. "I'm still one behind you."

"And you'll stay that way. I've had my fill of the local cops and won't get pulled over again."

"Maybe I do want to take a cab," I suggested.

Laura reached through the open window and opened the passenger door with the inside latch. "Too late. Get in."

The Tercel was looking at its better years in the rear-view mirror. The fact that I could see dents in the darkness suggested it wouldn't stand up to inspection by daylight. My feet rested on a rubber mat that lay directly on the metal floor. The seat wouldn't slide back. I folded myself carefully to keep from smashing my knees against the dash. There was no room for the daypack so I handed it back to Kerr to put on the seat beside her.

"Sorry," said Laura as she cranked the engine. It didn't turn over. "I would have brought Kevin's pick-up but he doesn't want me driving that downtown." She turned the key again and nothing happened. "It's new and he's positive somebody will hit him if he takes it off-base." Another try.

"Did you say, 'please?'" Kerr asked from the back.

"Oh, it always does this. It's Panamanian. You just have to be persistent so it knows it won't get out of driving us somewhere. Start, you bitch!" she yelled, slapping the dash.

The engine roared to life.

“You can tilt the seat back, I think, if you hold that lever away from the door.”

“No, no, it’s alright,” I assured her, but pulled the lever anyway to see if I could gain a few inches for my knees. The seat back shot back a foot and stuck there. No matter how far I yanked on the lever or how hard Kerr pushed from the back the angle didn’t change. I felt like any moment a dentist would lean over and ask me to open wide. “It’s alright,” I repeated, turning sideways to lower my head away from the roof liner hanging in my face. When I did that my left leg pressed against the stick shift so I leaned back to the other side. I found the seat belt but couldn’t figure out how to fasten it in the position I was without wrapping the shoulder harness around my neck. While fumbling with it I began to sweat profusely. I didn’t see an air conditioner represented among the few switches below the radio and my long pants collected heat from the nighttime air. This would be a fun ride.

Kerr laughed as Laura backed out onto the road. “Oh, God, he’s all scrunched up! Well, don’t worry, Mike. We’ll probably be in an accident before long. And by the way, welcome to Panama.”

The Tercel died and re-started twice before we reached the main road.

We turned left by the base movie theater and headed against traffic on a two-lane road. A hill rose on the right but everything not actually on the road passed by in deep shadow.

The jungle stood out for its utter lack of illumination. That and the sweet weight of the air told us it was there. Together the effect was so relaxing I could have fallen asleep.

“Up there is base housing,” Laura pointed. “You can’t see it but it goes back a long way, all the way to the hospital.”

“And there’s the spot where Laura killed a coatamundi,” her friend added, tapping me on the shoulder.

“Killed a what?”

“A coatamundi. It’s like a raccoon. She shot it.”

"I didn't shoot it," Laura corrected. "I skewered it. But not there. That's just where it died."

"Right. That's where it died after you wounded it and it crawled in pain through the jungle..."

"Oh, stop! You're making me feel bad all over again."

"...crawled right up to the road and keeled over, so everyone could see the arrow sticking out of it."

I looked at my driver. "You shot a raccoon with a bow and arrow?"

"They're vile creatures. You'll see. Here's our commissary."

The base supermarket went by on the right, its parking lot vacant and dark. Compounding the poor visibility to the sides was the view out front. It was hard to see anything with all the headlights.

"Um, do all these cars have their headlights on bright or is it just me?"

"No, they're all like that," said Laura.

A hand pulled on my seat back. "Oh, let me tell him," Kerr said, leaning forward between the front seats. She explained how Panamanians adjusted their headlights high and how government vehicle inspectors insisted on re-setting the lights on all U.S. cars shipped in until they matched Panamanian standards. She told how her husband had brought in a brand new Ford Taurus that the inspectors wouldn't allow past customs until he paid a fee ("It's just a bribe") for them to re-aim the car's headlights at an acceptable blinding angle.

"It makes driving at night interesting," Laura added. "I rarely do it." She had her left arm on the open window and kept her hand up to shade her eyes.

A bus passed, lit up like a float in a Mardi Gras parade. Colored lights flashed over its roof and sides while screams and waving arms flew out the windows

"That's a Chiva," Kerr explained. "They're old school buses from the States but the locals decorate them. Wait 'til you see one during the day."

We reached the main gate after a mile. A dozen cars waited there to enter the base. Three base cops checked IDs of the drivers while two others dealt with a line of women that formed at the side of the road waiting to get on a bus.

"Oh, it's going to be a busy night at The Pit," Kerr said behind me. "Box lunches all around."

"'The Pit' is the club?" I asked.

"The NCO club," Kerr replied. "Though they open it on Friday nights for all enlisted. The word is if you're an American guy you can have all the" – she waved her hand in spirals in front of her looking for the right word – "*whatever* in exchange for a box lunch."

"'Whatever'," I repeated.

"Oh, yes," Kerr enthused. "All the *whatever* you want. Steve has some great stories. The advantage of being married to a cop. But you'll have to look elsewhere, Mr. Mike, because you're an officer. I'm sure you can get *whatever* downtown if you want for the same box lunch but the enlisted club is out of your reach."

"All these women are here just to get to the bar on base?" I asked, examining the crowd of short skirts and heavy makeup. "Seems like the base creates a lot of work for itself by letting all the locals on."

"You, my good sir, have just captured the American presence in Panama in a nutshell," Laura sighed. She stopped outside the gate as two garishly-dressed women stumbled across the road in our path. One ignored the vehicle; the other gave us a look like we should watch where we were going. "We give more and more to the locals in exchange for....what is it again? For that observation alone you should be promoted and allowed to go back to the States."

"Any normal American women down here?"

They both shrieked. "Us!"

We passed a half dozen taxis parked in the grass outside the gate. The drivers gathered, talking and smoking, their white guayaberas untucked and loose in the heat. Music played from a cab with its doors wide open. The men looked uninterested in fares but very interested in the women across the road.

Beyond them the drive turned onto an entrance ramp to the Pan American Highway. Laura kept the speed up. With the Tercel's engine whining like a chain saw we entered a four-lane road heading off into the night.

3. Panama 2

THE ROAD WAS darker than a highway should be.

"So where is the city?" I asked.

"Straight ahead. You'll see it in a couple of minutes."

For two miles it was so dark that following the road was like tracing electrician's tape across a chalkboard. There were few signs and no exits. The right lane tapered away into what in the past must have been a shoulder but that now more accurately would be called a jungle transition point. At irregular intervals it eroded away entirely to dirt and high grass. Huge potholes gaped where the rain carved away even the dirt. At one point we passed a fifty-gallon drum standing sentinel-like on the crumbled asphalt of such a hole. It was dimly marked by the fading flame of a smudge pot but even so it came into view too late to avoid had that been necessary. A yellow and black placard leaned against it that said *"Peligro"*. Danger. In the darkness no further details were forthcoming.

The road itself was in bad shape: paved but in a patchwork manner that left no section of more than fifty feet at the same level as the next. It wasn't washboard but only because washboard roads were more predictable.

Separating the lanes of opposing traffic was an unmarked waist-high cement divider. It cut into each of the two middle lanes, making passing a dicey proposition. I began to understand why Laura rarely drove after dark.

Still, when we rounded a bend and the Canal came into view it was impossible not to take my attention off the pavement. The highway climbed as it neared the shore, ascended to meet the bridge, and then lost itself in a sea of lights.

The Bridge of the Americas stretched over the water in a magnificent steel arc, stitching together the shores of North and

South America with the only road this side of the continental divide. Even now, traffic streamed across in both directions coming to and from the capital. The moving lights of the cars complemented the lights on the structure to make the whole vision like something from a carnival.

On the opposite shore a black patch hid where the highway met land but the lights picked up again where traffic continued into the city. On that side of the water Ancon Hill loomed over the docks. Ancon was the home of Quarry Heights, the headquarters for American forces in Panama. After the Canal itself it was *the* geographic landmark on this side of the isthmus. At its top, bathed in light, fluttered an enormous American flag.

Panama City wasn't huge but at night, surrounded by the blackness of ocean on one side and jungle on three others, its lights were as bright as a major metropolis. Their glow reflected off the sky. There wasn't a skyline so much as an eclectic collection of high-rises that stretched along the ocean and parallel to the Canal. Where they stopped the lights stopped, too, with suddenness and finality. With such stygian borders the city could have been a galaxy lost in a corner of the sky.

There were lights in the Canal, too. Running through its middle and perpendicular to the bridge was a corridor of buoys for the ocean-going traffic; green on one side, red on the other. An enormous cargo ship bore down on the bridge from the locks side as we neared it ourselves from the west. It disappeared as we approached then reappeared as we drove onto the bridge itself. The size of the vessel ensured that part of it was in sight at all times as we crossed, even in the middle where I looked down and saw the bow thrust out toward the open waters of the Pacific.

"That's the causeway."

Behind me Kerr pointed. She pushed her hand past my ear and out the window to show me what she was talking about. At the south end of the Canal entrance a spit of land formed a breakwater.

"It's a good place to go jogging or biking. And over there," she pulled her hand back, "those are the locks."

Going up the near side of the bridge the road was four lanes wide, two in each direction. At the top, however, it inexplicably narrowed to three and Laura was forced to merge. Two cars there didn't want to let her in but after a bit of jockeying she slowed down to get between them and then just slid over. The driver of the second car hit his horn in protest. The fourth lane reappeared on the back side of the bridge, giving the road an hour-glass shape. I guessed correctly that rush hour there had to be interesting.

As if reading my thoughts, going down the other side traffic was backed up with a line of cars trying to get around a Chiva bus parked against the railing. As Kerr had described, it was an old American school bus but with a cheery red-and-white paint scheme borrowed from a parade float. This one was dark, its engine off, with no lights inside or out and no emergency flares or flashers to mark its position. It just sat in the lane as angry drivers on the downhill side fought with each other over the right to pass. Two men stood in front of the Chiva talking and smoking cigarettes. If they were concerned about causing a traffic hazard by putting an unlighted bus on an unlighted road, they didn't look it.

"Okay," said Laura as we left the bridge. We turned onto a curving road that led down to the causeway. There was no sign marking the exit. "I made reservations for you at the Hotel Panamá. It's downtown."

"If it's downtown, why are we getting off the highway here?" I asked.

"You're getting the scenic route because the direct route takes us through parts of the city I don't like."

The road ended at a T-intersection. There a one-legged man leaned on crutches in the middle of the lane. He held out his hand and Laura handed him fifty cents.

"Over there is Fort Amador," she said to me, continuing past the man. "A great place to play golf."

"Who's the guy on crutches?"

"I don't know. He doesn't talk. He's always there, though."

"How did he lose his leg? In the invasion?"

"No, he's been here since before then. I don't know. Maybe by begging on a dark road."

We put the Amador gate behind us and drove through a residential neighborhood. It stopped at an intersection overshadowed by an imposing stone building that had "Young Men's Christian Association" carved across the top of its late-nineteenth century facade. The traffic lights at the intersection were dark.

"It's hard to point out much at night but this is the Balboa area," Laura said. "It's beautiful once you get off the main drag into the neighborhoods. The Canal administration buildings and offices are here, too."

Three massive white-washed buildings with classical facades and tall windows went by on the left side. PANAMA CANAL COMMISSION was written in sturdy block letters above each entrance.

"The main building is that way," she said, pointing past my face off to the right. "This area hasn't been handed over to the Panas, that's why it's still in good shape. I know that sounds bad but you'll change your mind when you see the areas they *have* taken over."

"Ooh, for example," cooed Kerr eagerly from the back seat. "Right up here..."

We were heading north, parallel to the Canal. Coming up on the right was an overgrown lot with large, ill-defined lumps strewn in the grass. In the dark it could have been a herd of sleeping elephants.

"The national railroad," said Kerr.

"It looks like a bunch of train cars lying on their side," I said.

"That's because it's a bunch of train cars lying on their side."

The rail line kept pace with our route as we continued along the Canal.

"Does it run at all?" I asked. The grass was six-feet-high around the tracks.

"No. It was the first thing handed over to the Panas after the treaties were signed in '77. There hasn't been a moving train on those tracks since the early-eighties."

After another mile we saw a sign that read 'Diablo Heights.' It pointed to our left. Instead Laura turned right and we crossed the tracks. As soon as we did, we encountered bright lights and a military gate.

"Albrook Air Base," Laura explained. "As I said, you're getting the scenic route to your hotel. At night I like to stay as close as possible to American-controlled territory."

"So my hotel's on this base?"

"No, it's downtown. But downtown is on the other side of this air base so what we'll do is cut through the base and then go into the city the back way. There aren't too many ways to get there from Howard so if you don't go the direct way – which we're not – you have to go a long way *out* of the way."

I smiled, confused. "Okay. I just hope you can repeat the tour during the day so I'll know what I'm looking at."

The security policemen at the gate looked at our IDs, saluted me, and waved us through.

Albrook was dark, too. We stayed on the main road all the way to the back gate, a distance of about two miles, but with little traffic the street lamps fought a lost cause. What little I could see told me that Albrook was designed much like Howard. The street was smooth and the houses all had carefully-tended yards.

"There's a lot of jungle for being this close to the city," I commented. "The base police must have a fun time trying to patrol this area."

"They don't," Kerr said. "There are break-ins all the time on both bases."

Out the back gate we drove up yet another dark road. The headlights of the Tercel stabbed into the darkness and showed jungle on both sides. There was no traffic.

"Are there streetlights anywhere in this city?" I asked. "Where are all the lights we saw coming over the bridge?"

"I told you this was the back way into the city," said Laura. "This is actually a park we're driving through right now. The *Parque Nacional Metropolitano,* the national city park, if that makes any sense. It's kind of a buffer between the city and the bases. We'll pop out in a minute and be on one of the busiest roads they have here. Believe me, the first time you encounter traffic in this country you're going to wish all the roads were like this."

"It's that bad?"

"It's so bad," called Kerr from the back, "that you have to drive just like the locals or you'll get killed. Don't be nice. Chip Harmon was nice and he had to buy some drunk a new car."

"How's that?"

"He's a scheduler in the squadron," she explained. "A C-130 navigator. He was on his way back to his apartment two months ago at about ten o'clock at night and stopped at a red light..."

"Ha!" Laura cackled. "Never do that."

"...There he was, waiting. Two drunk guys in a pick-up truck with no lights plowed into him and totaled his car. Fortunately Harmon drives a Bronco so he was shook up but not hurt. He went to court, explained how he was *stopped,* not moving, sitting still, minding his own business, when these guys hit *him,* and you know what the judge ruled?"

"It was his fault?"

"'You gringo, you pay.'"

"The judge said that?"

"Yup. And no kidding, he had to. Four hundred bucks. The Panas wanted more but even the judge had to agree that their truck was a piece of junk. As far as they're concerned it doesn't matter whose fault it is. You're an American and you have money so you're going to fork it over if you're in an accident and stick around to do things the right way. So don't."

"Don't get in an accident?"

"Don't stick around if you do, or hope the other person kills himself so he can't identify you." Kerr smiled sweetly.

We broke out of the trees and saw lights ahead.

"What's the name of this road?"

"I don't know," said Laura. "I just call it 'the back road by Albrook.' There aren't a lot of street signs in the city so everyone gets familiar with landmarks. For example, there's a McDonald's up here where we're going to turn."

"This one coming up?"

"Yes. It's the only one."

We pulled to a stop by the McDonald's even though the light in the intersection was green. Laura nudged forward toward the corner, stopped again, and looked to her left. As if on cue, two delivery vans approached from that direction racing at top speed. They didn't slow down as they neared and shot through the intersection in front of us, the rush of air from their passing enough to rattle the Tercel. I was about to say something when I noticed *they* had a green light, too. All the stop lights were green, regardless of direction.

Laura peered down the street for more delivery vans. When I pointed out the lights, she nodded but said, "I never look at them anymore."

We turned to follow the vans. The new street was called *Tumba Muerto*, which has no literal translation but could be taken to mean "it falls down dead."

"Watch the guy!"

Two men appeared out of the darkness at the side of the road. They hopped off the curb in a manner suggesting haste but half-way across the first lane one apparently decided hurrying wasn't for him. We were too close to stop but with a flick of the wheel

Laura cut to the outside and missed him by inches. He looked in our direction and yelled something unintelligible.

"Nice job, idiot!" yelled Kerr. To her friend she added, "Good driving, chica."

"Yeah, nice," I offered as calmly as I could. We had come very close to spreading the guy all over the road.

"Hey, Mike," said Kerr. "Why did the Panamanian chicken cross the road? So its owner could collect $4. That's what they cost if you hit one."

I wondered what you owed for hitting a fat man outside a McDonald's.

For two miles the women pointed out sites of interest: the RostiPollo fried chicken restaurant, the corner where Laura had gotten her first Panamanian traffic ticket (for changing lanes without signaling, she sniffed), the dip in the road that flooded daily during rainy season, the turnoff for the Trans-Isthmian highway that you *didn't* want to take (even though it was legal) because the police would always pull you over and say you were being unsafe, and the Circle of Death.

"The what?"

"The Circle of Death," Kerr said matter-of-factly. "It's coming up at the bottom of this hill."

"You won't appreciate it because it's so late and there's hardly any traffic," Laura added sadly. "But during the day it's ridiculously dangerous." She perked up. "It's a roundabout except there are no rules. You just try to get through it as fast as you can without hitting anyone."

There was in fact a roundabout at the bottom of the hill. Three streets converged on it at different angles, one of them branching off to join the entrance to the Trans-Isthmian highway. The highway itself passed over the intersection on a viaduct, providing the added distraction of cement support pillars flanking the curving road. Even without the pillars it was a six-spoked wheel with the hub hiding in the shadows of a bridge. Like the other streets, Tumba Muerto descended to the circle and then rose up another hill once past it. The image was of a bowl with each street heading downhill to join a giant swirl at the bottom. I wondered aloud what the rain did to traffic here.

"Turns it into a harbor!" Kerr laughed. "People still try to get through and there are always a handful that end up floating until the water drains away."

Having few cars to compete with at this hour of the night, we caromed into the circle like a satellite entering orbit. The Tercel used the bottoming energy to launch itself at the hill on the other side. Kerr pointed out the university on our right.

"The University of Panama. When they're in session it's supposedly a good school."

"Are they *not* in session a lot?"

"Students here protest. The whole university closes down once or twice a month. Last year it was the Liberty Battalions you had to worry about, this year it's rock-throwing students."

"What do they protest?"

"The standard student stuff."

"Us?"

"No, but avoid them anyway. If they see a car with a military sticker on the windshield or a "2" on the license plate you're probably going to become a target."

"Why a '2'?"

"All plates registered to foreigners start with a '2'."

Laura swerved around a pothole you could have mined coal from.

"Mostly it's government corruption or student benefits that gets them mad. Endara proposed a decrease in academic grants at the beginning of the summer and that closed the Trans-Isthmian road for two days. He proposed a law changing retirement rules and that closed the roads again. They even protested when both laws failed. You can't please everyone. That's why you hope for rain when you drive downtown."

"So they can't see you?"

"No, they don't protest in the rain. Strictly fair-weather types."

The light worked at the intersection just past the university, the first operational one we had seen. Apparently Laura did look at this one because we stopped.

"So," I collected my thoughts as we waited for the light to change. "Traffic here is dangerous, students are violent, rains are torrential, and the government is corrupt. Is that about it?"

"That's about it."

"You must hate it here," I told them.

Laura smiled. "No. The place grows on you."

The lights of the Hotel Panamá shone through a wall of palm trees, orange neon letters spelling out its name against the dark sky. As we approached it, however, Laura had an idea.

"Let's give him a tour of downtown," she urged her friend.

"Maybe he doesn't want one," Kerr replied. "He's probably tired."

In fact, I did want to turn in for the night but Laura was adamant. "No, we'll make it quick. We shouldn't just dump him off like a bunch of luggage. You drive, girlfriend, because you know this part of the city better than me.

We pulled over a block from the Panama and the women swapped seats. I could see the spray of a fountain at the entrance to the hotel. The beat of a salsa reached my ears. Patience, I told myself. Just a quick tour of the city.

Kerr drove us past the hotel, turned right on Via España and then left up a hill onto Federico Boyd, a darkened boulevard with mature trees down its middle. Dodging a sawhorse that stood inexplicably in the middle of the road, she pointed out a Chinese restaurant. "The Don Lee," she announced. "Good menu but the second-worst food poisoning in the city."

"Where's the worst?"

"La Cascada, over on the bay. We'll show you."

On the back side of the hill, Federico Boyd came to an end. It bisected a boulevard and stopped. Beyond the t-intersection was pitch black. The ocean.

The boulevard was Avenida Balboa, one of the main thoroughfares in the city. It ran along the shore but its location granted it no special dispensation as far as electricity – it had no more streetlights than any other street we'd seen. There wasn't a night life, either. All the businesses in either direction were closed. An enormous blue sign for Panasonic towered above the street a mile to our left. It flashed on and off in a display that intermittently broke up the darkness on that side of the street, but that and a few cruising taxicabs were the only signs of activity. The land curved past the sign, making the bay about five miles across and maybe a mile deep. Over there was a forest of high-rises capped by the lighted letters (also blue) of the Plaza Paitilla Inn that stood at the base of a squat peninsula. The rest of the buildings had a scattering of lights in each that implied they were apartments but overall that side of the bay just faded into the ocean.

A bay that in any American city would have been the centerpiece of the town was here an abyss that started on the sidewalk and stretched out as far as could be seen. The only lights on the water were far to the right, behind where the land curved to form a small peninsula. Ships waiting to enter the Canal.

We turned right. Nothing was open in that direction, either. The only well-lighted building was the U.S. Embassy, quietly ensconced in a classic building with a colonnade facade. Across the boulevard from it a pleasant boardwalk ran along the bay, bordered by a low wall and wrought iron lamps. The walk was deserted.

"This part of the city empties out at night, huh?"

"The safe parts do," Laura affirmed. "And it's the weekend. Most people have left town for the countryside."

A mile past the embassy the road narrowed and curved into a congested area of apartment blocks and cobblestone streets.

One restaurant was open there, marked by a constellation of Chinese lanterns. Open and crowded. Between the bougainvillea-covered trellises we could see it was standing room only.

"La Cascada," Kerr explained. "Great food but it might kill you."

"It can't be too bad," I commented, swiveling in my seat as we passed. "The place is packed." Even the parking lot was full. A guard leaned against one of the cars, a rifle looped over one shoulder.

"Take our word for it," insisted Kerr. "Your First World gastrointestinal system won't stand up to their Third World cuisine. Steve and I know only one guy who has eaten there and still been able to walk the next day."

"Food poisoning?"

"Big time."

"You don't get used to their germs after being down here a while?"

"Maybe after twenty years."

She studied how to turn around.

"Well, shoot, where's the street with the embassy?" she complained, peering at each corner that we passed.

"The U.S. Embassy?"

"No, some Arab country. It's on a corner and has a good street to go around the block."

"I don't know," Laura answered. "We passed the one I was thinking of. It was by the school for the blind."

"What school for the blind? There's no school for the blind."

"The school for the blind, that curving street – how does anyone get around down here without knowing street names?" I asked.

"Um, dearie, we'd better turn around because we're heading into El Chorillo."

"I know, but that last street was the only street I know. We'll have to go back on Balboa. Where's the next turn-around?"

The only street that appeared didn't look like it went anywhere. It angled off to a cobblestone square in the middle of which was a bus disgorging passengers.

"Oh, shoot! Laura, what do I do?"

"Why can't we go straight?"

"Because we'll go into El Chorillo," Laura repeated. "The people there don't like gringos. We'll get lost and we'll get killed. Laura, get in the left lane and make a U-turn."

That made sense. All we would have to do is turn around and follow the sea wall back the way we had come. But as we approached a break in the median another obstacle appeared. This one was a barrel placed in the middle of the eastbound lanes. Leaning against it was a policeman.

The cop barely looked up as Kerr passed, thinking we intended to turn left into El Chorillo. Not until Kerr turned all the way around did he sense something out of order in his world. He barked at her. She stopped. He waved his finger and shook his head.

"But we need to turn around," Kerr pleaded.

On hearing English, the policeman craned his neck to see our license plate. Then with sudden energy he pulled a ticket book from his back pocket and stood up.

"Oh, bullshit," exclaimed Laura.

Kerr straightened the wheels and hit the gas. We shot forward onto the hill street. As my head scraped the roof liner I heard the policeman blowing a whistle behind us.

"Oh boy, oh boy, oh boy, oh boy," Kerr said quickly. "That wasn't good. That was definitely not good. I should've just paid the bribe. That was not good."

Laura pulled herself up from where she had been tossed in the back.

"You might say that," she snapped. "You who were giving me all that grief about *my* tickets!"

I kept quiet. Visions of a high-speed chase by machine gun-toting Latinos in mirrored sunglasses flashed through my brain:

Thelma and Louise were going to get me killed before I had moved into my hotel.

"Oh, what did I just do?" Kerr exclaimed, slapping the steering wheel with her palm.

The street became one-way. There weren't signs but it got too narrow to be anything else. By the time we climbed the hill it was impossible to see the waterfront behind us.

We drove into an older section of the city, what looked like it might have been the downtown area of an earlier age. The buildings on either side leaned over the street. All were shuttered for the night.

Kerr rounded corners with abandon, putting distance between us and the whistle-blowing traffic cop. In about four turns I was no longer sure where the water was let alone the street that would lead us out.

"You might want to slow down," I advised. "I can't see around these corners and if we run over somebody we're going to have a serious problem."

"Yeah, slow down, babe," said Laura. "That guy didn't even have a bike. He's not going to follow us."

Kerr slowed to ten miles per hour but not before we slammed into a patch of street that was missing all its bricks. My head hit the roof so hard I thought I would break through.

A church appeared and we pulled over to the curb. Kerr needed a minute.

"Sorry, guys," she said, aiming her apology at me. "I don't normally do that."

Laura laughed from the back. "Steve's going to kill you! Steve's going to kill you!" she chanted.

"Well, he ticked me off!"

"How could he tick you off? He didn't do anything!" Laura slapped her friend on the side of the head. "If that happens again just stop, *I'll* pay the ticket."

"It wasn't *paying* the ticket, it was getting it! What the hell was he going to give us a ticket for, other than being gringos? He could have just told us how to turn around or let us pass."

"We should avoid any cops now," I suggested. "If that guy has told his buddies, they're probably going to haul us in somewhere if they see us again. Do they have radios? Can he call somebody else or is it even worth it to them?"

"I don't know," said Laura. "I don't think so. I guess we'll find out."

"There's a car coming, we're going to have to move."

Kerr looked in the rear view mirror. "Is it the police?"

"I can't tell," was Laura's answer. "Do you want to wait and see?"

Kerr put the car in gear.

We drove a block into a square fronted by another church. It was empty. I wondered where everybody went on Friday night.

Kerr turned right, then had to drive up on the sidewalk to get around trash bags piled in the street. She sped up and took the next left.

"Okay, where the hell are we?" she asked. "I can't tell which way we're headed."

"Don't ask me," I replied. "I haven't seen a street sign since I got into the country."

"I think we're near Old Town," Laura suggested.

"Honey, we're *in* Old Town, I just don't know where."

"Well, it's a peninsula, right?" I suggested. "If we just keep going one way we'll hit water and then be able to figure out which way to go?"

"Yeah, but the idea is to get out of here because this area isn't a whole lot better than El Chorillo."

"Then how about we stop and ask someone?"

Kerr hesitated. "Um, I'm not thrilled about three gringos stopping to ask 'How do we get out of your neighborhood.' Last year an American chick was raped in here. Damn, here comes traffic."

A car crossed our path and disappeared down a cobblestone alley. Kerr followed him. Immediately we found ourselves stalled behind four cars that waited on someone up front who we couldn't see. Cars two and three were already blowing their horns. Kerr tried to back up but before she could a taxi swung in behind us.

"Come on, damn it! Move!" she shouted. Whoever it was four cars ahead of us gave no indication of being pressured by her impatience, but she did attract the attention of people standing outside a *tabaqueria.* One man called something back to her that I didn't understand and they all laughed.

"Oh, good," she muttered.

"Don't worry, Mike," said Laura, patting my shoulder. "Panas are mostly wimps. They don't start fights with gringos unless there's about fifty of them."

I looked up the street. Some of the *tabaquerias* in this neighborhood were still open and people were out and about. They could probably scrape together fifty without much trouble.

The car in front of us moved. Kerr shoved the Tercel into gear and followed on its bumper. When the line bogged down again we were farther into the neighborhood than ever. People leaned over balconies and stared at us. Others walked by and did the same. From somewhere came music.

"Is this some kind of holiday?" I asked. "Maybe it's a block party."

"I don't know, but I'm baking back here," Laura complained. "And I don't like being stuck in this traffic. This isn't safe."

Kerr gave the rear view mirror a look that said 'Tell me something I don't know.' She moved forward and to the left to peer around the car in front of us. The driver of that car thought she was trying to squeeze past and blew his horn, making wild motions with his hands. Kerr blew her horn in return and yelled for him to shut up.

Traffic inched forward. It could do no more since people were starting to walk between the cars. More than once someone pushed against us or leaned on the Tercel in passing, enough to shake it and make Laura start. Some teenagers on a balcony saw Kerr's blond hair and called to her, making lewd gestures. The staring was the most nerve-wracking.

Then the rock hit the windshield.

Actually, we heard the whistle first. It came from behind us – shrill, piercing blasts. We jumped and Laura shrieked. Not knowing if it was the police I assumed the worst. Then the windshield got hit. It cracked the glass at the top on my side and bounced up onto the roof.

"Tour's over," Kerr announced, and stomped on the accelerator.

We lurched forward and clipped the bumper of the car in front of us. People jumped out of the way as Kerr accelerated through the tiny space between the other cars and the building. She wrenched the steering wheel at the corner and made the turn onto the next side street.

Behind us people yelled and waved their arms. A couple of men made half-hearted efforts to run after us but Kerr floored it.

Laura curled up in the back seat and slapped the driver's headrest like a jockey wielding a crop. "Go!" she shouted. "They're chasing us!" Then she stopped to look out the back window and added, "No, they're not! No, they're not! They're not chasing us!"

The next street was brick, sunken in the middle like a rain gutter. The cross streets were concave, too, so when two roads met the rain gutters converged and the intersection became a free for all of ridges and valleys. Kerr hit the first intersection unknowing and when she did the Tercel became a bucking bronco. Only momentum and a racing engine carried us through. I bounced in my seat like a rag doll.

Finally, her panic subsided and we slowed down. There was still no obvious way out of the labyrinthine neighborhood but our current street was quiet. A *chunk-chunk-chunk* came from the right front wheel.

We passed another barrier and at this point thought nothing of driving around it. At the next corner I looked right and left. The streets paralleling our course were closer. In fact, they were converging. And the music from earlier became louder.

"We're going the wrong way," I said. "We're heading to the end of the peninsula."

"I don't think so," said Kerr.

"I know so," I said. "Take the next right."

"Let's put some more distance between us and them first," Kerr replied.

"I don't think we can," I said. "What's at the end of this thing?"

Neither of them answered. Laura was still glued to the back window and Kerr went back to driving as fast as she could.

On the next block, our street curved to the left. An alley split off at a forty-five but we stayed on the main road – and immediately hit the brakes.

"Found 'em!" I said. "So that's where everybody is."

We had run into a parade. From the looks of it an entire county fair was coming at us down the street. People stretched back as far as we could see, dancing and singing as they moved forward. A cattle truck carrying a band led the procession.

Two men danced in front of the truck, waving Chinese candles that spat flame and sparks. A third man beat on a drum. A woman on the truck added to the din through a bullhorn. She was trying to keep time with the music but had no obvious ability to match her enthusiasm so the result was sheer volume. Crunched over the wooden slats, she exhorted the crowd nonetheless, including the police.

The police. There were two that I could see. The first one looked up as we screeched to a halt in front of him. The second one continued dancing with a woman by the truck's grill, moving along with everyone else and careful not to spill the beer he held.

Kerr flung an arm behind my seat to back up. The first cop broke from the crowd and walked toward us, waving his hand for us to stop. The guys with the fireworks trotted in our direction as well. That attracted the attention of everyone else.

"Keep going," I said out of the side of my mouth, smiling at the policeman as though I understood what he wanted and was working hard to fix the problem. "Faster would be better," I added.

She backed up ten feet but then the transmission popped out of reverse. We coasted to a stop. While she pumped the clutch, the policeman picked up his pace. His waving became an angry motion.

"Let's go!" came the urgent whimper from the back seat. Laura slapped at the headrest again.

"I know, I know, I know, I know!" Kerr shouted. The shift popped into place.

We sped in reverse to the alley. The policeman reached the middle of the street and fumbled for his whistle. The crowd behind him roared. One of the dancers was almost on top of us. His goal seemed to be to shower sparks on our car before we could get away. He just missed the hood when we backed up the second time and now he ran full tilt, leaning forward with his flares overhead like an Olympic runner bearing torches. Kerr hit the brakes, shifted gears, and lunged forward again. The dancer tried to leap out of the way and strike the car at the same time but she cut to the right into the alley, scraping a rock wall and throwing up sparks of her own as she did. He lost his balance and fell in the street behind us, a hard, sprawling fall on the bricks. The candles clattered to the ground, flame shooting sideways into the curb.

"Okay," I said with a deep breath. "I've seen everything now. You can take me home."

The street we were on ran straight, which meant we headed away from the parade but not as fast as we could if we could turn around. As we passed an alley that bisected ours I looked left and could see the aft part of the parade only a hundred yards away. For all I knew we were only cutting around behind the procession.

But then the street came to an end and we popped out at the edge of the water. It wasn't the water we'd started on: it was the opposite side of the peninsula. We couldn't even see the water it was so dark but we could see across it to land on the other side. It was a small bay that lay between the old town area and the base of the Fort Amador causeway. A quarter of a mile away the lights of the Army post twinkled. San Francisco never looked so good from Alcatraz.

The street we came out on ran straight back into the city.

"Oh, oh! I know where we are!" Kerr cried.

"Big deal, so do I," I said. "That way."

We flew down the new street as fast as the Tercel would go. It eventually took us back into El Chorillo and for a moment I thought we were lost again.

"Great! Here we go again."

"No, this'll be really short," Kerr promised. She'd caught the scent now. We started cutting in and out of streets like a prairie dog searching his burrow.

"Down the next one," urged Laura, pointing. "Go to the *'Ventas, Ventas'* sign and turn by the dry cleaners. Then take that street to Central." She pronounced it the Spanish way, Cen-*tral.*

"Yeah," agreed Kerr, like she was planning a raid. "Then we can take the short-cut past the *Rey* store over to the bus station."

There were people out and about now but no one paid attention to us. And for all their expressed fear of El Chorillo the two Lauras paid no attention to anyone outside, either, consumed as they were in the search for the fastest way out of the area.

"No, not that way! That's the pedestrian mall," Laura counseled just as Kerr was about to commit herself to a left turn. "Stay straight, and turn where that one-way sign is."

"That's one-way *this* way," I pointed out.

"I know, but it's faster. The taxis block up the street we're supposed to take. See?"

I looked where she told me and had to admit she had a point. The impossibly narrow side-street we were passing was choked with cabs. One side of it was filled the length of the block with bars.

The one-way street was clear. A car tried to pull into it at the other end while we were only half-way down the block, but the driver saw Kerr barreling toward him and backed up. He settled for a blast of his horn and a vigorous arm-wave as we passed.

"We - are - not yet, not...yet," Kerr repeated to herself, still looking for one more turn. We drove down the best-lighted street I'd seen yet in the city. Perhaps for that reason, for the first time we began to compete with real traffic. The roadway was three lanes wide and traffic moved in both directions, creating an obvious conflict of interests as well as math. The three lanes were illusory, anyway, implied by the width of the pavement rather than physically painted on the asphalt. No one kept to one side or the other. Rather, cars moved forward the way water flows around rocks: when a space opened up or a weak point showed in opposing traffic, drivers rushed to seize it and then build on that advantage. The only reason this worked was because all the maneuvering slowed traffic to a third the speed that an organized system would have allowed. Cars drove around and among each other like ants going up and down a jungle path, impeding each other so much that everyone fought to find a shortcut around whoever was in front. The whole mess could have been dismantled in seconds had everyone just stayed in single file on their side of the road but it was one of those situations where the solution was a vicious circle: without universal participation, any individual's attempt to set an example would be ignored and treated like another obstacle; yet no one would even consider the idea unless someone led the way.

A Chiva bus rocketed through the intersection in front of us and Kerr slowed to follow it. In the lights it was finally possible to get a good look at this unique Panamanian creation. An old Blue Bird school bus, this one sported a paint job that would have done a Bronx viaduct proud. Red and white predominated, from the sleek horizontal lines that ran the length of the bus to the glossy, thickly-hedged trim around the windshield flanking the words "DR. DOOM" in bold script across the top of the glass just above the driver's head. Flames leaped aft from the grill. They gave way to an oasis scene behind the passenger door. There water shimmered beneath a desert sun while palm trees clustered at the shore, their leaves bending over to offer fruit and shade. A pair of dolphins frolicked in the water. Animals gathered, a swan stretched its wings, and a deer leaned its nose out to inspect an apple proffered it by a large-breasted mermaid just breaking the surface. Cultures, not to mention ecologies, collided in this image. The varying quality of the drawings and their placement on the available panels of the bus suggested it had been a group effort, as though each artist had been called in separately, surveyed what had already been done, and then said, "You know, this picture needs a (fill in the blank) right there." By far, the preponderance of time and most accomplished talents had been expended on the anatomy of the mermaid. For this part of the work the apprentices had obviously given way to craftsmen, the full-fledged members of the Chiva Guild. Not only was the mermaid beautifully drawn and given every advantage the layout and construction of the bus afforded, she was also in full view. Not used to seeing enormous breasts displayed on city buses I felt obligated to give these their due regard.

The mermaid was followed by cartoon characters for most of the rest of the bus. They gave way before the end to a brief infusion of religion in the form of the Virgin Mary. Dark-skinned with Hispanic features, she rose on angel's wings above the rear axle, her face serene, arms open to welcome all comers. Above her head was the elaborately-scrolled legend, "*La Madre del Mundo.*"

The bus passed and I saw the artwork didn't end with the sides. The rear windows were obscured with starbursts and fireworks and the kind of slogans that high schoolers and struggling artists share an affinity for: "Life is Death," "To Struggle is to Win," and the enigmatic "The Way is Always Free." But most interesting to me was the rear door. After the hood over the engine it was the most open, flat spot on the bus and the perfect place for a detailed portrait. Whoever had commissioned this vehicle must have thought so, too, for there in full color was a tall, bare-chested Mexican with bulging muscles and a washboard stomach. He wore black pants and boots and a red bandanna wrapped around his flowing black hair. He also carried an absurdly large machine gun and had a machete strapped to his leg. Before I read the caption I saw the face, and it looked so familiar that I knew I should recognize who it was. The whole picture was saying something to me but steeped in my new world I tried to relate it to Panama and it wasn't working. Then I saw the title the artist had put helpfully above the handle of the door: RAMBO. I looked again. The features, the hair, the heavy eyebrows, the cut of the jaw. *He's Mexican,* I thought. *Latino, anyway. He doesn't even look like Sylvester Stallone.* The bus tore down the street with me staring after it.

The Chiva had come from a bus depot up the hill on our left. I could see more buses lined up in a semi-circle at an on-load point. Whatever this area was it was crowded, not at all like the empty streets we'd puzzled over in the old town sector. Here it was Friday night in a big city. Had I been familiar with the city I'd have recognized that we were at the base of the back side of Ancon Hill.

As soon as Kerr made the turn to follow the Chiva, both of them collapsed back in their seats. They had no doubts where we were now. "Yes, we are," she sighed in triumph. "*Golden.*"

The women dropped me off at the hotel just after midnight, the Tercel limping up the driveway like a war veteran. The windshield had spider-webbed, one of the front wheels was off-center, and the entire right side was scraped clean of paint and trim. The parking lot attendant did a double take as we rolled to a stop by the fountain.

Kerr and I examined the damage, then she went into the lobby to call her husband and let him know they were on their way back. If the women didn't return to the base within an hour Steve and his cops would head out to look for them.

"Thanks for the ride," I told Laura, trying to sound sincere.

She eased behind the wheel again and gave a slight wave. Her bubbliness was gone.

Kerr came back. She couldn't get the passenger door to open so she climbed in through the window like it was the most natural thing to do. Laura may have been in shock but Kerr took it all in stride.

"Mike, you'll have a good time here in Panama," she said. "It's a funny kind of place but like Laura said, it grows on you."

"I'm sure," I said.

"Maybe we can come back next weekend and hang out with you again."

"Do that," I replied, thinking that gave me seven days to change hotels.

She tapped her friend to get going. Laura put the car in gear. Slowly, rocking with every turn of the right wheel, they rolled down the driveway.

When they left I sat by the fountain for a while, tired but needing my nerves to relax and enjoying the heavy, humid evening. I also wasn't quite ready for my first night in-country to end.

The doorman paced on the driveway. He chatted with a dozing guard stretched on the grass between parked cars. The street outside the lot continued to be busy. As late as it was, a cafeteria there, Manolo's, was doing great business and cars squeezed down the narrow street in front of it in an unbroken line. It was a comforting bustle, made more tolerable by the balmy air. And no one seemed in any real hurry. Drivers made a show of being impatient but it was all in good fun. They would get there when they got there. And if they weren't in a hurry, I told myself, how could I?

I relaxed. This was Panama. I couldn't wait to see it during the day.

4. The Problem with Panamanians

"THE PROBLEM WITH Panamanians," he said, forking too much pancake into his mouth, "is they're lazy."

I glanced around. The dining room wasn't crowded. It was early on a Monday and one of my first lessons in Panamanian culture was that Mondays weren't taken seriously. Still, there were people about.

My companion was American. He was about forty, overweight but with a tan that looked like it had been acquired through working outdoors rather than lying in the sun. He'd overheard me asking at the desk for the nearest place to eat breakfast and invited me to join him. His name was Bob Clammett. He didn't like eating alone, he said, and it became obvious why. He liked to talk. When he found out I was new to the country he leaped at the opportunity to share his observations. I just wished he would keep his voice down.

"Actually, lazy doesn't do them justice," he continued. "They're *actively* lazy. They're *creatively*, actively lazy. They would rather make an effort to avoid doing something than spend half the time doing it. As a culture, they're a joke."

I drank some papaya nectar and peered over the glass to see if anyone was listening.

"I like coming down here, don't get me wrong," he said, wagging his fork at me as though I had gotten him wrong. "The country itself is incredible. Have you seen the jungle yet? No? Go out to the Botanical Gardens by Gamboa. You'll get the Reader's Digest tour of everything they've got growing here. It's incredible. Awesome. They've got stuff in these jungles science hasn't discovered yet. They've got a zoo there, too, right by the gardens. You'll never want to walk in the woods again. Birds, bugs, big snakes – they've got a jaguar the size of a horse. And they're right around here, too. Not in the city, of course. Hell, the locals have eaten everything in the city, but right outside. You said you're at Howard, right? Howard? Yeah, you'll see stuff over there because *it's right in* the jungle."

I made a mental note to go to the zoo. If Panama really did have ten times as many poisonous snakes as the United States – in an area smaller than Texas – I wanted to know what they looked like.

"How long have you been here?" I asked.

"This trip? Two weeks. But we've had the contract for eight years so I've been down here off and on since '82. This coffee's cold." He grimaced at his first sip and looked around for another pot. None was nearby so he got up to search at the buffet.

I checked my watch. After two weeks of rushing to get things done for my move from the States it felt unnatural not being in a hurry to go anywhere. I would have to report to the base at some point but saw no reason to do it before people there had a chance to recover from the weekend.

Clammett came back with a new pot of coffee. "See?" he said. "How many people are in here and they can't have even one waiter around? And this is a 'nice' hotel."

Indeed, the Hotel Panamá was one of the better hotels in the city. On the outside it was unimpressive, occupying half a city block but surrounded by other buildings just as tall. Painted the color of a guava fruit, its facade had all the attractiveness of a rose-colored Soviet apartment block. Inside, however, a tropical retreat beckoned. From the driveway that curved past the entrance guests passed through a mini-mall of expensive shops and bubbling fountains leading to the lobby. The marble floor and teak paneling channeled light from chandeliers. The spaciousness of the lobby lent it a calming feel: after negotiating the hemmed-in streets of the capital it was soothing to walk past potted palms and listen to voices echo off the walls. The air conditioning made a difference, too. It escaped to the outside through the open lobby but touched anyone passing through, allowing them to breath, relax, and sigh like a tired swimmer. Beyond the lobby were more shops, the hotel casino, and a walkway to the swimming pool and courtyard restaurant. At night tiki torches lit the area around the pool, their light flickering off the water and disappearing into waving leaves of palms. It was possible to sit there in the evening air and forget you were in a city.

Unfortunately, the efforts to create an oasis stopped at the elevators. The rooms were unexceptional. The only distinguishing feature of mine was its size. With two king-size beds and an armoire large enough to hide a phone booth, my room had enough space to host a soccer team. The balcony was tiny. It overlooked a rundown tennis court and the backs of commercial buildings on the nearest big street, Via España. In all, the hotel had the feel of a place trying hard to look upscale but not sure how to do it.

Appearances aside, the Hotel Panamá was as centrally located as one could wish to be in the capital. Via España was *the* commercial street in the city: besides ritzy clothing stores boasting the latest European and North American fashions, the thoroughfare was flanked by electronics galleries, high-priced jewelers, and crowded cafes. A block away was the beautiful, castellated Iglesia del Carmen with its twin spires and string of copper bells.

The dominant feature on España, of course, was the banks. The main reason that Panama mattered to anyone in the world (besides the Canal), banks from around the world stood on every corner of every street throughout the downtown area. The Bank of Boston stared me in the face as I looked across from my balcony, as did the Banco Nacional de Panama when I looked east. Farther down the street was Panacambios, another local bank; BancoPopular, a Spanish holding; and Banco del Pacifico, who I knew nothing about other than there was a headline in the morning paper about it being investigated for laundering money. Closer than those stood DeutscheBank, the Korea Development Bank, the Bank of Scotland, and the stern facade of Bank

Mandiri where "Indonesian National Holdings" was carved into the marble. Finally, in the distance was the Bank of Switzerland – known locally as the 'Torre Swiss.' It was a 30-story white tower that loomed over a residential neighborhood north of Calle 50.

The Hotel Panamá's success was due to the fact that it was close to all of these banks. In fact, it was close to everything.

"They're very fashion-conscious," Clammett said, comfortable now with his new pot of coffee. "Kind of strange. They want to be like the big guys but here they take it to an extreme. All the young people want to look and act like Americans at the same time they complain about everything American. The older people like European styles, a more conservative look. Nobody just wants to be Panamanian, so when they try to be nationalistic and talk about "being Panamanian" they look foolish because it's obvious *they* don't even know what that means. How do you think Noriega got away with it for so long?"

"Got away with what?"

"Staying in power. I mean, yeah, he killed a few people and had his goon squads beat up more, but most of his support he got just by standing up to the U.S. It didn't matter to people why he was standing up to us, just that he did it. It gave them something to pin their Panamanian-ness on. They didn't stand for anything, they stood against something. And now that he's gone they're at a loss again. Endara's a better president but he doesn't have something obvious to stake an identity to – he's just the elected leader. In this country that's not enough. Not yet. And he's too willing to cooperate with the U.S. to get things done. Already people criticize him with a view to the next elections. It doesn't matter if they have any plans or suggestions of their own: it's clear that the next president will be picked from the group that whines the most about how he hasn't stood up to anyone. And Endara's no politician. He tries to get everyone to get along – he'll be ripped apart when '94 rolls around. My take on it, anyway."

The little I knew about Panamanian politics I learned because of our invasion the previous December. Since then news of the country was sparse in the U.S. as the media turned from the boring aftermath of war to more exciting stories, like the return of locusts to the Midwest and how they tasted when barbecued.

"How's he doing? Endara?"

"Alright given what he's got to work with. But...," Clammett shook his head for emphasis, "he's in a no-win situation. The people who never liked him to begin with now see him as a puppet of the Americans. The people who do support him expect him to work miracles now that he's replaced Noriega. After all, it took an invasion to put him in office so if he's worth that to the U.S. they think there must be something special about him. Don't forget, that whole thing rocked people's world down here. It was the biggest event most of them will ever see. Now they associate it with Endara so he'll have to deliver. And I think from reading the papers up north that people there expect a lot from him, too. There's just no way."

"What is it everybody expects him to do? Anything in particular?"

"No, just make it better." He put down his fork and ticked off a list on his fingers. "Better roads, better schools, more jobs for the university students – who riot about twice a month – more services for the poor, safer streets, lower taxes, increased trade: you name it, some editor in the daily paper whines about it. But there's no way. Even with Noriega gone the government thrives on corruption. Hell, most of the people in office are still the same as last December. And there are twenty-three families in this country who control the wealth – they won't give up their perks just because there's a change at the top. Maybe in a hundred years their idea of how to run a government will change but," he sat back with his coffee, "your tour should be over by then."

I thought about the invasion. I hadn't taken part in it but knew people who had. The flying must have been good.

Clammett said there were still signs of the destruction if you knew where to look.

"A lot of it's been repaired already. Most of the fighting was localized, anyway. The barracks on Fort Amador looks like Swiss cheese but there's almost no damage downtown. Except El Chorillo, of course. The gunships blew it to bits and then it burned. Folks there hold a grudge so keep your distance."

From my balcony I could see construction in the city. Buildings – high-rises – were going up all over. Somebody had money to build. I asked about that while Clammett swept away crumbs from a croissant. He shrugged like it was a pointless subject and instead told me about the Canal.

Bob Clammett was an engineer. His work involved maintenance of the Canal locks. There were three, two on the Pacific side of the continental divide and one on the Atlantic. For half an hour he gave me a verbal tour of their history and construction, from the spillways to the mule trains to the effect they had on Lago Gatún, the freshwater lake that provided the water for their operation. He was a man who loved his work.

"Did you know the whole thing is mechanical?" he asked. "Not a bit of hydraulics involved in opening the locks. Not a bit. They work the same way they did when the whole thing was built eighty years ago. That's why I'm here. The locals are learning but they're not into maintenance. Hell, you can see that by looking at everything we've turned over to them since the '77 treaties. Everybody's afraid that when they do finally get the Canal they'll screw it up so bad it'll have to be shut down. Everything right down to the pulleys and cables on the locks was designed a certain way and a certain size – there are companies in the U.S. that still make replacement parts from the original designs. If the Panamanians don't keep everything at a certain standard – you know, inspections, overhauls, spending the money they'll need to keep all the machinery up to snuff..." He snapped his fingers with a dismissive gesture to illustrate what would happen.

"And you don't think they can do it?" I inquired.

Clammett was eating again but pointed at the coffee pot as his answer. When he finally swallowed he said, "It's a question of standards. No. Well, hell, I don't know but I doubt it. The government's too corrupt and our little invasion isn't going to change that. The people are lazy and there's a culture of dependence. Not on us, on anyone who's willing to let them be dependent. Everyone thinks it's because the nasty Americans have held them back but if you go back in history you'll find that in the 1880's the French were writing home saying they would have to get Canal laborers somewhere else because the locals couldn't cut it. There are good people here, of course, but my guess is my company will have a contract for a long time to come, no matter whose name is on the deed to the Zone."

His lack of confidence in the Panamanians notwithstanding, Clammett loved the country. When I asked about the Canal again he forgot all about his breakfast and proceeded to tell me its history. From the original French attempt to build a sea-level pathway between the Atlantic and Pacific, to Theodore Roosevelt's adoption of the project and the grand opening in 1914, to the 1977 treaties signed by President Carter and Omar Torrijos, he led me through the highlights of the isthmus' last century, peppering the facts with asides about the principal characters. The physical construction of the Canal was his forte but he brought forth enough names of people involved in the original project and later to demonstrate that the waterway wasn't just a hobby with him. Before he reached the present time and his own involvement with the Zone I wished I had taken notes.

"It's an incredible story," he said, looking at his watch to see that we had passed more than an hour at the table. "Big! This Canal carries a lot of people and history with it. You should read up on it. You know, a lot of people travel and never learn anything about the places they visit, going home with pictures and nothing else. Don't be like that. Your time here will help a lot of things in the world make sense. And the Canal...well, it's the reason we're both here."

He gathered up his things.

"I'll be here until the end of the month so maybe we'll see each other around. Right now I've got to run. I'm already late." He signed the check and stood up awkwardly, realizing he had eaten more than he planned. He smiled and patted his stomach.

"Getting to be like the locals. Must be the climate."

5. Peligro

My first car ride in Panama told me that driving there resembled driving in the States the way herding cats resembles ballroom dancing. But that ride – when the two Lauras took me from my plane to the hotel – happened at night. It was so dark then that I had to assume the phantom cars and chaotic conditions were due only to the shadowy streets. During the daytime, I was sure, the roads would show more discipline. They would be more welcoming to the faint of heart.

On Monday I got to find out.

At mid-morning the base sent a van to the Hotel Panamá to shuttle people to Howard. A colonel and his wife climbed in before me, leaving me the option of crawling over them to get in the back or taking the passenger seat up front. I rode shotgun. The driver welcomed us cordially.

"Buenos días, señora y señores. Welcome to Panamá."

"Gracias," I said. "You can take us out to the base?"

"Oh sí, señor. I am professional driver. The best in Panamá. I take you now?"

"Yes, please."

Our first surprise was that there were few traffic lights in the city and most of the lights that did exist didn't work. No problem: there was an impressive collection of stop signs at most intersections. Unfortunately, nobody paid attention to them. Nor did anyone heed one-way signs, or the signs that cautioned traffic to merge, or the ones that prohibited turns at certain corners. Signs that said "*No entre*" or that prohibited parking were universally ignored.

There were few street signs, too, the kind that identified a particular way as Avenida Roosevelt, for example, or Via Brasil. Traditionally in Panama these were high on the side of a building at the corner of an intersection where Americans had installed them early in the century. Where the occasional one could still be seen it imparted a quaint, ordered feel to the road. But most signs outside the Canal Zone disappeared long before 1977 and those in the Zone were pilfered or destroyed during the invasion. So it was hard for me to track our progress.

Of course, it might have been difficult to track anyway. The street map I took from my hotel room showed three different streets with the name of Calle 33. It showed projected roads where none existed. It also showed Avenida Central turning into Avenida 1 Norte and then into Avenida Simón Bolívar but didn't specify where the transitions occurred. You just had to know.

The only signs in abundance were small yellow ones with black lettering that read "*Peligro,*" which means "Danger." The signs never explained what danger was approaching or how near it was or whether it was temporary or permanent. They just announced its existence: *Peligro.* Sometimes these warnings were mounted close to an obvious obstruction like a fifty-gallon drum with a lighted smudge pot on top of it – whose presence was often unclear as well – but sometimes the signs were mounted on a sawhorse with no further explanation. You could drive down a street and suddenly come upon a placard leaned against a tree, at the curb, or in the middle of your lane. *Peligro.* They were an existential reminder that danger lurked everywhere.

Lanes were another eye-opener. A concept more than a reality, they were painted on only some of the major streets. This left the width of other streets open to interpretation, especially the heavily-traveled side-streets that everyone used for shortcuts. On these it was difficult to drive even in light traffic. The pavement was narrow and the *Estacionamiento Prohibido* zones in residential areas were always jam-packed with parked cars. If you encountered a vehicle coming from the opposite direction, forget it. Someone had to yield and go in reverse or bodywork would be in order.

And bodywork was in order a lot. Not that people tried to hit each other – it was more a Hobbesian mentality of inevitable conflict that descended on the driving population whenever they faced a choice of yielding or forging ahead. Instead of getting out and pacing off steps to decide if they had room to pass most drivers made an instant determination and then floored it.

On streets where lanes did appear their function wasn't so much to separate traffic as to provide a reference for its unpredictable motion. Cars ducked and weaved and merged and raced and inevitably stopped for long periods everywhere there was pavement. That included the sidewalk. Our driver lurched along with the flow, stopping short then gunning the engine the instant the vehicle ahead of us moved up an inch. To keep from being thrown against the seatbelt all the way to Howard I propped my foot against the dash.

"This is incredible," I heard the colonel's wife whisper. I turned and with a smile offered her the front seat. She declined.

From the El Panamá we went north up Calle 49 and then cut left a block to get on Tumba Muerto. I remembered Laura had come in on that road Friday night and was hoping the driver would go back through the Circle of Death so I could get my bearings. But he didn't. Instead he turned left down Tumba Muerto (no mean feat since it was a boulevard with no breaks) and drove back to Via España, where we then forced ourselves through the logjam at the intersection and seized half of the sidewalk to continue west. I heard two "oh!'s" from the colonel's wife and one "Watch it!" from him. I would have offered my own outbursts except my teeth were clenched.

I wanted to talk to the driver to practice my Spanish but didn't. Besides my clenched teeth, I was afraid of distracting him and causing a fiery crash and 97-car pile-up. In turn, he ignored us. That was okay since he talked to himself the whole trip anyway. Or rather, he had one-sided conversations with the drivers around us. He addressed the windshield non-stop, calling this person a fool, screaming at that one about his mother, and baiting a third with challenges like, "Oh, you think you can get in there, do you? Does it look like I am not here? You cannot push that boat wherever you please! Don't even try it. Don't even try it! Don't...! *Puta de madre!!!*"

"Oh!"

"Watch it!"

From España we leaped onto Avenida Central where traffic really exploded. Central went all the way through El Chorillo and into the Santa Ana district where the Lauras and I had gotten lost the Friday before, but between us and those neighborhoods it turned into a pedestrian mall. Inconveniently that mall blocked access to where everyone wanted to go – the bridge road – so cars popped in and out like roaches from the side streets that abutted it. They came from all directions, including our main road, converging on the street where the stores began and creating multi-directional gridlock. Cars radiated outward from that single most coveted patch of real estate in the city, the drivers all revving their engines and honking their horns and gesturing from behind closed, air-conditioned windows. From overhead it would have looked like a giant magnet somewhere on the street had pulled in cars for a mile around. Or maybe a rugby match is a better metaphor, for like a scrum in a cloud of exhaust the mass of honking, smoky cars seethed back and forth across Cinco de Mayo Plaza, fighting with the pedestrians and *chivas* that crowded the bus stop there. Progress happened but only by chance: if a driver found himself close to Avenida 3 Sur he could seize the moment and cut over to Calle K or Calle J, narrow paths of broken concrete that would take him to freedom. Or depending on how crafty he was feeling and how impossible the situation at Cinco de Mayo looked, he could race down Calle 24 Este to Avenida Balboa and try to dart across the mall south of the Napoli Pizzeria. There Calle 17 Oeste would take him up the hill to the Avenida de los Martires, the bridge road. The city was a maze, the bridge was the cheese, and every driver was a hungry, frustrated mouse. The only choices we had were to give up and walk, or stay and slug it out in the plaza.

This morning our driver slugged it out. After twenty minutes of monologue in which he alternated dry commentary with raging outbursts, he finally squeezed us between a van advertising Bimbo Bread and a Mazda pick-up stacked with electrical conduit pipe that hung so far out the back of the bed it scratched a following car and instigated a Pana-fight: no violence but lots of yelling and dramatic gestures.

We turned up 3 Sur, a side-street cratered with potholes and flanked by crumbling tenements. Laundry hung from windows. Antennae and electrical wires crowded on the balconies. On one corner as we went up the street a demolished house lay in a pile of rubble twenty feet high. Out of the rubble a skinny dog appeared and trotted across the street directly in our path. He didn't look up as we missed hitting him by inches.

In the back the colonel's wife sat rigid in her seat. This was not the country welcome she'd been looking forward to. To take her mind off the traffic her husband quietly explained how this neighborhood had burned after the C-130 gunships pounded it during the invasion. Our street being clear for the moment, I took the chance to ask the driver.

"*Este, no,*" he replied, not taking his eyes off the road which reassured me. He pointed over his shoulder to the left. "*El Chorillo. Todo el barrio se quemó. Todo!*"

It had all burned because a year before the buildings there had been wood. When troops from Howard poured across the bridge onto the Avenida de los Martires, Liberty Battalion snipers hidden in the apartments opened fire on them, prompting the Americans to call in gunships. A few rounds from the Spooky's 105mm howitzer set the whole area ablaze. Building after building burst into flames, forcing snipers and residents alike to flee, running down streets in terror as bullets rained down. The slum tenements, the derelict stores, the whorehouses and bars and kiosks selling liquor and gum all went up in smoke. The densely-packed neighborhood that had festered in poverty since the 1950s became a bonfire of nobody's vanity. In the sense of urban planning, however, that wasn't all bad. Like the Great Fire of London clearing out the plague, within hours Chorrillo was no more, its long overdue renovation halfway resolved. Halfway, for in March the U.S. cleared away the ashes and built anew. Army engineers and contractors descended on the neighborhood and in two months rebuilt three square blocks of apartments.

"*Allí, véalos,*" the driver pointed proudly. He pulled far enough onto the bridge road to block the oncoming traffic that wouldn't have let him through anyway and gestured toward the new neighborhood down the street. It was an uninspired but functional collection of square concrete buildings painted coral green and blue. The laundry and antenna collection was similar to what we had just seen but the absence of pirate electrical wires running in through every window suggested the locals were finally wired to code. Clean and bright, the new Chorillo leap-frogged past the areas either side of it.

Forcing our way across two lanes of traffic that only at the last second decided an accident was more inconvenient than giving way, we turned onto the bridge road and headed west.

The west lanes were clear. Most traffic was coming into town and we were heading out. For the first time since leaving the hotel we could drive without it being a struggle.

Our driver clapped his hands in anticipation, meaning he took them off the wheel which caused my heart to skip a beat.

"*Ahora vamos a recuperar el tiempo que perdimos!*" he cried and pushed the accelerator to the floor. The van lurched forward.

I hastened to point out that we didn't need to make up time but it made no difference. A clear road in Panama is like a rain shower in the Sahara. You don't consider whether you need the water. You just drink.

The Bridge of the Americas was choked with cars in the inbound lanes. By contrast our lane was almost empty.

We raced across the canal, the chipped and cracking asphalt bouncing us like a cattle guard and creating echoes through the steel span of the bridge. Below, the water of the canal stretched left and right. A container ship moved under us toward the Miraflores Locks, its decks stacked so high with 18-wheeler-size crates that it seemed I could have stepped down from the bridge to ride it to the Atlantic.

The speed with which we covered the length of the bridge and then the two miles of Pan American Highway until reaching the Howard Air Base turnoff could have calmed me down. I could have forgotten the jams in the city and relaxed in the knowledge that now on the open road traffic was just like anywhere else. But that would have been a waste.

Our van was a Mitsubishi. It didn't have a lot of power. Climbing up the city side of the bridge our driver used momentum to squeeze past a half-ton flatbed truck just before our two lanes merged into one. In the back of the flatbed, locked in by wooden slats braced around the sides, were a large pig and a dozing farm worker. In the front was a driver who was about to teach us a lesson.

In the States Americans coined the term "road rage." Panamanians didn't call it anything, although expatriates called it "pana-jacking." And for the locals pana-jacking carried a significance out of all proportion. It went beyond not letting others merge into your lane. It went beyond moving into the intersection even though you knew the light would turn red and you would be stuck there, blocking other traffic. It went beyond turning right from the left lane. Panamanian drivers wanted whatever piece of pavement you were trying to inhabit and would move heaven and earth to get it. That included passing.

On the long downslope of the bridge we gained on a small Mazda pick-up carrying firewood. Suddenly the pig truck shot by us close on the left, horn blaring. It caught all of us by surprise, including our driver. He swore and waved a cupped backhand at the truck driver who continued on past the pick-up. We then moved into the left lane to pass the pick-up ourselves. The pig driver, however, saw us change lanes and immediately slowed down to block our way. He slowed until he was abeam the pick-up truck and stayed there. The pig and the farm worker – now awake – struggled for balance, caught on a swaying platform already moving faster than the chassis was comfortable with.

Our driver continued swearing while the colonel and I tried to calm him down.

The driver of the pick-up didn't like being in the middle of our conflict. He tried to speed up to get away from us but the pig driver was having none of that. He sped up, too. Both vehicles had tremendously inefficient engines so when either driver stamped on the accelerator the first reaction was a plume of thick exhaust out the back. Our driver careened from one lane to the other in the smoke, looking for an opening.

In the meantime a fourth car appeared on the scene. A dark blue Mercedes with tinted windows roared up behind us all and squeezed into the left lane while we were on the right. My first thought was that this was an elaborate set-up for a hit, that any second the window of the Mercedes would roll down to reveal a machine gun pointed at our tiny minivan. But I could only dream of such a deeper motive. No, the Mercedes was just a wealthy driver in a hurry who wanted all of us to get the hell out of the way. He weaved and bobbed behind the pig truck, pounding his horn and flashing his headlights. The pig driver answered by weaving and bobbing himself to block everybody's way. His morning was thoroughly ruined and he wanted to share the feeling.

The poor driver of the pick-up had the worst of it. As he dodged to the right to avoid being side-swiped by the larger flatbed, his right wheels went into the emergency lane. Now, as explained earlier, the emergency lanes on Panamanian roads weren't there for you to drive onto should you have an emergency. They were there to cause an emergency. With their deeply-rutted gravel surface, gaping potholes, and unpredictable obstacles like stray rebar and old wheel hubs, they existed only as a more exciting alternative to the normal road.

In this case the pick-up driver momentarily lost control of his vehicle. He lurched right, then left, then – realizing he was about to be mashed by the pig truck – back to the right again. The motion sent chunks of chopped firewood sailing off the pile and into our path. One log hit us square in the grill with enough force that I expected it to come through the engine block and land between the front seats. Our driver squealed like the pig in the truck and applied his brakes – a novel concept that so far had appealed to no one in our little group of road warriors.

The pick-up truck, too, slowed down, but not before dropping a hefty log that landed under the rear wheels of the flatbed. The pig truck bounced over it at full speed. The sudden upheavel sent the pig crashing into the wood slats. They splintered and the pig went over the side.

"Oh!"

The farm worker dove for his charge and grabbed the pig's hind legs just as it was about to drop to the pavement. The truck careened across both lanes completely out of control. Through the window of the cab we saw the driver wrenching the steering wheel this way and that.

The Mercedes stayed with him, looking for an opening to pass.

Paradoxically, the pig was the calmest of all of us. Though he hung face down out the side of a pickup with his snout only inches from the pavement, the look on his face suggested he'd seen worse. The farm worker was too small to haul him back into the bed so the pig hung there, swinging back and forth and occasionally around the corner to the rear as the truck careened down the highway. Once he swung so high that he was looking straight at us, his front legs stretched out in front of him like Superman. I waited to see him come flying at us and right through our windshield.

Finally the pig driver scraped the cement barrier dividing opposing traffic. That stopped his weaving and let him get the steering wheel moving in only one direction. He pulled over into the cause-an-emergency lane and slowed down, watching over his shoulder as much as he looked out front in order to keep an eye on the pig he might lose at any second. The sudden deceleration threw farm worker and pig back into the truck to land in a heap amongst the splintered wood. Lives and livelihood survived intact.

The Mercedes driver gunned his engine and shot ahead. In seconds he was out of sight.

Our driver didn't stop, either. Satisfied the log hadn't done any damage he stayed on the road and maneuvered to the left lane against the concrete barrier. We passed both the pick-up and the flatbed, the latter getting a full dose of Spanish invective and a blast of the horn as we did.

Our turn-off was a hundred yards ahead.

At Howard's gate traffic was orderly and polite. The trim security guards with spit-shined boots stopped each car and calmly checked each person's ID. People waited patiently in line.

In the back seat the colonel looked ready to explode, his face a purplish-red. His wife cried. When we pulled up in front of the wing building he jumped out and stood there shaking, torn between beating the driver to death with his bare hands or simply having a nervous breakdown. His wife decided on the latter: in tears, she walked past her husband into the building. Eventually he followed her.

My t-shirt was wet in a long V down the front. I massaged the indents that my death grip on the door handle had put in my hand and climbed out of the front seat. No, I decided. The faint of heart need not apply here.

The driver watched the couple go.

"Hay algo malo?" he asked me, confused.

"The ride," I explained. "It was a little much."

"Cómo?"

"The traffic," I tried again. "Maybe that was not safe, the way you drove."

His expression went from bewildered to worried, realizing that whatever I was referring to could cost him his job. "No!" he insisted. "I drive good! *Ven conmigo.* You come with me now. You see!"

"Right, well I..."

"A qué hora vuelvo?" he demanded.

"Pardon?"

"A qué hora vuelvo? At what time I come back for you?"

"Uh, no need for you to come back. I can get another ride..."

He grew frantic. He jumped from the van and came around to grab me by the shoulders. "I drive good! I show you!" he insisted.

Through the doors of the headquarters I heard the colonel shouting into a phone. In a minute he would come storming outside and probably do the same to the driver. I looked at the man so afraid for his job and wondered if I didn't just need to put things into perspective. We had made it to the base alive, after all.

"Okay," I said. "Come back at four o'clock. *A las cuatro.* You can take me back to the hotel."

The driver squeezed my shoulders in thanks. He climbed back into the seat, realizing now it was in his best interest to leave quickly. Rolling the window down, he shouted gracias again and assured me I had made the right choice.

"I am professional driver," he reminded me. "The best in Panamá!"

6. A Cast of Many

LIEUTENANT COLONEL RASMUSSEN was brief.

"You're here to fly. You're here to make good decisions in bad situations and take responsibility when things go wrong. You're here to work with a lot of strange people and not talk about it. You hear that? This isn't national security but it is need-to-know, so if someone doesn't need to know something then you don't tell them. You're here to do what I tell you. You're NOT here to cause problems. You get in trouble doing your job, I'll back you up. You get in trouble because you're fucking around with one of my airplanes, then God help you because I won't. You have any questions?"

"No, sir."

"Anything you want to say?"

"Sir, I'm here to fly."

"Good. I'm glad to have you. You come well recommended."

I didn't believe that. The only recommendation he could possibly have received was *"You'd better take him far away before he gets into more trouble."*

"Thank you, sir."

And that was it. It wasn't that he was curt, there just wasn't anything more to say. As I was to learn over the coming months, my new commander was sincere, professional, and friendly to the people he worked with, especially with his pilots. But as a commander there were only three things that mattered: what had been done, what was being done, and what was going to be done. Everything else was window dressing.

"You talk to the colonel?"

Major Chip Harmon was waiting for me when I left the commander's office. Harmon was my flight commander, meaning he was my supervisor, but that was true only in a paperwork sense. Harmon belonged to the C-130 side of the squadron and had nothing to do with my flying. He wasn't even a pilot, he was a navigator, a position that any good flyer thought should have been phased out in the late 1970s and replaced with a two-dollar computer chip. And he had just been promoted to major so everyone else in the squadron was used to treating him like a captain except me. But when I walked into the squadron Monday morning he was the friendliest person I met, getting up from his desk by the scheduling board to say hello and boisterously welcome me to Panama. He also informed me that my additional duty – what I did when I wasn't flying – was scheduling. That meant I worked for him. He said it like it was a gift.

Harmon was a nice guy. He was a good ol' boy with big teeth and an Elvis leer that made them look even bigger. He was also big in body, being an amateur weightlifter except not disciplined about how he went about it. Judging from his build he was unconcerned about apportioning time to each muscle in turn and instead just worked on whatever grew fast. The upper body, mostly. His shoulders, arms, and chest were massive. His back was wide and his traps grew together to look like one big muscle. They arched in a massive bow behind his shoulders so that he appeared to have no neck at all, just an average-size head that sat on his torso and looked around with misplaced confidence in his coveted physique.

Below his waist, however, the major was skinny. His legs were as thin as mine. Legs are a tough part of the body to work and from the looks of Harmon's he didn't try. His were runner's legs, long and lean despite supporting a top-heavy build that weighed in sixty pounds heavier than I did soaking wet. As I grew to know him over the coming months I found that the normal position for Harmon's feet was propped up on his desk by the ops counter. That was as much workout as they ever got, as Harmon casually munched Power Bars and directed activity around him. When he wasn't finessing numbers on the board he declaimed on weightlifting and women to anyone who would listen. Sometimes it seemed like that was all he knew to talk about. But he ran a tight schedule.

"Yes, sir, I did."

"And?"

"And what?"

"And what did he have to say?"

"He's glad I'm here, he expects a lot, and, uh...well, that was about it, I suppose." I couldn't help looking over his shoulder to the scheduling board where the week's sorties were written in grease pencil the length of the wall. Different missions were written in different colors so the board had a festive look: blue for training in the local area, red for test flights to make sure systems on the plane worked as advertised, and green for trips down to the Amazon. In case anyone was unsure, to the far right the codes were explained: *Local*, *FCF* (for Functional Check Flight), and *The Jungle Express.*

"Uh-huh." Harmon looked at me like I was holding out.

"Was there supposed to be something else?" I asked.

"Oh, no. I'm sure you talked about whatever you talked about."

He slipped around behind the ops counter and made a show of disinterest as he went back to work. Clearly he felt I had jilted him somehow.

When Charlie Manson appeared later to show me around I asked him about it. He laughed his signature sardonic laugh.

"He's a one-thirty puke. He's paranoid."

"I thought you used to fly -130s," I said carefully.

"I did. I don't now."

"So what's he paranoid about?"

"The 155th," he explained dismissively, "used to be here for one reason: DV airlift. Used to be. The CINC Southern Command had his T-43 and the wing commander here at Howard had his C-21. Kind of dumb, I know, an entire squadron to carry around 'Distinguished Visitors' but hey, that's how it was. Then last year the C-130s arrived to do surveillance over Colombia. A different mission. Not too dramatic – all they do is fly circles and take pictures and listen in on phone calls, but it's more respectable than serving coffee to some four-star. So for a year *they've* been king. Herc guys are always looking for somebody to look down on and here they had the DV pukes as their water boys. They ruled."

"So?"

"So now *we* show up," he continued. "Uh-oh, new kids on the block! Some black hole in the Pentagon dreams up the C-27 and adds it to the mix down here. The -130 guys are scared. We already outnumber them in pilots and planes, and worse – " he looked around to see if anyone else could hear him "– they're not sure what we do or how long we're going to stay. They're afraid they're going to be pushed into the background. Which," he smiled happily, "they are."

I nodded as though I understood.

"And what is it exactly that we do?"

Manson looked at me in mock horror. "You don't know?"

"Uh, no."

He grinned wickedly. The man had a face for it. "That's the beauty of it. Nobody does. Hell, I'm in charge of tactics and even I don't know. Rasmussen might but he's keeping it to himself."

"Well, what?" I asked. "Drug raids, troop re-supply, radar sites?"

"Probably all of the above. Keep guessing. Maybe whatever you come up with we'll add to the list. That is, when we have a list. Until then we're going to make it up as we go along. Which suits me fine. It's hard to screw up a job if you never had it to begin with."

The 155th Tactical Airlift Squadron operated out of Hangar 1 on the flightline. There were two hangars on the Air Force side of the ramp, which was most of the ramp. Down at the south end were two more hangars, smaller structures where the Army garrison of Fort Kobbe kept its UH-60 Blackhawks and UH-1 Hueys.

Manson walked me across the hangar to the Replacement Training Unit. The hangar was a cavernous girder-and-sheet metal structure with a cement floor and four-story-high sliding doors on two sides. Two floors of enclosed office space had been built onto the walls of the long axis. On the east wall was the operations side of the squadron, on the west side was the RTU. The RTU looked like a double-wide trailer turned on end. Its bottom portion was a store-room while upstairs the tiny space was shared by Manson's office and a classroom. A metal staircase led up the far wall.

"It's not much but this is what we have to work with," he explained, stopping at the bottom of the stairs. "Eventually we'll use the classroom for a three-week ground school followed by three weeks of flying. We don't have enough guys for that yet, though, so you'll do both at the same time."

"Three weeks is still a good amount of time," I offered.

"Yeah, well, you probably won't get that, either," Manson scoffed. "The Chuck is new and everybody's asking for it. Rasmussen wants to get as much visibility as soon as we can so somebody in that same black hole doesn't change his mind and cancel the program. We need guys to fly the line so you may do a lot of your training OJT."

On-the-job training sounded alright to me. It beat sitting in a classroom looking at overhead slides.

"But how could they cancel a brand new program?"

"Easy. They've already scaled it back. The original order was for 18 planes but we're not getting 18."

"How many are we getting?"

"Many."

"Say again?"

"No one knows. There are three out there on the ramp right now. Bob Harcourt's supposed to bring another one down next week and more are promised but nobody will give an exact number. So all we know is we'll have more than three. You ever hear of the Piraha?"

"The what?"

"The Piraha. An Indian tribe in Brazil. They had an outbreak of plague a few months ago. You didn't hear about it?"

"Uh, no."

"Well, now you have. One of our first missions here was to fly them antibiotics which it turned out they were allergic to. We ended up killing more of them than the plague did," he laughed. "Irony, that. But the point is we tried, and the other point is they don't count in numbers. Everything up to three is 'a few,' and any more than that is 'many.' So guess how many planes we're getting?"

"Many?"

"That's exactly right! We're getting 'many.'"

"But if you don't know the number of planes, how do you know how many pilots we'll need?"

"Oh, I know exactly how many pilots we'll need."

"Many?" I guessed again.

"Exactly."

"That's got to make managing a squadron difficult."

Manson pointed to me like I was the bright pupil in the class.

"You've got that right," he said. "It's above my pay-grade but how anyone expects Rasmussen to build a flying unit when they won't tell him the number of aircraft he gets, the number of people, or his budget is beyond me. He's already cut back on people since the planes are late. That's why some of the pilots we were supposed to get by now were re-assigned to other bases. You squeezed in under the wire. It's bureaucracy and money. Also, we're attached to Tactical Air Command down here. TAC hates anything that's not a fighter. Nobody here will shed a tear if we disappear as fast as we showed up."

"What about the new Special Operations Command they just created?"

"Don't hold your breath. That command is dominated by C-130 guys. They'll see us as competition and try to destroy us rather than help."

"Competition? That makes no sense. We don't do the same job."

"Tell the -130 guys that. Believe me, I spent three years flying the Herc. The whole community is as insecure as a virgin at a convention of porn stars."

"And what about MAC?" The Military Airlift Command controlled most of the airlifters in the Air Force.

"Same thing. The C-130s *there* will see us as interlopers. They're part of the reason we only get ten planes instead of eighteen. They told the Pentagon we were unnecessary."

"How can they say that when according to the books the C-27 can land at five times as many airfields as a Herc?"

"They can say it because the Pentagon asked them for their opinion and they're the experts on tactical airlift."

"They lied," I said bluntly.

"Or they just didn't take the time to learn the truth," Manson offered. "But probably you're right – they lied. I told you, they're insecure. It's fun to mess with them for just that reason."

The door to the Supply office was unlocked. Manson ducked inside and fumbled for the lights, then mumbled "Ah, screw it," and moved around by feel. The sound of collisions and curses reached me but eventually he popped back outside, brushing dust off his flight suit. He held out a handful of patches.

"Here, throw these onto your flight suit. Boat on the left, kickin' chicken on the right."

He gave me two copies each of three patches. One was the Tactical Air Command patch to wear opposite my name tag. Another showed a 15th century sailing ship with the logo "24th Wing – *Los Profesionales.*" The last displayed the outline of a bird in full braking action as though it was desperately trying to reverse course or, worse, had already smacked a picture window.

"What is that?" I asked in disbelief, amazed that anyone would wear it on their shoulder.

Manson grinned his evil grin.

"The Group patch," he explained in triumph. "Designed by the Group commander's wife. Since we're a composite squadron he wanted all airframes to wear the same patch and coincidentally his wife has no artistic talent so she got to draw the design. Kind of a reverse capitalism, where lack of supply meets demand. Supposed to be an eagle or maybe a phoenix, I forget which. To me it looks like a chicken being dragged to the fryer. We call it the 'kickin' chicken.' Wear it with pride."

I would wear it with dark sunglasses.

"And the boat?"

"The *Santa Maria.* Colombus' boat. How that fits with '*Los Profesionales*' I don't know."

"The Professionals," I mused. "Are we professional?"

"In every sense of the word," Charlie answered. "Though professional *what* is open to debate."

From the RTU we walked back across the hangar and found another staircase. This one led to the floor above the orderly room. There we found the tactics shop and a single large room broken up by gray cubicles. On the door to the tactics office was a picture of John Wayne glaring into the camera. The caption read: "Life's hard, son. It's harder if you're stupid."

"Training, Supply, Pubs, Mobility – all that stuff," Manson explained as we walked through the large room without stopping. Nobody was in any of the cubicles since most of the squadron was still on post-mission crew rest from last week's trip. Several of the offices were still in the construction stage as well: the publications corner was a masterpiece of disarray with books and boxes stacked waist-high on the floor. An unplugged Commodore 64 computer peeked out from behind the vines of a potted plant.

One thing that was up and running on the second floor was the air conditioning. It was super-efficient, cold enough that I shivered. Condensation formed heavy enough on the windows that they were opaque.

We exited the cubicle room through a stairwell on the far side, walking back into blessed heat. We were now in the northeast corner of the hangar.

"And back here, confined to the attic like the red-headed stepchildren they are," Manson announced as he opened the last door, "are the glorious fliers and professional suck-ups of the DV side of the house." We walked in without knocking. A lieutenant and a captain were in the office looking at an enroute high chart of Costa Rican airspace. The captain didn't miss a beat.

"But not to you, Charlie, not to you," he said cheerily. "And don't forget the coffee and inflight meals. If you're going to make fun of our mission at least get it right."

He got up to offer me his hand. He was tall with golden skin, Latin features, and a hesitant smile that suggested he knew he was meeting yet another tac airlift pilot who would make fun of his job.

"Hey, Todd Bainbridge, welcome to Panama."

"Thanks," I said. "I'm glad to be here."

He looked at my nametag.

"Bleriot...Bleriot..., now why does that name ring a bell? Wait, where are you coming from again? Travis? Ohhhhh, that's why I know it. You're that guy from the C-5. The one who flew with the colonel! A buddy up there told me about it. No wonder they sent you to Panama."

He laughed out loud. I mumbled something about overblown rumors.

"You guys are really hidden away up here, aren't you?" I said to change the subject.

It was Bainbridge's turn to grimace.

"Yeah, well, we *used* to be downstairs. We *used* to be a lot of places. Every time somebody new shows up we get moved farther and farther away. Nothing personal, though..."

"Oh, no. Of course not," Manson chided.

"Hey," said Bainbridge, "at this point I'm just grateful we're still allowed in the hangar. One more plane gets here and they'll probably send us to Kobbe to live with the Army."

"McCaffrey would like that," Manson smiled. McCaffrey was the four-star commander of SOUTHCOM. An Army four-star.

We left the DV office by a back stairway.

"Yeah, I heard about your little attitude problem up in California," Manson said casually.

"Attitude problem?"

"Yeah, your little cockpit mutiny. Taking the controls from an O-6. Not a recommended career step for most lieutenants."

"Being dead isn't much of a career, either. He almost killed us."

Manson shrugged. "Hey, I wasn't there. But a colonel's a colonel. Just think it's funny, that's all. So that's how you escaped the C-5 in only a year. They sent you down here to get you out of his sight?"

"Pretty much."

"What did your buds up there think about that?"

I thought back to my ops officer in the C-5 squadron who turned pale when he heard I was leaving. "Don't go to the C-27, Mike," he urged me. "It's too new a plane. Never fly the A-model in anything."

"They thought it was a bad move."

Manson reached the bottom of the stairs and held open the door.

"Well," he said. "That is yet to be seen."

CHARLIE WAS GOING to give me a tour of the C-27 but was intercepted at the last minute. As we were heading out to the flight line Garb Taylor called down from Group Headquarters with an emergency.

Garb was a C-130 pilot who'd come to Panama to fly C-27s but who, like so many others, hadn't impressed Lt Col Rasmussen with his wit or wisdom. He'd flown C-130s for six years and now when flying the Chuck he just couldn't get the Herc out of his head, trying to fly the same way he always had and confusing ops limits between the planes. Twice he oversped the flaps and the gear on 91-104. On a good day he could hit the landing zone once every five tries. In his first month in country he almost crashed by mistaking the engine condition levers for the throttles – momentarily shutting off fuel in flight. And he was just as coordinated on the ground. On a mission to Honduras he ended up in the hospital when he tried to help the loadmaster off-load a pallet. Luz, another of the Puerto Rican mafia, didn't need help, certainly not from a pilot, and told Garb to stand clear.

"No," Garb insisted. "I'll watch the right side."

But he didn't just watch. He ended up on one end of the pallet when the forklift driver backed up too quickly. The pallet tilted and fell off the ramp, throwing Garb up against the cargo door (which knocked him unconscious) and then down to the ground (which broke his leg).

Since Garb was a nice guy and a good staff officer Rasmussen didn't boot him back to the States. He also didn't let him back in a plane. Instead he offered Garb a job at the Group. Garb accepted, being the kind of pilot for whom flying was nice but not necessary and honest enough to know that staff work was his strong suit anyway. He served the squadron well, too, as the whipping boy for the Group.

Group was the next command level up from the squadron. It was headed by a full colonel, Colonel Hunley, who was a navigator by trade. Hunley didn't interest himself in daily flying operations. That made him a great overseer for an independent soul like Lt Col Rasmussen.

Unfortunately, Colonel Hunley had a deputy by the name of Buncheman. Colonel Buncheman was a professional training pilot, a rare bird who had risen through the ranks flying only trainers like the T-37 and T-38. He'd never flown an operational aircraft in his life and so had a mission-focus more oriented toward dotting i's and crossing t's than in putting bombs on target or hitting a landing zone on time. He didn't have anything against the C-27 program but he didn't trust it, either, since in his mind any weapons system that consisted of only ten aircraft was suspect. He made a point to keep an eye on everything the 155th did. The result was that whenever there was a bureaucratic obstacle threatening to delay our flights, more often than not it had Buncheman's name on it.

Today it was the technical orders, what pilots call the "Dash 1." Tech orders are the instructions for how a plane works, the basic manual for what parts make up a plane and how you're supposed to make them all work together to get it into the air. Garb was calling to give Manson a head's-up that Buncheman had found out that the C-27 Dash 1 was written in Italian. Since the C-27 was an American modification of the Italian company Alenia's G-222, all the original manuals were written in the designers' language. The Air Force and Merrill Technologies were supposed to have translations by now but so far only a few drafts had made it to the squadron. Now Buncheman was threatening to ground the aircraft – and one plane was off-station in Colombia.

"Engines aren't in Italian," Garb told him. "Electrics aren't in Italian. We have mechanics so good they can build a new C-27 out of a toaster and a shopping cart. Just let them work." But Buncheman found that argument lacking.

Manson sighed and handed me off to Bob Harcourt. Growling something about 'paper-shuffling desk-rectums,' he headed across the street to Group HQ.

Bob Harcourt was...calm. Tall with an awkward frame and a lined face that made him look older than his thirty-five years, he was one of the last people you would notice in a crowded room, one of the last you would talk to, and the very last one who would talk to you. Not that he was unfriendly, just that his absolute-zero on the placidity scale made him as accessible as a room with a locked door. He had just made major against his will, having hoped to be passed over for promotion so he could leave the Air Force with an exit bonus. Even that didn't bother him much. Bob had mastered the art of complete indifference and didn't give a damn about anything.

Blindsided by Manson, he glanced at me like I was interrupting a hard-earned hangover.

"What is it I'm supposed to do with you?" he sighed.

"Uh, well, Capt Manson was going to show me the plane."

"The plane, huh?" He squinted across the field. "*Captain* Manson. Okay, we can do that."

We walked in blazing heat across the ramp.

If you saw everything on the airfield in relation to the runway, Hangar 1 – where the 155th was based – was about two-thirds of the way up the strip on the right side. The C-27s – only two now since one was away – were parked at the north end of the ramp with their noses poking over the grass. Since the runway was eight thousand feet long that meant we had half a mile to walk to reach them. Half a mile over steaming white cement that reflected heat like a stone griddle. Over the mountains small cauliflower clouds were building but it would take an hour yet for them to mass large enough to fill the sky and drop their afternoon rain. Until then the sun was free to abuse the earth. By the time we reached the planes I was dizzy like a lost trooper on an Arabian campaign.

"Hot?" asked Harcourt when we arrived, the monotone not giving indication that he cared. He was sweating, too, but since he'd looked like hell when we started out that wasn't much of a change.

"Roasting," I gasped. "How long will it take to get used to this heat?"

"A lifetime. Pace yourself."

The crew entrance door was open so we climbed up into the shade of the cabin. That got us out of the light but with the ramp and cargo door closed the air there was even more stifling than outside. The first thing Bob did was lean into the latrine opposite the crew door and pull open the emergency exit hatch. At least then the air in the cabin could move.

The cargo compartment was empty except for the cloth fold-down seats that were set in place on each side all the way back to the troop doors. Enough light came in from the porthole windows to see that the plane was spotless. The floor was steel and painted gray with the inverted pallet rollers three stripes of silver running the length of the cabin. On the walls and overhead there was gray noise-suppressive padding. It looked like we were inside a gigantic oil pipeline, the round, tubular interior just three feet higher than I was tall. And it was new. Every other cargo plane I had ever seen had been stained with hydraulic fluid, dirt, and years of use. This one looked and smelled like it just came off the showroom floor. It was exciting to stand there and breathe the smell in, knowing we were in on the ground floor of a new weapon system.

Bob stood at the front and put his hands on his hips, unsure where to start.

"The cargo compartment," he said finally, then paused. "You're a pilot. Don't come back here."

Seeing my confusion, he gave in and walked me around anyway, first down the right side all the way to the ramp and then back up to the front.

“Latrine. Self-explanatory. Piss-tube only. Nobody uses the shitter, it’s not polite. We call it the honey bucket, by the way. If you do use it it’d better be an emergency and you’re going to clean it when you land.”

The latrine was tiny. It would have to be an emergency for anyone to want to go through the yoga contortions to get in there. On the floor behind the honey bucket was something that looked like it belonged on the front of a safari guide’s truck.

“Yup, it’s a winch,” Bob affirmed. He lugged it out of the corner and laid it on the floor of the cabin. “Sixty feet of cable. We bolt it down here, run the cable out the back, and pull stuff in.”

“What stuff?”

“Heavy stuff.” Switching topics, he pointed at the red fold-down seats.

“These seats aren’t comfortable. Don’t sit in ‘em unless you have to. They’re designed for guys wearing chutes so you get no back support. You don’t have a chute, three hours into the flight you’ll never walk straight again.” Moving on, he pulled back a flap in the wall padding. “Cargo straps. The chains are on the ramp. Straps and chains. Learn how to use them and get used to it. Your job’s not over once you land.”

“I thought you said pilots don’t come back here,” I reminded him.

“I lied. You land, you get back here and start moving stuff.”

That sounded alright to me. Maybe Garb Taylor couldn’t help out without killing himself but I could.

“Troop door,” Bob continued, reaching the back right side. “It slides up.” He slid open the door, raising it along its tracks until it hung high on the roof. “When they jump if you’re out of trim they’ll bounce against the side.”

“The paratroopers? They’ll hit the side of the plane?”

"Yeah." He reached outside and pounded his fist rhythmically against the fuselage. "It sounds like someone banging his head against the wall. Know why? Because they're banging their head against the wall."

"Uh, does the Army know about that?"

"Oh, yeah."

"Don't they get hurt?"

"Nah. By then they're already going a hundred miles an hour the other way. And they got the ground coming up so scraping the tail's the least of their worries."

We went past the troop door and up the ramp. A canvas shroud hung there from the roof to the floor, blocking view of the ramp and the back side of the cargo door. It was there partly for heat conservation as the back of the plane was always the coldest in flight, and partly for aesthetics. Bob took one side and I grabbed the other. Together we pulled it out of the way.

When the ramp and cargo door of the C-27 were closed they met halfway on a thirty-degree angle up from the cabin floor. Or rather, they met two-thirds of the way. The cargo door was longer and made up most of the aft section of the cabin. When closed it revealed its hollow back side, where tightly organized recesses provided storage space for miscellaneous accessories like the ramp toes for rolling stock, a hydraulic jack, tie-down chains, a bag of survival gear, and cans of engine and hydraulic oil. When activated to open the door pivoted up from its top side, folding inward until it raised high enough to be flush against the ceiling. The ramp, on the other hand, opened out, pivoting on its bottom hinge until locking either at 90 degrees (level with the cabin floor) or when it had lowered far enough to reach the ground.

"Next troop door," Harcourt went on, keeping the tour moving up the left side of the cabin. "See these rails?" He leaned down and pulled up on a tab in the silver rollers. The whole rail came out of the floor, six feet long and weighing twenty pounds. "They're rollers. Flip 'em over, pin 'em back in, and voila! You've got thirty feet of furniture coasters to slide the heavy stuff on. In or out. Don't need rollers? Have pax instead or maybe a Jeep or boxes of cocaine – oops, did I say that out loud? – no worries. Flip 'em over again and you have a regular floor." He put the rail back the way we'd found it.

"How many troops can we carry?"

"Twenty-eight. More if you put some on the ramp. More than that if they don't care about having a seat."

"What about weight?"

"What about it?"

"Well, twenty-eight guys – or more – is a lot of people. What do we gross out at?"

"Not people. You could fill this can full of Cambodian refugees – hell, make 'em heavier; Norwegian refugees – and still be able to take off. This plane's got power. Throw a fire truck in here then sure, you're going to have to start thinking about leaving the co-pilot behind but other than that there's no reason you shouldn't always be able to load the plane up and fly at least two hours. You'll cube out before you ever exceed the weight limits."

I stopped at the crew entrance door and looked back. Cubing out would be tough. The hold was nine feet high, eight feet wide, and twenty-five feet long.

"See this?" Harcourt asked. We came to the last item in the cabin. "The dual-rail locking system. It's what holds your pallets in place."

"I thought the straps and chains did that."

"No, they keep the stuff *on* the pallets. No straps, no chains, stuff flies around and falls over. The dual-rail system keeps the pallets themselves from moving."

"Oh."

"Get down on your stomach. Watch as I move this lever."

I stretched out on the floor and peered under the molding. Harcourt stood by the door and moved a crank that looked like a parking brake up and down. As he did there was a ratcheting sound. One by one a series of thick yellow hooks came down out of the molding beneath the seats. They hid inside a groove where the tongues of a pallet would fit as it slid aboard the aircraft. When Harcourt activated the crank the hooks came down in sequence from front to back on the left side of the aircraft. That allowed the crew to load one pallet at a time and lock it in place or, vice-versa, unload one at a time from the opposite end of the cabin.

"Now stay there. Look on the other side as I do this."

He climbed over me to the right side of the cabin behind the latrine where there was another parking brake. He threw that lever once. Immediately a whole series of locks fell into place the length of the cabin from that side's molding.

"The emergency locks," Harcourt explained. "The left side goes one-by-one. The right side goes all at once: all locks up or all locks down. Useful if you want to throw something out quickly. Combat off-loads or container airdrops. You know, like when the feds are getting too close and you have to drop your stash out over the water. Oops, there I go again, not watching my inner monologue."

We moved on.

Access to the cockpit was through a narrow opening with two steps built into the bulkhead. There was a curtain velcroed to the side of the opening but no door. I hopped up and on Harcourt's direction climbed into the left seat.

There were three seats in the cockpit. Pilot on the left, co-pilot on the right, and behind the co-pilot at a tiny navigator's table was a third seat on a swivel. I asked who it was for.

"Whoever wants it," Harcourt said with a shrug. "I guess the Italians have a navigator. You don't. We'll expect you to know where you're going without help. But if you've got somebody on board who wants to look out the window you can have them sit up here."

Above the table were three panels of circuit breakers for everything electronic on the aircraft. Above the panels were an oxygen regulator and quantity indicators for the emergency oxygen system. Across from the table, directly behind the pilot's seat, was the avionics rack. It was five shelves of radios and cryptographic equipment shielded by a padded curtain.

And in front of me was everything I needed to fly the Chuck.

"Mike, meet the cockpit," Bob introduced us. "Cockpit, meet Mike."

In twenty minutes in the cabin Harcourt had already spoken more words than he usually said each day so every syllable now became a chore. He put in a dip to ease the pressure, pulling back his lower lip to insert a plug of tobacco you could have fired through a rifle. The motion itself relaxed him. He took a deep breath.

"Merrill Technologies did a lot of things right when they bought this plane. Number one was they configured the cockpit with the pilots in mind. Look around. Everything is in reach. Everything is where one of us can get at it without getting up. Everything you need to fly a plane and run a mission is right in front of you, or above you, or on your left or right. Except for a fighter, you can't name another plane where that's true. You don't have a navigator, you don't have an engineer, and you've got more radios than on a B-52. And it's all within reach."

He was right. In some Air Force planes you needed eight hands or a cast of thousands to operate all the equipment. The C-130 "flight deck" – it was too big to be called a cockpit – had an engineer to work the throttles, a navigator to plot the course, and a radio operator, for god's sake, to make all the calls, because the equipment was spread out all over the place. In C-5s some of the instruments were so far-flung I couldn't have reached them without lying prone across the panel.

But in the C-27 I had everything within reach. Smack in front of me over the yoke was a bright blue and brown artificial horizon, a gyrocompass for flight through bad weather and dark nights. Flutie, an instructor who seemed stoned half the time, claimed it was better than the real thing.

Directly below that was the HSI, or Horizontal Situation Indicator, an ingenious device that superimposed a god's-eye view of the aircraft's position relative to a selected magnetic course on top of a rotating compass card. Simple as it was, it was only present in the newest of Air Force aircraft.

Surprisingly, there was an RMI in addition to the HSI. The RMI received more primitive radio signals.

"Why both?" I asked.

"Because someone was thinking," Bob said. "What's the most common navaid in the Third World? The NDB," he said before I could guess. "Basically an AM radio broadcast. And you can't read an NDB signal on an HSI. So we merge the new technology with the old."

In fact there were two RMIs, one for the pilot and one for the co-pilot. Each had two needles and a control panel that allowed it to receive two signals at the same time, one from its own transmitter and the other from the transmitter belonging to the other pilot. Add to that the Tacan I had above my right knee and I could be tuned to three navaids at once. I could also compare those signals with the information from the inertial navigation system, the INS, a gyrocompass that needed no outside signals. I would be hard put to get lost.

The engine instruments were aligned in two columns on the center panel. Nothing odd about that, except...

"Is that Italian?" I asked, pointing at the tiny labels beneath each gauge.

Harcourt leaned out the window to spit.

"Yuh."

When he didn't elaborate I asked, "They going to change that?"

He shrugged. "Oil's oil, boy. Don't let it worry you."

The radar screen sat next to the columns. Above it was the ground speed read-out and the display for wind direction. Along the edge of the dash were push-button indicators of everything from Fire Warning to the status of the aircraft doors. The buttons curved up and around the length of the front panel. The Stall Warning button was smack in front of the pilot's face next to the FIRE light. It only came on when you were about to fall out of the sky so the designers put it front and center. The instrument lights were smaller. They marked sequential milestones on an instrument approach and marched up the panel to merge with the autopilot.

"There's an autopilot?" I asked.

Harcourt looked over, searching. "I guess so," he admitted. "No one uses it."

The control yoke was intimidating. It had a small electronic screen and a series of buttons built into its face. Together they made up a clock. The primary mission of the C-27 being tactical airlift, accurate timing and navigation were essential. And although the plane had nav instruments to read radio signals, those only worked if there were signals to begin with. Since there were few radio beacons south of Panama and since we had only one INS to get us to all the places we needed to go, someone realized we would be doing a lot of basic flying: by looking at a clock, a map, and the ground.

The lower panel between the pilots was awash in radios.

I sighed and looked over everything I would have to learn. "There aren't a lot of warning lights," I observed.

"Then pay attention to the ones you have."

"Shouldn't there be more?"

"Look," he sighed. "There aren't a whole lot of things that can go wrong with this plane that will kill you. A lot of cockpits have flashing lights and bells and voices and horns and other crap that was designed by non-pilots who think you need the acoustics of a pinball machine in order to do your job. You don't. The most important skill any pilot develops is how to ignore all the unimportant stuff that competes for his attention. In this plane you don't have much of that. Pay attention to what you've got and you'll be okay."

Harcourt realized he'd forgotten to tell me something about the cabin so we hopped back out of the seats. He found a paper cup in the latrine to spit his tobacco into.

"The flight controls are manual," he stated matter-of-factly and pointed at the cables that ran the length of the cabin ceiling. "You have a hydraulic assist but you don't need it. You lose hydraulics, you can still fly."

I was used to the C-5's elaborate system where the huge control surfaces required hydraulics before they would even budge.

"Nope, don't need it," Harcourt repeated. "We ain't that big. You don't need a sledge hammer to push in a thumb tack. And the cables are redundant. That means you got more than you need."

I knew what redundant meant but I asked anyway. "Why do we have more than we need?"

He spit into the cup.

"In case they get shot up."

We walked outside to take a look at the exterior of the plane. The sun wasn't any cooler so we stood in the shade of a wing discussing the engines. While we were doing that a Merrill pick-up truck cruised by. The Merrill crew chiefs were always tweaking their planes one way or another and now, seeing us, two of them worried we had found something wrong. Or maybe they just worried. When a plane's on the ground, mechanics don't like to see pilots anywhere near it.

Dale and Tyrel hopped out. Dale was a crew chief, the chief mechanic of a particular plane. Tyrel was a hydraulics specialist. They wore polo shirts with their names sewn on so both of them looked like gas station attendants.

"Anything wrong, Bob?" Dale asked.

"Yeah," said Bob. "I'm not flying. That's wrong."

"So long as you not flying is because of the schedulers and not my plane. I can't fix the schedule – I *can* fix the plane."

"Dale, this is Mike. He's new."

Dale offered his hand and eyed me carefully. "Welcome. Don't wreck my plane."

"Thanks. I'll try not to."

"You like it?"

"Absolutely. It looks sweet."

"You should. It's a nice one. A nice one. Tough, new, *everything works.*" He said the last in a way that all military people understood – having a plane where everything performed as advertised was a rare treat.

Tyrel had smooth black skin and was as skinny as the crescent wrench hanging from his belt. He looked no older than twenty-two.

"Hi," he said when I shook his hand. "Please don't crash."

What the hell? Was there something about my face that made people think I was a lawn dart waiting to happen?

"Okay," I agreed.

"I just showed him the plane for the first time," Bob explained. He moved to one side and put his sunglasses back on. "As long as you experts are here, would one of you mind explaining the outside to the young lieutenant? I'm talked out."

"Absolutely." Dale clapped his hands together and darted over to the main landing gear. Nothing made a crew chief happier than the opportunity to talk about his plane. Bob sat down in the grass.

The landing gear were mostly in sight below the fuselage but by popping open a long cowling below the wing Dale could get access to the upper part of the tires, the struts, and the shock absorbers.

"Okay, the first thing you need to know about the gear," he said, "is that it was designed by Italians." Seeing my doubtful expression he added quickly, "No, that's a good thing. Now there are lots of things they didn't do so well on this plane but the gear is one where they were shack on. Up in Texas we beefed it up but the principle is the same. Look here."

The upshot of the gear was that it combined a strong strut with a powerful shock absorber to create a system that would soak up the punishment of hard landings. Dale claimed a sink rate of a thousand feet per minute was not out of limits.

"A thousand feet per minute?" I repeated, incredulous. That would wreck most aircraft. "The gear would come up through the floor!"

"Nope. See the scissors shape of the strut? It cants back at an angle so more of the pressure is dispersed. You know how on a Herc the gear jack-screw straight up, into the cabin? Passengers there have been killed by hard landings. Well, here the gear don't come straight up. They fold back at an angle. That's also the reason the gear doesn't come up all the way when you retract it."

"What do you mean?"

"I mean, even if you retracted the gear right now, while the plane is sitting on the ground, the belly still wouldn't touch down. The gear sticks out the bottom several inches while you're flying. The designers wanted to keep everything small and compact, reserving space for the cargo hold. They're up in flight but part of the tires stay down in the slipstream. Which means yes, you can land with the gear up." He tapped his head knowingly. "Someone was thinking."

He talked about the brakes, which were strong enough we could set them before landing to make sure we stopped quickly. The gear, Dale assured me, would never let us down.

We moved on to the rest of the plane. Dale talked about the engines, the props, and the wings. He talked about the forest of antennae on both the top and the bottom of the plane, including the HF wire that ran from the cockpit back to the top of the tail like an angled clothesline. But what struck me most was how small the plane was. Squat. Compact like a wrestler. From the outside it didn't look big enough to hold 35 pax or three and a half pallets or a dozen radios. It looked more like a sleek dump truck with wings.

"I know what you're thinking," Dale said with a grin.

"What's that?"

"The Flight of the Bumblebee. How does it fly, that's what everyone wonders."

"I guess." The dump truck analogy worked for me. A dump truck you took into unruly neighborhoods. "How far will it glide if both engines quit?"

"Halfway to wherever your nearest runway is. But don't worry, the engines won't quit. This is a good plane. We just have to convince the big-wigs to let it do its mission."

"Well, from what I've heard nobody seems to know what the mission is anyway. It just flies for whomever, whenever anything comes up.""

"Exactly," he nodded. "The best kind of mission to have."

Charlie Manson chose that moment to drive up in a flight line van.

"How's things?" Harcourt greeted him.

"*Bene*," Manson replied dryly. "*Tra bene*." He stayed in the van with the air conditioning at full blast.

"Why don't you come out here in the fresh air?"

"Because I'm not stupid."

"How's Buncheman?"

"The same. Worried about the right things but at the wrong time."

"Did you make him understand that we're all fluent in Sicilian and that all our mechanics trained for months at the Rome Institute for Flying Things before they came to Howard?"

"No, I made Garb understand that his job is to keep Buncheman from asking those questions."

"So we can still fly?" Harcourt asked.

Manson waved his hands like a street vendor hawking his wares.

"Diami il alfredo di fettucine e un vetro del vino di casa."

"What does that mean?" I asked when nobody else did.

"To the best of my knowledge, it means 'Give me the fettucine alfredo and a glass of house wine.' Oh, and by the way, your first local sortie's tomorrow. I just came out to tell you. Try not to get heatstroke before then."

I looked at the C-27, then at the faces around me to see if Charlie was making a joke. Nobody looked surprised. How could I fly tomorrow? I hadn't had a class yet.

"Tomorrow? What...uh, what are we going to do?"

Charlie rolled his window back up. As it sealed him off from the heat outside, we heard him say, "Fly, my boy. We're gonna fly."

8: Impossible

I DIDN'T FLY the next day or the day after that. Despite Charlie's best efforts, for a week Colonel Buncheman and the Group staff came up with reason after reason why the C-27s shouldn't leave the ground. While Charlie and the commander fought that battle Major Harmon told me to hit the books and find a place to live. Since I didn't read Italian I concentrated on the latter.

I also met one of the new copilots, a stocky second lieutenant with a hangdog expression and a mass of black hair that hung in his eyes no matter how often he had it cut. His name was Rolo. He arrived in Panama only days after me and was just as lost. In fact the first time I saw him he was sitting upstairs in the Pubs cubicle, staring at a waist-high stack of photocopied manuals for the G-222 that Maj Harmon had told him to organize.

"I can't read these," he replied when I said hello. He stared at the stack some more, mouth open, willing the Roman script to reveal itself. It never did.

As the first weeks went by Rolo and I kept running into each other. We in-processed together, learned our way around the base, met people in and out of the squadron and figured out who was worth knowing and who wasn't. Everyone in the squadron fell into the former category, of course. There was Walt, of course, one of the line instructors. Line instructors were experienced pilots who taught new guys how to fly off-station down to Colombia and Peru. They took over from RTU instructors like Charlie and Mike who taught basic aircraft mastery by flying in the local area. Josh was another line instructor, as was Flutie. Flutie also headed up the Pinheads, a group of four single guys who lived downtown and spent as much time drunk as they did in the air. Lowell and Kurt lived downtown, too, and also partied a lot. Manny, one of our few basic aircraft commanders, not yet an instructor but above a copilot, didn't drink nor did he live downtown. He lived on base with his wife and kids and was happy to stay inside the gate.

But everyone we met had been in Panama at least a few months and was well-established in the squadron. Only Rolo and I were new. We went through all the new-guy experiences together: the welcome briefings; the menial tasks to fill our dead-time like moving old lockers out of the hangar and doing an inventory of flight kits; even qualifying at the gun range. Eventually we started at the RTU together and then began flying at the same time. By the time we hit the flight line we knew each other as well as we knew anyone in Panama and decided that we might as well watch each other's back.

Besides, everyone else in the squadron already had a place to live. So when we got an apartment together it was for reasons other than friendship. In the next three years Rolo and I were never best buddies – we just got along. For my part, I talked too much, didn't follow sports, and was a neat-freak. For his, he never wanted to go out, kept the kitchen a mess, and walked around in his underwear. I was a snob and fancied myself intellectual. He was blue collar and hadn't read a book since college. But we made it work.

The great thing about Rolo was that even though he wasn't the coldest beer in the fridge he knew it and used the fact to his advantage. Because no one ever expected him to get the better of them he could be disarmingly blunt, even rude, and get away with it. For example, when late that summer we were ordered to the base theater to attend a briefing on the Air Force's next-generation fighter, and a visiting colonel proceeded to tell us that because of the fighter's unpopularity with Congress he needed all of us to express enthusiasm for the project, Rolo raised his hand and inquired, "Why is that, sir? Is it because buying such a fighter is a colossal waste of money?" I respected that.

The first reason we moved in together was convenience: we were looking for housing at the same time and were both desperate to leave our respective hotels. Rolo was still living in the El Panamá while I was in the Costa del Sol. The El Panamá was nice because it was fancy and upscale but there were no cooking facilities. You had to eat out in a restaurant every night which was expensive and tiring. Even Manolo's, the popular cafeteria across the street that specialized in sliced hot dogs, got old quickly.

The Costa del Sol was where I moved after two weeks in the El Panamá. It was in the same neighborhood but boasted a kitchenette in every room so at least there I could cook for myself. However, it had its downsides. There were roaches, the air conditioning failed regularly, and it was loud. Specifically, it was loud outside where garbage trucks rolled through the alley outside my window each morning at four o'clock. Because the windows had to be open when the a/c failed, I heard every shout, every clunk of a trash barrel, and every shift of gears. After the trash haulers were gone a fruit vendor retraced the same route at six o'clock. Bawling *"piña, papaya, banana!!"* at the top of his voice, he would stay in the alley until at least three hotel guests leaned out their windows and purchased something.

Another reason Rolo and I linked up was financial. Rents were through the roof for Americans living in Panama City, an average of $2000 a month for a decent two-bedroom apartment. As a first lieutenant I received $1,200 a month from the government for housing: Rolo, a second lieutenant, got $1,000. It made sense to pool our resources.

One last factor drove us together. Most of the guys who lived downtown were robbed on a regular basis. The crews flew so much and spent so much time out of the country that everyone's home sat empty sometimes. Having a roommate cut that window of vulnerability in half.

Some guys were hit more than others. People who rented houses rather than apartments were the usual targets. The Pinheads, for example – Evan, Jem, Tommy Goode, and Flutie – shared a spacious four-bedroom bungalow on Calle 54 Este, just down from Josh in the Torres Bahia Vista. Even in that respectable neighborhood they had narrowly prevented three break-ins simply because one of them was almost always home. But then they had bad luck with houses anyway. Their first place out in Rio Abajo was partially destroyed during the invasion, targeted by a gunship when somebody in the back yard took potshots at aircraft flying overhead. This was before they moved in, though, and they didn't know about the damage when they called about the ad since the owner insisted during several phone calls that it was "new, very new, with only *un poquito de construcción*" remaining to be done. They moved in only after Evan, Tommy, and Flutie ganged up on Jem and convinced him that the collapsed wall adjoining his bedroom was really a good thing since it afforded him a better view of the street. That lasted two months, until the second floor gave way entirely and dropped half their household goods into the kitchen. Their second house, a sprawling three-floor pad across the street from Patatus Club, had an even shorter lease. Six weeks after they moved in the owner returned from Colombia in a panic wailing, "I need a place to hide! I need a place to hide!" Even a Pinhead could read the writing on that wall.

T.J. and Skinny Steve fared no better. They were cleaned out twice when they rented a one-story house off Tumba Muerto. Their maid tipped off her relatives the first time the boys left town and within hours her family members pulled up in moving vans to help themselves. Eventually the guys moved to the more exclusive and less accessible 24th floor of the El Dorado towers. There a thief would have to be a cat burglar with alpine climbing skills to break in.

So the problem with houses was that they were easy to get into. They sat open to the street with at most a short fence or low wall to protect them. Apartments, on the other hand, could be twenty floors up with their entrance guarded by armed doormen and security cameras. The doormen were mostly for show but even so no Panamanian thief wanted to trouble himself going up and down stairs or making several trips on the elevator. So almost everyone who lived downtown eventually retreated to the protective aeries of highrises. Besides the Pinheads, Lowell Hendricks and Kurt Norris were the only other squadron members to persevere in keeping a place at ground level. They were robbed once – losing a box of tools and a broken microwave before the thieves were scared off – but instead of moving they solved their security problem by hiring two guards: one man to watch the building and a second man to watch the first.

Despite all this, Rolo and I still wanted to get a house. We had a misconception that local apartments were small and cramped while all houses had pools; more importantly, we each wanted to grill. It was the tropics and grilling outside in beautiful weather was key. You can't grill in an apartment: therefore, we wanted a house. To guard it we reasoned that if we flew on different schedules one of us would always be there to protect it. Or we could hire guards. We were sure it would be no time at all before we found the perfect bachelor pad of luxury in our new tropical home.

Like so many things in Panama, it just wasn't that simple.

"Imposible. Uds. no tienen dinero. Lo que tienen no es suficiente."

With that greeting, the housing office on base poured the first bucket of cold water on our plans. Staffed by U.S. and Panamanian civilians alike, the office had long ago lost its collective patience with anyone trying for a sweet deal downtown. The harried agents wanted only to match names with places as quickly as possible and then lock the doors.

Unfortunately, the housing office was its own kingdom on base. Rolo and I had to go through it to arrange somewhere to live. There were forms to fill out, logs to record which places we had seen and rejected, allowance applications to take to Finance, brochures to guide us through the legal maze of Panamanian rental contracts, and more. The irony was, the staff didn't want to deal with us anymore than we wanted to bother them. Things would be easier, they sighed – ten minutes into our first appointment – if we retained a local real estate agent to guide us through the bureaucracy as well as the city: why, yes, they would be happy to suggest a few.

The first suggestion was Olivia, a bustling, energetic, non-stop talker of a woman who epitomized every business consultant the world over: everything she said was technically true and of no help whatsoever. My first encounter with her was in the crowded parking lot outside the housing office. I was crossing the lot on foot and had stopped to let a vehicle pass. As the driver maneuvered carefully into a parking space, Olivia broadsided him with her Mitsubishi.

It was Olivia who first used the word "impossible."

"What do you mean we don't have enough money?"

"One thousand two hundred plus one thousand is two thousand two hundred. It is impossible to get a house downtown for that much money. *Imposible.*"

"But we know people who live down there who pay less than that."

Not to mention that thousands of Panamanians lived very well in the city and paid half what the Americans did, if not less. It was an example of the gouging Americans accepted in order to keep down the grumbling about stationing troops on the isthmus.

"Si, pero es raro, muy raro."

"Well, that's why we have you! Because you're the expert who can find us those 'rare' cases."

"*Imposible.*"

When Olivia had a line of reasoning that was rational to her but made no sense to us, she talked only in Spanish, rattling off all the obstacles that prevented us from renting such-and-such a place in the hopes that such manifest logic would transcend linguistic barriers and make us understand. Usually I could follow her; Rolo would wince like he had an ice cream headache.

Olivia had an agenda: we would see whatever she wanted to show us.

Between training flights in the RTU Rolo and I drove into town with her to see what her research had found. For two weeks we let her take the reins on our search. She would pick us up on base in her clunky sedan and chauffeur us into the city.

For Rolo that was hell. He was allergic to perfume. Not only did Olivia wear perfume the way oil riggers wear crude but the plush leather seats of her car were dotted with air fresheners and the puffy sprigs of plastic flowers, each of which spat out the chemical likeness of some nectary fragrance. We didn't know if she was trying to mask some smell of the car or create an idealized olfactory environment in which she could comfortably drive, but either way the effect was sensory overload. The experience was worsened by the profusion of mascara-smeared tissues that littered the car. Olivia applied and removed make-up on her daily drive to the base, enough that to climb into the seats Rolo and I had to sweep away kleenex strewn like gauze from a botched operation.

Rolo would have driven himself around if he could. But he couldn't. His car, a brand new Geo Storm that he bought leaving pilot training, arrived from the States two days after he did. Driving it up from the docks he struck an open sewer hole and broke the axle. He had the damage repaired at a local body shop but the promised 'like-new' axle fell apart of its own accord five minutes after pick-up. Its third failure in a month came when Rolo offered to drive me up to Balboa so I could inspect a Bronco that was for sale there. Abeam the *Parque Botánico* and in a driving rainstorm we splashed through a puddle that masked a two-foot deep pothole. With that impact the front half of his vehicle nearly separated from the rest. So for now he was stuck riding with Olivia. Approaching her car alone made him break out in hives. The worst part was it was suffering to no avail. The places she showed us never resembled in the slightest what we wanted to rent.

At first we wished to live in El Dorado. El Dorado was close to the back gate of Albrook, had easy access to Tumba Muerto which could zip us downtown (and at the time was one of two streets we knew), and was a quiet, almost American neighborhood. But Olivia discouraged us. Nothing happens there, she claimed. It was a boring place. The residents suffer high crime. The garbage doesn't get picked up. The noise from the street is intolerable. Car fumes give it bad air. And...she didn't have any listings there.

No matter. She had listings downtown.

"So what's this area?" I wheezed, straining to reach the top of my window which I surreptitiously cracked open during the drive. Rolo didn't even wait for the car to stop as Olivia pulled up to the curb. He threw open the door and gulped in a lungful of hot perfume-free air.

"*Este es San Francisco.* A beautiful neighborhood!" our guide exuded. "The ocean is right down there...—" she wagged a finger down the uneven street toward some ramshackle houses "–...and the *Parque Recreativo,* the big city park, is right up there." Another wag. "I think you will like this place."

'This place' was a two-story building with a railed balcony encircling its four units. It sat at the top of a hill on a curving section of Avenida 1a Sur. My first impression was that the building was uneven, that the concrete slab on which the apartments sat sloped downhill toward the water. That was noteworthy, since my first impression should have been of the electric-futia color which the owners had painted the place. It was so bright it must have glowed in the dark. When Rolo stopped gasping for air and stood straight to look at the building, he took a step back.

"And the color is unique," Olivia beamed.

"It's not a house, Olivia," I pointed out. "We want to rent a house."

She dismissed my complaint with a wave of the hand and guided us inside.

The interior didn't improve our first take on the place. The rooms were drab and square with torn wallpaper and chipped tile. It looked like a cheap motel on Route 66.

"No," said Rolo, and walked out.

Second on her list was another apartment. This one, she claimed, was "just like" a house.

"It's another apartment building," Rolo sighed, stepping around broken glass on the street to look up through the trees at the high-rise.

"No! *Bueno, sí, sí,* but it's very beautiful. You must look at it."

A fallen tree branch blocked the entrance. We entered the lobby through a side door.

"What's with the tree, Olivia?" I asked. "Are they pruning?"

"Oh, yes, yes. Come, you must see the apartment."

The building was the *Condominio Miraflores,* right on the water on the west side of Punta Paitilla. It was a new building, white on the outside with gleaming windows and polished chrome trim. Apparently it was so new the builders were still working on it because several windows on the first floor had plywood over them or were taped up.

"Here we are!"

We exited the elevator on the 14th floor. In the tiny, marble hallway you could go left or right. At either end was a door.

"And here is 14A!" Olivia pressed before us to unlock the door, her pear-shaped frame so wide it blocked our view of the door itself. When she swung it open she swung with it like a slapstick comic.

"Go!" she said enthusiastically, gesturing inside. "Look! See for yourself, it is a *beau*tiful home!"

For once she was right. The apartment was almost a house, it was so big. The floor plan was airy and bright and expansive by anybody's standards. The walls were white, the only decoration a narrow tapestry hanging opposite the entrance. The floor tiles were white, too, so that with the uncovered windows entering the main room was like walking into a spa for light therapy. The kitchen was by itself on the left but the dining and front rooms blended into each other to make one large area to enjoy the view. Since the apartment took up this half of the whole 14th floor all the bedrooms and bathrooms were enormous, too. I was impressed.

"Wow!" exclaimed Rolo. "Look at this view!"

The windows were floor to ceiling. Below us the Bay of Panama stretched across to San Felipe and the old quarter, with Avenida Balboa tracing the shoreline on the right. The tide was in so that when I cracked a window the air smelled fresh. Hot, but fresh. An amazing view, an amazing apartment.

Olivia hadn't left the doorway. Her smile in place, she raised her eyebrows in question.

"You like it?"

I hated to admit it but I liked it.

"I'm amazed," said Rolo. "I have to admit it's really...hey, what's on the wall?" He pointed to the plaster behind the tapestry. Olivia slapped a hand on the rug.

"What? Where?" she said, looking over my shoulder to the other side of the room.

"Here." Rolo pulled her hand and the tapestry aside. The plaster and cement behind the rug were pock-marked worse than General Noriega's face. A circle the size of a car-tire had been knocked out of the wall.

"Oh," said Olivia with elaborate surprise. "My, that must be fixed right away. I am sure they are just doing touching up here and there." She started mumbling in Spanish and side-stepped to put the tapestry back in place. "It is nothing. We will get it fixed before you move in."

"Hey!" I said. "What's up with the door?"

Olivia looked up in alarm and moved back to the door but Rolo pushed her out of the way. The heavy wooden door had a hole in it at waist level big enough to pass a watermelon through. Splinters of wood still hung at the inside edge. The hole was directly in line with the carved up wall. It didn't take a scientist to do the math.

"That's a shotgun blast!"

"Yeah...it is," said Rolo in awe. "Are those included in the rent?"

"That's a shotgun blast!" I repeated.

This wasn't something we encountered every day. Rolo got down on his knees and peered at the loose chunks of wood.

"Oooooh, I'll bet that hurt," he said.

"That's a shotgun blast!" I said for the third time.

"Oh, nooooo. No, no, no, no, no," babbled Olivia and promptly let loose a torrent of more Spanish, this time disjointed phrases that would have served well as filler for the holes in the plaster. Most of it involved how there was a simple explanation and gosh, no one at the agency had told her anything and the people who lived here before were very nice but my, look at the clock isn't it time to go...

The branch was still on the street when we left. A policeman was taking pictures of the broken glass.

We kept Olivia as our agent for a week even after finding out about the murder attempts at 14A. It was just a drug-related attack. The accountant who bought the place but never moved in had done the books for the wrong people who, dissatisfied with his figures, rang his doorbell and started shooting, then concluded the evening by blowing up his son's car when the latter pulled up downstairs. That explained the tree branch and the boarded up windows. But the cartel didn't get the accountant himself until some days later when he boarded a flight for Miami out of Colón. The plane blew up after takeoff and dropped 21 people into the waters off the north coast. When I read that I wondered what the pilot was thinking as he fell.

When Olivia spent another seven days showing us nothing but apartments we gave her one last chance.

"Okay," she announced defensively one day. "You want a house. I have found you a house. *Es una casita bonita.*"

It was, in fact, a house. A beautiful house, an estate-like house, a house so grand and aristocratic that it merited its own half of a city block a mere two hundred yards from the Gran Morrison Shopping Center in Punta Paitilla. It was built of black stone in the traditional hacienda style of Spanish nobility, half of it a one-story sprawling affair that connected like the lazy bottom of an L to the more formal two floors of living quarters, all of which curved around a flag-stoned compound. Gorgeous and ridiculously expensive, the entire structure sat on a natural forty-foot bluff of basalt and black granite smack on the border of Punta Paitilla and El Cangrejo and at the base of yet another twenty-story block of condominiums that was under construction. The bluff gave a sense of aloofness to the already distinguished, luxurious home. I had no idea why Olivia was showing us this place. Its financial inaccessibility slapped me across the face like a displeased princess the instant we drove through the wrought-iron gates.

"It's not much, is it?" cracked Rolo. "I mean, I've had better."

"An unassuming little place that someone likes to call home," I added.

Olivia, already impatient, missed the sarcasm.

"It is a very beautiful place," she insisted. "How can you say it is a little place? It is not little. Many important people have lived here. But the big house is not for you. Oh, no, no, no, no, no. That is much more than your money has. You rent the little house."

The 'little house' was servant quarters close to the entrance gate. It was a low, narrow barracks in the shadow of the outer wall, spitting distance from the guard shack. We knew this because after the gate closed the guard ambled behind his booth to spit on the tiny barracks lawn.

"Who lives here?" I asked Olivia.

"No one lives here. That is how it is for rent."

"No, I mean who lives in the main house? Who are our landlords?"

"Oh, a very old, very noble Panamanian family lives here. But you do not deal with them. You will pay the agency."

"What's so noble about them?" Rolo asked.

"Pardon?"

"The family in the big house. What's noble about them?"

"They are very, very rich."

"And that makes them noble?"

"They own many industries in Panama. They own the *cervecería*, all the *cerveza* in the country."

"That's noble enough for me," I said. "Maybe they'll give us free kegs."

"Big deal," Rolo huffed, "so we've got Marge Schott living up the driveway."

Olivia frowned. "I do not know who that is."

"If they're so rich," I asked, "why are they renting out servants' quarters? Why aren't their servants living here?"

"The family does not live here very much. Only sometimes," Olivia explained.

"Well, when they are here do we ever get to see them?"

"Oh, no! No, no, no. They do not like to see the people here. When they are here sometimes you may have to leave."

"Excuse me?"

"Sometimes when they come here, they are here *dos o tres semanas*, two, three weeks. Sometimes they have many people and they need to use the space, all space, including this house."

"So you're saying we might have to move so they can stay here?"

"*De vez en cuando.* Only sometimes, not all the time."

Rolo laughed.

"What if *we* have guests?" he asked. "Will the owners move out so that our guests can stay in the big house?"

Olivia took a moment to understand the question and then looked horrified.

"Oh, no! No, no, no! No, you may not go to the big house, even if no one is there."

We bade farewell to Olivia that afternoon and found a new agent.

Lucinda.

Lucinda was middle-aged like Olivia but more down-to-earth. She liked Americans, kind of. She had the ambivalent attitude of many Panamanians that liking us wasn't the same as liking us being here in the country. We couldn't begrudge her that. Her memories were vivid of the Christmas invasion.

"I looked out my house and ooooh! The whole city was on fire!"

"But the city didn't catch fire," Rolo would remind her. "It was only eight months ago. Look around. Most of the city wasn't even touched."

"Ooooooh, but it *looked like* the city was on fire! And those trucks everywhere – the big Jeeps..."

"The humvees?"

"Ooooooh, *sí*, the hum*vees*." (She said it to rhyme with 'geese.') "But the most scary, the most wonderful, is the specter."

"The what?" I asked.

"The specter," she repeated in a hushed voice. "The big plane in the sky that sees everything and kills those one peoples however it wants. Ooooooh, it is the Angel of Death looking down, stealing life from this one but leaving that one alone."

Lucinda stared into space, seeing a vision in her mind. Her voice lowered to a dramatic whisper as she channeled the spirit of a bad Victorian actress. *"The specter sees all!...."* she hissed.

Rolo and I looked at each other, not knowing what she was talking about and thinking the woman had had a ghostly encounter in the dark confusion of that first night of fighting.

"It is so powerful," she continued in a hush. "I saw with my own eyes the police station it blew up. The church and the *crèche* – not even a scratch."

Then we understood. The AC-130 Spectre – the new gunship version of the old standby, the Spooky – had made a name for itself during Just Cause. It flew at night and used its TV optics and infrared cameras to pinpoint and destroy vehicles, anti-aircraft sites, and even a few boats. Its 50mm howitzer and 7.62 miniguns wreaked havoc among the PDF, the Panama Defense Forces, the more so because all the destruction came from a dark sky in which they could see nothing. The H-model plane's motto was "You can run but you can't hide," apt for those people unfortunate enough to be on the receiving end of its firepower. The Panamanians would have been pleased to know the Air Force was building a new version, a pressurized plane with even more precise targeting devices and more powerful guns. It wasn't off the ground yet but it already had a motto of its own: "You can run but you'll only die tired."

The gunship was legendary among the Panamanians mainly for one shot. When snipers holed up in a police station in the Balboa district, a U.S. infantry platoon called for fire support. The AC-130 overhead banked left, pointed its howitzer, and leveled the building. So contained was the damage that a chapel right across the street, with a Christmas manger scene out front, stayed untouched.

Horrified by our flying brethren though she was, Lucinda nevertheless tried hard to find us a place to live. Yet with her, too, we soon got a feeling there was a failure to communicate.

"Do you like this? It is beautiful, is it not?"

She walked up the driveway to the house and spun around, gesturing with arms outspread. We were on a *finca*, a farm on the road to Penonomé twenty miles west of the base. The house wasn't big but that hardly mattered. We were *twenty miles* from the base.

The property took center stage. It consisted of forty acres of lush grass, fruit trees, and stands of bamboo beside a trickling stream. Most of it rolled out of sight behind half a dozen low knolls that bordered the lime orchard. The orchard itself flanked three fish ponds, each of which was forty yards in diameter and stocked with carp. The ponds were on the way to one of two pastures where even now cows grazed under broken clouds. A wide *bohio* with a concrete slab and built-in grill stood in the grass between the house and a barn. It was a rural paradise.

It was also the sticks.

"Didn't we say we wanted to live in the city?" Rolo muttered from behind a hand as he pretended to yawn. "We're in Iowa out here."

"Yup," I replied quietly.

"I mean, we can get to the base fast enough but it would take us an hour to get into the city. And we would have to get into the city if we don't want to end up playing banjos on the porch out here for entertainment. There's....there's....well, there's nothing out here!"

"Nope."

"We could throw a hell of a party but we wouldn't be able to talk anyone into coming. They would be afraid to come out here at night. Hell, I'll be afraid to come out here at night."

"Yup."

"You have anything else to say?"

"Nope."

"Rural atmosphere getting to you?"

"Yup. Country folk don't talk much."

"They also screw their sisters. Let's go."

I looked around. Afraid to come here at night? I was nervous being out here during the day. We were a mile off the road, which was another mile from the Pan-American Highway, and the nearest house was somewhere on the other side of one of the hills. The invasion was only eight months in the past. I had visions of grudge-bearing Noriega supporters swarming out of the orchard to hack us to death with machetes. Were we to live here we would be sitting ducks every time we turned on a light.

We passed on the farm.

Lucinda also showed us an apartment downtown. This one was on Avenida Balboa, across the street from the Panama Yacht Club. It was an adequate flat, nothing exceptional, but the experience of seeing it stood out because our interest required a visit to the owners.

The owners met all prospective renters. They were a middle-aged couple who lived alone in El Cangrejo but for the purpose of our interview they invited the extended clan to be present. Their apartment – the entire top floor of a four-story building – was intimidating enough. It was so packed with furniture and tropical plants that the impression was of a movers' convention in a botanical garden. Framed paintings and gilded mirrors occupied whatever wall space was not taken up by oaken armoires, dressers, china cabinets, or bishop's chairs. Three cages of tiny, fearful-looking tropical birds hid behind potted palms and the tumbling tendrils of spider lilies and wandering jews. The effect was so claustrophobic I loosened my collar walking through the door. Yet the feeling of being hemmed in, of rooms coming alive and closing in on us, wasn't limited to the walls. The shag carpet in the living room was so thick I got tired wading through it. Ceiling fans and chandeliers kept us in a constant crouch to avoid knocking our heads.

The family awaited us in the dining room. There were eleven people altogether, enough so that when Rolo and I entered accompanied by Lucinda everyone had to stand up and do a Chinese fire drill of swapping seats and moving chairs so that we could sit near Señor and Señora Mendez Mosquera.

A somber air prevailed. The clan was pleasant enough in the sense that nobody grabbed a broken chair leg and leaped screaming over the furniture to attack us. But nobody smiled. The women wore thick make-up and the men open shirts with lots of jewelry. With the proximity of so much perfume and chest hair, a football huddle in a Turkish prison couldn't have been more uncomfortable.

Señora Blanca Mendez Mosquera was the matriarch. She was sixty years old but looked like she had an additional ten behind her. Large, imposing, and prone to talk through anyone else's conversation, the instant she opened her mouth the other members of the family visibly shrank – most notably her husband. Thin and ascetic, Luis Mosquera never said a word.

Which was okay by his wife. She had enough words for both of them. She started by telling us the history of the family, their move from Colón to Panama City, her struggles to raise four children, her instinctive grasp of the real estate business, her minor fortune that subsidized the living standards of the entire family, her unenthusiastic acceptance of the economic circumstances that forced them to rent the Balboa apartment, and her concern to have only the best tenants. During this soliloquy Lucinda tried to interrupt twice and both times retired under the imperious gaze of the señora. Rolo stifled yawns. I was afraid to look at my watch.

Eventually Señora Mosquera sighed and listed what she expected of anyone she allowed to live in their "second home." Among other things: no parties, no music, no more than two visitors at once, no extended absences, and weekly reports to her in person on the state of the building. Also, just to be safe – although we looked like respectable gentlemen – she would have no choice but to require three months' rent as deposit for any damage in addition to the month's deposit that would be held at the base. In other words, a mere eight thousand dollars out of our own pocket just to move in so we could begin paying rent. A mild cough from one of the statues behind me suggested even her kinfolk thought Blanca was daft.

Rolo chewed a fingernail, convinced he was in the midst of inbreeds.

"How about sex?" he asked. "Can I have sex with my girlfriend or do I need to check with you first?"

We didn't rent the Mosquera place.

Lucinda was followed by two Marias. One Maria was a freelancer not associated with any real estate office. She was pretty, talkative, and constantly promised to show us dozens of places to live – but she never did. It became obvious after a while that she wasn't an agent at all but simply wanted to hook up with Rolo. Rolo decided he needed a house more than a woman so we moved on.

Maria Number Two was a friend of Josh's girlfriend at the time. We had wanted Josh's girlfriend Irena to help us out herself – after all, she had found the place Josh was living in – but Josh was reluctant to share. He feared that if we spirited Irena away long enough for her to find us somewhere to live we might decide to keep her. He allowed her only to fix us up with a fellow agent, Maria.

Maria had long hair and a dancer's legs and never stopped moving any of them.

"*Bueno*," she said with a toss of her head. "I will find you a house but I do not recommend you live there. You should be in an apartment. But I give you what you want. *Vengan*."

And off she went. For three days straight she bustled us from one end of the city to another, fighting traffic, rainstorms, and obstinate security guards to show us places she'd heard, read, or otherwise found out about being on the market. True to her word, they were all houses. Houses of all shapes and sizes, houses of all levels of quality, and houses that varied across the price range. Most ended up being more than we could pay but that wasn't Maria's fault, it was simply an economic fact of life. The ones we could afford we inspected with a fine-toothed comb. And whether it was a subliminal influence from Maria, a growing weariness with the search, or our own plain demanding natures, for some reason we just never found one we liked. Our standard was the Pinheads' palace with multiple bedrooms, interior courtyard, and built-in pool. The reality was the Pinheads had gotten lucky. Even the best places Maria showed us didn't measure up to their pad of decadence. More and more we started to think that an apartment might be best after all.

Once we made that decision Maria really excelled. She knew the apartment market in the city the way grocers know their shelves. Soon we were back in Punta Paitilla, navigating the forest of high-rises in search of a place to live. And there were many places. Paitilla was Panama's Manhattan. Apartment buildings towered there like sequoias and somehow contractors were building even more.

There were so many buildings between the overpass on Avenida Balboa and the shoreline that the only way to see the sun from the narrow, twisting streets was to look straight up. Breezes from the ocean got confused working around all the monuments of mirrored glass and reinforced concrete. But it was a lively area of the city for just that reason. People were everywhere, shops and cafés abounded, and the tree-lined streets mixed with the greater shade of the buildings overhead to lend the area a quiet, neighborhood charm. And just for local color, the Vatican embassy – where soldiers had serenaded a holed-up Noriega for days with blaring rock music – was just off Balboa at the entrance to the district.

One hot afternoon as the one o'clock rain shower was starting, Maria pulled up to the Condominio Tamanaco. The three of us piled out of her Toyota hatchback.

"This one is the last I have today," she apologized, hurrying us up the steps and into the lobby. "It is not the best quality and it is not new, but it is big – *gigante* – and you said you wanted a big apartment."

The apartment was on the 23rd floor, the highest we had seen an offering yet. In fact, it was one floor below the penthouse. Part of our floor was taken up by the small swimming pool belonging to the people upstairs. Maria was right: the apartment was huge.

"Hey, nice!" was Rolo's first reaction. Even more than me, he was frustrated with not having a place to live and had hinted at being willing to settle for less-than-perfection. Rolo was all about being settled. He liked to cook and needed a kitchen. Living in a hotel was driving him up the wall.

The Tamanaco apartment *was* nice. Not great, not horrible – just nice. As Maria said, it wasn't new and buildings in Panama aged quickly due to poor construction and minimal maintenance. Yet the main room was spacious and so was the kitchen – a big plus for Rolo, the aspiring chef. The bedrooms were at the end of a long hallway. Their windows looked out over the city.

What sold us was the balconies.

"Holy acrophobia!" I exclaimed, going out on the south balcony where I felt vertigo just stepping outside. The entire wall of the main room consisted of sliding glass doors that led to a six-foot-wide ledge. The ledge stretched the length of the apartment and had a four-foot iron railing. Beyond it was a two-hundred-fifty-foot drop to the street. More than that, however, the Pacific Ocean began a mere city block away and stretched out as far as the eye could see. The distant ocean was purple and dotted with sea-going vessels; the closer water was blue and shimmered with the currents. Through the rain we saw whitecaps forming over the breakers as waves moved ashore. We had the finest ocean-front view of anyone in the city. It was awe-inspiring.

"Mike! Mike! Look at this side!"

The opposite balcony was just as big only its view was of the city. Because the Tamanaco building was on the edge of the point, close to Paitilla Airport, it lucked out in having neighboring buildings on only one of its four sides. Thus the view to the city was as jaw-dropping as the one over the water. Much as I liked to knock the Panamanians at every opportunity and curse the traffic and urban sprawl and pollution, there was no getting around the fact that the city skyline was beautiful. Viewed from twenty-three floors up, away from the noise and car exhaust, it was a strikingly white, clear-aired, wonderfully-jumbled metropolis bordered with forest green. And with the downpour in progress the streets and parking lots below reflected the sky above, giving the entire picture a glossy aspect as though city designers had just finished their work and put it out on the showroom floor.

We competed to point out prominent landmarks. There was the Iglesia del Carmen, the twin-spired church on Via España. There was the Hotel Panamá, and over there the Tocumen

Airport. There were the towers at El Dorado and to their left the giant hangars and heavy jungle of Albrook Air Base. Farther away we could see the red-tiled roofs of buildings on Fort Clayton. Howard Air Base was hidden by hills beyond the canal but an arriving C-5 pointed unmistakably to where its runway lay.

"We'll take it!" Rolo announced.

"Whoa," I cautioned. "Not so fast. This place is old. And we don't even know the price."

Maria checked a slip of paper from her office. "Two thousand dollars," she answered.

"We can afford that," Rolo pointed out. "Look, your grill will fit right here in the corner of the balcony."

"It's kind of dirty," I persisted. I liked the view, too, but the place just didn't strike me as being worth two grand, even if it was coming out of the government's pocket instead of mine.

"They'll clean it up," Rolo said confidently. "Won't they?"

"I'm sure they will," Maria nodded.

"But the walls. They look dingy, too."

"I'll talk to the owner. I'm sure he'll repaint them."

"And the water heater?" We had noticed it was electric – ancient electric – and electricity bills in Panama were notoriously lofty.

"It's old. I'll talk the owner into getting a new one."

"You see?" Rolo proclaimed. "No problems. Be as pessimistic as you want, Mike, but we've found a home. Look at this place. It's huge! It's high! It's just waiting to have a ton of drunk people and the smell of grilling steaks fill it up." He leaned over the railing to look down at the street below where Maria's Toyota sat like a toy car. "And if nothing else, we can toss firecrackers onto people below."

I had my doubts. Like Rolo I wanted to see the bright side but our fantasy of perfection had eroded over the weeks to a resigned acceptance of reality.

"I was looking for a place with more character," I muttered.

"We'll load it with all the character it needs. Come on, what do you say?"

Maria perched behind him with a pleading smile. She wanted to get us off her hands. In truth, I was tired of looking.

"Well, if you think it's alright..."

Rolo rubbed his hands anxiously. "We won't regret it. I know it! Mike, let's take it. The first dinner's on me. I'll grill up Grandma Metzger's famous traditional secret recipe for spaghetti!"

"Your grandmother came from Dublin."

"She traveled a lot. Come on, you want a place as much as I do."

"Maria, do you think you can get the owner to take care of those things?" I stalled.

She nodded reassuringly. "*Por supuesto.*"

"You're sure?"

"*Sí,* I am sure!."

"Alright then, I give up. If they fix those problems then I agree to take it, too."

Maria sighed with relief.

"In the meantime, Rolo," I added, "I wouldn't lean on that railing if I were you. It was probably made by the same guy who fixed your axle."

9. Flight

Mike Vaneya was easy to fly with. He was thirty-one years old with curly hair already turning gray and an attitude that nothing in life was worth getting upset about. His sense of humor was quiet. His favorite joke was to get in the cockpit and put his headset on before anyone else. Then when the other pilot clicked into the intercom system, he would pretend to be caught in the middle of a conversation.

"...biggest asshole I've ever flown with... – *uh, that's a roger, tower, we'll take Runway 36,*" he would say. Or, "...hope his wife doesn't find out, she...uh, never mind, I'll tell you later."

His second-favorite joke only worked when he had passengers on board. He had an old bottle of Jeremiah Weed that he kept half-filled with iced tea; somewhere on climb-out he would lean over the center panel (where anyone in back could see him), take a giant swig and proclaim "Damn, that's good!", then drop the bottle into the cabin where it could roll into everyone's view.

Mike was part of the initial cadre of C-130 pilots selected to test the C-27. He was a captain and spoke Spanish. He liked calm and didn't get wrapped around the axle over particulars. That helped him in his job at the RTU where he, Charlie Manson, and Erich Fetterman trained new guys to fly the Chuck.

"What do you want to do today?" he asked whenever I flew with him.

That was simple. I wanted to fly, not crash, and see cool stuff. Mike always found a way to do all those things and teach something at the same time.

On my second ride in August we flew a low-level through the Azuero peninsula in search of an unimproved strip marked on the map by a blue circle. The ride took us over every type of terrain Panama had to offer: mountains, beaches, jungle, farmland, volcanoes – it was a lightning tour of the isthmus.

We flew west and south past El Valle and Penonomé, south over the salt flats at Aguadulce and along the coast to Las Tablas, inland over pastureland slashed-and-burned from the native forests, and finally hooked around the tiny Oria mountains to approach our target, Las Minas, from the north. But when we got to Las Minas there was nothing where the map said the strip should be. The INS counted down the distance remaining on our run-in, our clocks ticked toward our time-on-target, but at the moment when we should have seen an airstrip there was nothing below but fields of corn and grazing cattle.

I felt betrayed.

"Let this be a lesson to you," Mike said. "These maps are old. Their information is out of date. Rivers move, dams get built, the jungle spreads. Sometimes things aren't as you expect. Have a back-up."

We shot an approach anyway after circling the field. I turned base using cows relaxing under a ceiba as my reference. The cows looked up as we passed through fifty feet. Green filled the windscreen.

"Go around," said Mike.

I pushed the power in. The engines leaped and let the props tap all their power. We climbed back to three hundred feet.

"Good approach," he said as though expecting nothing less.

I had a second route planned to get us home: north through the peninsula, over the continental divide, and up the Parita River. But Mike had other ideas. He took the map and picked off points, telling me where to fly.

We flew into the foothills and turned west.

"Twelve o'clock, see that lone tree?" he asked, pointing out front.

I looked. A ridge curved down out of the mountains. On it was a thin trunk with few more branches than a telephone pole.

"I've seen that before," he went on. "Come around it and aim for that gap over there."

We climbed the divide, heading for a dark triangle of forest that marked a canyon with flowing water. Our shadow skittered across the ground as though trying to escape us.

At the top of the divide some houses appeared on the sides of the canyon. Beyond them was a dam. The reservoir it held back looked as blue and calm as a swimming hole.

"Hey, we're learning all sorts of things this morning," Mike said, studying the reservoir as we banked over the dam.

"What's that?"

"This place isn't on the map. The village is but not the lake." He took a marker from the pocket on his shoulder and scribbled down the outline of the lake. Later he would update the squadron's master charts.

We ducked down the back side of the divide beneath clouds building over the spine of the isthmus. As the sun rose higher more heat rose from the jungle. The heat carried moisture and offshore winds pushed both up against the mountains. I felt sweat running down the inside of my flight suit.

Bunny Elpole felt the heat, too. He was our loadmaster for the day. Bird was the regular RTU loadmaster but he was busy this morning with a bank official on Fort Clayton. Bird's wife was a Panamanian woman from a small village who had trouble understanding credit cards. She had spent eight thousand dollars that her husband didn't have so now Bird had some negotiating to do.

Bunny was built low and wide with short legs that were wholly out of proportion to the rest of his body. He looked like one of the puppet elves you see in parades, the ones who bob along and blow kisses with big lips. I hardly knew him but right now he didn't look well. He was sweating from every pore in his body.

"You okay, Bunny?" Mike called over the intercom.

Bunny squatted in the third seat with a neckerchief in each hand to mop his face dry.

"Oh, y-y-yes, sir. J-j-just fine."

Bunny stuttered, too.

The mists and fog of the morning dissipated over the jungle. The air on the north side was as clear as a freshwater pool. Except for a few hills there was nothing to see between us and the coast.

"Where do you want to go from here?" I asked Mike.

"Well, let's see," he said, studying the map. He turned it one way, then another, then lay his plotter across our course and pulled out his whiz wheel. "Try 060 for a few minutes while I figure this out. I want to show you an emergency field."

I held course while he spun the numbers on the wheel. The EA-9 flight computer was just a circular slide rule that pilots had used for generations. Some understood it more than others, some used it more than others, and it was a slowly-dying art in the age of inertial navigation and global positioning systems. For C-27 operations it was indispensable. With an INS that drifted and no funds to install a GPS, clock-to-map-to-ground procedures weren't going away anytime soon.

"Okay, got it. See this ridge coming down on the right? See where it leads into those two breast-shaped hills? Fly between them and then come left to 010 degrees. I'll call the hack."

Bunny laughed over the intercom, trying to sound cool. "He said, 'breast'," he giggled.

We flew around the jungle for another fifteen minutes navigating solely by dead reckoning.

"A-a-are we g-g-going to Coclecito?" Bunny inquired.

"That's right," said Mike.

"Okay," said Bunny. "I'm going to be in b-b-back."

"Okay," Mike acknowledged. "Take a walk around and make sure everything's secure."

"Roger."

"What's at Coclecito?" I asked.

"I'll show you."

"I haven't studied that field, just so you know."

Mike shrugged. “Then you’ll get the most out of it. There’s no substitute for a lack of preparation.”

We cruised up toward the coast then turned back inland. After several minutes Mike was satisfied that he knew where we were. He took the controls.

“I have the controls.”

“Roger, you have the controls. You need me to read the map?”

“Naah. I can find it naked. You ever landed on grass?”

“Uh, no.”

“What does the Dash 1 say about landing on grass?”

“It says your landing distance will be longer.”

“How much longer?”

“Up to fifty percent.”

“Why?”

“The tires won’t have the friction they would on pavement.”

“What else?”

“For landing? Not much. If it’s dry grass and a prepared strip that should be it, but if it’s wet or the ground is soft or you’re not familiar with the landing area you have to watch out that the nose wheel doesn’t dig in. Keep the controls full aft while on the roll out and while taxiing. Try to keep moving so you don’t have to keep pushing the power up to get started again. If there’s a lot of loose stuff in the grass you don’t want to be sucking it into the intakes.”

Mike nodded while I talked, keeping his eyes outside. He wore military issue sunglasses, the ones with silver rims and straight arms that made him look like a staffer in the Kennedy administration. As far as I could tell he was the only guy in the whole Air Force who wore them.

“There it is,” he said. He pointed off the nose. Four miles in front of us a cleared knoll stood out against the jungle. A cabin with a thatch awning stood at the left of the clearing, a curl of smoke rising above it. There was a paddock of spindly wood and a clothesline. The green of the clearing was lighter than the trees but I couldn't be sure how large it was.

"That's our LZ?"

"That's Coclecito," Mike affirmed. He put his left hand on the power levers. "We'll start the approach at one-point-five. Bunny, you ready?"

Bunn reappeared on the cockpit steps. He wore a Kevlar helmet.

"Ready, sir. Is he out there?"

"Don't know yet. We'll see in a minute."

"Is who out there?" I asked.

"Farmer Brown. Two miles out. Stand by on the flaps. At 180 knots I'll call for ten, at 170 for mid. Approach speed is 108. When I call for gear throw the gear down first and then go right for the flaps to full. Be quick."

"Roger."

The wind was off our tail but not enough to matter. Mike held the speed up until he judged we were a mile and a half from the clearing. By that time I could see tire tracks etched into the grass. To the right two cows grazed on tethers. A few brown spots moved on the grass by the clothesline. As we got closer the brown spots focused into chickens.

There was nothing noteworthy on the ground to mark the one-and-a-half-mile point: Mike just chopped the power levers to idle when it looked right.

"Flaps ten."

I pulled the flap lever out to clear the detent and then down.

"Ten."

"Flaps mid."

"Mid."

The airspeed dropped faster as the flaps lowered into place.

"Gear down, flaps full."

"Gear down."

As the gear swung into place Mike pushed the propeller condition levers all the way forward. The props responded immediately by going to an almost flat pitch and spinning like mad. Now anyone who couldn't hear us coming had to be deaf.

He shot a textbook assault approach. With the power levers in idle the airspeed dropped like a rock. When it hit 120 he moved the power levers up. The airspeed continued down and then stopped at 110. With some fine adjustments he worked it to exactly 108 knots.

We were level at three hundred feet above the trees until three-quarters of a mile out. At that point the forward edge of the clearing sank to the lower third of the windscreen and Mike held it there to capture his glide angle. He made it look easy but I noticed he was no longer talking.

The nose never wavered until we cleared the front trees and descended through twenty feet. Then Mike pulled back on the stick, shifting the aim point to the far end of the clearing. Our descent rate slowed. Our relative velocity, now that we were closer to the ground, sped up. For two hours the image out my window had walked past me at a comfortable pace. Now it accelerated to a run. I saw the cows raise their heads, mouths in mid-chew.

The main gear hit with a *whoompf!* We slammed into the clearing with all the subtlety of Ty Cobb tackling a catcher. The shock absorbers and the grass minimized the impact but even so I felt myself compressed into the seat.

Grass flew up from an invisible bow wave. Behind us the gear scraped off the first few inches of topsoil. The roar of the props discarded any pretense of grace – fifty thousand pounds of man and machine came to earth and there was no way to disguise the fact.

Mike lowered the nose gear and advanced the power levers. As soon as we were down we were on the go.

We flashed by the cabin at a hundred miles per hour. The laundry never wavered but the curl of smoke bent our way when we roared by. It was during the rotation as Mike lifted the nose wheel off the ground that I saw a figure run out from behind the building. I wanted to turn to look but the approaching trees were more immediately important.

"There was somebody down there," I said when we had climbed back up to four hundred feet.

"Your turn," said Mike, finally speaking.

"Okay, my controls," I answered. I banked the plane around to the left to keep the clearing in sight. "There was somebody down there," I repeated. "Doesn't he get ticked that we're landing on his front yard?"

"We're not landing on his front yard," Mike replied, adjusting his baseball cap. "He's living on our runway."

"Yeah," came Bunny's disembodied voice from the back. "He's on *our* runway."

"No kidding?" I said. "He moved onto the runway?"

"It was a helicopter pad originally," Mike explained. "Not a pad but a clearing that helicopters used. Then someone burned off a bunch of trees around it to graze cows. That lasted a few years. Then the Panas had a Twin Otter they brought in for a while – nobody knows why. This guy only moved onto the field last winter. I call him Farmer Brown. He doesn't like us."

"Did he shoot at us?" came the voice from the back.

I raised my eyebrows. "Shoot at us?"

Mike waved his hand. "Fly your pattern. He's only kidding."

I flew the pattern to the left about half a mile out. I tried to stay low but there was a hill where I turned base that made me climb a hundred feet higher than the level of the landing zone. When I completed the turn I was too high, so I started the checklist and pushed the nose over to get down where Mike had initiated his approach. My airspeed climbed. Now I was too fast.

"Don't make it hard," Mike said calmly. "One step at a time – keep it flowing."

I was going to flow right past the LZ if I didn't slow down. I chopped the power levers to idle at three-quarters of a mile. The airspeed fell below two hundred but then stagnated. Why the hell had it fallen so easily for Mike?

"A hundred aaannnnnd...eighty," I announced. "Flaps ten."

Mike moved the flaps and we went quickly through the configuration steps as the airplane slowed down. Still I delayed too long and stayed fast. If we continued I would make it into the clearing but too far down to be safe. The approach wasn't salvageable.

"We'll be going around," I said in frustration.

"That would be a good idea," Mike agreed. Bunny looked over my shoulder and nodded vigorously. I paid no attention to him until at some point while adjusting the power levers my elbow knocked against his chest – which felt like a steel plate. I glanced back quickly and saw it *was* a steel plate: Bunny had donned body armor. With the helmet it made him thirty pounds heavier. Just standing on the steps he puffed from the exertion.

"We're not going to touch down – flaps back to mid," I directed, turning my attention back out front.

It was as Mike moved the flaps that I saw the running figure emerge again from behind the cabin. We were almost abeam the structure and moving fast so I only had time to glimpse his outline: pale shade of pants, dark shirt, a stained white hat with a rag or bandanna tied above the brim – and a shotgun.

"Holy s—!" I started to bank to the right but hadn't even moved before there was a rattle at my window, a sound like rocks thrown against the plexiglass. I hunched and threw us into the turn.

"Whoa!" yelled Mike and got on the controls. I felt extra pressure as we rolled out with the cabin forty-five degrees of the tail. We headed toward the foothills of the divide and pushed over to get down to the trees.

"He shot at us! That guy shot at us!" I called into the intercom.

Bunny ducked back down into the cabin. We didn't have kevlar blankets on board so instead he sat on the crew chief's toolbox, his butt protected by wrenches and screwdrivers.

"I knew it. I told you he would," he said.

"Wow," said Mike, impressed like someone observing automatic windows for the first time.

"Wow? You don't sound surprised – you guys were expecting him to do that?"

"Here, let me see." Mike took the controls and pulled us up and around to the right to get the field back in sight. We were outside even a wide pattern by now. Once he got oriented he brought the gear and flaps up and dropped low enough that we had to follow the compass to know where the clearing was. He put his hand over to bring the props back to a quieter setting.

"You're going back?" I asked, incredulous.

"Just to see," he shrugged.

See what? I thought. What do you have to see about a guy with a gun? I looked to Bunny for support but he hid in the cabin.

Mike set up a third approach, this one faster even than the one I had gone around from. He came in at an angle to the runway to take advantage of lower terrain. The clearing was above us until we reached the half-mile point, meaning (we hoped) that the farmer couldn't see us coming. I wondered, though: our tail stuck up another twenty feet. For all we knew he was following it like a shark's fin cutting through the trees.

At half a mile Mike cut the power. This time we were screaming along, though, and here Mike taught me another maneuver. Because we were offset from the direction of the runway he used the late turn to final to kill off our extra speed. So close to the threshold that we should have been set to land, he banked hard and pulled. The airspeed plummeted. I threw down the gear and flaps and by the time we passed over the near treeline we were only ten knots hot. He never pushed up the props. Without that thundering roar in the blades we all but crept up on the landing zone.

"Anybody see him?" Mike asked. "Anybody see the farmer?"

"There!" Bunny pointed between us. He climbed back up on the center steps.

"I've got him."

The farmer had lost us. Either that or he decided we had gone for good. His back was to us and he was on one knee doing something at the bottom of one of the laundry poles. He wasn't deaf, though, and we weren't totally silent. When we crossed back into the clearing he looked back over his shoulder. I couldn't see whether he was shocked or surprised but I did see him fumble for his gun.

"What are you going to do, land on him?" I asked. The way things were going I wouldn't have been surprised.

"Not at all," Mike murmured. We were only thirty feet off the ground but he leveled off so as not to touch down. If we stayed straight down the tire tracks the farmer would pass just under our left wing. Finally Mike pushed the props to max.

The farmer had his gun in his hands but was nervous and rushing. He hadn't finished re-loading.

We roared over the short strip. Mike dipped his left wing. From the ground it must have looked like the farmer would catch a face full of propeller.

"He's got his gun."

"He won't hit us."

"He hit us before."

"Well, he's on your side."

We were almost on top of him. I pulled the adjust lever on my seat and slid back as far as it would go. That still left me by a window but at least now I had more room to duck. For the first time I wished the designers had put less glass and more steel around the cockpit.

The farmer brought his gun up. Then he saw the wingtip and the enormous prop leading the left nacelle bearing down on him. He staggered backwards and fell. The gun came up and fired just as he landed on his back, the chickens scattering behind him. I threw myself to the right.

"Ha, ha!"

Mike yanked back on the controls and we shot upwards as though launched off a rail.

"Flaps mid!"

From my hunched position I reached to move the flaps. The clearing dropped behind us.

"He hit us?"

"I don't know. Bunny, he hit us?"

There was a dragging sound on the intercom as Bunny picked up his headset. On the climb-out he had fallen over. Unable to stand in his tortoise-shell of armor he'd slid all the way aft to the ramp.

"I-I don't know. L-l-let me check."

"Doesn't look like it," Mike said, confidently scanning the engine instruments. He was pleased with himself. "Good thing, too. If he'd hit us twice we might not be able to go there anymore. Once is a lucky shot. Anyone can do that. Twice is a trend."

I had trouble believing he was serious. In flight school trend items were such things as forgetting a checklist or not turning on your landing light on final. No one ever included ground fire in that category.

"It was a shotgun," I volunteered, not knowing what else to say.

"Yeah."

"Does he always shoot at us?"

"Only when he's home." Mike sighed, wondering what else he could show me on this ride. Then, sensing that answer didn't satisfy me he added, "Usually he doesn't come close. He must be practicing."

10. Howard

I WENT FOR a run one Thursday afternoon once the window of peak cancer hours had passed. PCH ran from 11 a.m. (10 a.m. if you were really being careful) until 3 p.m. and was inviolable for athletic activity on the base. There was no formal rule put out by the base commander but common sense and the fear of heatstroke made it just as effective. Unless you had grown up in the jungle or had spent your youth herding camels in the Sudan, the sun was just too damned hot during the mid-day hours to do anything outside. It goes without saying that Panamanians observed the restriction, too; in fact, for extra safety most of them extended their window of inactivity to the other nineteen hours of the day as well.

Running on the base was easy and safe. The air was clean, traffic was light, and the jungle imparted a sweetness to the air that you could taste anywhere on the complex. There were also several routes to keep things interesting. An asphalt bike path ran from the passenger terminal all the way to the front gate, a distance of two miles. It wound up and down the terrain and through long stretches of trees where on a quiet day spider monkeys chattered in the branches and cicadas buzzed in the heat. There was also a dirt track behind the horse stables that cut into the jungle near the approach path to Runway 18. Unlike the paved path that road was little used. I would run it if someone was with me but usually shied away from getting too far into the jungle, worried about two-stepper snakes and spiders that spun webs at face level.

A road barred to vehicle travel ran abeam Farfan, the Navy's housing area which sat across the main road from the elementary school. I called it the Swamp Road. It led through more jungle out to one of the few sections of perimeter fence that the locals hadn't stolen, one that bordered a mile-wide swamp. Even on sunny days it was steeped in shadow, over-arching trees keeping it cool.

After settling into the squadron I made time to run several days a week. Partly that was my way of dealing with the stress of a new job and a new country, but I got more regular about it once Manny convinced me to train with him for a marathon. Manny was another pilot but one with a lot more discipline than me. Clean-cut, clean-living, in fact just all-around clean, Manny approached running with an evangelist's passion and a scientist's rigor for efficiency. He was a machine on the road, focused solely on his pace and his stride, whereas I was content just to be outside getting exercise. But such were his ardor and his charisma that when he found out I ran it took him all of five minutes to sell me on his latest training regimen.

Often we ran together. Sometimes I went out on my own. Our hangar was across the street from the gym where I could change my clothes, replace boots with sneakers, and be outside and running in ten minutes. Whenever the fluorescent lights at the scheduling desk got too much for me that's where I headed. Even if it was raining, there were days when my legs got jumpy if they were trapped behind a desk. I would fight the urge for a while but eventually turn to Major Harmon and tell him I needed some exercise. Since the base gym to him was like Canterbury Cathedral to a pilgrim, he always smiled and egged me on. "Good on you," he would say. "Lift a few for me."

The urge came upon me one Thursday. Up the hill from Hangar 1 I ran, past the legal office, past base operations and the passenger terminal with its parking lot. The motor pool and ATOC came next. ATOC was the Air Terminal Operations Center, a long title which meant it was the home of the guys who loaded and unloaded aircraft. Their K-loaders and forklifts were parked neatly on the ramp, lined up and ready to roll as soon as the next C-5 landed.

Past ATOC the street gave out and the bike path started. To its left lay a border of grass that kept the jungle from reaching out and snatching hapless passers-by. To the right was an immense lawn a thousand yards across. At its far edge was the main road with which the bike path eventually converged. The grass on the lawn was always kept short, rain or shine, due to the persistent efforts of an army of Kuna Indians wielding machetes, weed-whackers, and wide riding mowers. They were a perpetual sight on base, working in bands from early in the morning until late in the afternoon. With baseball caps trailing home-sewn towels and bandannas to protect their neck and shoulders from the sun, they would descend on a patch of overgrown grass and shred and cut and hack and mow until nature had once again been tamed. Then they would move on to another section of the base. Such was the rain and the never-ending growing cycle that they enjoyed perfect job security. The grass grew so fast you could watch it.

The bike path curved down between the lawn and the jungle until it entered a copse of zapateros. In the trees was a short bridge across a creek. The creek ran through the center of the base and was essential to flow and drainage of the local watershed, sluicing away hundreds of thousands of gallons during every afternoon downpour. In the mornings it trickled quietly; you could step across its few inches of water. By two o'clock it was usually Class 3 rapids.

Past the creek were the horse stables, then several stretches of meadow, trees, meadow, trees until the path popped out on a course paralleling the main road.

As I passed the creek it began to rain, a gentle hiss that started all around as the trees intercepted drops with their broad leaves. Past the stables the trees opened up and by the top of the hill I was soaking wet. But the rain was warm and gentle, not the vindictive downpour that usually happened at mid-day. It felt good and I kept running.

I always treated the stretch thus far as a warm-up. It was half the distance to the main gate and even with the rain was a soothing, relatively cool jog through nature. At the top of this second hill was when I settled into the long haul. 'Long' in this direction was only a couple more miles but since the path remained exposed to the road as it climbed and descended runs there were less personal and more pressured. The path was also open to the sun. I didn't want to be puffing and wheezing and looking on the verge of heatstroke in front of passing motorists – some of whom would know me. I wanted to look like I knew what I was doing.

So it was a relief just past the school to cross the main road and hide again on the bypass leading around the naval facility. Once over its barrier the gloom and quiet of the Swamp Road let me relax and think only about my stride and breathing. The trees intercepted the rain again so for a while I trotted in shelter, dodging puddles and listening to the background hiss.

Visible through the trees were abandoned ammunition storage bunkers whose access had been the road's purpose in years past. Now they were just suspicious hills of thrown-up dirt sitting like burial mounds in the forest. Trees grew on them, signs that that same forest was reclaiming them as its own. Cement walls covered with moss, dark entrances and thick steel doors encased in vines – all were grown over and sported hideously wide spider webs wherever a man-made hole remained.

The webs were forbidding. From the road they weren't always visible but came and went depending on sunlight. The light had to hit the silk just right, or dew from the morning or rain in the afternoon had to cling to the strands heavy enough to mark the geometry of ever-expanding circles. Whether the webs were visible or not, their owner always was. The spiders hung inverted on the strands, large wolf spiders the size of my hand or thin, hairy-legged banana spiders with yellow torsos and bulging eyes. It was startling enough to make out such creatures at a distance – to see them hanging from nothing only a few feet away, suspended in the green tableau, was enough to alter my stride.

At the end of the road the trees gave way, parting to allow in light. I emerged to find...swamp. Acres and acres of grass and bamboo and cattails taller than a man and waving in the breeze. The road eked through this new expanse, water lapping at its edges, everywhere the smell of rot and decay. It only stopped at the base perimeter. There I encountered a cement barrier, a warning sign, and then the chain link fence beyond which lay the Pan American Highway.

I always hurdled the barrier and trotted up to the fence to enjoy its presence, to look out and feel the colonist's gratitude that the disorganization of the locals couldn't intrude past this point. I did it every run and never felt guilty, running to the fence deliberately to think the same thought. There was just too much order on one side of the border and too much anarchy on the other not to feel comfortable having a barrier between.

From the fence my run went back the same route. Crossing the bridge I could turn left and cut across the baseball fields in a direct line toward the commissary. The road past the store went into base housing, the beautiful duplexes of terra cotta roofs, cream walls, and red trim that spread across the hill on the south side of the base. The houses filled the lower and middle levels of the hill, grouped vaguely by rank in winding streets and cul de sacs with swathes of lawn and pruned outposts of jungle available to every home.

Near the top of the hill was the Officers Club. At the very top was the hospital, perched at the summit to face the whole of the air base stretched before its main entrance. Behind it lay the forested back slope of the hill at the bottom of which lurked the Veracruz swamp that I had just left. There was no path or road down the back side of the hill, no road into, out of, or through the swamp.

The road up Commissary Hill was tortuously steep for the first hundred yards. After that it settled into a series of smaller inclines along the ridge, a switchback that toured the west slope. The inclines interspersed with flat stretches through the neighborhoods which made the road and the climb even longer.

The size of the housing area never ceased to surprise me. From the base – the passenger terminal, say – the hill looked like a modest affair with only a few houses poking their way through the trees. But the trees hid much. There were streets and streets and then more streets, flanked with well-kept homes each of which had a name plate beneath the number: "Colonel So-and-so" or "Captain Such-and-such". The names went on forever. There was a lot of geography on that hill.

The perimeter road worked its way through the houses until reaching the final run up to the summit and the hospital. From there it curved down again to the parade ground and to the barracks of Fort Kobbe.

Fort Kobbe was tiny. It shared the same territory as Howard Air Base without so much as a gate to define the border between the two. It was really like a small room in the back of a large house, one where a cousin lives and keeps to himself. For the Army did indeed keep to itself. In our operations we only saw the soldiers from a distance, usually taxiing past on our way to Runway 36.

Kobbe supported an engineer battalion, the 87th Infantry, and the 228th Aviation Regiment, a UH-60 and CH-47 helicopter squadron that flew infantry and medevac support for Army posts around Panama. In fact, the 228th was *the* Army air presence in Central America.

The amazing thing about Fort Kobbe was that it had over a thousand people assigned to it, something that was hard to believe sometimes. On any given run at whatever time of day I rarely saw enough people to make me think the garrison was half that size. But then the Army being the Army kept to itself, the soldiers either intimated by or just not desiring to mix with the larger Air Force presence only yards away.

But because it was quiet, Fort Kobbe was as good a place to run as the Swamp Road. The main road on this side of the base kept a straight line through to the motor pool, past which it ran into the perimeter fence again. The fence here had been put up on the *base* side of the jungle rather than the Veracruz side – in other words, it didn't try to keep the locals out but was there to keep grunts from going exploring. I got that far and turned right, following the fence road out to Gate 2.

For a while there was nothing but jungle on both sides. Then an obstacle course appeared on the left, outside the fence in a clearing of its own. On the right a picnic area came up, slick and shiny from the rain. Then more jungle. The road veered left, heading back toward the runway. The entomology research office appeared on the right, off in a cutout set back from the road. Like grounds-keeping, entomology was another never-ending job in Panama. There were probably more bugs within a ten-minute walk of that building than there were in all of North America.

The road crossed a creek, dipped and curved left, and suddenly broke into the open again, the approach end of Runway 36 ahead in the afternoon light. The rain tapered off. Over the ocean clouds parted to let blue sky through.

At this point the fence on the left disappeared and was replaced by swamp. Another popped up on the far side of the road to protect the runway itself from intruders.

As I broke from the trees a C-130 roared in off the water and descended overhead, close enough that I covered my ears. Its nose raised in a flare, its landing gear reached toward the ground like the feet of a duck coming in to splash down on a pond. The pilots aimed for a spot a thousand feet past the threshold where rainwater had collected so deep it was a wonder they could see the runway markings.

I watched the plane through touchdown. Then I jogged around the overrun to where I could look straight down the field where the now distant plane shimmered in reflected light from the puddles. Behind me hummed the approach lights that guided the aircraft in. Standing in a row that started half a mile away at the beach, they were mounted on pylons that stood above the murky swamp. From here they looked like deformed street lamps but it was easy to imagine them as though on final approach myself, blinking in rapid sequence toward the runway, the last one leading right to the overrun whose own lights then took over. On a clear afternoon they were superfluous but when the weather was bad they were a pilot's best friend. Whenever the field was open they welcomed landing aircraft, defining the airspace inbound from as far out as one could see them as a gateway to America, another sign of that clear, linear order that made returning pilots feel at home.

Gate 2 was another few yards on. There a lone sentry monitored traffic in and out from this side of the base. There wasn't much traffic to monitor since outside the gate there was nowhere to go. Veracruz was a rundown fishing village. The beach itself had some *bohio*-type restaurants, shacks that offered cheap fried fish and shade. Other than that and the water there was no reason to come out here. On Sunday afternoons the beach was party central for the city's poor but every other day it was deserted.

"Going out?" called the airman at the gate.

"Nope. This is far enough. Any more and I won't make it back."

He waved. I turned around to head back to the squadron. The round trip would be close to seven miles and if I made it without stopping I would be satisfied. Manny would have kept a better pace but he wouldn't have seen as much along the way.

11. Flight 2

*"*SHARK *11,* ARE *you requesting a turn in holding?"*

"That's a negative. We'll take the approach from present altitude."

"Shark 11, roger. You're cleared for the HI-TACAN approach, runway 36. Winds at Howard are two-eight-zero at five, altimeter 30.12. Report final approach fix for frequency change to tower."

"Shark 11, 30.12. Understand cleared the approach and we'll report the FAF."

We were twenty-four miles south of the base, over the waters of the Pacific at an altitude of twenty thousand feet. It was the highest yet I had been in the C-27. Though I had already made two flights in Panama they were both at low-level, never more than five hundred feet. Already I was getting used to that picture. Suddenly twenty thousand feet seemed way too high. My days in the C-5 when we routinely flew at thirty thousand or more were fading rapidly from memory.

"Alright, just hit the initial approach fix and then hold your altitude," said my instructor. "I'll tell you when to descend."

I was flying with Charlie Manson on my third flight of training. It was still unclear how many flights I would get with the RTU but so far the only consistency was that there was no consistency. My first flight had been with Captain Erich Fetterman on an orientation flight around the local area. Fetterman flew fine but he yelled a lot. Not that I scared him, he was just tightly wound. Anything that didn't go exactly according to plan set him off. If the crew bus showed up late, he yelled at the driver. If the airplane's forms (where the mechanics recorded all their work) weren't sitting on the pilot's seat when we got to the plane, he yelled at the crew chief. If the sun was too hot, he yelled at the sky. He yelled at me, he yelled at the tower, he yelled at other aircraft – it was his default method of conversing with the world. He screamed at students especially, often beating the dash so hard to emphasize a point that flecks of green plastic flew off and sailed through the cockpit. Fetterman was as patient as a Prussian drill instructor and half as tactful, believing that the careful application of terror is a form of communication. Sometimes he screamed because you didn't learn something the first time he mentioned it and he hated repeating himself. Sometimes he screamed even when he wasn't repeating himself but because he had a point worth emphasizing. Sometimes he screamed just because he was a hyper-emotional stress-case who had no other instructional technique. We got used to it. It bothered me but not as much as his insistence on reminding people that he was a Major-select. I wanted to remind him in turn that another word for Major-select is *Captain* but didn't, figuring I should pass my check ride first.

Fortunately, Fetterman paid little attention to me. Since I already had six hundred hours of experience in the C-5 he granted me some benefit of the doubt for knowing how to fly. That didn't make sense since flying the C-5 was as much like flying the C-27 as driving a bus was like racing Indy cars. But I didn't argue since it removed some of the pressure of flying with him.

That extra pressure fell on Rolo. Rolo was usually the target whenever Fetterman vented his spleen, which was about every twelve seconds. Nothing Rolo did was right and the fact that he was doing it for the first time earned him no slack. After the second landing on our inaugural ride where he flared high and dropped the plane onto the runway, causing the aircraft to shudder like a boat slamming into a pier, Fetterman seized the controls.

"Jesus Christ, Metzger!" he howled in fury. "Do I have to stick a piece of Plexiglas in your stomach so you can see out when you have your head up your ass?!"

Rolo hated Fetterman as a result. He decided that if ever he was about to crash, the last thing he wanted anyone to hear on the cockpit voice recorder was "Fetterman's a nazi!" In fact, he started saying it whenever he was stressed while flying. It caught on with other co-pilots, too, all veterans of Fetterman's unique instruction. (Except for Lowell Henderson, who vowed that in the seconds before he crashed he would shout into the microphone, *"What was that? That purple thing with the tentacles??"*) I suppose it was better than having all these guys turn to their pilot and say, "I've always loved you," but still I had horrible visions that one day in the future after a string of accidents investigators from the FAA would be left shaking their heads in confusion.

Nobody much liked Fetterman which was a shame. He was a decent pilot, he had a sense of humor, and he was loyal to his friends. In fact his loyalty is how he ended up in Panama. Before coming to Howard he'd had a promising career going in the C-130 world that ended one day up at Duke Field, Florida when he embarrassed a group commander who had shafted one of Fetterman's friends. The friend got into minor legal trouble and instead of supporting him the group commander nixed his promotion. Fetterman saw that as betrayal. Later, on a day when the colonel needed a check ride – *really* needed it to avoid going non-current and losing his flight pay – Fetterman was his evaluator. Fetterman knew the man wore a toupee so he dug up an obscure passage in Regulation 35-10 that prohibited flyers from wearing wigs in-flight and brought it out during the brief, when all the rest of the crew, the weather guys, and various others were in attendance. The commander was humiliated. He fumed, then protested, then threatened – and then shrank away to the latrine to replace said hairpiece with a hat. Not long after that Fetterman was made to go far, far away. That's how he ended up on my first flight.

The second flight I had was with Mike Vaneya. Vaneya's approach to instruction was as relaxed as Fetterman's was apoplectic. He just liked to get shot at.

Now this third flight was with yet another instructor, Charlie Manson. The goal was to get familiar with flying instruments in the C-27, something you do when the weather or darkness doesn't let you see out the window. So far, Charlie was in a category all his own. His humor was all sarcasm and he didn't like small talk.

"Isn't your first name Theodore?" I asked.

"Yeah."

"So why does everyone call you 'Charlie' Manson?" I asked.

"Because I remind them of Charles Manson."

"How so?"

"I use drugs, founded a cult, and killed a bunch of people." He pointed to the center panel and changed the subject. "If you set 600 foot-pounds of torque in the pattern, that'll fly you at 180 knots," he stated matter-of-factly. "When you drop the gear and flaps it'll slow you to 150."

"Is that in the book?" I asked, referring to the flight manual.

"You mean the Dash 1? No. Nothing's in the book."

"Well, not to be a chicken but I've never done this steep an approach before."

"That's okay, it's a technique."

"What do you mean, a technique?"

"A technique is something that somebody teaches you because they did it once and it worked."

"Oh. And when does something stop being a technique?"

"When you've done it twice. Then it's a procedure. For now, because it's technique you don't have to do it but it works so take it for what it's worth."

The flight had been enlightening. Uneventful but enlightening. We flew three approaches into Howard and three into Tocumen International. Since both airfields used the navaid on Taboga Island the controllers were constantly vectoring us out over the water or telling us to navigate there on our own to start the next approach. The repetition made it easy to learn local procedures. The navigational aids, the frequencies, and the limits of the control zone around Panama City all coalesced into a big picture. So did the instrument panel on the dashboard. It was like driving around a strange city for a few hours in a new car.

I was comfortable flying instruments. Flying instruments is all about precision and procedure and there's a lot of predictability to it. If the pilot does this, then this other thing will happen. If the plane is here and the course is over there, then obviously this is the heading to fly to reach it. There's very little variety. If you follow the procedures, you'll always get where you want to go.

And getting there was made easier by the fact that everything on the C-27 was new, including the instruments. The artificial horizon gleamed from its center position on the panel. The Horizontal Situation Indicator, the HSI, was also so clean it made me feel guilty to look at it. The Bearing-Distance-Heading-Indicator, the HSI's back-up, was more modern than the primary instruments on the C-5. The radar altimeter was digital. So was the barometric. Even the clock was electronic. That in itself wasn't rocket science but it was a huge leap forward from the wind-up clocks on every other Air Force plane, the ones with the second hand that always jammed and the stopwatch button with its admonition to PUSH HARD.

The panel on which the gauges were mounted was spotless. Everything worked and everything was redundant, bundled into a tight package repeated on both sides of the cockpit. The beauty of that was that one pilot could fly an approach using one system and be backed up by the other pilot on a separate one. Screw-ups were still possible but now it would be harder to blame any mistakes on the plane.

Mistakes like descent rates.

"Two miles to the initial approach fix," I prompted Charlie.

He nodded but made no response.

I looked at the approach plate clipped to the window above my right knee. It gave a god's-eye view of the ground track we needed to fly to get to the field as well as a profile view to explain our descent rate. It was a TACAN approach and one of the steepest I had seen.

A TACAN is a radio beacon that transmits its signal in every direction at once. The signal is broken down into 360 pieces, called radials, that project outward from the station like spokes from the center of a wheel. The receiver in an airplane identifies which radial the plane is on. The same receiver calculates slant-range distance from the transmitting station. We were on the 178 radial, almost directly south of Howard, at 23 miles. Consequently the heading we needed to fly was north. No problem. As soon as I crossed over the 21-mile marker, the initial approach fix that marked the beginning of the instrument procedure, that's what I would do. I would also descend. But we were still at twenty thousand feet and the approach plate said we should be at fifteen thousand.

"There's the IAF," I announced as the distance marker in the BDHI rotated past twenty-one.

"Roger," said Charlie. "Hold your altitude a few more miles."

I looked over at the approach plate again. Its predictability – the predictability that I liked about instrument approaches – was already shot to hell. The profile view showed us starting our descent from fifteen thousand feet at twenty-eight miles. Even at a ground speed of 180 knots – three miles per minute – we would have to descend more than fifteen hundred feet per minute to get to the runway in time to make an approach. And that was just to make the runway. Technically we were supposed to meet an altitude restriction at the final approach fix, the FAF, which was five miles sooner. We were five thousand feet higher than the profile allowed and still doing two hundred knots. I started to back off the power.

"No, no, keep your speed up," Charlie insisted.

"Uh, how long do you want to stay up here?"

"Start the approach at twenty."

Twenty miles out. I quickly did the math. Three miles per minute, twenty miles, twenty thousand feet. We would have to descend at more than three thousand feet per minute. Not exactly a free-fall, but definitely a malfunctioning elevator.

"Um,...I know I've already referred to the book once today but shouldn't we have started down by now?" I was thinking of the paragraph that recommended descents not exceed 1,000 feet per minute.

"Book, shmook," replied Manson. "I want to show you something."

"Another technique?"

"You got it."

"Shark 11, confirm you are commencing the approach?"

Even the radar controllers at Howard had doubts.

"I've got him," Charlie said, keying the mike. *"Yes, sir, that's affirmative. We're delaying the descent a little but we're on the approach."*

"Roger."

This wasn't something we could ever do at a civilian field. It was also something we would never want to do in real weather conditions. Such a huge descent rate in bad weather could induce spatial disorientation, the belief that we were doing one thing when actually the plane was doing another.

Fortunately today the weather wasn't a problem. The sky was cobalt blue with a scattering of wispy clouds. We could see the runway far out in front of us where the ocean met the land. It looked small and quiet, a brownish litmus tab stretched beyond the beach that moved lower and lower on the windscreen as we got closer. The Canal was in sight off to the right. Beyond it was the city. The bank buildings along Avenida Balboa glistened in the sun and the high towers of Punta Paitilla looked as though they had been white-washed in the bright light. It was a beautiful day for a space shuttle approach.

My mouth began to dry up as I watched the runway disappear beneath the nose.

Our loadmaster was Leonard Mondavi, he of the massive frame. Leonard was an amateur body builder who could display rippling muscles even through his flight suit. He sat in the center seat facing the front and craned his thick neck to keep the runway in sight.

"We gonna land?" he asked innocently.

The circular distance indicator on the BDHI slid through sixteen. Charlie glanced at it, indifferent, as though the instrument had let him down. Then he tapped his finger on the approach plate as if he were seeing it for the first time.

"Okay, start your descent."

I pulled the power to idle and watched the nose fall to try to keep the airspeed. The runway came back into sight. To keep it there, however, I had to keep the nose pushed over. I couldn't do that without the airspeed climbing. There was no way we could make the runway that way – the math just didn't work out. The faster we went the sooner we would eat up our fifteen miles, which meant we had to descend faster. But to descend faster meant we would *go forward* faster which meant we had less time... I pulled the nose back up and slowed so we could lower the flaps.

"That's it," said Charlie. "Put as much drag on the plane as you can. That's what I wanted to show you. This baby will drop like a rock if you do it right."

I didn't do it right. Within seconds he was putting a finger on the yoke to push it back forward.

"Ah-ah-ahhh. Keep thy airspeed up lest the earth rise from below and smite thee."

'Doing it right' in this instance meant the opposite of what Chumley had taught me so long before in Arizona. Here it meant getting the plane as 'dirty' as possible – full flaps and gear – so it could go as slow as possible. The flaps did most of the work. Fully extended they reached down into the slipstream and acted like giant speed brakes. When I finally got us in the right speed range to drop them it felt like we had thrown out an anchor. Then I brought the nose up again to keep the airspeed exactly on our computed final speed of 104 knots. That slowed our progress across the water and helped us to descend even faster. We plummeted to earth like a chicken clutching a bowling ball.

"You can also help yourself by pushing the props up."

I advanced the propellers to max. With the blades rotating about the hub to an almost flat pitch, they now spun in the air so fast they created two solid disks to resist the wind. I prayed to the god of drag.

"Shark 11, uh, we show you on course but still, uh, rather high."

"Roger," Charlie radioed back calmly. *"Training in progress."*

That was the blank check. Tell a controller 'training in progress' and you could get away with anything.

We crossed 10 miles above fifteen thousand feet. The vertical velocity indicator was pegged on the low side, which meant at six thousand feet per minute. The elevator's cable had definitely now been cut. The needles on the altimeter swung around like a clock gone mad trying to keep up with our fall to earth. The pressure in the cockpit changed so quickly that every few miles I had to pinch my nose and blow to clear my ears. Leonard Mondavi did the same.

"Good thing I don't have a cold," he commented. "Thanks for asking, though..."

Approach Control called and told us to switch to Howard's tower frequency. I looked out the window and shook my head. There was just no way we would make it. Charlie changed the preset frequency on the UHF radio and smiled.

"Have a little faith."

"Faith is one thing," I muttered. "You're an optimist."

"Hardly," he replied. "George Bernard Shaw said the optimist invents the airplane while the pessimist invents the parachute." He pointed over his shoulder toward where our parachutes hung in the cabin. "I'm firmly in the parachute category."

"But have you done this before?" His pedantry was getting on my nerves.

"No," he admitted. "I've never started down later than sixteen miles. You can do it, though."

"Can I push the nose over more?"

"You can," he said, "but that'll overspeed the flaps which might cause them to break off the aircraft and cause catastrophic failure to the wings. Personally, I try to keep the plane in one piece when I fly. Again, that's technique only."

I wanted to punch him.

"Maybe the problem," I suggested, nervously watching the VVI spin around, "is that the plane doesn't want to descend this fast."

Charlie drew 8's in the air as though conducting an orchestra.

"The C-27 doesn't *want* to do anything," he scoffed. "It's an airplane. Airplanes are emotion-less. They don't care about you, they don't care about your mission, they don't care about flying. They're hunks of metal and they do whatever you tell them to. Your job is to learn to demand everything the airplane will give you. That's what makes a pilot a pilot."

"And what if I demand more than it will give me?"

"Then you're a fool. And you'll crash."

The ocean was still so far below us that the swells on its surface looked motionless. They scored the surface like ripples on wallpaper. By leaning forward only a bit in my seat I could look straight down on them.

"Whew!" sighed Leonard behind me. "I'm getting woozy." He shook his head from side to side.

We were also looking almost straight down at the runway. I toyed with the idea of making sharp turns left and ride to help us descend faster but then decided against it. The last thing I wanted to do in such a freefall was turn the aircraft on its side.

"Howard tower, this is Shark 11 with you on the Tacan approach to three-six for a full stop."

"Shark 11, you're cleared to land Runway 36. Uh, sir, we have you on radar at six miles but you're not yet in sight."

"Give him the landing light," Charlie said to me. I flipped the switch. Powerful beams shot out from the leading edge of the left wing. We passed five miles screaming through seven thousand feet.

"Oh, THERE you are," came the voice of the tower controller. There was a short pause while he obviously debated whether or not to say anything. In the military, controllers are reluctant to question pilots but eventually this one decided he had to.

"Um, Shark 11, ahhh... you seem rather high. Are you going to be able to make the runway?"

Charlie laughed out loud and slapped the top of the panel in glee.

"I love this!" he exulted. Then he quickly composed himself to sound as unconcerned as a policeman at a fender-bender. *"That's affirmative. Not a problem."*

Tower wasn't convinced. There was another long pause. Three miles, four thousand.

"Well, um, in that case Shark 11 is cleared to land."

The unspoken tag was "*and I'd love to see it.*" I sensed everyone in the tower move to the window to watch our approach. My hands began to sweat.

"Roger, cleared to land," Charlie repeated happily.

"Uh, Charlie, this doesn't look..."

"Faith, faith," he counseled. "Keep doing what you're doing. Just hold it steady until you get on what you feel is a normal glide slope."

Which ought to be about four feet prior to touchdown, I thought.

Behind me Leonard swiveled his seat and locked his shoulder harness. He probably did that all the time but on this approach it sounded like he was preparing for disaster.

Two miles, twenty-five hundred feet. Charlie reached up and toggled the pressurization switch. There was a soft *whoosh* as a butterfly hatch opened on the cargo door and vented the aircraft to outside air. I pinched my nose again.

"How does this look?" he asked.

"High!" I said defensively. I pushed the nose over more to aim it at the threshold. The airspeed climbed to 110 knots but that was now the least of my worries. The large 36 painted at the beginning of the pavement seemed absurdly clear and high in the windscreen. Worse, it was growing like an expanding balloon. One mile, one thousand feet. I was still six hundred feet higher than I should have been.

"Remember to lead your power," Charlie prompted. He sat casually in his seat but out of the corner of my eye I noticed he moved his hand closer to the throttle quadrant. "Give the engines about two seconds to break the descent."

Then the incredible happened. Passing over the beach, with water still in sight to the right and left and nothing filling the windscreen but the runway overrun jutting out of the swamp, all of a sudden the picture looked almost normal. The parameters I had seen on previous approaches started to line up. We were still high – way high – but the descent rate acquired perspective as the ground came into view on all sides. A usable glide angle formed in my mind. The imaginary line from cockpit to runway presented itself to my eyes in a way I understood. We could land after all.

"There! There!" he prompted, seeing the angle himself. "Where are you going to land?"

"On the numbers," I barked. Now wasn't the time to ask me questions. I was no longer falling, I was flying.

We crossed over the overrun like an eagle reaching for a salmon. I nudged the power levers up. The engines, which for fifteen miles had languished in idle, purred a response. There was a slight pressure in the seat as the descent rate slowed. I nudged the levers more.

The solid line of the threshold shot past eighty feet below. Long hash marks followed it, then the numbers that had loomed so large a few miles out. In my peripheral vision I saw the lighted digits on the radar altimeter drop to zero.

"Power," said Charlie. "*Poweeerrrr...*"

He was afraid that with the ground rush I would be tempted to break our descent by pulling the nose up. That would make us fall faster and hit harder. But while I may not have been way ahead of the plane I was at least finally keeping pace. At what I judged to be ten feet I shoved the power up and killed our descent entirely just as we touched down. The tires met the pavement as the VVI swung back toward the positive range. There was a bump and lurch as the shocks absorbed the impact, then we were down. I pulled the power levers to idle and called for reverse.

"See?" Charlie said in his most sarcastic tone as we rolled out toward Bravo taxiway. He was easily one of the most pompous people I had ever met. "You didn't believe we would make it, did you?"

"No, I didn't."

"Neither did I," said Leonard, climbing out of his seat. From the cabin he reached up to straighten it on its tracks and slide it out of the way. "I couldn't even *see* the runway. A *damn* good thing I don't have a cold – you would have blown in my eardrums."

"Blown your eardrums, hell," I said, still trying to clear my own right ear. "We would have crushed your head."

"Oh, ye of little faith..." Charlie mused into the intercom. He hummed to himself and took the controls to taxi us in.

Mickey met us at the far end of the ramp where we cut the engines. As Leonard rounded up the chocks and Charlie climbed out of his seat, I asked him how he was so sure we would descend in time.

"Easy," he oozed condescension. "I'm never wrong."

"Really? Anything more substantial I can bank on in the future?"

"No." He slid out of his headset and hopped down into the cabin to stretch his legs. There he let out a loud groan straightening his back.

"Come on," I insisted. "Nothing? That picture was wrong all the way down. What's the technique for doing it again?"

He sighed. "Technique? Not everything's a technique. You have to figure it out yourself."

"That doesn't help."

"Tough. What do you want? You want me to scream, or maybe go find someone to shoot at us while we fly? I just showed you what the plane can do. It's up to you to figure out what to do with it from there."

"Yeah, but... I *don't* know what to do with it."

He chuckled. Then, perhaps feeling a twinge of conscience that as an instructor he should actually instruct, he put his foot up on the steps and leaned into the cockpit.

"Okay, you want something to help you know the plane will do what you want it to do?"

"Yes."

"A *technique* for knowing things will work out halfway through every maneuver?"

"Sure. At least halfway."

"A fail-safe, no-brainer, absolute guarantee that when you do something you won't screw it up?"

"Yes."

"Uncle Charlie's secret recipe," he continued, "for dropping the plane out of the stratosphere and putting it onto Brick One of the runway every time, on time, without killing the passengers or turning into a flaming pile of Italian engineering?"

"Yes! For god's sake, just tell me!"

"Okay, then. Here's the secret of my success." He leaned forward, his thinning hair showing the headset marks around his ears. "When you get close to the ground," he whispered, looking around to make sure no one could overhear, "and there's a runway, land. If there isn't, don't."

"You're no help at all," I told him.

He shrugged. "It's gotten me this far."

12. Grandy

"Hey guys, what's up?"

He sat down without asking. Josh stopped what he was saying about the stock market and said hello.

"What're you guys, TDY? Where're you from?"

I didn't like him right off the bat. It wasn't that he didn't introduce himself, or that he sat down at our table without asking, or because he talked with food in his mouth and we got a bird's-eye view of his lunch on the way down.

"No, we live here," said Josh.

He was just a jerk.

"No kidding. What do you fly? You're not -130s." His tone implied he would have recognized us if we were.

Josh smiled the way a man would if a doctor told him he didn't have HIV. He was an instructor, one of the few line flyers who hadn't come from C-130s, and an unrepentant snob. I met him at the scheduling desk and he offered to take me to lunch and tell me what he knew about the C-27. Instead he'd spent half an hour declaiming on the merits of price-to-earnings ratios as a means of rating equities.

"Noooo," he chuckled, "we're not -130s."

"Too bad. That's the bird to be in down here. Great theater, great flying. You must fly VIPs, then. The C-21? Or C-12? What is it they have down here?"

His name tag said Matt Grandy. The patch on his shoulder showed a C-130 Hercules making a fist and looking tough. Below the plane were the words *Georgia Air National Guard.* Below that was a small velcro square that said HERC in red letters.

We were in the snack bar above the Base Exchange. Grandy had ordered a sandwich and was waiting for them to call his number, though why he decided to bless us with his presence I couldn't guess.

"They've got both," I told him. "The Army's got the KingAir and the wing has a Lear. The four-star has a T-43, too." The T-43 was the SOUTHCOM commander's plane, a decked-out 737 from what I heard though I had never been inside it myself.

"Oh, yeah? So how is it serving coffee? Getting prepped for the airlines, huh?"

Josh made a poor effort to hide his disgust. It was bad enough we'd had to change the subject: Josh loved talking about money and investing. It's a given that if you get two pilots together within ten minutes they'll be talking either flying or money but Josh cut that time in half.

"Who *are* you?" he asked.

Matt Grandy pointed to the *Matt Grandy*. "Matt Grandy, Herc driver."

"Really, a Herc driver," I said mock-admiringly. He was eating popcorn out of the basket on the table and dribbling crumbs down his front. Picking them off his flight suit distracted him from noting my sarcasm.

"Yeah, greatest job in the world, greatest plane in the world. Only part-time, unfortunately. I've got a job with a shuttle back in the States, pullin' down some good change. *Cha-ching!* Get trips like this once a month to punch the pension ticket." He made a punching gesture and winked at us. "Should be with the big guys in not too long."

"'The big guys?'"

"Yeah. You know, the airlines. American, Delta. They haven't hired me yet but they will. You know why?"

"Because you're quick with the gear handle and always take the fat chick?" Josh guessed.

Grandy started to nod and then processed the words.

"No, dumbass. Because..." – he pointed at his patch again – "...I'm a Herc driver. We're a breed apart."

"Thank god for evolution."

"Well, of course it doesn't compare to pouring coffee..."

"Wouldn't know," Josh said quickly.

I looked at the goof, half-amused and half in disbelief. He was the worst stereotype of both C-130s and the Guard. The sloppy flight suit, zipped only halfway up with the dog tags flopping out; the flight cap shoved into the thigh pocket instead of the one on the bottom of the pants leg; the rounded gut. This guy was barely thirty and he looked like a washed-up master sergeant.

"I thought you said you flew VIPs."

"No, you said that."

"What do you fly?"

"Why, the Jungle Express," Josh said, as though there was nothing else.

The -130 guy looked confused. Then the light bulb went on.

"Ohhhh, you mean those little things down on the flight line? Right. Heh-heh. Looks cute."

"It gets the job done."

"What job? You embassy support?"

"A lot of different jobs," I said, now defensive. "It's pretty versatile."

Grandy looked at his watch and then over his shoulder to the lunch counter.

"Well, you want good flying down here you need to try a Herc. We pretty much own this theater. They want something taken into the tough spots they don't call the big guys. Nope, they go with the four fans of freedom."

Josh gagged on his soft drink.

"The four fans of freedom?"

I had heard the phrase but thought it was a joke. It sure sounded like one.

"*The four fans of freedom*?" Josh repeated and laughed out loud.

Grandy looked like we had kicked his dog.

"So which tough spots do you fly into," I asked, "given that of all the known airstrips in Central and South America a C-130 can operate on about fifteen percent?"

"Huh?" Grandy looked dismissive. "We can go anywhere."

"Like?" Josh pressed.

Grandy ticked them off on his finger. "Bogotá, Guayaquil, Lima..."

Josh ticked them off, too. "Ten thousand, eight thousand, ninety-five hundred..." he called out the runway lengths in feet. "Those are international airports. Every one of those places can land a DC-10."

"That's not it," Grandy sneered. "You ever hear of a place called Yurimaguas?"

"Was there last week. Almost six thousand feet, paved, wide as a parking lot."

"Yeah? Well, how about Esmeraldas?"

"Ecuadorian Air Force Base. Come on, dude, they fly fighters out of there. How tough can it be?"

Grandy looked impatient for his sandwich.

"It's probably not too tough if all you're flying is a little puddle jumper doing milk runs. Hell, that thing's probably an ultralight you can land on my front lawn. But if you've got your hands full of airplane doing a real mission it changes things a little."

The guy was unbelievable. We were going to have to write that sentence on the wall of the squadron: "when you've got your hands full of airplane..."

I remembered another rule of Air Force pilots – everybody needed somebody to look down upon. Fighters looked down on heavies, heavies looked down on tankers, tankers looked down on trainers, and within each of those groups there was another hierarchy. F-15 pilots hated F-16s, for example, who in turn thought little of A-10s. In the heavy world C-5s were king, followed by C-141s, followed by C-130s. Everyone looked down on helicopters, which made no sense since helos are just plain cool.

Even with the various hierarchies, though, C-130s had still acquired a negative cachet. Trash haulers looked down on them as being the lowest of the low. The -130 guys always whined about that when I was in C-5s but lo and behold, here I was learning that as soon as a Matt Grandy found out there was somebody smaller he was going to try to reverse the tables. I supposed we in the C-27 would have to find somebody smaller to turn up our noses at. Maybe a Cessna?

"Yeah, you're right," said Josh. "You guys probably do have a tougher mission." He wanted to be through with this guy. "How long does a runway have to be for you to land on it? Three thousand?"

"Are you kidding?" Grandy chuckled. "Three thousand on a waiver, maybe. We can do five thousand, though."

"You probably have no enroute weather restrictions, do you?"

"Of course we do, we..."

"And you do hundred-foot low-levels?"

"No, five hundred's our min..."

"And blacked out night assaults, of course?"

"Once you're qual'ed..."

"Airdrop?"

"Some guys in the unit have..."

"HALO?"

"I heard we might start..."

"And you can land on roads, right?"

"What?"

"Well, then." Josh stood up. "Seems to me you've got one hell of a mission alright. Try not to let it put you off your appetite." He pointed at Grandy's stomach and winked.

We left. We were schmucks for engaging in the "my job is better than your job" game but Grandy hadn't even tried to have a normal conversation.

Still, he managed to salvage his dignity. As we headed for the door we heard him get in the last word.

"Yeah. You guys aren't -130s."

13. Flight 3

Of course it was Walt who taught me assault landings. He flew with me on my fourth ride in the RTU, a scheduling fluke that left me struggling to remember all the techniques and idiosyncrasies of the first three instructors. Consistency would have made for better training but with the 155th still settling in there was no way around flying with whoever was available. Beggars can't be choosers and I was definitely a beggar. I wanted to fly missions. To fly missions I needed a check ride. To get a check ride I needed to complete the course syllabus. To complete the syllabus I needed assaults.

"There's a trick to assault landings," Walt shouted over the roar of the engines.

"What's that?" I called back. I could have keyed the mike, I suppose, but since he was shouting I did, too.

"I don't know. I haven't figured it out yet."

The trick to assault landings was to bring a twenty-five-ton aircraft out of the sky doing 120 mph and smack it into an area the size of a suburban front yard. The actual landing strip could be thousands of feet long but because of any number of factors including aircraft weight, the surface of the strip, the air temperature, or the altitude it was vital to have the tires impact at the very beginning. The zone the C-27s trained on was hand-painted on Howard's runway. It was 60 feet wide and 300 feet long. A narrow football field when looked at from the ground, it was the size of a postage stamp when hurtling towards it with fifty thousand pounds of metal beneath your seat. I was learning to do carrier landings in a parking lot.

"The first thing is the takeoff," Walt explained. "Yes, we land in small spaces but we can't land unless we intend to take off again. Soooo,..."

We turned onto the runway at Delta taxiway and lined up in the center facing north. Walt stopped the plane with the main gear abeam the white blocks that were painted onto the beginning of the assault zone. In front of us I saw pairs of smaller blocks at five-hundred-foot intervals that outlined the rest of the strip-within-a-strip. They extended two thousand feet down the larger runway to just past Charlie taxiway. The idea was to be airborne before those blocks ran out.

"Ready?" Walt asked.

"Ready."

"Good. Watch this. It's so cool."

He pushed the power levers up to 1150 foot-pounds of torque. The power levers were the throttles – I don't know why we called them power levers except that that was the literal translation from the Italian manuals. They controlled fuel to the engine but only indirectly. Mostly they told the propellers how much power to use from the already-spinning turbines. The props converted the power into torque which created the lift to pull us through the air.

The engines wound up, pushing the propellers to their max rpm. Their wash over the wings hit the elevator and forced it up so that the whole plane canted forward like a sprinter in the starting blocks. Walt's feet mashed the brake pedals to keep us from moving. In the humid air contrails flew off the propeller tips, swirling in a vortex behind the engine nacelles so that we trailed opaque cones from each wing. We rocked and shuddered under the power of the engines, the Mighty Chuck struggling to lurch forward. It felt like if we didn't let the plane go it would shake itself apart.

Walt took his hand off the yoke long enough to point two fingers at the columns of instruments down the middle of the center panel.

"Everything's in the green."

Just then Tower responded to our earlier request for takeoff clearance. Walt immediately released the brakes. At the same time he hacked the clock on the front of the control yoke.

The C-27 reacted like a thoroughbred released from the gate. Up front Walt was thrown back against his seat by the acceleration. I would have been had my seat been locked but the catch slipped and the whole frame slid back ten inches on the rails, banging me twice as it slammed back into the rear guards and I slammed into it. Leonard Mondavi was our loadmaster again and helped me forward as we continued to charge down the runway.

The first distance markers flashed past as the airspeed indicator came off the peg. When the next blocks went by the needle was passing sixty-five knots.

"Speed's good!" Walt yelled. I had forgotten to check the clock.

Seconds later he pulled back on the yoke. The nose rose into the air and the rest of the plane followed. We were airborne in twelve hundred feet.

"Whooo-hooooo!"

We climbed out on a forty-degree angle. All I saw out front was sky.

The north end of the runway was flanked by hills so the effect of our steep climb wasn't as pronounced as if we had gone, say, the other way, out over the water. But it was still impressive. What the Chuck did better than anybody else was takeoff and land. Almost immediately Walt was pushing forward to keep from climbing through the traffic pattern altitude at one thousand feet.

"Okay," he said into the intercom once we had made the turn to downwind. "If you noticed, I kept the speed at best climb all the way. You have your minimum controllable speed on the ground, your min controllable speed in the air, then best angle of climb, then best rate of climb. You should follow them in order. Always, always, make sure the best angle is higher than Vmca. Remember, we talked about it in class. You lose an engine on takeoff while you're below min controllable airspeed and it's going to be a self-critiquing event. Understand?"

I nodded.

"I'll demo this landing," he offered.

We flew over the swamp down the hill from the hospital and cruised on out to the beach. I was in the right seat. Through my window I could see the wing headquarters with its twin flagpoles, the U.S. and Panamanian flags flapping gently in a northerly breeze. The BX complex across the street from the parade ground passed next, then the Army administrative buildings and the broad picnic area alternately used as tent city for visiting ground troops. Just outside the south end of the runway, beyond the approach lights perched high in another swamp, ran Veracruz road and the beach. Passing over the sand Walt pulled the power and started his approach.

"Okay, just like anywhere else the runway is your primary reference for an approach. But you can still use some local-isms to get the procedures down. For example, I start my approach going over the beach at one thousand feet. Power back to 500 ft-lbs of torque, nose up to bleed off airspeed, flaps ten. Let the plane start down. Then start your turn."

He called tower to request clearance for the approach then made his turn along the beach.

"On base turn go to flaps mid. Lower the gear. You can put the flaps all the way down if you want but keep in mind you'll need more power if you're not ready to descend."

Final was clear, so was the rest of the pattern. It was eleven o'clock in the morning but it was a Monday – on Mondays hardly anybody got up early. It was a nod to local culture. Downtown most businesses wouldn't open their doors until after lunch.

Below us waves rolled onto the beach as though they, too, were tired from partying all weekend. The water was beautiful but Veracruz Beach looked like it always did after Saturday and Sunday: filthy. Beer cans, food wrappers, and all kinds of garbage littered the area. This was the morning we had to watch out for bird strikes. Thousands of sea gulls, ospreys, and herons flocked around the trash, not to mention the clouds of darker birds from the jungle. The beach was usually clean by mid-week so for all I know it was the birds that did the dirty work. I couldn't imagine Panamanians coming out to pick up the litter.

"Look out your window. See the blocks coming into view? You want to line yourself up on them as far out as you can because by the time you roll out on final you're going to have other things to think about. Right turn."

"Clear right."

We rolled out crossing the beach. By this time we had descended to eight hundred feet. Walt lowered the flaps all the way but left the power where it was until the extra drag pulled our airspeed back to 105, our computed speed on final. We were half a mile from the beginning of the runway – "the numbers" – but a mile still from the assault zone where we intended to land. It didn't look far, though. It never did.

He pointed out the front window and then placed his fist on the dash.

"See where the blocks are in the window? Imagine a beer can up here – or a fist. Put the blocks halfway up the beer can and keep them there. Or keep your aim point at the top of your fist. That's all there is to it."

Well, yeah. That *was* all there was to it but it was easier said than done. Most of the time the C-27 was a stable airplane but on final it sat like a four-year-old in church. The nose tracked left and right, the airspeed bled off, the sink rate tried to increase if not watched. The problem was all the drag we had and the slow speed we were trying to hit the ground with. In the slow-flight regime any plane feels like a wallowing boat. The controls get mushy and the pilot has to make big inputs to effect little changes. More than ever you have to anticipate what will happen next. Imagine driving through traffic with a loose steering column.

Walt didn't make it look easy but he did make it look fun. He leaned forward in his seat to see over the nose and kept both stick and throttles moving. He was happiest whenever he was on the controls.

"Small changes, small changes...the plane wants to go where you point it...keep the nose coming down. Where people screw up is at the end where they let the nose rise. That makes you float past the zone or worse, stall out too high and drop it in. Just keep it down...aim short if you have to. That way when you pull it up to flare it carries you between the blocks."

I tried to follow his monologue but by the time he described what he was doing he had already done it and was moving on to something else. So instead I fixated on the approaching zone. I hoped to get the picture in my head for the next time around the pattern.

Walt brought the plane down as promised, looking until the last instant as though he was going to prang the nose into the concrete a hundred feet short of the first set of blocks. Then at thirty feet he pulled it up just a hair and pointed it down the runway. The C-27 kept descending but now its vector changed.

We slammed into the middle of the zone in what could best be described as a controlled crash. The shocks on the main gear absorbed the brunt of the impact so that all we felt up front was a tremendous compression as though we were riding a large spring. Walt pushed the nose over. When the nose gear touched he stomped on the brakes and simultaneously lifted the throttles over the aft detent to send the propellers into reverse. We roared and shuddered for nine hundred feet, decelerating all the way. Had I not been wearing my shoulder harness I would have been thrown against the instrument panel. This plane could *stop.*

"We can do better than that," Walt said matter-of-factly when we finally came to a halt. He dropped the throttles back into idle and the shaking ceased. The plane quieted down.

I knew he was pleased with his landing by the way he brushed it off as nothing special. In fact it *was* what we were supposed to do every time. But just as doctors are supposed to save every patient and NBA players are supposed to sink every free throw, there are landings and then there are landings. A good one looks even better when you pretend it isn't anything at all.

"Your turn."

I didn't make things look easy. With the power levers full forward I fought the controls like a novice on a bucking horse. The control yoke shook like a living thing as prop wash struck the elevator.

"Don't fight it," Walt advised. "You look like you're trying to choke it. Just control it."

"I'm trying."

"We're rolling," he pointed out. "Hold the brakes."

I *was* holding the brakes. At least I thought I was. My boots were mashed on the top of the rudder pedals and my knees were almost locked out.

"Now, scan the instruments. Make sure you've got good engines. You don't want to find out on climb-out that you don't."

I nodded quickly. My legs were getting tired.

"Then, when you're ready, just hack the clock and go."

Again, I had forgotten about the clock.

We didn't use a refusal speed per se for the C-27, a speed that once reached committed us to a takeoff or to an abort so that we could stop by the end of the runway. Instead we used a variation on CEFS, the Critical Engine Failure Speed. CEFS is a speed that, once attained on takeoff roll, gave us the option to continue the takeoff or abort and stop regardless of whether we did either before we ran out of pavement. Ideally, that number was low enough that we could stop before the runway ran out but that wasn't always the case.

During pilot training in Phoenix, Arizona, one of my fellow students tried to takeoff one day when it was so hot the runway was barely in limits for his jet to operate. To make things worse, he miscalculated his takeoff data. The result was that when he lost an engine he could neither take off nor stop before the end of the runway. The crash net caught him before he careened into the desert but the aircraft and a promising career were damaged.

The problem for us in the 155th Tactical Airlift Squadron was that our whole reason for existence was to operate on runways where refusal speed was usually lower than CEFS; in other words, where the runway available was shorter than the Critical Field Length, the runway we really needed. The fact was, sometimes runways were just too short to attain a number that would guarantee us the ability to stop *or* takeoff before plowing into the trees. Bumpy dirt strips are hard to accelerate on. Throw in a hot day and a heavy airplane and now we might reach the stopping speed long before we met the one that would allow us to takeoff after losing an engine. So we relied on a riskier proposition.

Instead of waiting for a speed that we knew would get us airborne, we figured a speed twenty knots lower and calculated how long it would take us to get there. If, say, after twelve seconds we were in fact at or above that acceleration check speed, we figured the plane was doing what the books said it would. If it wasn't – if the books said we should be doing 80 mph after ten seconds but we had only reached 75 mph – then we could abort in time to keep from plunging into a ravine. It was complicated but it was our lone backup, a comfort factor that the Dash 1 and the sharpened pencils of aeronautical engineers assured us would work. And it all depended on the clock. You had to hack the clock.

"Ready, ready, hack!"

I released the brakes. My feet sprang away from the pedals as the C-27 once again launched itself from the starting blocks.

"More, more!" Walt prodded, his left hand helping me pull back on the controls. His right hand guarded the power levers. "Pretend you've got a tree out there."

We did have a tree out there. We had a whole lot of them in fact. And we would have cleared them at half the rate of our initial climb. But that wasn't good enough. I was learning to max perform the aircraft so I had better do it.

"That's better. Get the nose up there. You see how it wants to accelerate even with a climb like this? That means you have to climb even steeper. Pitch controls the airspeed so control the pitch to keep the speed where you want it."

I tried. Our best angle-of-climb speed was 97 mph. I shot past that to 105 mph when I didn't rotate far enough right off the bat, so now I tried to correct. I worked the airspeed down to where it should be, reaching 97 just as we hit traffic pattern altitude.

"Level off. Level *offffffff.* We're going to the moon, Alice! To the moon!"

Damn. I pushed over on the controls and we all lifted out of our seats. Walt whooped like he was on a roller coaster. Behind us Leonard chuckled.

"Hey, that felt good. Do it again."

I felt like a complete tool. I knew how to fly but now I looked like a brand-new student.

"Okay, nice takeoff," Walt lied. "Any questions? We'll do a few more of those, don't worry. Now, set up for your landing."

I turned crosswind abeam the base front gate and picked a point on the distant city skyline to head for. The point of the traffic pattern was to fly a rectangle using the runway and its approach and departure paths as one of the long sides. After a one-potato, two-potato of aiming just north of the Bridge of the Americas I turned to a downwind. Below us was the perimeter of the base, with the hospital sitting on a hill at the east end. Walt pointed it out.

"Don't fly over the hospital if you can help it," he warned. "Depending on who's there, they'll complain. I do it all the time," he added with a look over his shoulder at Leonard, who laughed and nodded agreement. "I figure, if they're in a military hospital then they're military. And it helps their morale to know the rest of the military is still out here working. So that's why I do it. But I get talked to a lot so I recommend you fly outside it."

We flew over the motor pool of Fort Kobbe and then out over the beach. I pulled the power levers back to 500 ft-lbs of torque just as Walt had done. With the loss of power the nose wanted to drop so I held it up and clicked the electric trim switch for assistance. When we had slowed below 170 mph I asked him to bring the flaps halfway down.

"Flaps mid," he repeated cheerfully.

Leonard did what all loadmasters did on these local sorties. He watched disinterestedly and tried not to doze.

We turned final. I called for flaps full down.

"Flaps full," Walt repeated.

The flaps helped us slow down so quickly that I pushed the nose over to catch the speed. Pushing over made us descend so now I had to bump the power up to 700 ft-lbs. Bumping the power made the plane want to climb so again I had to push over, which made us speed up. Everything I did affected something else and I felt like a juggler as I tried to duplicate Walt's performance.

What had he said? Imagine a beer can on the windscreen? That image did nothing for me since I immediately started thinking about how hot it was and how a real beer would taste good right about now. I put my fist up on the panel instead. Peering over it, I picked a spot on the runway that I judged to be 100 feet short of the blocks that marked the beginning of the assault zone. Then I tried to keep that spot in the same place on the window. It was tougher than it looked.

"Don't fight the plane," Walt said for the third or fourth time. "Get the airspeed first, then the aim point, then the glide slope. Airspeed, aim point, glide slope. In that order."

While he coached I continued to jockey both the controls and the throttles until we were well off every parameter we needed to land in the zone. The glide slope was the hardest to maintain. I couldn't tell before descending to about two hundred feet whether we would make the zone or not, and by two hundred feet it was too late to correct.

"Okay, we're way high," Walt pointed out. "Unless you can hover us down like a helicopter I suggest we go around."

"On the go." I tried to say it calmly but my exasperation was obvious.

"No, no, don't worry about it. We have to do a go-around anyway for the syllabus. You're just working it in sooner than I planned."

How considerate of me. I felt like a dunce.

We flew around the traffic pattern again. This time I set us up on a longer final to give me more time to find the right glide angle. Walt nodded his approval.

We configured again. This time I crossed the beach at six hundred feet and almost immediately found myself low. The picture out front looked good except that now the glide angle was too shallow. I pushed power up to try to hold altitude but didn't do it enough.

"Okayyyy," Walt started. "Well, this might work but it's going to be harder to see the zone..."

Yes, it was. I aimed for the first set of blocks but ended up bringing my nose up to do it, so far up that the front part of the zone disappeared. I also sank too fast at the bottom of the approach. When I pushed the power up to recover we shot right past the entire football field and touched down gently on the far side. It was a landing that would have pleased the airlines. Unfortunately, we weren't flying for Delta.

"Too far. Go around." Walt ordered.

I let the nose come down but pushed the power forward. We rotated and climbed out without ever slowing below 90 mph. Passing four hundred feet Walt raised the flaps to mid and then brought up the gear.

"Two things on that one," he said. "First, *always* go around if you land long. No 'that was close enough' or 'maybe we can stop in time,' – just go around. You missed it, try again. Second, you saw how we climbed out? Did you notice we did it with the flaps down? That's the power this plane has. Don't waste time or take chances trying to move the flaps if you have to go around in a hurry. Just do it. The plane will fly even with all that drag."

I mumbled okay. The day was just getting worse. Two screwed-up approaches! Two! Most guys got it right the first time, or at the very least on their second attempt. Me, I was already on number three. Maybe I wouldn't get the picture at all, ever. Maybe this type of landing was beyond my abilities. The thought of being sent back to a C-5 caused a wave of nausea to wash over me. The bright, hot cockpit suddenly felt cool as a cold sweat broke out on my forehead.

"Okay. Number Three is the charm," Walt enthused. "You've gone high, you've gone low. This time just recite the basics and set yourself up on a good final. Eight hundred feet at the beach, 105 mph on final – oops, 104 now – and a solid aim point. No problem."

He sipped coffee from his Bambi cup and began to whistle. To show how unconcerned he was about my flying, he and Leonard pointed out rocks in the water and discussed which of them was big enough to be exposed when the tide retreated.

Basics, I chanted to myself. Basics. Airspeed, altitude. Just like flying a Cessna.

On the next approach I pulled power over the beach as before but turned to a base leg sooner. The flaps went to mid and the gear came down at 150 mph. I made the turn to final early, keeping it shallow. Crossing the sand with its ever-growing crowd of vagrant birds, I cracked the power to three hundred foot-pounds and left it there. To keep from inadvertently moving the levers around I opened my hand and just left it on top of them, wiggling my fingers to stay relaxed.

"Good," Walt prompted. "Now wait for the glide angle."

We were in a descent but I could still use the nose to make adjustments to the picture. My hands were too busy to sight a fist on the dash but I imagined it there. Amazingly, this time the picture didn't change much. Leaving the power alone seemed to do the trick. The C-27 descended in a quiet glide, wings outstretched and gear poised.

My eyes darted from the airspeed indicator to the runway. At one hundred feet there was a brief moment of panic when I thought we would land short, but Walt's "wait..., wait...," calmed my nerves. At twenty feet on the radar altimeter I pulled the nose up. At the same time I killed the power. The combination of getting more from the wings and less from the engines kept our sink rate the same but re-directed the vector into the middle of the zone. The rear tires smacked onto the pavement just as the tail cleared the blocks.

"Nose down! Nose down!" Walt urged.

I allowed the nose to fall and pulled on the power levers. They stalled at the detent but Walt's hand was already on the move, raising the levers on his side so that I could bring the props to reverse. Together we slammed both levers to the bottom of the throttle quadrant.

"Brakes! Don't forget the brakes!"

Walt was enjoying himself. I slammed on the brakes as the blades on the props reversed their pitch. I didn't do it evenly so we careened left and right as the brakes sought to bring us to a shuddering stop. But stop we did, on a drunken angle just short of Taxiway Delta. It was a violent, loud, and utterly marginal performance.

"Alright!" Walt proclaimed, and reached across the center panel to shake my hand. "Nice job. Smack in the center of the zone. Of course, you used more runway than I did and drove all over the place once you were down but hey, for your first assault that wasn't bad. Not bad at all."

Behind me, Leonard clapped me on the shoulder.

They were both overdoing it but the sense of relief and exhilaration I felt could not have been sweeter. Bringing this beautiful machine out of the sky and slamming it to a halt in little more than a city block was more exciting than I expected. I was sweating up a storm and my arms trembled from the death-grip I'd had on the controls. It was work, challenging work, and it would only get more demanding once I tried doing it on a zone that wasn't painted onto a runway. C-5s *suck*, I repeated for the thousandth time to myself.

The C-27 purred beneath me like a speed boat tied to the dock.

"Want to try it again?" Walt interrupted my reverie. He spoke as though we had anything else to do over the next two hours. For him there simply was no better way to spend the day than max performing an aircraft.

My arms stopped trembling. I wiped the sweat from my eyes.

"Damned straight," I replied and pushed the throttles back up.

This was going to be fun.

14. Check ride

I WAS SUPPOSED to have a fifth training ride but it was getting to be late in the summer. Anxious to make room in his RTU for newer students, Charlie Manson pronounced me ready for my check ride. It sounded like a screw job but he really did it to help me out. Because the only planes on the ramp were about to go to Colombia for three weeks, the alternative was to wait until they returned to fly again, at which point I would get one training ride – my fifth – and *then* the check. This way I could go into the evaluation with continuity in my favor.

Check rides suck. That should be clear right off the bat. In both civilian and military flying, check rides are the most stressful thing that most pilots will ever encounter. This is true despite the fact that on paper they're nothing but an opportunity for a pilot to prove that he meets the standards of whatever organization he's flying for. In the civilian world the standards are set by the FAA, the Federal Aviation Administration. In the Air Force the standards are set by the major command that controls whatever aircraft a pilot happens to be flying. Those standards are published, taught in training, and no secret to anybody. But that's like saying that what you need to do to qualify for the Olympics is no secret. Knowing what you have to do is one thing. Doing it, and doing it in front of an evaluator, is another.

No two evaluators are alike but there are types. Most are normal guys who become evaluators through hard work and experience. Some are jerks. In the civilian world, a lot are old fat guys who deny their irrelevance by berating new flyers. At least half the FAA evaluators I tested with when getting my civilian ratings started off the interview by growling, "You military guys think you know how to fly. Well, let me tell you..." But there are people like that in uniform, too. They want to show you that they know more about flying than you do. It has simply never occurred to most flight examiners that the examinee couldn't care less for his opinion.

During my pilot training in Arizona I never failed a ride until late in the course. Then one day a T-38 evaluator named Breck looked at my folder as we stepped to a jet.

"You've never busted a ride?" he barked.

"No, sir."

"How's that? Everyone busts at least one."

"I've been lucky, sir."

He threw the folder on his desk.

"Your luck's about to change."

Sure enough, he failed me on that sortie, claiming that I tried to lower my landing gear above the allowed speed. We both knew it was a lie but there was nothing I could do about it. It was the kind of claim that was impossible to dispute.

In Panama, we had two check pilots in the 155th. One was Erich Fetterman, he of the loud voice. The other was Brad Giverson. Either one could have administered the check ride for me and Rolo. Rolo, who managed to finish his fifth ride and was scheduled to be on the same flight as me, hoped that it would be anybody but Fetterman, which was a mistake because although Fetterman was loud he was fair. And Fetterman was in fact the first choice to check us. With no warning, however, he recused himself saying that since he had instructed both of us already on training rides it would be a conflict of interest for him to evaluate us now. So Major Harmon scheduled us to fly with Captain Giverson.

Brad Giverson wasn't in the squadron. He was up at the Group with Garb Taylor and therefore a mystery to us new guys. Taylor being our standard, we assumed that anybody at the Group was an idiot. But Giverson wasn't an idiot. He was a three-year captain who had come to the C-27 program as part of the first group of instructors and now was on a fast track to early promotion.

Nobody knew quite how he got into the program. Manson, who didn't like Giverson, thought it was in part due to geography. As a C-130 guy based in Abilene, Texas, Giverson wasn't far from Waco, where Merrill Technologies received the G-222s and re-built them to Air Force specs. Giverson was political and ambitious and Manson suspected he had sweet-talked somebody at Dyess AFB into getting him an instructor appointment, seeing it as an opportunity to put the magic words 'initial cadre' on his performance report.

It wasn't clear yet what Rasmussen thought of Giverson but there was no denying he was giving the man a good deal. Any flying squadron has a Standardization-and-Evaluation office and that office reports to a parent office at the Group or Wing level. In coming to Howard with a new weapons system Rasmussen had to make appointments to both. He made Fetterman the chief pilot in the squadron and then, perhaps detecting discord in the ranks, sent Giverson up to the Group. In a way that was strange since it put Fetterman, a senior captain, in a subordinate position to Giverson, a relatively inexperienced pilot, but on practical terms it satisfied the squadron's immediate training needs. It kept experience at the squadron level and put a guy who was more interested in padding his resume into a position that did just that. Rasmussen wasn't deliberately helping Giverson but the results were the same.

Rolo and I didn't care about the office politics. We cared about passing the check ride. Rolo was particularly nervous because he had done four of his five rides with Fetterman and had nearly developed an ulcer from the experience.

"He didn't teach me anything," he insisted the day before our check. "You remember our first ride. He just yelled."

"Come on, he must have taught you something. You can fly the plane, can't you?"

"If someone's yelling in the background, sure. If not, the silence will freak me out. I'll roll inverted and crash."

I had gotten lucky and flown with different instructors for each ride. That was good because it showed me several styles of flying. But it was also bad because everybody had their own way of doing things. Charlie Manson, for example, liked to cruise on downwind at a set six hundred foot-pounds of torque then drop flaps and gear on the base turn. Walt adjusted the torque constantly and configured on downwind. Mike Vaneya did his assault landings by going as fast as possible until the last moment and then hoping he could slow down by the time he hit the zone. Fetterman set his assaults up with obsessive precision, hitting every parameter before moving on to the next step. If he didn't turn final at exactly one mile and seven hundred feet, he would curse and shake his fist and abort the approach. As Mike explained it, we were all writing the book and nothing was procedure yet. 98% of the instruction was technique.

That was good if you were already qualified in the aircraft. It was bad if you weren't. The first word in StanEval is 'Stan,' which stands for 'standardization.' A StanEval – or 'check' – pilot wants everybody to do things exactly the same way. Technique is bad.

Walt helped Rolo and I prepare for our check ride. We had to fly two parts: a basic portion, where we flew a couple of instrument approaches and then simulated emergency procedures to the runway; and a mission profile, where we flew an hour-long low-level over the countryside to hit a time-on-target at some landing zone. We had to meet the TOT within thirty seconds. I guessed that would be our toughest hurdle so we spent most of our time searching for a good airstrip and tracing a viable route on the map.

With Walt's prompting we decided to use the airstrip at Fort Sherman as our destination. It was a strip we were familiar with. Also, unlike the little blue circles that dotted the map, it was a runway we knew we would be able to land on. Working backward from Sherman we chose turn points every 20-30 miles. The turn points were geographic features we could recognize from the air:

river bends, hill tops, the end of a mountain ridge. The goal was to fly low enough that observers wouldn't see us from the ground and turn often enough that even if we were seen nobody could report reliably what direction we were heading. Beside each leg of our flight route we penciled in what looked like the outlines of a house. "Doghouses," they were called. Inside the outline we wrote the heading to fly, the distance to the next waypoint, the time to the next waypoint in minutes and seconds, and the lowest altitude we could climb to without hitting anything in the immediate vicinity. It was a summary of the most important things to know for a pilot who only took his eyes off the terrain outside long enough to glance at a map folded on his knee.

As we had for our training flights, we prepared two maps for navigation: one for the pilots, one for the instructor/evaluator to follow along. Rolo had better handwriting so he drew our routes while I figured out how to make sure we landed on time. When we finished the maps were works of art: flight route in black, doghouses in blue, emergency escape altitudes in red. Rolo had gone to town with his Sharpie markers, proving that kindergarten teaches valuable skills after all. Aesthetics aside, the maps were now officially charts and they were masterpieces of concise information. Any pilot could pick one up and know everything he needed to fly a successful sortie.

On the day of the check ride Josh picked up Rolo and me downtown and gave us a ride to the base. He quizzed us on ops limits – *What's the normal temperature range of the APP? What's the maximum acceptable torque for a single-engine go-around?* – and told us what we could expect based on his check ride three months earlier.

"I flew with Walt as my co-pilot," he said. "The weather was perfect and we did all our approaches to the runway at Howard. No problems."

I looked out the window as he drove. The weather wasn't perfect today. A rainy season haze hung over the city. That wasn't a problem by the coast but it could affect our flying in the mountains. It was an axiom of check rides that conditions were always different from when you had trained. So far the day was starting out that way.

"Maybe the ride will be short," Rolo said wistfully.

"Maybe," Josh agreed. "Good check rides should be like skirts: short enough to be interesting and just long enough to cover the essentials."

"Was yours like that?" I asked.

"Pretty much."

"Who was your check pilot?"

"Fetterman. He yelled but at the controllers, not me. Mostly he just sat in back and watched. It was his first check ride in a C-27 and I think he wanted it to be a good one no matter what I did. No Q-3s."

A Q-3 was a failed ride – a bust, a taco, the big goose-egg. A grade of Q-1 was good. It meant you passed the check ride with no problems. A Q-2 meant you passed but had some bugs to be worked out. Q-2s were rare. Pilots are a simple bunch. You're either good enough or you're not.

"Was he friendly? I mean, you know, was he a jerk or basically nice?" I asked.

Rolo scoffed at the idea that Fetterman could be friendly. Josh thought about it, remembering.

"He was alright. Just remember, as long as you're competent there's not much an evaluator can do to you. Remember the goal: finish the ride and get the bastard off your plane. But he's also looking at your attitude. No matter how much of a jerk he is, you need to be a nice guy because otherwise a lot of things won't go your way.

"Be nice?" I repeated.

Josh nodded.

"Be nice."

When we arrived at the squadron Brad Giverson was already there. He was in the planning room, studying a terrain chart spread flat on the wide oaken table.

Rolo went in with a friendly smile.

"Hello, sir! Except for the weather, it's looking like a good day to fly!"

Giverson took his time before looking up, tracing his finger over some point on the map. When he finally did he paused before speaking, looking at Rolo as though he had spoken in a foreign tongue.

"There's nothing wrong with the weather, lieutenant," he said. He put enough surprise in his tone to suggest he was confused how Rolo could even think so.

Rolo's placid expression registered only a tiny change. *Cock*, he was thinking, and I didn't blame him. The problem with saying there's nothing wrong with the weather when bad weather is forming is that you look like a jackass.

Giverson was medium-height with jet-black hair and a hirsute complexion that suggested a five o'clock shadow would appear by noon. His eyes were sharp and he made a point of staring right at you when you spoke, almost to the point of distraction. Yet his most distinguishing feature was how young he looked. I figured that as a captain and an Academy grad he had to be at least 26 but even with the stubble-to-be his face suggested instead that he was still teetering somewhere in his late teens. We got the feeling he realized it, too. Other people might have been happy to lag years behind time but Giverson saw it as a handicap. He tried hard to fight the impression of inexperience, making a point of being serious to make up for his youth. Very serious.

We introduced ourselves. There was no small talk. Giverson produced our training folders and laid them on top of the map. They were standard forms that recorded which events we had accomplished, accompanied by a narrative write-up from the instructor explaining how he thought we were doing. Reading upside down, I saw Charlie Manson's quick scribble at the bottom of one page saying I had achieved proficiency in all events and was ready for a check ride. Below his initials were Erich

Fetterman's, approving as the head instructor. At the very bottom was Lt Col Rasmussen's signature.

Giverson read through the folders, bent over the table to peer at each page in turn. He studied them with the intensity of an accountant on his first audit. It wasn't long before he was shaking his head.

"The syllabus calls for five rides," he sighed like a disappointed teacher. "Five. Not four. You...can't...teach...someone to fly this plane...in...four...rides. I've explained that to Captain Manson I don't know how many times. I don't know why he signed you off."

"Looks like you'll have to explain it to Lt Col Rasmussen, too," I replied without thinking and immediately regretted it. I meant to be sarcastic, in a funny way, but it didn't work. *Shut up, you idiot. Shuuuutt uuuup.*

Giverson lifted his head and gave me a long stare. Trying to recover I did my best to look respectful. Next to me Rolo maintained his open-mouthed, hangdog look, probably wanting to fall over laughing.

"Lieutenant Metzger," Giverson said slowly, lowering his head again and moving on to the next folder. "I see you *did* complete the syllabus." He paused, waiting to see if I would fill in the silence with another ill-considered comment. I didn't.

"Uh, yes. Sir," Rolo acknowledged.

"That's good. The syllabus is there for a reason. This isn't a C-5."

Oh, god, I thought. There it was again. The C-5 stigma, shoved back in my face like the evidence of a crime. For a second I considered snapping back, "How would you know?" but didn't. I didn't know if Giverson was jealous of the big-jet time or if he hated C-5s as much as I did. He just wanted to make the point that whatever I thought I knew about flying wasn't enough.

"Let's talk some ops limits," Giverson suggested. He closed the folders.

Damn. He surprised me. We had to have a ground evaluation, a quiz session where the evaluator probed to find out what we knew about the plane and the rules we had to follow. Rolo and I expected that. It was just that we had been hoping Giverson would put it off until after the flight. With the skies turning ugly we wanted to fly as early as possible while the day was cool. If we could get down before noon the storms might not have a chance to build. Then we could talk ops limits all day while the rain poured. Maybe Giverson knew that, maybe he didn't. Whether he did or not we spent the next three hours sitting in the planning room while the air outside heated up.

The ground eval was straightforward. Giverson alternated from me to Rolo, asking one question after another, moving from one system to the next, fuels then engines then electrics and so on, doing the standard evaluator technique of finding out how much we knew before moving on. The trick for us was to show confidence and answer the first questions with ease. If you could do that most evaluators figured they needn't waste time on that subject and went on to something else. Giverson was especially prone to that maneuver since he seemed to want to find a subject we were weak on in order to show us how smart he was. I answered quickly and concisely to every question. Unnecessary words had already hurt me so now I conserved them like a Scottish preacher.

Rolo never quite grasped the strategy. He treated every question like it was a set-up, repeating it carefully to make sure he understood what Giverson wanted and then asking questions of his own to make absolutely sure he was on the right track. At first that attracted Giverson's attention the way blood draws sharks. He peppered Rolo with follow-up questions, getting deeper and deeper into the subject. When Giverson asked him the fairly easy, "What's the diameter of the propeller blades?" (which I thought a stupid question because, frankly, who cares?) and Rolo responded with, "What do you mean?" it opened the door to the whole propeller system. We went from a simple answer of 14 feet to the much more difficult task of describing the hydromatic blade control, the low pitch stop assembly, the feathering system, and how it all ties in to inputs from the power levers via the fuel control unit. Finally we had to break out pencil and paper to draw everything else hidden underneath the spinner. I wanted to kick Rolo in the ass.

In the long run, however, Rolo's molasses pace produced a trade-off. It took Giverson so long to figure out that Rolo wasn't stupid, just slow, that he never got to some of the subjects he wanted to talk about. He finally looked at his watch and said that if we wanted to fly at all today we had better get to it.

But he had one more surprise.

"We have to go to Cañazas. We'll do your qual check here at Howard to get the instrument approaches then Captain Harcourt and I will hop into the seats and fly out to Cañazas to survey it for an LZ. You two will fly the mission part of your check ride from there back to Fort Sherman."

Rolo and I looked at each other in disbelief. Cañazas? Where the hell was that? And what about the route we had drawn up the day before? The one we spent four hours planning and knew from memory?

"You've got thirty minutes to draw up a new route. And try to stay away from the coast. I don't want to drone down the beach like we don't know where we're going."

We looked where he was pointing at the table. Thirty minutes. And don't drone down the beach.

Giverson saw our surprise and savored it.

"Things change," he said, his voice suddenly deeper. "In this job you have to be able to react."

"I'll react," Rolo whispered the minute Giverson left the room. "I'll react by getting that arrogant little pecker in a choke-hold and twisting his head off!"

"Yeah, he's got issues," I agreed.

"Issues? No, my girlfriend has issues. This guy has a severe case of cranial flatulence. Who does he think he is? *'In this job you have to be able to react.'* He says *this job* like it's rocket science what we're doing here. And give me a break, he came from C-130s!"

"And he doesn't like C-5s," I added.

"Oh, yeah. Nice job, by the way, with that crack about Rasmussen. Did you throw that in because you thought the check ride wouldn't be hard enough already?"

"You're right. I should have kept my trap shut. Condescending bastard set me off."

"'Condescending bastard?' Is someone talking about me again?" Walt entered the room behind me.

"A perfect example," I sighed. "Good thing it was just Walt."

"'Just Walt?'" Walt smiled. "Is that all I am? I see you guys have met everyone's favorite Captain-going-on-General. How's your check ride going so far? Do you hate the guy yet? It took me half a sortie to decide he was a jerk but he may have improved on his time since then."

"Walt, he wants us to re-do our whole route," Rolo whispered. "We've got half-an-hour – correction, make that twenty-seven minutes – to plan a new check ride. Can he do that?"

Walt pursed his lips, sympathetic.

"Yes. Yes, unfortunately he can. I wouldn't..." – he looked around, then whispered back – "because it's bullshit, but he can. You can do it, though. Don't worry about making it pretty. Just get the facts of the route down on paper and concentrate on making your TOT. If you do that he can't bust you."

"If we duct-tape him to a litter and airdrop him over Empire Range he can't bust us, either," Rolo muttered.

"Any advice, Walt?"

"Yeah. After landing, if it takes full power to taxi back to the hangar you probably forgot to lower the gear."

Neither of us thought that was funny.

"Okay, okay," Walt pointed at Rolo. "For you, this is a co-pilot checkout. Lots of hands, not so much head. For you," he pointed at me, "it's the opposite. More head, less hands. How you fly is important, of course, but it's more how you think. Make decisions and stay two steps ahead of the plane."

"Hands, huh?" said Rolo. "Okay, so long as I don't have to think."

Walt turned to go. "Break a wing, guys. Oh, and Mike?"

"Yeah?"

"Thinking's good, but remember Rule #1 of check rides: Never miss a good chance to shut up."

"Too late but thanks."

"Don't mention it. Oh, and one more thing: don't let him look at the 781s."

The 781s were the maintenance records kept on the aircraft. After every flight pilots recorded anything they noticed wrong with the plane. Maintenance fixed the problems and wrote down what they had done.

"Why not?"

"Just don't. Now get to work."

We tried. Putting lines on a map to mark where you're going to fly isn't, as Rolo observed, rocket science. If you're going from Point A to Point B it's easy enough to find a way to get there. The problem is that the best low-level routes are long-term, studied affairs that evolve through several iterations. After a year of flying at 35,000 feet it still took me a couple of hours at least of staring at contour lines and terrain features to decide whether my best option for flying undetected was to cut around a ridge and down a river valley or avoid both features entirely and instead cross a road at 90 degrees. The best I could hope for in half an hour was to come up with a plan that was modestly tactical and that avoided the larger concentrations of people in the country. Intelligence I could claim but nobody would ever accuse me of being a lightning read.

Half an hour later Giverson returned with Bob Harcourt in tow. Bob said hi then sat in the corner by the weather terminal and kept silent. Though it was past eleven he looked as though he had just gotten out of bed.

Our evaluator hunched over the new map in his favorite pose, lacking only a green eyeshade for the full effect. It wasn't long before he was displeased.

"What information is this in the doghouses?" he asked.

Rolo leaned over to look. "That's heading there at the top, sir. Then timing, distance, and minimum safe altitude."

Giverson pulled out a thick red Sharpie and lined through each one.

"It should be heading, distance, *then* timing," he said. "Get it right." He pointed to the third turn point along the route. That would be mine to field, I knew, since I had picked them.

"This here. Number three. What is it?"

"It's a fork in a river, sir. That river comes out of the mountains here, then meanders until it splits right there."

"Yes, it's a river Y. But it's a river Y in the jungle. Do you really think you're going to see that from the air? How are you going to know you're even getting close?"

Because there's an 800-foot peak right next to it, I wanted to say, the only one within ten miles. Since I couldn't think how to phrase that without sounding insubordinate I settled for, "Yes, sir. Well, the terrain kind of funnels us into it."

Giverson made a show of rolling his eyes. "We'll see," he chuckled. "Some people just have to learn things the hard way."

I fought the urge to smack him over the head with a stack of maps.

For his last edit Giverson pulled out a ruler. He laid it perpendicular to each leg of the route and started measuring distances on either side.

We knew what he was doing. For each leg of a low-level flight we computed a minimum safe altitude, an MSA. If we were flying and suddenly became confused about our position, or accidentally flew into bad weather and could no longer see outside, the minimum safe altitude was a height above ground that we knew was far enough up that we wouldn't hit something – at least for a minute or two. It was a knee-jerk reaction, a number that we could announce at each turn point so that for the next twenty or thirty miles we would know that, say, 3700 feet above mean sea level was what we would immediately climb to if we got disoriented. We figured the MSA by adding 500 feet to the highest obstacle five miles either side of the route leg.

For several minutes Giverson slid the ruler forward and back, checking each leg of our flight and then checking them again. Finally there was a satisfied clucking from the table. The serious look glared at both me and Rolo.

"Who taught you guys how to figure MSAs?" Giverson asked.

Rolo struggled with that one. "Uh, all the instructors we've been flying with, sir."

I liked that answer.

"Uh-huh. Well, I don't think any instructor taught you this." He slid the map over to me – with the ruler – and said, "What's a good MSA for that leg from Waypoint 5 to Waypoint 6?"

I left the ruler on the table and read what was in the doghouse.

"4400 feet MSL," I answered.

"No, it's not. Measure it."

"I already measured it when we made the map," I said flatly. "It's 4400 feet."

He gave me a frosty glare, realizing I thought he was a jackass. He slid the map back to his side of the table and picked up the ruler. Measuring carefully, he took a red pen and circled a mountain peak on the map.

"That peak is 4080 feet," he stated carefully. "It's within five miles of the leg that you say is safe to fly at 4400 feet. By my math, 4080 plus 500 is 4580. That puts you 180 feet too low."

Rolo leaned over the table to look. He had trusted me to figure the altitudes.

"Uh, sir. That peak you circled is, uh, past the leg. The next leg covers it. Its MSA is 4700 feet."

I leaned over, too. Rolo was right. Giverson had circled a peak beyond Waypoint 6. By the time we got near it we would be operating on the next leg's information.

"What does the regulation say?" Giverson insisted. "It says 'within 5 miles of the route leg.' That peak is exactly five miles from the leg from Five to Six."

"It's five miles *past* it," I repeated.

"It's within five miles," Giverson snapped.

This wasn't good. We hadn't even stepped to the plane and both students were already arguing with the evaluator. I glanced toward Harcourt. He looked like he was listening but his eyes were closed.

"Another thing," Giverson added. "You've rounded off all the MSAs. Like this one: the controlling obstacle is here, right? The spot elevation on the ridge? It's at 3164 feet. So the actual safe altitude is 3664 feet. You've rounded that off to 3700 feet. Why? Who told you you could do that?"

That was a legitimate question. Rolo and I shared blank looks. No one had. We had done it automatically, without giving it a second thought. Our barometric altimeters were analog instruments, needles that swung around a dial. You couldn't read them with precision to less than fifty-foot increments: I certainly couldn't tell a difference of *thirty-six feet* on one. Trying to remember a number like 3664 feet didn't make sense so we rounded it to 3700. That was a number we could see when we were climbing to avoid terrain.

"So, in other words, all your MSAs are wrong," Giverson concluded.

"I guess so," I admitted, while Rolo added a "yes, sir." Neither of us sounded contrite.

Giverson nodded, then quickly transitioned to a disappointed shake of the head. It was clear there were a lot of things he had to fix.

The second Giverson released us Rolo and I sprinted for our lockers. Then I stepped outside with my gear.

It was too late.

The sky was gray. It wasn't showering at the field but rain shafts stood like truant bullies over the ocean. They stretched south and west in a long formation of cumulus build-ups. Straight across the airfield the cloud deck scraped the summit of the hill above Veracruz.

"I'm sick," Rolo announced, coming out of the hangar.

"With what?"

"I don't know," he said, looking at the clouds. "With whatever will get this check ride postponed to a day when the weather's better."

"No kidding. What happened to the sun?"

"You mean the one that was out for all my other flights? I don't know but I wish somebody would find it quick and drag it back here before Giverson starts going on about how whoever taught us instruments did everything wrong."

Flutie, the strangest of the Pinheads, poked his head out the door just then to check if it was dry enough to make a lunch run. He saw us standing there looking pitiful and looked thoughtfully at the sky.

"Just remember," he said gloomily. "If you crash because of weather your funeral will be held on a sunny day."

We got to the plane. Remembering Walt's advice, I did my best to hide the 781s from Giverson. As soon as I saw them I knew why.

The 781s, known as "the forms," are a logbook where pilots note any mechanical functions encountered during a flight. They're a means of communication between aircrew and maintainers. The old joke is that planes are designed by PhDs, flown by college graduates, and maintained by high school dropouts. It's not always true, of course, but it illustrates the point that good communication between the groups is important. Some pilots never figure this out. They treat mechanics like hired help rather than professionals in their own right. Further, they assume the mechanics are mind readers who will understand what the problem is even if the pilot doesn't explain it well. Looking at the forms, I could see that Giverson was one of those guys.

He had flown our aircraft three times in the previous week. On Tuesday after landing he wrote in the "Discrepancy" block: "Something loose in the cockpit." What a dumbass. What does that tell a mechanic? Obviously nothing, because the crew chief for that day investigated the problem and then wrote in the "Action" block: "Something tightened in the cockpit." On Wednesday Giverson flew again and followed up that sortie with: "Weird noise from behind the panel. Sounds like a midget banging on something with a hammer." Again, this wasn't much to go on. Where on the panel was the noise coming from? When did it start? Was it noticeable in all stages of flight, with power on and off, when the pilot moved the controls or activated certain switches, etc.? You couldn't tell from the write-up, and the mechanics' reply was: "Hammer taken away from midget."

By Friday of last week Giverson must have been frustrated because he concluded that day's flight with the complaint, "Aircraft handles funny!!!" The crew chief wrote back: "Aircraft slapped around some and told to be more serious!"

I slipped the forms under my seat but when Giverson showed up he stomped through the cabin until I coughed them up. His face turned red when he saw Friday's write-up.

"Get ready to go!" he shouted at me before going back outside. I watched him through the cockpit window as he stalked across the ramp looking for a line supervisor to yell at. He didn't find one and finally vented his spleen at a mechanic named Harry who had nothing to do with our plane or its write-ups but who happened to be working nearby. From the looks of it the venting didn't do Giverson any good. He tried to shout Harry into contrition but only got more frustrated when Harry refused to stop grinning. I wasn't surprised. Harry's normal expression was a smirk that would have pushed Mother Theresa over the edge.

I flew first. Giverson sat in the right seat, promising to be a normal co-pilot for required items like checklists but not one who would go out of his way to warn me if I was doing something wrong. *Great.* Rolo and I had counted on being able to back each other up. Now Rolo had to sit quietly in the cabin, monitoring our conversation on headset and anxiously awaiting his turn to fly.

We backed up to Alpha taxiway, turned ninety degrees, then drove forward to taxi down the parallel to Runway 36.

"Not so fast," Giverson rebuked me as we rolled along.

I put the props into Ground Idle, their lowest pitch.

"You're still too fast."

I tapped the brakes.

"Don't ride the brakes. You'll heat them up. Ever have a brake fire? They're not pretty."

I took my feet off the brakes.

"You're too fast again. You know, there could be other traffic out here."

I put the props into reverse. It was the only other thing I could do to control my speed. He was right that there was other traffic on the airfield. A C-12 was taxiing clear of the runway at Delta and an Army Blackhawk helicopter sat in the birdbath near the hammerhead. But it wasn't like they were leaping into our path. They were a quarter mile away. We could also see them, I thought of saying, *because we have a piece of advanced technology called a front window!*

But if Giverson was trying to unnerve me I determined to stay calm.

We ran up our engines to check power. Then I briefed my departure and the first instrument approach I would fly. I chose the ILS approach at Tocumen International because it would be nice and slow and give me time to warm up.

The tower controller cleared us on to hold. We lined up, the ocean now off our tail and the long asphalt path of the runway stretching out in front of us until it ran into the jungle at the north end. When the controller said the magic words, "Cleared for take-off," I pushed the power up and away we went.

Giverson stayed quiet for the most part. He didn't trust me: that was obvious in the way he muttered little corrections even as we rotated and started to climb out. When we went into the clouds at twelve hundred feet he put his hand on the yoke as I started the first turn, apparently worried that I already had the leans and was succumbing to spatial-disorientation. When I leveled out at 3000 feet he again helped me push over, thinking maybe that I would miss the altitude and climb into someone else's path. But still he didn't say anything. I managed to get all the way through the first turn in the holding pattern before he couldn't take it any more.

"What are you doing for wind correction?"

I explained how I used the triple-drift technique, crabbing into the wind on the outbound leg of holding in order to keep my racetrack pattern from looking more like a bent paperclip.

"That doesn't work," he said. "You always end up flying in a curve. You have to correct on the turns."

Whatever. Almost every pilot used triple-drift and it worked fine but to side-step an argument that I would certainly lose I acknowledged that his method was also a good technique.

We got cleared for the approach and I crossed the VOR inbound. The HSI presented such a clear picture of our position relative to final that I could hardly take credit for flying a good approach. We stayed in the clouds until coming down through a thousand feet, at which point the twin parallel runways of Tocumen airport appeared in the distance through our rain-spotted windscreen.

"What's your missed approach point?" Giverson barked suddenly.

My eyes were fixed on the course needle of the HSI and the small glide-slope indicator to its left. So long as I kept both of them centered we stayed exactly where we wanted, descending on a three-degree angle toward the right runway.

"Decision height," I replied, not looking up.

"Which is what?"

"233 feet."

"What if you lose your glide-slope?" he asked. No sooner were the words out of his mouth than a red-and-white barber pole fell into view on both my artificial horizon and on the HSI. Under the pretext of adjusting his seat, Giverson had leaned back and pulled one of the circuit breakers associated with the ILS. Now I had only course guidance. The glide slope was out.

"Wha..?" I wasn't afraid of losing the glide slope but I was ticked off. The point of the check ride was to show I could fly instruments, not to deal with a bunch of artificial emergencies.

Giverson was pleased. "So, now what?"

I counted to ten before responding.

"Now we transition to the localizer approach," I said in an even voice. "As I briefed."

"So what's your missed approach point?"

"1.2 DME. And that's at the new altitude of 420 feet." I readjusted the pointer on my radar altimeter and kept descending. Now the approach was different. Instead of descending on a constant angle all the way to 233 feet, the new approach called for us to descend to 420 feet. Once there I would level off. If I got within a mile of the runway and didn't see anything (or the instructor told me that the imaginary weather kept me from seeing anything) I would have to climb again to a safe altitude.

We descended and leveled off three miles out. All I had to do was hold altitude. But something was wrong. Giverson looked entirely too smug.

"So," he said, "your new missed approach point is 1.2 on the DME?"

DME was our distance measuring equipment, a fancy way of telling us how far we were from the runway.

"That's right."

"What if you lose your DME?"

Oh, jeez. Give it a rest, buddy.

"Then I revert to back-up indications."

"Which are?"

"The first is the inner marker. The light on the center panel will flash when we're over it."

"True, but can you use that?"

I knew what he was getting at.

"I can," I said, "if it's backed up by timing."

"Ah-ha!" Giverson almost broke his finger against the overhead instrument panel as he leaped in his seat to prove his point. "You have to have timing for a back-up! And you don't have timing."

We were one mile out.

"Yes, I do," I replied. "I hacked the clock at the final approach fix. Timing at our ground speed is three minutes and ten seconds inbound."

"You did *not* hack the clock."

"I hacked the clock," I repeated and pointed to the clock right in front of my face on the control yoke, the one with the stopwatch feature that was currently running and just passing three minutes. "Just as I briefed I would."

"You didn't call it out."

"Okay. But I hacked it."

"How do I know you hacked it on time?"

This time I looked away from the instruments to see if he had really just accused me of lying. I gave him a withering look and debated whether to observe Walt's #1 rule.

"Because I said I did. We're at the missed approach point. Do I see a runway or not?"

Giverson looked away. "No. There's no runway. Go around."

We climbed out and re-entered the radar pattern. I called the controller and requested a VOR approach to the north runway at Howard. First Giverson had me perform a fix-to-fix to a radial-DME off the Taboga VORTAC, a maneuver that I did well in spite of myself. I guessed a heading to fly at the outset and then after several measurements found that it was dead on. Giverson criticized the whole way – or at least until we were within two miles and it became clear I was going to shack it.

We entered holding again over the island. This time when I hit the final approach fix inbound I said aloud what I had only thought on the previous approach.

"Time," I announced, and waited until he looked over before I pushed the button on the stopwatch. Giverson made a gesture with his hands to indicate that obviously I had learned from my earlier mistake.

I flew two more approaches, an NDB and a PAR. On both Giverson heckled me mercilessly. Sometimes he would pepper me with questions so much I had trouble concentrating on the controller's directions. ("Where are the circuit breakers for the transformer rectifiers? If you select VOR for steering will the Number 1 needle still point to the Tacan?") Other times he would announce that a certain part of the plane had "simulated failed" and then ask what I would do about it if the emergency was real. The worst was when he pulled the number two engine back to idle, forcing me to apply hard left rudder to compensate for the thrust from number one. He did it during the climb-out from the NDB so that I had to hold the pedal in for a full fifteen minutes while the radar controller vectored us out over the water and back around the pattern. Even with the electric rudder trim shoved all the way to the left holding the nose straight was like keeping a sumo wrestler pinned to the mat with one foot. My leg was cramped from the hip down by the time we landed. All in all it was a painful hour and a half. When it was over I felt comfortable with my performance but drained. I hadn't watered anybody's eyes but then nothing had been so catastrophically bad, either, that he could fail me. I would take the victories where I could find them.

"Well, I don't know," Giverson commented as I climbed out of the seat to make room for Rolo. "Metzger, let's get you up here and see if you can do any better."

Jackass, Rolo mouthed to me as we passed each other in the cabin. I nodded in agreement.

Rolo's flight was ugly. He tried to fly an identical profile to me but had the bad luck to hop in the seat just as the afternoon arrivals to the international airport began. Tocumen, whose southern approach path intersected Howard's, didn't get a lot of traffic but the dozen or so flights a day that did come in all arrived at once. Since the Panamanian controllers freaked out whenever two aircraft were on their radar scopes at the same time, local traffic such as us was the first to be ejected from their airspace when commercial arrivals began. Rolo couldn't get clearance for a long approach so Giverson threw him immediately into the Howard VFR pattern instead for some simulated-emergency patterns. That was unfortunate because Rolo didn't stress well. He needed time to warm up.

"Jesus Christ! My controls!" was one of Giverson's first calls. In fact, he said it a lot.

"Tower, Shark 14, request right closed."

"Shark 14, right closed approved. You're number 1 inside a Dash 6 on the Tacan final, 8 miles."

"*Shark 14.* Right turn."

"Watch your bank angle. Who taught you to turn closed like that?"

"Sorry."

"Roll out, then start your turn to downwind. Square off the patterns. That's better. Hey, don't fly over the hospital."

"I won't. I'm going outside it."

"You're going right *over* it. I can see it. You think I'm blind? Come left."

"Coming left."

"Don't stretch your pattern out so far."

"You just said to come left."

"Not that far left. Your downwind should never be so wide that you can't make it back to the runway if you lose both engines. Didn't they teach you that in flight school?"

"In Cessnas, yes, but here I can't fly over the base. There's no way I could make it to the runway from out here."

"Of course, you could."

"Okay."

"You don't believe me?"

"Uh, sir, can you see the Dash 6 out there?"

"Don't change the subject. You don't think you can glide to the runway from here?"

"No, sir."

"Okay, simulated two-engine failure."

Immediately the sound of the engines faded as Giverson pulled the power levers back to idle. Harcourt woke up and quickly rolled out of the web seats. We didn't do two-engine failures so his first move was to check the cockpit. He listened for a moment, then took a position by the window of the crew entrance door. I tried to get an idea what he was thinking but his face was a mask. If I was hoping for him to undercut Giverson in some way or drag him out of the seat for being a fool I was disappointed.

I peeked out the window on my side of the cabin. We were abeam the golf ball antennae by Hangar 4, overhead the eastern perimeter of the base.

Rolo started a turn toward the runway.

"Uh, sir, this isn't..."

"Watch your turn. Don't overbank. Slow your speed to 120."

"If I slow down I'll land short."

"What are you smoking? You'll land sooner with a higher airspeed."

"Yes, sir, but I'll go farther."

"No, just listen – did you call tower?"

"Uh,..."

"I'll get it. *Tower, Shark 14 is turning right base, gear down, for a touch and go.*"

"Shark 14, understand you're turning base now?"

"That's affirmative for Shark 14."

In my mind I could see the controllers reaching for their binoculars.

"Shark 14, are you having any problems?"

"That's a negative for Shark 14. Training in progress."

"Shark 14, you're cleared touch and go to Runway 36. Traffic is a Dash 6 on a five mile final."

"Shark 14, cleared touch and go. Keep your nose up! Where are you aiming?"

"You said to hold 120."

"Yes, but you have to keep your nose up or you won't make the runway."

"I won't make the runway anyway," Rolo muttered.

From my porthole window I could only see behind the right wing. The picture there was filled with the terracotta shingles of troop barracks on Fort Kobbe. We were low enough I could see in the third-story windows, too low to turn another ninety degrees with no power.

"This is stupid," Rolo said bitterly. When he got frustrated he backtracked to what he knew and went single-mindedly with that. "I'm going around," he announced.

"No! Hold your picture!"

"We're gonna crash! Power's coming in."

"Jesus Christ! My controls!"

We would have crashed. I had no doubt of that. Rolo getting frustrated and refusing to play Giverson's game merely let the evaluator off the hook.

Fortunately, after the go-around and a bit of arguing that Bob Harcourt had to mediate (he quietly offered to give Giverson a break, which brought our evaluator back to reality and seemed to remind him that Harcourt was on board), Rolo and Giverson squeezed themselves into the instrument pattern. That calmed things down again. Unless the weather is bad instrument work is fairly boring.

The ceiling over the water lifted enough that at two thousand feet we stayed just below the clouds, knifing in and out of the overcast in intermittent rain. The water was always in sight and Taboga Island with its eight-hundred-foot hill facing the city provided an easy reference point. Rolo flew all his approaches at

Howard. Giverson gave him the same problems he'd given me but backed off on the trivia questions, in part out of frustration. Rolo became task-saturated quickly and dealt with it by blocking out everything else. Holding one rudder pedal to the floor, compensating with bank, talking to the controller, and spouting boldface for a simulated engine failure maxed him out. He didn't have time or brain cells to spare to tell Giverson the range of the UHF radio or the width of the cargo compartment and greeted such queries with silence. Giverson, chastened anyway by Rolo's earlier antagonism, gave up trying. Damn, I thought. I wish I'd thought of that.

Besides, Rolo never liked instrument work. When you learn something new you tend to remember best the instruction you get first. In Rolo's case his first instrument teacher in basic flight training had been a former Army pilot who had never gotten over the Army viewpoint that instruments are an emergency procedure. The Army guy told him that if there are ever clouds in the sky you should always carry a cat and a duck. If the weather closes in, throw the cat into the air because it'll always land on its feet and thus tell you if you're wings-level. Then throw the duck out the window and follow it to where the weather is clear. For wind direction, he said, try to find a break in the clouds to look down on the ground for cows. Apparently he believed cows always face downwind. Rolo never got over that teaching experience. Watching him fly approaches now, I could see him glance desperately around the cockpit from time to time as though hoping a friendly member of the animal kingdom might show up to assist.

Closing in on three-thirty, Rolo finally swapped seats with Harcourt. He and Giverson were equally happy to see each other go.

My roommate held himself together like an unpinned grenade until Harcourt advanced the engines for take-off on the second half of the sortie. Then, covered by the reigned fury of the engines just outside the fuselage walls, he whipped off his headset and exploded in a torrent of invective. His fluency in filth surprised me. Until now I had seen only his domestic side. He cursed, he swore, he spewed abuse at the cockpit such that spittle shot halfway to the stairs. He recited all nine chapters of the holy book of four-letter words including the two that dealt with goats. He shouted himself hoarse and gasped for breath, then worked backward over the same material. What impressed me most was that he did it with such flushed, spluttering sincerity that a diner full of truck drivers would have applauded.

"You finished?" I shouted across the cabin when he paused for breath. The C-27 launched itself off the runway and we both grabbed at wall netting to keep from sliding aft.

"No! Who the hell does he think he is? 'My controls...' I'll rip his goddamn head off! I'll throw his ass out the window on a low approach! I'll gouge out his kidneys with a spoon and toss 'em in the intakes! I'll tear him limb from limb and roast him in pieces for the dogs in Chorillo!"

Ah, the cooking angle.

"Yeah, he's a cock, isn't he?"

"He's a cock's cock!" Rolo yelled, giddy with anger. He was red in the face and releasing pressure like an overstretched balloon. "He's a cocker spaniel cock! He's the cockiest, cock-sucking cock you could ever cock-block! I'd like to stomp on his cock with a chock!"

"And clean his clock!" I yelled back. "Knock his block off with a big fucking rock!"

We went on like that for a while.

The C-27 lurched and pitched around the sky. In the tubular cabin it was easy to lose all sense of direction. Sitting in the web seats I could see the door window only from afar, a porthole offering a dime-size image of whatever happened to be going by the plane at the moment. Mostly the picture was an amorphous grey. Occasionally, as the wing dropped, equally undistinguished green would flood the glass. It was easy to see how passengers got sick back there. I looked toward the ramp as we took another turn, the bank rolling me deep into the seat and then catapulting me forward against the belt at my waist.

Things weren't going well up front. Harcourt and Giverson had trouble with the weather. When I put my headset back on they were in the middle of a discussion about the best way to get around a series of rain showers that stood between the Parita Gulf and the mountains. After much maneuvering the only way turned out to be a deviation to the south. Far to the south. I wondered how much gas we were burning.

"Where are we?" Rolo shouted off-headset as jungle flashed by the window.

I pointed to the map.

"What are we doing there?"

"I think they're lost."

"Good! Does that mean our check ride's over?"

I shrugged, then decided it wouldn't be out of place to hop up in the third seat and follow along. I climbed back to the cockpit and buckled in.

Clearing my throat, I waited a few minutes and then asked cautiously, "We going to be able to make it to Cañazas?"

Giverson looked back at me like I was the little brother who had tagged along on a date. Flying with Harcourt he had calmed down, knowing he was with one of the boys now and didn't have to hold anyone's hand. I half-expected him to tell me to get back down in the cabin. But instead he ignored my question.

Harcourt, who was flying, said, "I think so."

The weather was junk. It wasn't bad if all we wanted to do was fly from Point A to Point B and so long as Point B had an instrument approach. But for staying below the clouds and out of the rain showers and finding a runway that was probably just a grass strip in a field it was junk. I watched over their shoulders as they deviated east and west, finally crossing the Pan American highway north of Las Palmas where the soil was rocky and Brahma cattle wandered the ravines. The ground sloped up to the continental divide, disappearing in the clouds.

"Checklist," said Harcourt. "Gear."

Giverson ran through the Before Landing items. "See anything?" he asked.

Harcourt shook his head.

We flew over a village perched on the flared *falda* of a hillside. I leaned from my seat to watch it go by the pilot's leg window. It wasn't big and we were past it in seconds. Giverson consulted his map.

"I'm pretty sure that was it," he said.

We circled.

The village sat on high ground between two streams. It was all of a dozen homes with corrals for livestock. The terrain was steep and if there had been an airstrip at some point in the past I wasn't sure where they would have put it except perhaps straight on to the mountain. I also wasn't sure why an airstrip would have been there in the first place.

But the village could have been Cañazas. The INS coordinates blinked on their display, saying we were close. There was another collection of houses further down the largest wash – it had flatter ground and more grass and might have been Cañazas, too. Worse, there were stone ruins by an intersection to the west: *that* could have been Cañazas. The INS, unfortunately, didn't pick villages. It drove to coordinates that we gave it from a map that was imprecise and out-of-date. Also, its accuracy drifted over time. So now even though it showed us within a mile and a half of our notional runway we had to take that with a grain of salt. Two grains, since there were three villages and not a runway in sight.

I suggested as much.

"You'll get your chance to fly again when we put you in the seat," Giverson answered without looking up. Translation: shut up and let the big boys do their thing.

Rolo smacked me on the back of the head. I sat back and crossed my arms.

Harcourt banked the plane to head us downslope, closer to the second village. Giverson stopped him.

"Head up north one more time. This is definitely it – the road stops here. It could be they covered it over on the far side of those canals."

Harcourt banked north again.

"What do you want to do on fuel?" he asked placidly. We were down to almost four thousand pounds which meant that depending on how much we wanted to push our landing reserves we had about an hour and a half of flight time remaining.

Giverson looked at the gauges. He had been so wrapped up in finding Canazas that he had forgotten about gas. Now he ran numbers in his head. There was no way he would be able to get both of our check rides done if he did us one at a time.

"Wellllll,..." he said, stalling.

Harcourt circled over the foothills. He looked so calm that you had to conclude he was thinking about five steps ahead of the aircraft and already knew what he would do about both the invisible waypoint and the dwindling fuel.

"We'll do this," Giverson announced. "Bleriot, Metzger, we'll put both of you in the seats. No, wait... Yes, both of you. I'll check you over the shoulder. Bleriot in the left and Metzger,... No, Metzger in the... Oh, whatever, both of you get up here. You both fly up to Sherman and swap the controls halfway. One of you shoot the TOT there and whoever's left will shoot one back down to Howard. Can you make 1730? Wait... No, how about this: you *can* make 1730, so that's your TOT to Sherman. You copy? You ready to fly? Come on, let's go!"

I was always ready to fly. Rolo would just as soon have grabbed a parachute and jumped out. He gave me a look that said "Can it get any worse?" and grabbed his headset.

It could get worse. Before Harcourt hopped out of the seat he had to slide south for a rain squall moving along the hillside. Giverson took the controls while I crawled forward but he spent most of his time staring at the fuel gauges. By the time I buckled in, the village was nowhere in sight.

"Where'd Cañazas go?" I asked.

Giverson waved vaguely toward the mountains. He climbed out of the co-pilot's seat to let Rolo up. I circled where we were.

Rolo sat down. He brought with him the chart we'd had in the back but Giverson grabbed it away and pointed at the one he left on the dash. It was the same chart – Rolo had drawn both of them – but when confronted with the fuel problem Giverson had folded his up and crammed it into the crack of the window to get it out of the way. Now suddenly we had a map explosion in the cockpit as Rolo pulled the TPC apart and tried to figure out where to begin. I circled some more and watched our fuel.

"Hey, sir," I said into the mike. "I can start heading toward Sherman but I need to know where the waypoint is."

"You were right over it. Are you lost already?"

"No, I was just wondering if you and Capt Harcourt ever decided which village was the right one."

Next to me Rolo disappeared behind his gigantic piece of origami.

Giverson was no help. A series of rain squalls moved in from the west and we had to make a decision either to leave the area or go IMC, Instrument Meteorological Conditions. IMC meant we would have to shoot for the stars climbing to an altitude clear of the mountains. If the deck above us was thick we would end up canceling our low-level and returning to Howard for an instrument approach. Check ride over.

A non-flyer might ask why we couldn't just fly through the clouds while staying low. The answer has two parts: One, we weren't allowed to. By regulation, we couldn't enter a cloud while flying low-level, not ever, not even for a couple of seconds. Two, it was unsafe. We navigated mostly by looking out the window – when you can't see out the window it gets real hard to know where you're going. So going into clouds while on a low-level flight was dangerous and a clean kill on a check ride, the fastest way to bust short of calling the evaluator an idiot. Which, come to think of it, I had already done.

So we had to leave. It was that or get caught in the approaching weather. I picked the nearest of the three villages that could have been Cañazas, flew over it heading northeast, and hacked the clock.

"You got us on the map, co?"

"Uh..."

"Cañazas...?" I prompted.

"Just a sec..."

Besides coming from the west, weather also tried to flank us from the north, moving down the mountains even as I looked for an opening to cross them. Within minutes of flying east I was forced to turn right.

I circled and tried again where the clouds were thinner. Again I had to turn for weather. The squall line successfully worked its way around us in the shape of a giant U. The mountains were socked in.

I tried a couple of holes but they were dead ends. They were also confusing. Because the clouds were drifting, the holes drifted, too. Each time I turned around to exit one the terrain was different, making it hard to know where we were. The rain squalls began to look the same. They also began to bunch up around us. The circle I was flying got smaller and smaller.

"Co?"

"Huh?"

I waited. He was navigating and being graded so I didn't want to push him. On the other hand, I was being graded, too. I had to get us to Fort Sherman. I needed Rolo to tell me which way to go.

Giverson loomed behind us in the third seat. "You guys know what you're doing?" he asked.

Rolo continued to study the map, his face pensive.

"Hey, co?"

No answer.

"Co?"

Nothing. I went for broke.

"I need to know our position, co. Where are we?"

There was a pause, then, "I don't know."

Crap. I felt like throwing my hands in the air. "Where are we?" is the third worst thing to say in a cockpit right after "Why is it doing that?" and "Oh, shit."

"Jesus Christ, what are you two doing?" Giverson shouted. He grabbed the map out of Rolo's hands. Rolo didn't want to give it to him and for a second or two I thought there would be a fight but in the end Rolo backed down. Now he had nothing to do. To keep him from seething I gave him the controls.

"Head south," I pointed. "We'll get away from this junk weather, evaluate our gas, then look at our options."

Giverson didn't like that.

"I *strongly* suggest we continue east," he said.

"No."

"You can't just ignore a mission because the weather is inconvenient!"

I held up a hand to cut him off. He didn't like *that*, either. My diplomatic skills, never strong, got worse when I was under stress.

But east? What was he smoking? While the wall of clouds in that direction didn't seem to bother him, it bothered me. One, I didn't know what was behind it. Two, the instant I touched it Rolo and I would both be Q-3. We flew south.

We flew ten miles before the squalls cleared out. The ceiling rose to six hundred feet.

Rolo turned us around. Now, at a distance from the hills, we saw that the wall we had run into wasn't thick. A tunnel of cloud flanked its back side and went up and over the divide. We could go around it and get over the mountains.

I took the map from Giverson, trying not to look at him for fear he would use the opportunity to start shouting. It was like pulling a sheet of paper from beneath a Claymore mine.

The beautiful colored lines Rolo had drawn earlier didn't seem as friendly now. Their very colorfulness pointed up the fact that we weren't anywhere near on-course. Worse, I found that when held at arm's length and viewed in the abstract the entire route formed something like a frowny face.

After a few minutes I figured out where we were. I pointed Rolo on an intercept heading for our ridge line.

The ridge we were looking for was hidden in the foothills so we didn't hit it exactly. But Rolo did some clever maneuvering over the La Yeguada Forest Reserve that got us close enough. He went up a box canyon, found it was socked in, turned on a dime with the help of a whifferdill maneuver that even Giverson seemed to like, came back to the entrance, and took the neighboring canyon instead of pitching back out to the flatlands. The move kept us in the ballpark. I plotted a new course from there and hacked the clock again. We were finally flying a route and not just wandering the sky.

But it was now two minutes to five. Meeting the TOT of 1730 was going to be tough.

"I'll speed up," Rolo said quietly.

"Yeah, hold 240," I replied. Speed never hurt. But going faster would only help us make up a minute or two: it wouldn't save us a quarter of an hour. I whipped out my whiz wheel and started doing calculations.

Rolo kept us on an angle to the top of the cordillera. At the summit, squeezing between earth and clouds, he pushed over on the controls and let us accelerate. From there it was a quick descent down the Caribbean slope where lush jungle prevailed all the way to the coast. Our ground speed, which had slowed in the climb, shot back above 200 on its way to 240. I hacked my stopwatch again but the more I watched the clock, the more I realized we didn't have enough time to fly the route. We had to cut off waypoints.

Fortunately, in building the route we had put in two significant turns. The first was just past the Belen; the other was another fifty miles on. With a slash of my pencil I cut them out, knocking more than forty miles off the distance we had to fly. I pointed out the change to Rolo. He nodded. Out of the mountains for good, we turned right, dropped toward the trees, and headed straight for Fort Sherman.

In the third seat, Giverson sat with his left arm across his lap, the sleeve rolled up so that his own watch was ostentatiously in view. Now that we were out of the bad weather he could relax somewhat and concentrate on doing what he did best: viewing us with contempt.

240 miles per hour is four miles per minute. A mile every fifteen seconds. We raced over the trees, their unending mesh of leaves sliding beneath our feet. Birds flew up but they were gone as soon as they appeared.

"Next waypoint is a hill," I said quietly. "A spot elevation of 802 feet. You can see it there at one o'clock."

"You want me to fly over it?"

"No. The INS is close enough. I'll do an offset update."

That should have earned us some points, I thought. You could improve the accuracy of the INS by occasionally reminding it where it was – bringing it back to the fold, as it were. Most guys updated the solution by flying directly over the waypoint but you could also do it while offset from a geographical feature. It wasn't hard but it was something most guys didn't remember how to do. Out of my peripheral vision I tried to determine if the sucking-up helped. Giverson paid no attention. Who was I kidding?

"Next waypoint?"

"A river Y. Where the Toabre meets the Coclé. Hit it and then go straight for Piña."

"Time?"

"It's good. Keep it at 240."

I sounded more optimistic than I felt. To get our gear down within the window we would have to keep the speed up until the last second. My whiz wheel was telling me that even at 240 knots we would get there with about 30 seconds to make an approach.

We shot over the Lagarto River, then jinked northeast to hit our initial point, a shipwreck just off the beach on the other side of the village of Piña. From there we had four minutes.

"Okay, my controls," I said, squeezing the map between my seat and the center console.

"Your controls." Rolo couldn't hide the relief from his voice.

"Run the Before Landing checklist but stand by on the gear and flaps. We'll need to keep the speed up until we turn final."

"What's your TOT again?" Giverson asked, knowing full well what it was.

"1730."

"Uh-huh."

I watched Fort San Lorenzo come into view, perched on a hill at the mouth of the Chagres River. Its cannon still pointed seaward, commanding the entrance to the river and the shallow bay. Once upon a time the pirate Henry Morgan had entered the river here, sailing upstream and eventually getting his forces to Panama City. Back in a slower age. I wondered if he had worried about meeting a time-on-target.

The bay came in sight. In the foreground I sensed more than saw the lagoon at the north end of the Sherman airstrip. Around the strip everything was green. Green and quiet. The fort might as well have been deserted.

"This approach is going to be fast," I said to forestall any hysteria that might break out in the cockpit when we started toward final. "I'll use the turn to kill off our airspeed. We'll have plenty of time," I lied. "Co-pilot, drop the gear and flaps on speed – *but not until* we're on speed."

"Roger."

I was no longer looking over my shoulder. I didn't want Giverson to see the sweat trickling down my face.

Two miles. One mile. We were ninety degrees to final and five thousand feet from brick one, still flying four miles a minute. We would have to kill seventy knots of airspeed just to drop the flaps. I looked at the clock – thirty seconds and we would be in the landing window – and took a deep breath. This was going to suck.

"Right turn!"

"Clear riii...."

I chopped the throttles and rolled right. Rolo's words dissolved as the C-27 banked ninety degrees and I pulled 3Gs to drag the nose across the horizon. Giverson's stomach must have leaped to his throat: it's impossible to stay level at ninety degrees so the horizon slid upward, giving us an ever-larger view of a lot of water.

"200..." Rolo called. "190...180, flaps 10 degrees! 170, flaps MID!"

The flaps shifted our center of lift and the nose tried to rise. I shoved it down and re-trimmed. My target was the short grass hugging the near end of the asphalt. It rose from the lagoon and marched toward the strip until meeting the pavement's edge, then stopped there like a crowd of protesters lining a fence. A Navy outboard sat tied up to the shore of the lagoon where the grass rose up. It pointed toward my touchdown point, the light wind making it rock and send ripples across the lagoon. The ripples were the only motion on an otherwise clear canvas that I intended to fly into and through. The short grass at the end. Put it a beer can up the screen and hold it...the short grass at the end...that's it...hold it there and we'll be alright...

The ground rocketed upward. Ten seconds. We needed ten seconds more for the gear.

"155, gear!" Rolo shouted, as calm as a woman giving birth. "150, flaps down! Flaps are down!"

The flaps were like barn doors. They dragged our airspeed lower toward the final approach speed I was looking for. The landing gear, on the other hand, didn't do much to create drag so it was hard to know when they were moving. Six lights up front told us when they were down. Right now the three red "Gear unsafe" lights were illuminated. That'll change, I told myself. They'll be there in time. They'll all be there in time...

"Your gear isn't down!" Giverson suddenly yelled. "Go around!"

I gripped the power levers in my right hand and held fast. Fifty feet to go. The gear would be there. I could feel the hydraulic pistons in motion. They were swinging forward, dropping the locks in place, hydropneumatic check valves at the ready.

Forty feet...

Thirty feet...

Twenty...

Come on...they have to come down...they're moving...

No lights.

It was now or never. Maybe we would have to go around after all...

The panel lit up with three green.

"Gear's down!" Rolo called.

I tapped the power and pulled the nose up, shifting my aimpoint to the end of the runway. The motion arrested our sink rate by half.

Whumpp!

"Nose is down. Reverse!"

The power levers slid over the detent and all the way to the bottom. Our props twisted to a negative angle and roared defiance at the forward speed. As briefed, Rolo put his hands on the control yoke the instant the nose gear touched to keep it from jumping about as I released it to guard the steering grip. But the props worked their magic together, reversing course simultaneously and not shoving us one way or the other off the edge of the strip.

"Brakes!"

I pressed the brakes but by the time I got to them it was all over but the shouting. Sherman's runway was two thousand feet long and we needed only half of that to stop.

"Time?"

I had forgotten all about the time. Rolo was asking which meant he had, too. I looked down. The clock said 1731:05, but when had we touched down?

"Uh...I don't know," I said, letting the aircraft roll to a stop. Belatedly I shoved the throttles back to Ground Idle, stilling the roar outside. In the silence and at rest I was suddenly unsure what to do, my adrenalin only slowly coming round to the idea it could relent. We were down. We were on the ground. The aircraft was stopped and the option of crashing and dying had evaporated.

"It was in the window," Rolo insisted quietly. He looked over his shoulder at Giverson, who glared back at him with contempt. That meant Giverson had forgotten to look at his watch, too, but then the way we had thrown him around I didn't blame him.

"1730:20," came Harcourt's voice from the back. He sounded bored, like he'd had nothing to do during the approach but stare at his watch – which was true. "You made it by ten seconds."

Ten seconds. We didn't shack it but it was good. It was in the window.

"Get out of the seat," Giverson said by way of congratulations. Speaking of trembling, he didn't look so good. The stop had knocked his headset off. He was red-faced and angry and we had scared the hell out of him. I remembered then that he had called for a go-around on short final – and that I had blown him off. I had scared him and ignored him on the same approach.

I assumed he was talking to me. My pleasure. I set the parking brake and popped the propellers into Ground Idle mode.

But Rolo sensed freedom, too.

"Were you talking to me or him?" he asked Giverson, watching me unbuckle my shoulder harness with envy.

"Both of you. Out of the seats. Bob, hop up here, will you?"

I shared a quick look with Rolo. Giverson had said Rolo would fly his own TOT back to Howard. We still had enough gas to do that but just barely. Not enough for him and Harcourt to do another joyride.

Down in the cabin Rolo had to ask. He plugged in to the headset there and said, "Uh, sir. What about my TOT? You still want me to fly one?"

There was a snort in response. Then the hammer came down.

"Take a seat, Metzger. You're both Q-3."

It wasn't a surprise. Often guys busted check rides for screwing up one critical detail after flying an otherwise perfect sortie. Rolo and I had done much the opposite: we made the time-on-target but in Giverson's eyes fumbled our way through everything else.

"So it started with the maps?" Evan asked the next night at the Pinheads' house. We sat in lawn chairs around the pool.

"It started when that peckerhead entered the room," Rolo muttered.

"The maps, then the grade folders, then the taxi-out," I listed. "The flying, the weather, the cloud clearance. The navigating, the time management, pulling 3 Gs – oh, and did I mention we blew him off when he called for a go-around?"

"*You* blew him off," Rolo corrected.

"You could have pushed the throttles up."

"I didn't want to mess with your carefully laid plan."

"My plan fell apart when I got up yesterday morning."

Evan yawned. "So other than all that, it was a good flight?"

"You name it, he didn't like it."

Tommy Goode had a mixed drink he was swirling with a straw.

"I heard Bob Harcourt say you guys flew pretty well," he said. "Then he said something about how flying well and flying for a check ride are two different things." He smiled apologetically. "My check ride with Giverson was awful. I sucked up a lot, though! Ask Jem."

Jem retrieved a beer from the cooler at his feet.

"Sucked up? Son, you were slurpin' so hard you could have pulled a bowling ball through a fire hose you were so anxious to impress: *'Yes, sir, Captain Giverson,'"* he minced. *"'Here's your map, Capt Giverson. I made two copies of each route and brought a blank one to be ready just in case you wanted any changes, sir. Was that acceptable to you, sir? Is your coffee hot enough, Capt Giverson. Why does my voice sound like this, Capt Giverson? Well, sir, it's because my nose is stuck so far up your ass, sir...'"*

Tommy's face reddened. "It wasn't *that* bad. But," he wagged a finger. "I passed. It's important to know your audience. Oh, by the way, here's something that might make you feel better: I was talking to Dale, the crew chief on your bird, and he said Giverson made another stupid write-up in the forms after you landed."

"Oh?"

"Yup. You guys must have been at low level for a while because he wrote, 'Dead bugs on windshield.'"

"What a jerk," Evan grumbled. "The Merrill guys would have noticed that and cleaned it up."

"Yup. That's why Dale wrote 'Live bugs on backorder' in the correction block and left it on Giverson's desk."

We all laughed. It was the first time I had done that in two days. Then I remembered the ride.

"Speaking of bugs," I grumbled, "the thing that bugs me is that I heard he was bad-mouthing our pattern approaches and the instrument work. I didn't see Rolo's but mine was flawless. Even the NDB approach. If he writes up any of those I'll protest."

"Hang on, there, son," Jem cautioned. "If he says you couldn't find your ass with two hands and a map, you just do a Tommy here and smile and nod and say 'Yes, sir!' Otherwise you'll find yourself with more problems than just one bust. You can't argue check rides, you know that. The only difference between wrasslin' a pig and arguin' with an evaluator is that the evaluator likes it, 'cuz he knows he'll just put you down for more."

Jem was right. No matter what had really happened, Rolo and I had no credibility yet.

Rolo sighed. He'd been doing that all night, slumped in his chair, staring at the beer he held in his lap, sighing with eyebrows upraised like a disciplined puppy. It's amazing there aren't more country songs written about Q-3s because busting a check ride is like losing your truck, your girl, and your farm at one go.

"Well, all I'll say is that if that peckerhead ever comes into my restaurant, I won't serve him."

Evan patted Rolo on the knee. "Hey, man. I don't like the guy, either. If I ever open a restaurant I won't serve him, either."

"Me, too."

"Me, three."

"Tommy?"

Tommy demurred. "Well, if he came all the way to my restaurant the least I could do is give him a sandwich in the kitchen, you know what I mean..."

Jem shook his head. "It's a wonder we need a vacuum cleaner with you around, Tommy. You know, son, by my rumor mill this Giverson monkey ain't gonna be around much longer so you had better choose who you're gonna suck up to: us, who're gonna record every depraved, inbred detail of your social life for the next two years so we can show them to your wife and kids later on, or him, until they send him to be somebody's office bitch at a staff job. Which is it?"

Tommy caved. "Oh, alright. I'll refuse to serve the bastard, then kick him in the jimmy for good measure."

"Here, here!"

We stared at the lights in the pool. It was a medium-sized pool in an hourglass shape. The Pinheads had bought one of those cleaning machines that worked its way back and forth along the bottom in random patterns. With enough beer, watching it was more entertaining than TV. Probably even without the beer.

"They going to schedule you for a re-take?" Evan asked.

I nodded. "Already have. Monday, with Fetterman. Any suggestions?"

"Keep the pointy end going forward."

"He's a hard-ass when he's instructing – I wonder what he's like as an evaluator?"

"Aw, he's fair," Evan promised. "He just wants to be liked."

"So if I promise to like him, he'll pass me on the check ride?" I asked.

"Only if you also fly good," he said. "Rolo, what about you? When's your re-take?"

Rolo raised his hand. "Tuesday, with Harcourt."

Jem couldn't hide a grin. He clapped Rolo on the shoulder. "That was Uncle Walt looking out for you, son!"

"Why?" Tommy asked. "You don't like Fetterman?"

Rolo shivered, horrified that someone could even think he might. "Tommy, just what the hell planet do you live on?"

Jem knew the answer to that. "Well, you see, son, it just so happens that Tommy gets along with Major-select Fetterman, too! Hmm? Now isn't that a coincidence? I wonder how he does it?"

Tommy reddened again but winked happily. "I'm a nice guy."

15. Declan

My re-check with Fetterman was a non-event. He gave me a short ground eval and a half-hour flight then signed me off as Q-1. He never mentioned Giverson but it was clear from his attitude (and from the short sortie) that he thought failing us the first time was a mistake. Not that Rolo and I didn't have a lot to learn, but Fetterman thought we could fly. He didn't even yell while we flew which for me was as much a compliment as the passing grade.

Then for several days after my check ride I did nothing. I didn't fly, anyway. The emphasis in the squadron was on getting two more aircraft down from Texas and since I was here, not there, there was nothing I could do to further that effort. Instead I moved into our apartment, tried to find a car to buy, and went into the squadron every day to hang around, study, and look at maps of the theater.

It was now late summer. With the return of the Peru gang the squadron started to flesh out. All of Rasmussen's recruits made an appearance. I was in town and already flying, Jebediah Crystal had arrived the week before, and Carl Diehrmann was expected any day. With the old heads like Charlie Manson, Bob Harcourt, and Mike Vaneya, and the various other fliers who were bringing the aircraft down from Texas and whose ranks Lt Col Rasmussen was aggressively culling, we were rapidly becoming a sizable flying group. The goal was to have twenty pilots by the beginning of fall.

Declan showed up that week. He wasn't supposed to but found it an attractive alternative to a court-martial.

His court-martial fed a rumor, one that began to circulate soon after the C-27 arrived in Panama. The rumor was that it was a hardship assignment, that the only pilots sent to fly the aircraft were guys who had made enemies or who had gotten into trouble. The first part of the rumor, that Panama was a hardship assignment, was laughable. Though in every branch of the military there are always homebodies who don't want to move overseas, among those who were willing to travel Howard ranked at the top of places to go. It was tropical, it was exotic, and with the exception of the occasional protest and major invasion, it was safe. Noriega took some of the sheen off that image but so many generations of military personnel had spent time in the Zone that only eight months after Operation Just Cause its reputation was coming back.

The second part of the rumor – that C-27 pilots were screw-ups and trouble-makers – was also untrue. However, here the matter wasn't so black and white. Like all good stories this part of the rumor had a kernel of truth. Declan went a long way to contributing to the myth.

Declan, like me, came from C-5s. Like me, also, he had been sent to the giant, lumbering aircraft against his wishes, or, as he described it, 'screaming like a whore being dragged to church.' He had wanted to fly fast and he wanted to fly something with guns on it – an F-15, maybe, or at least an A-10. He hated flying slow. He also hated flying with other people, believing that the true beauty of a single-seat airplane came from the quality of the social experience. For him the C-5 occupied an entire hangar of its own in Dante's hell.

Declan had done well in pilot training but when the time came to choose an assignment the Air Force, in its feast-or-famine approach to supplying aircraft, provided Declan's class with few choices. Lots of trainers, lots of heavies, lots of tankers – but no fighters. Declan was crushed. The way he saw it, the only choice for him was which particular torture chamber he would spend his career in. It was doubly painful because as an Air Force Academy graduate he and his classmates had had the opportunity to cross-train to the Navy upon graduation. Some friends had gone but Declan refused. The reason he did was summed up by a poster framed on his wall: it said,

"The Top 10 Reasons to Join the Air Force:
#10-Because Navy guys are fags.
#9-Because Navy guys are fags.
#8-Because Navy guys are fags..."

...and so on. The problem was that all his Navy buds eventually got to fly F-18s so Declan had to take the poster down. He would fly slow for the rest of his life.

On the reluctant theory that if he had to go heavy he might as well go *really* heavy, he signed up for the plane that even its supporters called FRED – the "fucking ridiculous environmental disaster."

Then he persevered for a year. He was sent to Dover Air Force Base in Delaware where he learned to engage the autopilot right after take-off. He studied for his master's degree while cruising at thirty-five thousand feet and listening to the other pilots enthuse about working for the airlines. He married his girlfriend, bought a two-bedroom house, and traded in his Jeep for a Honda Accord. For twelve months his life was uneventful. And over twelve months he went insane from the boredom.

Then he flew to Africa.

The mission was a series of relief flights for Kenya. Declan and his crew operated out of Cairo, flying supplies to Mombasa where the pallets were transloaded to Air National Guard C-130s that then ferried goods into the interior. Every so often the C-5 crew spent the night in Kenya and rubbed shoulders with their Herc brethren. Inevitably friction developed.

The bad blood resulted from three factors: money, flying, and attitude. Money was the least of them but it was a start. The Guard crews stayed in Mombasa for thirty days at a time, living out of an expensive hotel right on the beach called the White Sands. They rotated in and out every month, making seventy dollars a day in per diem and flying four or five times a week. Declan and his crew stayed in tents outside Cairo and, being active duty, made no extra money out of it, the U.S. government having worked a deal that required no funds for the airmen. So the Herc crews went home with $2000 in travel pay every thirty days while the C-5 crews earned only a case of the Pharoahs' revenge. That was one issue.

Flying was another. Even months after being assigned to Big Mac, Declan still seethed at the utter waste of his skills. You don't fly a C-5 so much as administratively manage it through the sky. The only time a pilot ever touches the stick is on take-off and landing and that's about as exciting as maneuvering a garbage barge against a pier. For a pilot fresh from T-38s – where breaking Mach 1 and doing Thunderbird rolls is typical – even the best flight in FRED was painful. I'd been there and knew how he felt.

In Mombasa Declan was forced to observe a slew of bragging, swaggering, pot-bellied C-130 Guard pilots take off and fly visual low-levels – in airspace that was completely uncontrolled! – through some of the most scenic terrain on earth. He listened to how they saw herds of wildebeest and chased giraffes through the brush. He heard how they landed on dirt strips where spear-carrying natives watched them taxi in and local authorities treated them like gods. He endured their stories of waterfalls and grasslands and mud-brick villages – and he knew there was no way he would ever have similar stories to tell because he saw none of that from seven miles up. He was jealous. It was disheartening and depressing. And knowing that he was in such a lame job that he was jealous of a C-130 flyer was the most depressing thing of all.

The last matter, and the worst, was the attitudes. Most C-5 pilots enjoy what they do and are therefore immune to the barbs of tactical flyers whether they be fighter pilots or theater airlift. To a jester's comments about engaging the auto-pilot a typical C-5 commander would cheerily respond, "Yeah, but the airlines will love me in a few years" and be happy with that. Declan couldn't do that. To him, having the airlines as a goal was aiming for rock bottom. Airlines paid well but just like the C-5 they were as stimulating as watching water drip into a sink. Just the thought made him want to slit his wrists. So when the two crews gathered at the

White Sands pool bar to trade stories, Declan inevitably fell into a funk that even the cheap gin-and-tonics couldn't assuage.

The Guard guys had a custom of buzzing the hotel when they returned from a trip to the interior. Larger aircraft flew carefully planned departures and arrivals that kept them high over the city but the Herc crews disregarded the route structure and flew wherever they wanted.

The hotel was on the beach a few miles from the airport. The -130s would extend their downwind over the water in order to race in over the luxurious structure with its wooden terrace and kidney-shaped pool. From the shade of the bar crews could look east through the palms to see a plane start its descent and then disappear behind the hotel. Minutes later there would be a low buzzing that grew to a roar. Glasses would vibrate, plateware would tinkle, and birds in the gardens would take flight. The pink flamingos in the aviary off the terrace would squawk their disapproval. Then the "four fans of freedom" would appear a thousand feet overhead, bringing whoops and cheers from the crews drinking down below. More than once Declan had to sit there watching a Herc pass over and tolerate the goading of drunken loadmasters and radio operators who deliberately sought him out.

"Ha, ha! See, that's what flying's about!"

"Can't do that in a FRED, can you?"

"Don't worry, airline boy! We'll take pictures for you next time!"

On his last trip into Mombasa Declan could take no more. When his crew – all 14 of them – piled into FRED for the trip back to Cairo, he maneuvered for a flyby of his own. On departure the aircraft commander climbed out of the seat to head to the latrine. Once he was gone, Declan banked to return to the coast. He called the approach controller to request a flyby. The controller refused, knowing that a flyby by a plane the size of a 747 was absurd.

Declan repeated the request. Again it was refused.

Frustrated, he asked a third time, this time framing it as "a fly-over in honor of the benevolent and most-just ruler of Kenya, His Excellency and Ruler-for-Life, the Commander-in-Chief and President, Daniel Arap Moi." The controller changed his mind.

But Declan screwed up. He intended to fly over the hotel no lower than a thousand feet but when he neared the coastline an Antonov 32 departed the international airport and climbed into his flight path. It was either climb and beat the Antonov – and give up on the flyby – or descend. So he descended. And he descended. And he descended. He saw 160 feet on the radar altimeter crossing the beach. In a C-5 that's low enough that if he had banked hard one way or the other a wing would have been in the trees. But he didn't bank. He headed straight for the hotel and passed over it within fifty feet of the satellite dish on the roof.

The blast from the four turbofan engines blew out every window on the fifth floor, raining glass on sunbathers by the pool. Tourists dove for cover. Alarms went off in the parking lot. Part of the mahogany bar collapsed and a dozen flamingos died from cardiac arrest. Security guards radioed for help. The huge aircraft cast an apocalyptic shadow over five acres as it passed. The Guard crews claimed later they thought the hotel had been shelled.

I was living in California at the time, at another C-5 base. The news of the flyby shot through the community grapevine so fast that I heard all the details within hours of Declan landing in Cairo.

So Declan was sent to Panama. For reasons beyond his control that only a bureaucracy the size of the U.S. military can produce, his court-martial turned out to be a non-starter. Politics, inter-command rivalry, the fact that he was 'just a lieutenant', and the desire of the wing commander at Dover to get another star, not to mention the sudden flurry of activity that accompanied the movement of troops to Saudi Arabia that summer, all conspired to sweep the event under the table and make people want to forget that it ever occurred. He also benefited from simple supply and demand: one year earlier the Air Force had needed fewer pilots and was encouraging guys to get out; this year it needed pilots to stay in and was reluctant to ground anyone. Declan was declared persona-non-grata at Dover, a Letter of Reprimand was placed in his file, and the square-fillers at the Military Personnel Center in San Antonio were told to send him someplace far away. They spun the globe and put their finger on Panama.

So in a way Declan was an anomaly in the 155th. Here was Lt Col Rasmussen weeding out people he didn't want in his unit and seeking out people he did, and all of a sudden the Air Force came down and said, "Take this guy." At first Rasmussen spiraled through the ceiling in fury. Then he re-considered. As sometimes happened, a black mark in someone else's eyes was for Rasmussen just another entry on the resume.

16. Driving

Americans moved to Panama pre-disposed toward the culture in one of two ways: open- or close-minded. Regardless of how we arrived, however, all who had regular contact with the locals evolved more closely to the latter. Stereotypes grew quickly particularly regarding traffic and driving. There were exceptions but most Panamanians fell into a common lot of lawless, dangerous, and flatly unpredictable motorists. "Pulling a Pana" became the stock phrase to describe an action so stupid it could only have been committed by a local.

The great truth of our prejudice, though, was its flat hypocrisy. We gringos adapted to the anarchic roadways faster than the Donner party acquired a taste for white meat. Don Redelkite's wife, Melissa, was a perfect example. She was so polite and demure when she arrived in-country that Don, one of our flight commanders, worried she would be crushed in traffic in minutes. To train her to survive he took her on practice runs around the city.

"Have no fear, baby," he instructed. "Whatever you do, don't show fear."

"But Don, I..."

"No fear, honey! Don't let them see you're afraid!"

They started on Sunday mornings and then built her tolerance through heavier and heavier traffic until she could finally pass the check ride he imposed on her, a Friday afternoon rush-hour transit to the Corozal Commissary and back. Under his watchful eye she drove as aggressively as her courteous Kansas upbringing allowed, gamely cutting off people who wouldn't let her merge and even driving in the opposite lanes when Don encouraged her. Yet still he doubted her will.

He needn't have worried. Within a week she became a beast unleashed, weaving through traffic and bouncing over curbs like an out of control slalom skier, screaming at Panas to get out of the way and flipping off those who didn't. Etiquette was forgotten. I saw that for myself months later on New Year's Eve when after much drinking Don and I needed a ride home from the Marriott casino. Two cars driving slowly up Calle Cincuenta refused to let her pass so after a flash of her headlights she drove into the one on the left, knocking off its rear bumper and shoving it sideways across the path of its neighbor.

"No fear, honey!" she exulted, punching a fist in the air.

Don cowered in the passenger seat, wondering what he had created.

Melissa wasn't the only one to go native. Like Hobbesian case-studies released to the wild we *norteamericanos* not only lowered our standards but set new benchmarks for others to beat.

Skinny Steve did his part. He shipped an '89 Ford Taurus to the base when he transferred in and immediately regretted the decision. Within three weeks of off-loading at the docks it had been side-swiped, rear-ended, keyed, dinged, paint-bombed, broken into, and stolen. Steve had no emotional attachment to the vehicle but the casual indifference that caused its demise brought out the Cro Magnon in him. It was the principle of the thing.

When he collected his insurance money he eschewed another Taurus and instead bought a used Pathfinder on over-sized wheels and 8-inch lifts. He installed a roll bar over the front seat and put mesh protectors before all the lights. He welded a guard across the grill, slapped a plate under the oil pan, and installed a cage in the trunk for security of baggage. On the rear hatch he hung not one but two spare tires. That way if he chose to back into someone he could do maximum damage to them with minimal to himself. He taped the windows. Then he went to war.

To be precise, he went to war daily. The Pathfinder was old. Its paint was chipped and patches of rust already showed beneath the doors. It had scratches and pits on the windshield. There was nothing short of a head-on collision that was going to reduce its value. Most of all, Steve didn't care.

When he drove into the city he did so with a mind at ease. Where lanes merged he turned on his indicator, waited five seconds, then merged. If a car refused to yield, oh well. When he was cruising in the right lane and someone tailgated him furiously, flashing lights and blowing the horn to get him to move, he slammed on his brakes. When someone cut him off he rear-ended them. He once nudged an Audi full of *rabiblanco* twenty-somethings into a ditch when they saw the 2 on his license plate and threw a beer can at him. Another time he squeezed a Montero against the bridge guard rail after the driver went around safety cones to get ahead of him. By the time Rolo and I hosted our apartment dinner Steve's Pathfinder looked like a Sherman tank that had fought its way through the Normandy hedgerows. He could have stamped silhouettes of its victims across the hood.

Steve wasn't our only champion. Kurt Norris easily had the most forbidding vehicle in the squadron. He, too, shipped a car south from the States but his was no sedan. It was his Oklahoma special, a Monster-Truck Chevy Blazer on absurdly large tires with shocks so long he practically needed a ladder to get in the front seat. On the streets of Tulsa on a Saturday night this behemoth wouldn't have looked out of place cruising mall parking lots with a load of beer-guzzling teenagers. On the streets of Panama City it fit in like a tractor in Beverly Hills.

Kurt didn't drive aggressively. He didn't have to. Traffic parted before his Blazer like a school of yellow fins making way for a great white. Panas feared a confrontation for the obvious reason that Kurt would drive right over them. To my knowledge he never did. But I was with him on one occasion where he silenced some verbal abuse by simply cheating right and brushing a massive front tire against the door of the aggressor's Pajero. The heavy squeaking of vulcanized rubber against sheet metal drowned out the driver's threats. It also left a sooty black streak wiped into an otherwise pristine paint job, reviving the age-old question of why fools in expensive cars believe others will suffer them gladly.

Not everyone drove like a madman. Jem had his Jeep CJ-7 with the rear-mounted gas cans and his Texas A&M Dixie Chicken sticker proudly plastered to the bumper. By all rights he should have attracted attention because Jeeps were a rare commodity south of the Rio Grande. When a CJ-7 drove down the road people could be counted on to notice. As they could whenever Senior Airman Tunkelman crossed the bridge in his banana-yellow MG. But neither Jem nor Jamie ever had any trouble in traffic. Jem was a polite Southern boy and that came through in his driving. The Man from Tunkel was just too fast.

I had my share of adventures on the road. Rolo's early experience with the cracked axle put me on guard from the instant I started looking for a car to buy. Partial to trucks by nature, the combative traffic conditions around the Canal made me more so.

After a long search I bought a GMC Jimmy from a soldier transferring out of Fort Clayton. I paid $4500 and he threw in custom-made speakers mounted in the trunk for free, so anxious was he to avoid haggling and get one step closer to leaving the country. He had bought the truck from a buddy of his on Clayton, who in turn had purchased it from his girlfriend who was a Zonie and had bought it new. Which meant the vehicle had Panamanian heritage. Six years old, it had never known orderly roads or smooth streets. It had cut its teeth in the rugged isthmian traffic. Now, like a ranch horse so accustomed to working cattle it follows a steer itself, this truck I trusted to guide me safely around the pitfalls and potholes, smog and snarls, and floods and fender-benders that were integral parts of daily driving in Panama.

It wasn't long before the city put us to the test. I bought the truck in mid-August. A week later a middle-aged man in a Toyota

Corolla backed into me. On the roof of his car was a placard that said *Escuela de Conducimiento.* Which driving school it didn't specify. Maybe Panama had only one.

Except for his crumpled trunk, the collision was minor. We were in the parking lot at the DMV so he wasn't moving fast and I was still parked. (I was there to pay the safety inspectors five dollars for re-adjusting my headlights upwards. The lights had pointed at the road which, they claimed, was too low. Now the lights pointed at a much safer angle – eye-level of approaching traffic.) The driving instructor tried to suggest I was at fault for being in the way when he backed out of his parking space but, as there was barely a paint smudge on my spare tire where he'd hit me, I smiled and waved him off. If that was the worst that Panatraffic could throw at me, driving here would be cake.

Cake comes in many flavors. Two days later I was sitting at a stop sign on Calle Winston Churchill, a block from our new apartment. I had turned at the wrong street and was trying to get back on Via Italia when suddenly, *BAM!* A Daihatsu compact flew down the parking ramp of a neighboring building and slammed into the Jimmy's left side just behind the rear wheel. The whole truck lurched a foot to the right.

I was fine. My first thought was that I needed to stop less often because that seemed to be when people came after me. My second thought was that someone in the other car might be hurt. But the woman in the Daihatsu was uninjured. She sat dazed at the wheel – shocked and on the verge of hysteria but unhurt.

Her car was a mess. The hood was folded back to the windshield. Glass from her front lights formed a glittering carpet in the street. The compact's grill was mashed lengthwise and wrapped around her car's own fender. As I helped her to stand her door fell off. She began to weep.

The Jimmy had a small dent above the gas tank.

She cried and cried and then ran into the building to call down her husband from upstairs. While she did I tried to disentangle her car from mine. Despite not even scratching my paint the grill and fender of her car somehow jammed behind my rear bumper. I pulled out piece after piece of Daihatsu from the corner of my car until it looked like a body-shop class had conducted a field survey. Still my truck was as good as new, minus one pressed-in panel and a toaster-size chunk of the compact's front end that insisted on staying put, jammed securely behind my bumper just below the turn indicator. It... wouldn't... budge... – so I gave up, leaving it in place as a trophy of war, half a parking light glinting in the sun. It stayed there for the next three years.

The husband came out. He was tall and dark with a moustache as black as the Jimmy's tires. His wife was upset but he was calm. Not surprising me at all, she followed him down from the lobby explaining in rapid-fire Spanish how I had cut her off and caused the accident. The husband looked with concern at the collision.

Then in a move that *did* surprise me, he said, "*Mi amor, es obvio – la culpa es tuya.*"

I was flabbergasted. He admitted that she was at fault? Then he asked if $100 would be sufficient to have my truck repaired.

I looked at the dent. 100 bucks? The panel was barely pushed in. I wouldn't notice it in a week.

"No," I responded, adding that I probably wouldn't even repair it. He could keep his money. So long as his wife was uninjured I was satisfied just to drive on.

Now it was his turn to be flabbergasted. Apparently we both believed that everybody in Panama did two things at an accident: laid blame and threatened legal action unless the other person coughed up immediate cash, and then departed the scene *muy rápido* before any police could arrive. We shook hands, wished each other good luck, and I left.

But that wasn't the worst scare I had, not by a long shot. Before the weekend, still only a fortnight from buying the Jimmy, more cake came my way.

I spent the day at the base trying to find out where the Traffic Management Office had stored my household goods. I wanted them delivered to the Paitilla apartment but the people in TMO couldn't find any record of which warehouse had stored them or even which boat had brought my belongings into the country. Returning downtown in frustration I explored a new route through El Chorillo, one that was ten times faster than navigating the Circle of Death. Faster except I got so lost a block past Napoli's Pizza that when I finally popped out by the bay a trained navigator couldn't have re-traced the twists and turns that got me there.

No matter. At the bay was Avenida Balboa. From there I knew my way home.

Traffic was heavy but moving well. That is, it moved well until I got stuck behind a van that was doing half the speed of anyone else on the road. Its roof and sides were cut away to make room for outsized tools, leaving a jagged frame that looked as though a tyrannosaurus rex had leaned down and taken a bite from the vehicle. I could see the driver in his seat. He was talking and smoking and doing everything but driving, having an animated conversation with co-workers beside him. Oblivious to his speed he and the van swerved left and right as he waved his hands to illustrate a story.

Traffic behind me backed up. We all wanted to pass. Abeam the statue of Omar Torrijos I succumbed to impatience and swung into the left lane to do it, squeezing between the van and the curb of the boulevard. Had the trees and grass not been there to protect me from opposing traffic I never would have tried the move but as it was I felt safe. A few bumps...a little overtake...the van swerved right...*there.* I had room to pass.

But then other cars behind the van erupted in impatient honking. The driver stopped talking and looked up. Seeing the Jimmy over his shoulder he pana-jacked me, flooring the accelerator until my overtake disappeared. Now instead of passing the van I was neck-and-neck beside it. The situation got worse when the driver looked over and met my eyes. *Trying to pass?* his look challenged, throwing down a visual gauntlet. Instinct moved him to keep me from succeeding.

Not wanting to be goaded into street battle I backed off the accelerator. But immediately a car horn blasted behind *me.* In my rear-view mirror there was a Montero on my bumper, flashing his lights. Now that I had established a presence in the left lane he wanted to use it, too. Traffic backed up in both lanes. Everyone wanted to move. My only way out was to finish what I had started and pass the van.

So together the van and I raced down the boulevard. Open lanes stretched before us while a long train of eager drivers chased from behind. We shot past the intersection at Federico Boyd doing forty and picking up speed, rounding the curve for the straight run all the way to Paitilla. I could already see the tall white swirls of the Paitilla Inn. The corner there at Via Italia would have to be my goal. If I didn't pass by then I would never make the right turn at the Vatican Consulate. It was either that or slow to drop behind the van and the traffic behind me would never let that happen.

We sped past the Mexico Lindo Restaurant on the left. On our right the tide was out, leaving behind two small, worn fishing boats to lean their weight into the mud. When I gained a few inches on the van I could see their masts, towering above the sidewalk and low stone wall and silhouetted against the flat Pacific. The sea waited in the distance, beyond the mud flats, gathering strength to wash back into the bay in a few hours and once again hide the smell that came from the city's sewers.

I was gaining. This was going to work. The Jimmy's timing was off so the transmission raced as it shifted gears but still it had more power than the jalopy next to us. The driver of the van knew it, too. He stopped talking and fixated on the race, foot clamped firmly on the accelerator, body hunched over the wheel with eyes locked down the road as though concentration alone could add horsepower to his engine. His companions in the cab did the talking for him, leaning across his back to wave and condemn my barbarian driving habits. But as my speedometer climbed through 50 mph I knew I would overtake them in a block or two. All his focus couldn't keep me from winning.

But someone else could. As we roared down the road toward Paitilla, toward the little bridge over the *Quebrada Iguana* which sat in the shadow of the Inn, where once-fresh spring water now carried trash into the bay, another driver set her sights on me. Or rather, she didn't.

There was only one break on this stretch of the boulevard. It was at the intersection with Calle 49E where traffic from the Marbella district could cross through the grass median. 49E ran from Via España down to the water and was lined with office buildings, banks, a newly-opened TGI Fridays, and most importantly the Bacchu's and Tabou nightclubs. Where it met Balboa there was an enormous blue Panasonic sign that was a landmark for us gringos. Normally 49E was little-traveled but now, at the foot of the sign, in the narrow gap in the boulevard where traffic could turn toward Paitilla, sat a gold Volvo with a elderly woman at the wheel.

No, I thought from a hundred yards away. She won't pull out. She can't. There's no room. Even a Pana can see that. Even a Pana wouldn't be so dumb. I eyed the traffic riding my bumper. *Come on, lady. Don't pull a pana...*

The woman peered through the window of her land yacht, surely seeing the tsunami of traffic washing toward her – especially the two idiots up front who were blocking both lanes. We were so close I could make out her coiffed hair, the lamé dress, the thick rings on all her fingers as they clutched the wheel at 10- and 2-o'clock position, the bracelets dangling from her wrists. So close she couldn't possibly turn into my lane, not even as she crawled uncertainly through the intersection, squinting up the road *right at us.*

She squinted again and moved up an inch. At 60 mph and 50 yards, I could see the lines on her face. The Volvo hunched like a tired mule beneath her, resigned to whatever course she ordered.

She moved another inch.

I looked right. If the van driver noticed the woman he gave no sign. He hunched and scowled. The passenger next to him practically crawled behind him to lean out the window and yell about my poor upbringing. Behind us the Montero leaned on his horn.

She pulled a pana.

Inexorably, like a train pulling into a crossing, the Volvo swung into the middle of our road in a wide left turn, straddling both lanes. If the woman could see us at all she was either supremely confident we would all crash to give way to her – or she simply had a death wish. There was no way we could avoid an accident now.

The van driver finally saw her. When he did he practically had a coronary. He sat bolt upright in his seat, smacking the passenger who was still trying to yell at me. Showing true survival instincts the first thing he did was lean on his horn. Other horns erupted behind me, the following cars being so close they could see what was happening through my own front window. No doubt they all considered with bitterness how the inevitable inferno would delay them from getting home on time.

I didn't hit my horn. In another few months I would evolve to that instinct but for the moment I simply decided I was a dead man. To my left were trees, to my right the van. I had nowhere to go and no room to stop. Brakes would only make me swerve. I would hit the Volvo anyway, the cars behind would smash into me, the van would go plunging into the bay, and the entire pile-up would burn for days. We had three cars and two lanes and the old lady was broadside to us both. We would hit and hit hard. That was a fact.

So I looked at the looming Volvo, now twenty yards away, and with a slight nudge of the wheel chose an impact point by its right rear tire. *If I hit her there,* I thought, *maybe she won't die...* It was the last real thought I had before our distance closed to nothing. Then I shut my eyes.

17. Tamanaco

Once Rolo and I agreed to take the apartment in the Tamanaco Building, there followed a flurry of paperwork between us, the base housing office, the finance office, and Maria's real estate agency. We also met the owners of the flat, an elderly Panamanian couple who lived in a condo of their own just down the street. Señor Fernando Hurtado Cabal was a tall, distinguished gentleman with white hair and wandering speech that hinted he was either only vaguely interested in meeting us or teetering on the edge of senility. His wife, Isabella, was confined to a wheelchair and never spoke to us directly, passing all her messages to the maid who passed them to Senor Fernando who relayed them to us. Not that there were many messages during our short visit. Both husband and wife dwelled on the amount of money they would be paid in rent and how promptly we would fork it over. Their own living quarters were spacious, plush, and sumptuously decorated so money didn't seem to be a novel possession for them, but I didn't enquire.

The bureaucratic and social demands being met, we were on our own. We had a place to live.

Except once again it wasn't that easy. According to the contract, Señor Cabal would arrange for our utilities to be hooked up. Three days later when we departed our hotels and moved into the Tamanaco, we had no electricity, no water, and no phone.

"I don't understand," said Maria when I called her from the base. "I will talk to Señor Cabal and see that it is taken care of."

A few hours later she called back.

"There was a misunderstanding," she explained. "He will take care of it this afternoon."

But two days later we still had nothing. Actually, we had water because Rolo found the main valve to our apartment behind a wall panel in the stairwell. But technically we were getting that illegally – and besides, it was cold.

"He will take care of it today," Maria kept telling us, each time sounding like she meant it *and why did we doubt her so?*

"Tell you what," I finally told her in frustration. "Amend the contract: we'll go downtown ourselves and get the utilities hooked up. We can't afford to wait."

This was the solution Rolo and I had been avoiding for it was well-known that dealing with the local utility companies was a bureaucratic nightmare. We made a deal. Rolo would get us electricity: I would take care of the phone and water.

I got the better part of the bargain. For one thing, both the phone company, Intel Panama, and the water company, IDAAN, had offices on Calle Gavilán in the Balboa neighborhood. Balboa, confusingly, wasn't anywhere near Balboa Avenue which ran along the bay but was instead at the base of the Bridge of the Americas, inland from Fort Amador and down the street from the buildings of the Panama Canal Commission. It was a less intimidating area to be in for an American because it was until the 1970s part of the strictly-controlled Canal Zone. Unlike Panama City, which evolved randomly over centuries from the time it was first burned by Blackbeard, Balboa looked like an American neighborhood born from the Northwest Ordinance. It had orderly streets, middle-class houses with shaded lawns, and stoplights and streetlights that worked. For me, going there was as easy as driving on base.

Rolo, on the other hand, was forced to seek an electrical contract at the offices of the *Instituto de Recursos Hidráulicos y Electrificación* (IRHE) in San Miguel, a jumbled district of unmarked buildings, random streets, and choking traffic. If he even found a place to park he could consider himself ahead.

Another way I lucked out by choosing water and phone service was that the Panamanians surprised the heck out of me with their service and efficiency. In just over two hours I was able to walk into both offices, talk to a clerk, fill out the paperwork, and pay my deposits.

It wasn't a cakewalk. The bureaucracy of both departments was intimidating. There was the blizzard of stamps that went on each receipt and order form. The clerks behind the desks slammed their inked markers with lightning speed and violence onto every carbon copy until I could barely read what I was requesting. The sound of *stamp...stamp...stamp-stamp-stamp!* reverberated through the offices like light artillery, each explosion making me fear that someone had discovered a reason why I couldn't shower at home after all.

But in the end they accepted my blank stares and studied casualness and completed my applications. I was done in half the time I expected. For fifty dollars I took care of everything in a single afternoon. Getting back in my car I found myself feeling ashamed at the stereotypes I had imagined at the beginning of the day.

Then the weekend arrived and we still had no service.

"So where's that phone you promised?" Rolo demanded as we sat in the dark one Friday evening, eating chips and drinking beer and waiting for Kurt Norris to pick us up so we could go to a restaurant and have a hot meal.

"You're one to talk," I countered. "Even if we had a phone we couldn't find it right now without a flashlight."

"Hey, I filled out their paperwork, I got the receipt. I did everything I was supposed to. They said we would have it by yesterday morning. What more can I do?"

"Well, the woman at the Intel office said we would have phone service by Wednesday so I did my part, too."

"Well, obviously not," Rolo laughed, tossing over another bag of chips. "Did you use one of those expeditors?"

"One of the what?"

"The expeditors. I've forgotten what you call them in Spanish. Evan said to use them so we wouldn't have to stand in line all day."

I stopped in mid-chip.

"Wait a minute. Are you saying you never dealt with the paper-pushers themselves? You paid some guy to do it for you? Then you don't even know what he did – if he even did anything!"

"Dude, that's how it's done here. You're not in Kansas anymore."

"Obviously. In Kansas they can see after dark. You got taken."

Rolo grabbed a piece of paper out of a pile of receipts on the coffee table. He held it aloft.

"I have a receipt," he announced triumphantly.

I took the piece of paper and clicked a lighter to read it.

"This is a letter from your mom."

"Hang on a minute." He rummaged through the pile some more, peering close to discern colors. "Ah, this is it."

The new sheet was in fact a receipt from IRHE. It did say that we were supposed to have power by now. I extinguished the lighter and shrugged.

"Well, I guess it worked, then. But something tells me you should have paid the expeditor more."

"Yeah, probably. Oh, by the way, on a related note some guy turned off our water today."

"Who?"

"I don't know. I came back this afternoon and there wasn't any pressure so I checked the valve in the stairwell. It was closed and wired shut."

"That doesn't make sense. I talked to the company on the phone this morning and they said we were all in order, that we should have water now."

"Well, they apparently didn't tell their meter guy."

"What'd you do?"

"I cut the wire and turned it back on. What did you expect me to do?"

A knock at the door signaled Kurt's arrival.

"You guys live in a hole," was the first thing he said. He brought Lowell Hendricks with him. The two of them stood in the light of the hallway looking around in distaste.

"It needs work," I admitted.

"That elevator is scary. We could practically hear guys on the roof tugging on pullies. It took four minutes to crawl its way up here."

"You in a hurry? Come on in."

They stepped cautiously into the darkened room as though anticipating an attack.

"What's with the lights?" asked Lowell.

"We're being romantic," Rolo called from the kitchen. "You guys want a beer?"

"Sure."

Taking his, Kurt grimaced. "It's warm."

"Yeah," grinned Rolo. "We like it that way."

"You guys don't have any electricity!" Lowell exclaimed.

I collapsed onto the couch. "Lowell Hendricks, master of the obvious."

"Okay, I'll bite. *Why* don't you have electricity?"

"The same reason we don't have a telephone or legal water."

"Which is?"

"We're pacing ourselves."

"No," Rolo explained. "There appears to be a problem with our paperwork at the utility company."

"Frickin' Panas," Lowell snapped. "Idiots."

"Yeah," I agreed. "But check out the view!"

"Hey, speaking of Panas, how are you feeling?" Kurt asked. "We understand you had a near-death experience."

I shuddered. "You might say that."

Rolo passed around a new bowl of chips.

"It was worse than that," he offered. "More of a very-near-death experience. A 'hey-how-you-doin'?-My-name-is-Death-why-don't-you-come-down-and-have-a-visit kind of experience.' When he came in the other day I thought he'd had surgery to remove all the color from his skin. You can't see it in this light but his hair's gone completely gray."

"That bad?" Even Lowell looked sympathetic. "Some Pana cut you off on the bridge?"

"Worse," Rolo continued talking for me. "She pulled in front of him on Balboa while he was doing about 90."

"No!"

"It wasn't 90," I corrected. "More like 65."

"Big difference."

"Frickin' Panas. You kill her?"

"No."

"You swerve just in time?"

"No."

"You stop?" he demanded.

"No."

"Well, what'd you do?"

"I drove right at her doing 65 mph and closed my eyes."

Lowell considered that. "Huh. Haven't tried that one."

"So how did you not hit her?" Kurt wanted to know.

I held up my hands in supplication, the image still scored in my memory.

"I don't know! I...have...no...fricking...idea! One second she's right there and we're all coming down on her like an avalanche, the next...I don't know. I closed my eyes and when I opened them we're all on the other side and everybody's slowing down like we just finished the hundred-yard dash. We must have swerved. We must have! Maybe just enough. But there wasn't any room! We had two lanes and about fifty cars. I don't know how we didn't all plow into her and close the street for days with wreckage."

"So where did *she* go?"

"I DON'T KNOW!"

Kurt and Lowell burst out laughing.

"Fantastic! Whoo-hoo, that's awesome! Didn't you go back and look? See if she got knocked up onto the parkway or anything?"

"I told you – there was NO collision. And besides, are you kidding? Go back? I had half the country behind me as it was. It was all I could do to change lanes and pull into Paitilla much less turn around. The only thing I can figure is – hell, I don't know. Maybe we all just missed her."

Lowell got serious. "Maybe it was one of those third dimension things. Or maybe, hey! Are you religious?"

"No, why?"

"Well, you know, maybe you had a guardian angel or something. Or maybe some mystical kind of transformation."

"Shut up."

"Frickin' Panas."

It was when we went downstairs to pile into Kurt's Blazer that I got my idea how to fix our electricity. Kurt had parked near the junction boxes in the parking garage. They were a Rube Goldberg affair, grey containers mounted any-which-way on the wall with fuses and wires protruding in a manner that one could only describe as Panama-entropic. Looking closely, it seemed to me that for our particular box – 23-A scrawled in crayon on the plastic cover – only three wires were lacking to complete a circuit.

The next morning I took out my toolbox and studied the junctions more closely. Three wires were definitely all we needed. They appeared to be the same gauge as those protruding from an unfinished outlet in our laundry room. I went upstairs, cut three lengths of wire out of the wall, and inserted them in our box. Standing back a judicious distance, I threw the switch. Nothing exploded. I replaced the box cover and went upstairs.

Rolo was still asleep. I tested the light in the kitchen.

It worked!

I promptly went to Rolo's room and plugged in the stereo next to his bed. Cranking the volume, I popped in a Guns & Roses CD: "Welcome to the Jungle" exploded out of the speakers.

Rolo vaulted from his bed in alarm.

"What the hell! What's happening? What's wrong?" Then, "Jesus Christ, turn that damned thing off! I'm trying to sleep."

I turned the volume down and stood there, trying my best to put the word "Voila!" into an expression on my face.

Rolo threw himself back onto the bed and closed his eyes. It was a minute before he opened them again in realization.

"Hey! Hey, hey, hey! We've got power! We've got power!"

We cranked the radio and danced around the apartment turning on every appliance we had.

Unfortunately, we couldn't work the same jerry-rigging magic with our phone service. We continued to live in lofty isolation without it.

Every now and then a diligent representative of the electrical company would swing by the parking garage and notice that we were stealing power. His response was invariable: disconnect the power, remove our wires, and put a lock on the junction box. Fortunately, Rolo and I were on different flying schedules most of the time so one of us was always home at night before anything in the refrigerator could spoil. Our response was to cut off the company lock and install new wires.

I called the power company several times and twice made trips to the office in San Miguel with copies of Rolo's receipt to find out where the confusion lay. What boggled our minds was how the company could be so diligent about removing our power but so unable to connect it, even when we stood in their offices with money in hand. Regardless, new deadlines for a proper connection came and went.

Telephone service grew to be more of a hassle. As a squadron scheduler, one week a month I stood overnight alert for the C-130s in the squadron. Most mornings they scheduled early departures to fly south and take pictures of suspected coca-growing regions. However, if the weather forecast was bad the AOC would call me at 3:30 am to cancel the mission: I would then call the members of the scheduled crew. Not having a phone for the AOC to call I carried a beeper. Whenever it went off I leaped out of bed, took the elevator to the lobby, walked down the street to the Plaza Paitilla hotel which had the nearest payphones, and started making calls. The hassle came when I carried the alert two weeks in a row and the weather down south was consistently bad. I ended up not sleeping at night, waiting fitfully for the beeper to go off so I could make my nocturnal trip down the quiet street. One night the AOC called when I *was* asleep. I dutifully took the message and then rolled back over without ever waking up. Needless to say, the C-130 crew was fit to be tied when they showed at 4:30 am for no reason. The commander chewed my ass.

Sleep or not, telephone or not, we were determined to make a go of the apartment. When the power was on and therefore when we had hot water and TV, it was a pleasant place to live. Grilling on the balcony worked like a champ. We enjoyed few pleasures equal to settling into lawn chairs with our feet propped up on the rail, drinking beer and eating whatever delicacy Rolo had cooked that night, watching aircraft take off from Paitilla Airport as the shadows spread over the ocean and the sun went down.

But Rolo still wanted to have a party.

"We need an official apartment-warming party," he insisted. "Everyone should come. I'll cook a spaghetti feast with Grandma Metzger's famous traditional secret-recipe spaghetti sauce. It'll be killer!"

Who was I to argue? If Rolo the wrestler, the football player, a man with more muscle than Venice Beach, wanted to play culinary socialite, more power to him. We scheduled a Saturday night at the end of the month for the event.

On the Thursday before the party he started to cook. The supplies required multiple trips to the store. From somewhere in the shipping boxes he had not yet unpacked, he produced a full-body apron and a chef's hat. I realized then that I had moved in with Julia Child. A hairy, cross-dressing, wannabe-Greek Julia Child.

From Thursday afternoon on I was persona non grata in the kitchen. Rolo had tomatoes, mushrooms, onions, garlic cloves, celery, avocadoes, bean sprouts, cilantro, and vegetables I didn't even recognize strewn around the kitchen. Though it seemed to me like an explosion from a farmer's market, he insisted there was a method to the madness. Five feet of Italian sausage from the Casa de la Carne (Paitilla's "House of Meat") snaked along the counter. It encircled an equal amount of ground beef from the commissary at Corozal. There were so many spices laid out in rows on the table that I felt ashamed over my reliance on salt and pepper. But Rolo appeared to know what they were for. He diced, chopped, grated, and pureed all afternoon and evening, the sizzle of simmering meat providing background music to his work and an aroma for the whole apartment.

By midnight he was done. He threw everything into a twenty-gallon copper-bottomed pot that had spent the day sitting on our electric stove like a misplaced pony keg from a fraternity party. He placed the lid on the pot, set the dial on the stove, and stepped back to watch his creation come to life.

Friday afternoon I flew a local sortie with Mike Vaneya and came home needing a beer. We got shot at again. This time it was at an airstrip near Jaque, southeast of the capital and fifty miles from the Colombian border. A Cessna 206 was sitting on the strip when we flew over and two men fired at us with pistols as we passed. Mike, not surprised, buzzed them twice in response.

When I got home Rolo was having his own crisis.

"Taste this!" he shouted the instant I came through the door. He held out a mixing spoon filled with sauce, stress causing his massive bicep to flex uncontrollably.

"Why? What's wrong with it?"

"I didn't say anything was wrong with it! Just taste it!"

I took the spoon carefully. One didn't argue with harried cooks who could throw you to the mat and apply the atomic hot-foot. I tasted. The sauce tasted fine, even good, until I swallowed it. Then a delayed smoky flavor crept in, growing until my mouth felt ashy. Rolo watched me like a police interrogator.

"Is it burned?" I asked cautiously.

"AHHHHHHRRRGGGH!" was the response. He threw up his hands and ran back to the kitchen. "I knew it! I knew it!"

"You knew what?" I followed him. "That it was burned?"

"It's not burned!" he replied, pointing at the pot. "It's not burned at all! It just tastes that way."

"How can it not be burned if it tastes burned?" I asked. "Did you leave it on all night? It probably burned."

"It...*didn't*...burn," he enunciated clearly. "I ran the spoon along the bottom. There's no burn. The food's not burned, the bottom's not burned, the stove's not too hot."

"So what's the problem?"

Rolo waved his hands in the air as though ready to catch something heavy.

"It's burned!" he shrieked. "I did that whole freaking recipe and everything burned! Ten gallons of sauce – useless!"

I didn't know he felt so strongly about his food. It was just a house-warming party.

"We could order pizza," I offered.

"AHHHHHHRRRGGGH!" he shouted again. "No! No, no, no, no, no...."

I got my beer and stepped around him carefully to get back to the front room.

"Dude, don't pop a vein over it," I said over my shoulder. "We'll make it a pot-luck and tell everyone to bring a dish."

He appeared at the kitchen door and glared in my direction. Pointing a wooden spoon like he was seconds away from dragging me to a crossroads and stabbing it through my heart, he said, "No pot luck. Grandma Metzger doesn't give up."

Julia Child on steroids.

He started over. The sauce went down the drain. Another trip to the House of Meat. Another trip to the commissary. More spices and vegetables and sausages and ground beef. More chopping, dicing, grinding, pureeing. I offered to help but was waved off – he was in the zone.

The next morning I went for an early run along the bay, something I looked forward to all week. Weekends were the only time it was possible. Weekday traffic on Avenida Balboa would either run a pedestrian down or choke him to death with carbon monoxide but on Saturday and Sunday the city was empty. On Friday evenings two-thirds of the capital's population traveled to "the interior" in an exodus that clogged the Pan-American highway for hours but that left the city a pleasant place to live.

The kitchen smelled good when I left. It smelled even better when I returned. Since Rolo was not yet up I took the huge risk of stealthily lifting the kettle's lid to get a sense of how things were brewing. The sauce smelled rich and Old World, with strong hints of basil and turmeric. Nothing wrong there. My boldness didn't extend so far, however, to taste it so I replaced the lid. Convinced my roommate's corrective action of the night before had been successful, I hopped in the shower.

But no sooner had I turned the water off than I could hear Rolo proving me wrong. His apoplexy at the stovetop carried throughout the apartment and kept him from forming complete sentences.

"How could it...?!!"

"I put all the...!!!"

"There's no way it could have...!"

"You're kidding me!!"

"Problems?" I called warily from the hall.

Big problems. The sauce had burned.

He started all over again. More sauce down the drain. More meat. More vegetables. More chopping, dicing, and slicing. By four o'clock that afternoon Rolo had spent the better part of three days wearing an apron. I worried that people might start to talk.

And by four o'clock he was near to having a nervous breakdown.

"It's this fricking stove!!!"

"How can it be the stove?"

"It's the stove!"

It *was* the stove. Somehow the electric coils on the top weren't getting a consistent current. Now that we noticed the problem we could see it for ourselves. If we set a burner on Low it would slowly warm up – and then jump to glowing-red hot for several minutes all on its own. Then it would cool down for a while only to heat up randomly again. Why this gave a charcoal flavor to the sauce was beyond me but there was no doubt the stove – and the oven, and the hot water heater, and the toaster, now that we paid attention – had minds of their own. If we wanted to cook something right we would have to stand there and supervise the process. But Rolo had had enough. He simply didn't have the energy or the time to produce Grandma Metzger's recipe again. And our entire squadron would be showing up in an hour. He was a grown man close to tears.

"They're going to kill me," he sighed, slumped forlornly in a corner with his chef's hat sitting on his head like a fractured Tower of Pisa.

"Over food?"

"They'll kill me."

"They won't kill you," I promised. "They'll just make fun of you until you throw yourself off the balcony in disgrace."

"That's worse. I would rather they killed me. I've been promising this dinner for weeks. Now they're going to show up and get nothing."

"We still have spaghetti."

"Okay, they'll show up and get plain spaghetti. And beer. Plain spaghetti and beer. Grandma's rolling over in her grave."

"I thought you said she was still alive."

"She is. But this'll kill her and then she'll be rolling over in her grave."

I thought he really was going to cry. Then I had an idea.

"Hey, Rolo! Buck up! I've got a solution."

"Forget it. They'll be here in an hour. I can't make sauce that fast."

"Yes, you can. Chop up whatever you have left. I'll be back in twenty minutes."

I ran three blocks to the Gran Morrison shopping center. I had never shopped there for anything except beer because the prices were so high but this was an emergency.

Back in the apartment I unloaded the bags onto the counter.

"Prego?" Rolo exclaimed in disbelief. He picked up a jar like it held a lab specimen. "Ragu? What's this?"

"Sauce," I explained. "Sauce right out of the jar. Instant salvation for people expecting guests in" – I checked my watch – "fifteen minutes."

"Forget it. You're not seriously suggesting that I serve store-bought spaghetti sauce for dinner when I've been promising Grandma Metzger's famous traditional secret recipe."

"That's exactly what I'm suggesting."

"Forget it!"

"Dude, we've got no choice. It's either that or dry pasta."

"Forget it! They'll recognize it as from the store. I'll be the laughing stock of the squadron."

I looked at my roommate dressed like Holiday Inn kitchen staff and left that one alone.

"Look, you can dress it up. You've still got tons of stuff here. All these jars are different styles and brands. Mix 'em all together in a pot and add your own ingredients. It won't taste like anything they've ever eaten."

That made him think. He stood for a moment looking from the jars to the refrigerator to the stove.

"The stove's still broke," he protested.

"I'll watch the stove. When it goes nuclear I'll move the pot to another burner. You handle the organics, I'll take care of the physics."

He weakened. Inside his head the hamster of imagination jumped back on its culinary wheel.

"Well, I suppose I could still fry the sausage up..." He read the label on a jar of Prego's Country Vegetable Favorite and grimaced, clearly worried that somehow his family back in Cleveland might see what he was doing.

"I'm telling you, Rolo, you give Lowell enough beer and he'll think this is the best thing he ever tasted."

"I'll know the difference."

"Then you get drunk, too."

He gave in. "Alright, let's do this fast and get it over with."

When Walt and his wife Sarah arrived some time later I was still hovering over the stove, oven mitts in hand and a beer not far away, in a private duel with the electrons within.

"Mike," Walt announced after watching me shuffle the pot of sauce from one burner to another to another. Nothing else. Just "Mike." The rest of his sentence he held back while searching for a diplomatic spin to put on it.

I tried tilting the pot. The coils on the current burner glowed irregularly but I found that, if I stood on the side closest to the wall, balanced just right with the pot in one hand, beer in the other, and my right knee pushing the rheostat, I could get all the coils on the outer rim to stay red. Newton and Einstein would have had a great time in our kitchen.

"Mike," Walt tried again, "if you can do that, how is it you can't keep your airspeed steady on final?"

"There's no beer involved," I replied.

"So next time if I put a bottle on the dash you'll shack your landing?"

"No question about it."

"Then I can go home now," he concluded. "I've learned my new thing for today. Who would have thought flight instruction could be advanced by watching a drunk man burn dinner?"

Lowell and Kurt showed up. Rolo got to them before they cleared the threshold.

"Hey, Lowell, have a beer."

"Why?"

"Just shut up and drink."

Big Bud came, as did Mike Vaneya and his wife Vayra, and Charlie Manson and Little Bud and Carl and Evan and Jem. Tommy Goode showed up with his stunning girlfriend Carla, she of the *rabiblancos* who normally didn't associate with Americans. Carla had two brothers who disapproved strongly of her dating a *yanqui* and who kept inviting Tommy along on high-risk adventures like para-sailing, rock climbing, and motorcycle racing in the hopes that he would get hurt or killed. Tommy, however, was blessed with as much good luck as he wasn't with common sense and prevailed at anything the brothers threw at him. Today they had come to the party from an afternoon of spearfishing off Punta Chame, where Tommy had been lured into free-diving (no tank) sixty feet deep in shark infested waters. He had speared a twenty-pound flounder and returned intact.

The more amusing dilemma Tommy had at the moment, at least for those of us who knew about it, was his efforts to cure a recurring rash on his groin that his girlfriend didn't know about. The rash had come from Peru where Tommy had taken a swim in the Amazon. Though assured by Doc Hinnaneman that it was not an STD and not contagious, it was still embarrassing when it flared up every few weeks. Tommy was trying to hide its existence from Carla. He had recently agreed to a drastic rash-removal program of Hinnaneman's that involved a nitrogen gun, a scalpel, and an ointment that resembled some cure-all mustard plaster of the 19th century. It also involved a three-week recovery period for the swelling and discoloration to disappear. According to Tommy, Carla was a sex freak but a moody one, a girl who would get mad enough on the slightest provocation not to talk to him for five days but then show up at his door wanting to rail like a sailor on leave. So Tommy's challenge now was to keep her angry for three weeks straight in order to protect both his pride and Little Tommy. He was two weeks into the deception when they came through the door at the party and, judging from the cool atmosphere between them, he was still surfing with the tide.

Josh walked in with a look of utter distaste. I hadn't flown with him yet but wanted to: he was so hilariously arrogant he had to be a good pilot.

"This place is a pit," he scowled.

"Hi, Josh! Thanks for coming. Glad you like it."

"No, seriously, you're getting ripped off. This building looks like it's about to fall down."

"Then you probably shouldn't go out on the balcony."

"And you don't know the half of it," Kurt added, handing him a beer. "Don't be surprised if the lights go off."

Declan arrived with his wife Sue. It was their first trip downtown.

"We carpooled with Mick Conner," he explained, not at all embarrassed to admit that he wouldn't drive off-base without an escort. "And followed Manny all the way. He only got lost once."

"I wasn't lost," Manny replied. "I was confusing the terrorists."

"It must have worked."

"I took the back way through Albrook. Made it up the hill, found the *RostiPollo* alright, the Circle of Death was no problem. It was when Tumba Muerto turned into a boulevard that I got confused. All those trees...when did they put those in?"

"Back in the forties," Josh answered.

"Ah, well. That explains it. I wasn't here in the forties."

For those who lived on base our new home was a novelty. The big draws were the balconies. The Pinheads rejoiced at the altitude and started throwing paper airplanes into the wind. At twenty-three floors up the better models disappeared from sight before hitting the ground. Soon everyone was in on the game, tearing up any paper they could find and launching from both ends of the building. A raid of paper bombers descended on Paitilla.

So many people were out on both ledges that nobody was inside the apartment when T.J. arrived. T.J. tipped the scales at a good two-fifty and never let a meal pass him by. Nonplussed to find the kitchen empty, he helped himself to a heaping bowl of spaghetti and was well into it before anyone noticed he was there.

"Hi, T.J.!" Rolo called out. "Make yourself at home."

The big boy gestured with his fork and grunted. "Thanks. Good sauce."

We served dinner. Everybody loved the food. Rolo showed admirable modesty when, like T.J., they professed the sauce was the best they'd ever tasted. Asked for the recipe he was vague.

"How's your phone doing?" Josh changed the subject, with an arch of the eyebrow that suggested he knew the answer.

"Ahhh. Has the conversation returned to making fun of our apartment?"

"Yes, I believe it has," Walt agreed. "And I can take part because I tried to call you last week and couldn't find a number on the recall roster."

"Why were you calling me?"

"I was going to put you on a flight. We were going to send a plane up to Changuinola and I needed a co-pilot."

"Why didn't you call me?" Rolo asked. "How come you were calling Mike?"

Walt considered. "Well, first of all you're in the same apartment so I couldn't call either of you."

"Yeah, but you said you were calling him," Rolo persisted. "Don't you like flying with me?"

"Rolo, I enjoy flying with you," Walt replied. "You know I do. It's just that you have those Fetterman flashbacks where you start pounding the dash and screaming at the top of your lungs – it unnerves me."

"I don't do it all the time."

"He screams?" Carla asked. She looked at Tommy. "You don't scream when you fly, do you, my sweet?"

"No, baby. I don't scream."

Carla's coolness evaporated. She looked with pride and naked longing at her confident boyfriend, who quickly put the situation back where he wanted it by adding, "Don't each so much spaghetti, honey. You're getting fat." At which point the temperature dropped again.

"And besides," Walt continued, "Mike's been patient. We need to get him flying."

"Yes, you do," I agreed.

"But about your phone," Josh cut in, returning to his topic. "What's the deal?"

Just then the lights went out. The stereo went quiet and we heard the water heater in the back room wind down. When it stopped entirely it clicked softly to itself, the sound echoing off the walls.

"And your lights," he added. "How're they doing?"

Rolo and I looked at each other in disbelief. It was Saturday. Almost seven o'clock in the evening, no less. How could the power company be out this late?

"Those bastards!" Rolo exclaimed and leaped to his feet. He grabbed his shoes with the intention of rushing downstairs to the parking lot to catch the inspector.

"Hey, relax, son," called Jem in his calm drawl from the south balcony. "The city ain't going nowhere."

The sun had disappeared far to his right. Now the water behind him slipped from blue to gray as he leaned on the railing and contemplated the view. Overhead the last streaks of light shimmered their way through deeper and deeper hues. Below, shadow filled the canyons between the high-rises and climbed like a black tide on their walls. He sipped a Soberania and enjoyed the Kodak moment.

We gathered at the balcony to share. Down below the only lights belonged to two Boston whalers bobbing in the waves off the point. Electricity had failed all over Paitilla.

"Ohh, how romantic!" cooed Sarah.

"You're not going to think that when you're finding your way down twenty-three flights of stairs with a candle," Declan pointed out. "You guys do have candles, don't you?"

"Are you kidding? After three weeks of this we have enough to stock a church."

"I would call somebody for help," Mike Vaneya suggested. "Ooooh, that's right. You don't have a phone, either..."

We lit candles around the room. The breeze made them flicker in fitful abandon. In a few minutes our apartment looked like a crowded chapel perched high on a windswept cliff, everyone gathered around the coffee table like pilgrims at an altar while shadows danced on the walls. Or so I tried to force the image. It really looked like a Third World apartment with the lights out.

The last glow faded over the ocean. The horizon disappeared, making it hard to tell which lights were boats on the water and which were stars in the sky. Jem and Evan kept flying planes into the slipstream, now dripping wax on them and betting whose would get the farthest before exploding. Against the blacked-out buildings the tiny tapers let us track the aircraft as they soared over the city.

I looked around and was suddenly glad Rolo had insisted on having a party. In the dark and quiet, with no music or TV or even light to distract us and just people we knew sitting around and laughing, it was easy to see who our friends were. Conversation flowed effortlessly. Jokes bounced back and forth. It was clear that the most memorable part of this assignment would be the people we were with right now.

"You know," Josh said with a sincerity whose irony only he missed, "In the dark like this your place doesn't look so bad. Really, with everyone here and all the candles and stuff, it's almost a nice place." He lifted a glass. *"Salud."*

Maybe the place had character, after all.

18: Isla San Telmo

I WANTED TO fly. I was *burning* to fly. After our disastrous check ride I felt like such a failure that I needed to get airborne in anything just to remind myself what it was like to be a pilot. I needed confidence that I wasn't the buffoon Giverson claimed. The repeat check ride with Fetterman helped, of course, but knowing there would always be a Q-3 on my record scorched my ego. The only way to treat that scorching was to drown it in more flights.

But more flights weren't in the offing, at least not right away. The squadron still didn't have all its planes and Walt was using the ones he had for training other guys. So there was only one option left to me: I went downtown and rented a Cessna at the Paitilla airport. Unusual times called for unusual measures.

That phrase came from Harry, who I met at Paitilla.

Paitilla airport was only blocks from our apartment, perched on the tiny peninsula whose name it bore and now threatened by the popularity of the same. Once comfortably situated and blessed with ocean breezes, by the time I came to Panama it was besieged on three sides by the city. Its single strip was short and cramped, long enough only for light planes used by well-heeled executives to get in and out of the downtown area without having to commute to Tocumen International further up the coast. The runway began at one end of the field next to Calle 32 and ended half a mile later at a jumble of boulders where seagulls nested and waves beat on the shore. Operations were so crowded that on takeoff a forest of high-rises loomed over each wing and a car-choked street pushed the tail. More so than even at Howard, it felt liberating to sail out over the beach and climb into wide-open air above the ocean.

All the bigwigs used Paitilla. Noriega had kept a plane there; in fact, a couple of Navy SEALs had died during the invasion trying to blow it up. But the field was still rundown: the tower leaned; the asphalt was pocked and broken. The city wouldn't upgrade either because the mayor wanted the airport to fail so developers could move in and put up more high-rises. Until that happened any upgrades were catch-as-catch-can.

The only commercial enterprise was a tiny flight club in one corner of a rusty hangar. It taught flying but also rented out planes so I became a member. Guys at the squadron thought I was crazy and I didn't blame them. Join a Panamanian club? Who would knowingly trust Panamanian equipment? A Panaplane might fall out of the sky at any minute from poor upkeep. But I was desperate.

From then on I flew whenever I could, taking a plane out sometimes just to clear my head. I didn't go far, up and down the coast mostly and occasionally out to Contadora, one of the Perlas Islands sixty miles across the water. But just getting in the air helped me forget the bad experience with Giverson. I felt like a pilot again.

Harry also flew at Paitilla. He was a crew chief on the C-27s but like several of the mechanics he had a handful of business ventures on the side. Harry's specialty was in rebuilding planes. In fact, he started going to Paitilla to work on other people's aircraft. At first few of the regulars would even talk to him. He was an excellent mechanic, had a Panamanian wife, and even spoke some of the local language, but until he owned his own plane the Panas treated him like he was domestic help in antebellum Georgia.

Then one day a drug-runner crashed his Skymaster on Veracruz Beach. The DEA confiscated the wreckage and sold it at auction – to Harry, who restored it to mint condition. So now he had his own toy to show off. Soon everyone at the airfield became his friend. Not that the Panas wanted to mooch rides or anything. It was just that most of the people who hung out at Paitilla had money and planes and weren't going to waste time associating with someone who didn't. Having a Skymaster showed Harry to be a man worth talking to. And Harry, once talking, made friends.

Around the time I joined the club one of those friends mentioned that there was great fishing off of Isla San Telmo, another island in the Perlas but farther south. Unlike Contadora, nobody lived on San Telmo. It was a 500-acre paradise covered in forest and decorated with white beaches, stunning coral, and billions of frigate birds, boobies, and pelicans.

The plan was for Federico the banker and Alfredo the restaurant owner (he owned *Las Bovedas,* the former waterfront dungeon where you could enjoy lobster bisque in the same rooms where prisoners once waited to drown) to take their boats out Friday night and position them in the Bahía San Telmo. Then Harry would fly out with a few other moneyed companions on Saturday morning. They would all link up for a day and night of fishing and drinking.

It was a good plan until Thursday afternoon when an AeroCharter Seneca ferrying people to San Blas landed at Paitilla and made a wrong turn at the end of the runway. For some reason the pilot thought there was a taxiway attached to the gravel road that led to the carports where Harry's Skymaster and a number of other planes were parked. There wasn't, and when he spun the plane to reverse course he sprayed gravel against five aircraft and broke the windscreens on all of them. Harry blew a gasket. Then he called me and asked if – since I was a member of the Paitilla aero club and he wasn't – would I rent a plane to fly him and his friends out to San Telmo Saturday morning?

"It's got a dirt airstrip," he explained. "Word has it the druggies use it so it's probably in good shape."

I'd never been to San Telmo but of course said yes.

At the Paitilla flying club Jorge the Elder frowned over his schedule and found a Cessna 182 for me to fly Harry's friends. The 182 was larger than the 172 Jorge used for most of his students. It had more room for guys with fishing gear. It also flew faster with a bigger engine and retractable gear.

The 182 was a good plane but few people rented it. Smaller planes were cheaper. Smaller planes also had fixed gear, meaning the local pilots didn't have to remember to put the gear down each time they landed. That sounds silly but it was true as Jorge could ruefully attest. More than once in the past two years he'd had to replace engines and props because someone ignored the gear warning horn and bellied the plane onto the runway. Recently the 182's only use was by Jorge's twenty-two-year-old son, Jorge the Younger. The son used it in a side job where he shuttled fresh fruit and strippers between Changuinola, San Blas, and the capital. So far he had always remembered to use the gear.

Jorge frowned a lot but it was a good deal for him to rent me his plane. His student load was down and people wrecked his planes so often that he constantly needed cash to get them fixed.

I felt sorry for Jorge – it was the nature of his clientele that most wanted to learn how to fly without working too hard. Rich kids from the city, they bought lessons up until their solo flight and then took off with wild abandon, confident they could "slip the surly bonds of earth" and maneuver like a pro. Usually they couldn't.

His current wrecks were due to solo flights where the students worried less about procedure than image. One was a 152 that the student landed hard, hard enough that he dinged the propeller against the runway, flipping the plane up onto its nose and then over onto its back. He landed hard because he was arguing with his girlfriend who he'd snuck on board so they could fly out over the ocean and join the mile-high club. However, a 152 is small. Having sex in its cabin is as comfortable as in the trunk of a mini-Cooper. Once airborne the couple found that any position conducive to romance was inconvenient for flying the aircraft, so they argued, slapped each other around a bit, and then came back to land in various stages of undress. Harry was on the field that day and said the only good part of the whole incident was getting to help a naked hottie from the wreckage.

The other damaged plane was a 172, the newest in Jorge's fleet. It ran fine until a student pilot returned to the pattern one day and pulled the carb heat lever as he set up to land. Carb heat allows heated air to go to the carburetor so that induction icing doesn't build up at low power settings. The heated air causes an engine to run rougher than usual but that's okay – the plane still flies. Unfortunately the student forgot that. Though he had done exactly as he was supposed to do, he panicked at the sudden change in noise and became convinced the engine was about to fail. *With the airport practically underneath him* he turned west and made an emergency landing in the mud of Panama Bay, a mile from the runway and mere steps from my apartment. It was a nifty bit of flying, we had to give him that. A tricky landing, too, that he was able to walk away from since the tide happened to be out. Unfortunately it was all unnecessary. It would have been easier and less scary just to land the perfectly-running airplane on the runway. Instead, two days and nights went by where a glistening two-year-old Cessna languished in the mud off Avenida Balboa. Until Jorge was able to get the money and the equipment to pull it out, the tide came in twice daily, picked up sewage from the city, swirled it around the forlorn plane in a toxic brew, then retreated with mocking abandon and let the stench ferment. Local fishermen and clam diggers parked their boats alongside the plane to take pictures, steal antennae, and write graffiti on the fuselage. Like I said, I felt sorry for Jorge.

But on that Saturday he was making money and I was getting to fly so any problem with wrecked airplanes was water under the bridge. At daybreak I met Harry and one of his pals at Paitilla. We took off to the south before even the seagulls nestled in the rocks began to stir. The air was calm and heavy and the city sparkled in tropical heat as one by one the lights along Avenida Balboa winked off.

"Mikey! You like beer?" Harry asked. "Anselmo owns Cerveza Panama, he can hook you up!"

The thin man in the back seat corrected Harry that he didn't *own* the brewery, he just managed it, but he smiled nonetheless. It was a thin smile since he was nervous. His eyes almost popped out of his head on take-off and once at altitude the small cabin and high whine of the engine didn't instill any confidence in him that we would make it across a hundred miles of ocean. He also clearly didn't trust me since I didn't own the plane we were in, I just flew it. But he was pleasant enough – Harry didn't hang out with jerks.

We got Isla Pacheca in sight after leveling off at 5,000 feet. Over Contadora we descended and island-hopped at a few hundred feet until getting near the south end of Isla del Rey. Anselmo's eyes went buggy again as he saw the pristine beaches and turquoise water outside his window. This time I didn't blame him. The Perlas chain was heaven as far as I was concerned. In all directions the world was marine blue, emerald green, and corn silk yellow. We were flying around the tropics for free, with no rules to follow or anyone on the ground to complain.

"I think it's over there," Harry pointed.

"Don't we have two more islands to pass? That's what the map says."

"Oh, yeah. Yeah, it's that one, not that one."

"Which one?'

"That one. No, that one over there."

"You don't know where you're going, do you, Harry?"

He smiled. "No."

"Do you at least know which way the airstrip goes?"

He nodded his head vigorously, then shook it and said no to that, too. Fortunately, I knew where the island lay. It wasn't hard – San Telmo was the last in the chain.

We came in from the west and crossed its lonely beaches at five hundred feet. There was a lake in the middle of the island. The lake sat in a bowl surrounded by jungle three hundred yards from the beach. Groups of birds clustered near its edges and stragglers dotted the surface toward the middle. Most flew up as we passed, great clouds of pink, white, and blue that circled the perimeter of the lake and then landed again where they'd taken off.

"There's the strip."

The runway stretched along the beach on the eastern shore. It was less than two thousand feet long with one end stopping at trees and the other open to the water. Federico's and Alfredo's boats were parked in the lagoon nearby. Somebody was in the water. Whoever it was looked up and waved.

"Ah, sweet!" Harry rubbed his hands together. "I like this place already."

"*Paraíso,*" Anselmo nodded. The beauty of the island subsumed his nervousness. He gripped the window edge like a kid shopping for candy and peered down in anticipation.

"You guys picked a great place," I agreed. "Let's see about getting down on the ground."

I set up for a right downwind to land to the north, over the beach approach to the airstrip. Our first approach was just a flyover to give us a chance to see what the surface looked like. Harry was right: it was in decent shape. We looked down and could even see recent tire tracks. Sand and dirt with patches of grass but not even a coconut from the nearby trees to serve as an obstacle. One thing you could say about drug runners: they took their work seriously.

As we flew upwind and turned toward the ocean we passed over another beach half a mile from the lagoon. In the shallow waters offshore was a rusted hulk.

"What the heck is that?"

Harry gestured for me to bank the plane more.

"I don't believe it! It looks like a...like a..."

"*Submarino,*" Anselmo said. Now that we were in a bank his nervousness returned and he looked out the right window from across the seat. "A Japanese submarine from the war."

"You're kidding."

"No. There is good fishing there."

A Japanese sub in Panama. The country surprised me every day.

We circled the wreck and set up for a downwind. The sun threw our shadow across the beach as we passed abeam the airstrip, turning final one mile out.

"Oh, good approach...good approach...nice...smooth...good centerline," Harry rambled as we slipped down final. "Keep it in trim...that's my boy..." I looked at him to suggest he shut up but he directed my attention back out front. "No, no...don't look at me...look there...nice, nice..."

We landed inside the sandbar of the beach, on short grass that fringed the palms. I left the power in to touch down gently but needn't have worried. The sand was firm.

We rolled our way downfield until the grass opened up and showed us the glassy surface of the lagoon. Men from the boats waded ashore to greet us. I smiled. It was only seven a.m. and I was landing on a tropical beach. Life didn't get any better.

"Ohhhhhhhh,..." was all Anselmo could say. He was enraptured with the setting and ecstatic that we hadn't crashed. I wondered how much he got out of the city. He found the jungle on our left side more exciting than the ocean on the right. As soon as we stopped, he crawled out of the plane and trotted over to the trees to stare at them.

"*Magnífico!*" Federico cried as he rushed up to the plane. "*Magnífico!* The landing was *perfect!*" He kissed his fingers and bowed to Harry. "And you are right on time!"

Harry raised his arms and accepted all the praise but then introduced me and admitted I had been flying.

"Federico, this is my friend Mike. *Miguel.* He flies with me at Howard and also at the Paitilla Club. He's going to run back and get Tio and Jacobo."

"And Lincoln!" Federico added.

"Who?"

"Jacobo's son. He's fourteen. He is coming, too. We will show him how men party when our women are not around!"

"Lincoln?" I asked.

"He's a nice boy," Federico insisted. "A little..." he held his hand out limp at the wrist.

Limp-wristed or not, that made three guys I had to fit into the 182.

"You told me there were two," I reminded Harry.

He shrugged. "Two, three...you can make it work."

I hoped they were small and didn't have luggage.

Everyone was nice. I met the whole crowd. Federico and Alfredo had brought a fair number of people with them. Including the two I'd just brought in I counted nine – and there were still two guys waving from the boats. That's when I noticed that Alfredo's boat wasn't just the normal 20-foot fishing toy. It was a yacht, blue with white stripes and seventy feet long if it was an inch. A small crane angled off the bow to lower a dinghy. There were chairs mounted at each side for fishermen to sit and guzzle beer while they waited for sailfish to strike, and a small cabin that sat high amidships for the captain to survey his domain. Plenty of room for a bunch of dudes to party. Federico's boat lacked the accoutrements of Alfredo's but was almost as long. It was white with maroon lines and had a forest of antennae above the cabin that suggested he was never out of touch with his banking affairs. But for a banker the man had a sense of humor: on the stern where owners printed the name of their craft Federico had printed – upside down – *Mí Primer Barco.* My First Boat.

No one offered to have me join them. Nice as they were, I was still the hired help, somebody Harry contracted to fly in their friends. No problem. Had there been women in tiny bikinis anywhere in view I would have begged my way into the party. A dozen guys and beer, though – even in such a pristine setting – held no attraction for me.

"Harry, I'm going to walk down the field and check it out, then head back for the others. I should be back by nine-thirty."

Harry lugged the last of his bags off the plane and nodded okay. He held up his ever-present VHF radio.

"We'll be here, Mikey. Call me when you're inbound."

I ambled upfield to where the cleared surface ended at the jungle, looking for holes or rocks or anything that might trip up an airplane. Then I walked back down the way we had come in to make sure there weren't any hazards there. Anselmo ran over to hug me and say thank you for the wonderful flight. His hands were sandy because he kept picking the stuff up and running it through his fingers. He seemed to be a sensitive type, more enthralled with the birds and the fresh air than the prospect of sipping scotch on the open ocean as night fell. I told him, "Anytime, anytime..." and he went back to join the others on the beach.

The strip was as secure as I could hope for. When I got to the approach end and found no problems I turned back for the plane. The only things of interest were a few trails that led off the cleared area into the jungle, trails that I couldn't see along more than twenty feet into the trees and had no desire to explore. No doubt they ran to the lake.

Getting close to the 182 I saw there were still bags sitting under the left wing. Then, closer still, I saw they weren't bags.

It was a crocodile.

Jorge the Elder had told me there was a crocodile on the island. He said there were rumors that at least one drug-runner or his fuel supplier had been munched and dragged off into the brush over the years. I assumed that was an urban myth until one day a farmer near Barbacoas made the news by being dragged into the canal by a caiman. If a caiman could snatch a human, then a croc just down the road surely could.

Whether or not the island had only one crocodile, if this one had friends he still had to be near the top of the food chain. He was easily ten feet long and two feet across. He must have moved quickly to get out of the brush but now he seemed comfortable in the shade of the wing, resting there without moving, his head off the ground and mouth slightly open.

I stopped and tried to remember what I knew about crocodiles. They could run fast, ate anything, and had no predators. That was about it. Staying fifty feet away, I decided it was enough.

The sun was now well above the horizon. The morning grew hot. Waves on the south shore crashed against the beach with regularity, every sixth or seventh one catching the one in front of it to allow a teasing silence behind both before repeating the cycle. The waves weren't big and neither were the rocks they beat against so the noise was unassuming. It was soothing, in fact, especially since it balanced the cheerless silence of the jungle to my left. These two worlds, the ocean and the jungle, faced off like this without relent. Every hour, every day, every night. The ocean was steady, infinite, and omnipotent; the jungle was secretive and brooding. To imagine them merging was to think of mixing oil with water. It was impossible to imagine for they held the world in balance just as they were. I squatted between them on the sandy airstrip and wondered what to do.

The crocodile was on the left side of the plane near the pilot's door, which I'd left open.

Crap.

No way in hell was I going over there. I looked at the guys on the beach two hundred yards away and thought about calling them over, then decided not to. Most were probably like Anselmo in that they never left the city. If they saw a croc one or two of them might try to pet it or pose nearby for pictures. The last thing I wanted to do was make an emergency run back to the city with a double amputee aboard.

Could they jump, I wondered? I thought back to any nature shows I'd seen where crocodiles dragged wildebeest into the water. No, of course they couldn't jump. Look at those feet, you idiot. Briefly I considered throwing rocks at it to get it to move, then decided that making a modern-day dinosaur mad was probably stupid.

How to get inside my plane?

I inched closer to the tail of the aircraft. The croc didn't move. It wasn't easy to make out if he was looking at me or just staring off into the distance. His eyes were the size of golf balls and protruded from heavy-lidded sockets at an angle to his body. They sat immobile in his head just as he sat immobile on the ground, mouth raised above the dust and open slightly like he was remembering a good joke. The whole animal could have been the product of a taxidermist. For a second, just a second, I considered that this might be an elaborate, fantastic joke and that somebody in the high grass was watching me make a fool of myself. But that moment passed. The eyes were real. They were real and big and as nerve-wrackingly blank as a professional poker player's. They could have been glazed over or reading the label on my guayabera shirt for all I could tell. But they were attached to a croc whose snout was two feet from the left tire so I watched them carefully.

The 182 had tricycle landing gear, meaning it had two main gear and a nose gear. The main gear was directly beneath the pilot's seat but the rest of the fuselage and then the tail stretched a long way back from there. The empennage, the part of the plane between the cabin and the tail, was six feet long itself. Because of that and because it ran parallel to the ground, the tail hung suspended three feet above the sand. It gave me an idea.

Very slowly I moved up to the tail, putting it between me and Godzilla. Getting in front of it, my eyes never leaving the creature under the wing, I leaned my weight on the horizontal stab. More, then more, then...

The nose wheel extended on its strut. With a heave I pushed myself up on the empennage just in front of the tail. The whole aircraft tilted back on the main gear as the tail fell to the ground with a thud.

At the sound the crocodile seemed to wake. He moved his head toward me a fraction of an inch, a small movement that sent a bolt of panic through my body. Only then did I realize that what I was doing wasn't the best idea in the world. I was two feet off the ground and prone, gripping the slender empennage like a retarded stowaway. Stupid, Mike. Really stupid.

But if it was stupid it was time to get it over with. I shimmied up the empennage to the back of the cabin, going around the radio antennae and making my way to the center of the wing. As I got there the center of gravity shifted again. The aircraft flopped back forward onto the nose gear.

Thumpp!

The croc swished his tail as every rivet of the airframe squeaked its protest. Jorge really wouldn't appreciate what I was doing to his plane. But who cared? I was now six feet off the ground and less likely to be eaten.

Nobody on the beach looked my way. The guys were obsessed with the boats. The two men on Alfredo's yacht were struggling with the winch that lowered the dinghy – why they needed it was unclear since both boats sat in only five feet of water and everyone could easily swim to them. But they were wealthy bankers and restaurant owners with two days to kill so the exercise kept them busy.

For a while I sat on top of the plane and watched them. What to do next? From time to time I peered over the left wing in the hope that my companion would remember he'd left his genuine human handbag back at the swamp and go back to get it. But the crocodile returned to statue mode. His head stayed where he'd turned it, pointing toward the tail as though nothing at the nose had happened. One big eye ogled me every time I peeked down from above.

Can I get inside, I wondered? Will the croc try to join me?

I decided to try. The 182 had handles forward of the wing so the pilot could climb up to look in the fuel tanks. I used them to go in the opposite direction. The right front door gaped open so with great care not to fall I climbed down to the right wing strut. From there I could see through the cabin to the far side where the croc seemed content to lie in the dirt.

I needed my plane!

Taking a deep breath I swung across the strut and into the right seat. Instantly I slammed the door behind me – which made no sense since the croc wasn't on that side. The 182 jolted and wobbled. For a moment the left door swung loose on its hinges above the croc's head. I tensed, waiting for a reaction. There was none.

Can he come inside? I asked myself that over and over, crouching down so he couldn't see me. Hell, I didn't know. It probably depended on how hungry he was.

Gingerly, trying not to move the plane, I leaned over the left seat and grabbed the closest part of the open door. With a heave I swung it shut.

BAM!

THAT made the croc move. Not much, but as the door closed I saw his tail through the window. It swished from left to right and panicked me so much I yanked my fingers away from the window to keep them from being bitten off. But the croc didn't attack. He just repositioned, facing the plane now on an angle with his snout only inches from the main gear.

"*Harry, is your radio on?*" I called on fingers-freq, getting the battery up and running.

I looked toward the beach. After two more calls I saw Harry turn away from the water and take his handset out of one of the bags.

"*Hey, Mikey! What's taking so long? You should be gone!*"

"*Uh, yeah. Hey, can you come here for a minute?*"

Harry started up toward the airstrip. Once he was far enough from the other men that they couldn't overhear, I stopped him and told him about the crocodile.

"*No!!*" Harry stood stock-still for a second and then did exactly what all men would. He jogged up the beach to get a closer look. Exactly why I didn't want everyone to know...

"*Well, will you look at him!*"

"I already have. You should have seen what I had to go through to get into the plane."

"I'll bet. What are you going to do?"

"Take off, I guess. I'm assuming he'll move. I just wanted to let you know he was here so you guys don't wander up this way and get munched."

"Yeah! Hey, yeah, that was a good idea. Man, he could eat a horse! Okay! Well, maybe don't land there next time. Stop a little further down."

"Um, I'm thinking there might be more than one, Harry. Just so you know, when I land next time I'm not getting out. Those dudes can haul their own bags."

"Oh, yeah, right. Don't get off the plane. Never get off the plane."

"Alright. See you in a couple of hours."

I stayed in the right seat, starting the engine while leaning over to look out the window and see the reaction. The croc didn't like it at all. Whether it was the noise or the blast from the prop, he turned away immediately and sauntered off. Not fast, not scared, and not far. He moved with the confidence that since no one in the last sixty million years had posed a threat to him this thing probably didn't, either. But it was annoying so he moved.

I taxied forward to the end of the runway and turned around. Out of habit I wanted to use the whole distance. The crocodile stopped, though, just to the right of centerline and didn't move any further. I had a vision that the plane would get up to thirty or forty miles per hour by the time it reached him and he would lunge into the way, causing a crash. Maybe he had experience in this kind of thing. He'd crash a plane and his buds in the grass would high-five each other while they prepared for a hot meal. With that in mind I taxied slowly back down the strip, going around him and sacrificing 300 feet for peace of mind. The croc watched me pass, eyes moving level from left to right like a bail bondsman sure that I'd be coming back to him soon enough. I ran up the engine from there and released the brakes.

"*Good job, Mikey,*" I heard once airborne. "*I'll see if I can chase him away by the time you get back.*"

"Harry, I recommend you leave him alone. Unless you packed a 30.06 in your bag he's more likely to make a meal out of you than you are to make wallets out of him."

"Well, if you call inbound I'll at least tell you if the strip is clear."

"Good enough. See you later."

The skies were quiet heading back to the mainland. Not a cloud marked the horizon in any direction. It was too early even for moisture to rise off the lush Perlas islands and form tell-tale cumulus caps that sailors in centuries past watched for in their search of land. Unhindered, the sun flared in the eastern sky and made the highrises on Punta Paitilla gleam. They were a beacon I could see forty miles away.

Flying in over the bay I made out only a few cars moving on the streets. Panamanians didn't do mornings on Saturdays and Sundays – or Mondays, for that matter. Other days Panama City began stirring by six o'clock but on weekends and the first day of the week those who had stayed in town didn't bother to get up and about before ten at the earliest. On Friday nights there was an exodus from the city as anyone with money headed west along the Pan-American highway to get to their country home, their *fincas*, or to the beach. On Sunday night there was always a migration in the opposite direction. The bridge over the canal at those times was jam-packed. Now, though, on a Saturday morning, the city was mine.

My passengers were ready when I arrived. They stood by the hangar where Noriega's plane had met its end at the hands of the SEALs. None of them was small...and they had a small mountain of luggage

Tio smelled of alcohol. He mumbled hello, then crawled into the back seat and immediately passed out. Jacobo mumbled something about him having a fight with his mistress. Lincoln also got in back while I loaded the luggage. His father took the seat next to me.

"*No me gusta volar,*" was the first thing Lincoln said as we started to taxi. *I don't like to fly.* His father nodded in agreement, implying the concept was clearly insane.

Then why didn't you take the boat, I wanted to reply but instead said something disarming about it being a short flight.

Jorge the Elder walked outside as we started up again. He waved an inquiry: "How's everything going?" the gesture said. I smiled and waved back, hoping he didn't notice the dirt caked on the tail.

We taxied out to the runway, the 182 moving sluggish under the heavy load. The tower controller's microphone button became stuck when we reached the end of the runway so I used the delay to recompute our take-off data for a second time to make sure that we still had enough power to fly. We did, so when the radio opened up again after several minutes of listening to the official describe to a companion how drunk he'd gotten the night before, I called for departure.

"You are a pilot?" Jacobo asked as I pushed up the engine for take-off. It seemed an odd question given the circumstances.

We lifted off to the south, skimming the rocks that lay beyond the crumbling wire fence at the end of the runway and climbing past the gulls who were now up and about. The plane rose smoothly into the warm air, grateful to be off the ground. I banked right to curve a course parallel to the shore, thinking my passengers might like to see the city from this vantage.

"Es tranquilo en la ciudad hoy día," I commented as we leveled off at two thousand feet.

Jacobo looked up from a notepad he was scribbling on and took a quick glance outside. Whatever he saw didn't interest him. He returned to writing. I looked over my shoulder to see if Lincoln, at least, appreciated my efforts. The boy was as prone as the unconscious Tio and the small back seat would allow, having stretched himself across a couple of backpacks that we hadn't been able to fit into the baggage compartment. He pressed his face against the bottom of the window in a valiant effort to enjoy the view but it was clear his heart wasn't in it. His forehead was damp, his cheeks ashen.

"I don't like the city," he croaked. Even as I watched he swallowed hard several times.

"Then look at the ocean."

"I don't like the ocean."

He panted like a dog, mouth hanging open with saliva at the corners. I pointed out the window, hoping he'd look that way and not make me a target of any projectile vomiting.

"Um," I said, trying not to make a big deal of his airsickness. "You know, a lot of people feel off-balance in small planes. If you think you might want to get sick, try to use this." I handed back a couple of heavy-duty paper lunch bags that I'd brought along for just that reason.

Lincoln raised a hand weakly and took the bags, then lunged forward and puked all over the floor behind his father's seat.

"Ay, mi hijo," Jacobo said, embarrassed but not surprised. That was the extent of his reaction and he soon went back to scribbling. I glanced over to see what was so important but it was just a page of numbers. The smell of vomit filled the plane. Lincoln started to apologize but then heaved again, in the same spot on the floor and no closer to either of the lunch bags. The morning was still young and the air calm so there wasn't any turbulence to throw off his aim but I made excuses for him anyway, trying to be nice.

"I don't like turbulence," he agreed in a dying gasp.

I handed back a dish towel that I had brought to clean the windows. Lincoln took it and wiped his mouth. He spewed twice more on the way to the island, the third time yet again on the floor but the fourth time finally into one of the bags. I twisted the swirl cup on my window so the blast of outside air hit me full in the face. It helped but I knew the flight home would be painful.

Ten miles into the flight Jacobo looked up from his note pad and stared at the engine instruments as if one of them had said something rude. He asked me questions about why they read what they did. There isn't much to a 182 so I explained the ops limits to him. His interest was flattering at first but he kept asking "Why?" and that grew annoying. Why is the tachometer at

2200 rpm? Why is there no fuel pressure gauge? Why did the oil pressure have to be at 25 psi instead of 20 psi? Why did I need a turn and slip indicator? The questions were odd. He wasn't asking, for example, how a wing worked – which I could have told him. He was in essence asking why the plane's designers had made it the way they did. Hell, I don't know. Because they did. No matter what answer I gave he came back with "Why?" until I felt inadequate and wondered if I would make a bad parent. Finally, his interest waned. Clearly doubting my abilities, he gave up and returned to his notepad. He didn't seem scared but the way he avoided looking out the window suggested he thought our chances of making it to San Telmo were only fair.

The rest of the flight was uneventful. It wasn't even any fun for me. Normally I enjoyed having passengers because it was someone to share the beauty and adventure of flight with. But today I had a drunk, a skeptical accountant, and an airsick teenager who wanted nothing more than to be back on the ground. And the plane smelled like a slaughterhouse. We stayed above two thousand feet since island-hopping would have been a wasted effort. It might also have sent my passengers into a panic.

"Mikey! Hey, good to see you! We scared the crocodile off!"

Harry called when we were five miles away. Because of our altitude he could see us from the beach. In turn I pointed out our destination to my passengers. Lincoln moaned weakly from the back seat. Jacobo looked up and adjusted his glasses but zeroed in instead on the radio.

"What did he say?" he asked.

"He said the runway is clear."

"But did he say crocodile? *Crocodilio*?"

They had enough on their minds so I lied.

"Oh, no. Crocodile? No, he said, um, they cleared the 'blocks and tile' off. There was some stuff in the way earlier. He's just saying the strip is clear."

Jacobo looked at me out of the corner of his eye. The radio crackled again.

"Yeah, boy. That crocodile was a big one. Easily a man-killer. I think we made him mad, too. But don't worry. We chased him away."

Shut up, Harry.

"Crocodilio?!" Jacobo snapped at the radio.

Before I could say anything there was a shriek from the back seat.

"No me gustan crocodilios!" Lincoln cried. Forgetting his nausea, he sat up in the middle of the seat and gripped the headrests.

"Uh, well, it was just a small one. Don't worry, you won't be staying on the island anyway. You're going on the boats. Let's get ready to land."

"I DON'T LIKE BOATS!"

I looked down as we flew over the airstrip to see a group of men standing in the grass that bordered it. Far from being prudent and staying clear, Harry had alerted the others to the crocodile's presence. Predictably, they'd converged en masse to throw rocks and shout to chase it away. A few were still hefting stones as they peered cautiously into the high grass, looking for a target. The croc was nowhere in sight. Jesus, I thought. Darwin was right.

"Gotcha in sight, buddy! You're clear to land!"

"Um, okay."

There's not much to flying a Cessna 182. To land you just lower the gear and flaps. I turned out over the beach still at 2000 feet and dropped the gear handle.

Nothing happened.

I raised the handle and dropped it again. Nothing.

No problem. I kept flying on a downwind heading and checked the circuit breakers mounted on the dash. There were a dozen of them and they were all in. I pulled out the one marked Lndg Gear and reset it, then tried the gear handle again. Nothing.

Hmm. I tried to figure out how I could have a complete electrical failure to the gear and only the gear. Everything else on the plane was working fine. The flaps, for example, came down smoothly. Nothing came to mind. To buy time, where I should have turned to a base leg in the pattern I just started a wide circle a thousand feet up. I put the gear handle down again and jiggled it.

Jacobo chose to look up from his notepad just then. He watched me play with the gear handle. Before I could say anything he said quietly, “Oh, my god. We’re going to crash.”

The reaction from the back seat was swift.

“I DON’T WANT TO CRASH!” his son wailed.

“Would you two shut up?” I snapped, losing my patience.

Clearly the heavy taxing and the load of an extra passenger had bounced something out of whack back at Paitilla. This is what I got for being a nice guy. Thanks, Harry.

Leaving the gear lever down I reached between the front seats and extended the bar of the emergency gear extension handle. The bar worked like the jack on a car: it was hooked directly to the hydraulic system of the gear and by pumping it you got the gear doors to open and the wheels to come down. You couldn’t raise them again but who cared about that?

With about twenty pumps I got the left main gear in sight out my window. Pressure on the lever grew heavier. Eventually I couldn’t move it anymore. That meant the gear was as far as it was going to go. The only problem was I should have gotten three little green lights on my dash and so far the light for the right main gear stayed out.

“Sir, can you see the landing gear out your window?”

“I don’t know.”

“Well, why don’t you look?”

Jacobo raised his hands to signal that was something he couldn’t do.

“I am not a pilot,” he explained.

I bit my tongue, wondering how these two functioned in the real world. Leaning past him and his computations, I glimpsed the main wheel but couldn’t tell if it was as far out as it needed to be.

"Hey, Harry. We've got a bit of a problem. The gear wouldn't come down so I manually extended it."

"We've got a problem, too. The ice machine on the boat is kaput."

"Did you hear what I said?"

"What, about the gear?"

"Yeah. I'm not sure if it's down."

"Okay."

"I don't get a light for the right main. It looks like it's out but I can't tell for sure."

"The light's out?"

"No, the light works but it's not on. It's not illuminated. The gear may or may not be out, though."

"Huh. You didn't bring any ice, did you?"

"Harry, can we talk about the gear for a second?"

"Okay. You pumped it all the way down?"

"As far as the handle would go."

"So the handle won't move anymore but you don't have a light?"

"That's right."

"Well, you're fucked, then. No, no, just kidding. Fly by and I'll take a look."

We buzzed the field a hundred feet up. Half the men on the ground waved – Harry stood by the sand with the radio held to his ear, watching us go by.

"*Uhhhh,*" he hesitated. *"Come by again. It looks like it's mostly down."*

Mostly down? I did a one-eighty over the submarine and flew back down the strip in the opposite direction.

"*No, it's not down,*" Harry confirmed with confidence. *"It's a few inches short. That's why you're not getting the light."*

"Is the over-center lock engaged? Could you see that?"

"I couldn't see it but there's no way it's engaged. The strut itself isn't straight so there's no way the lock could have fallen into place."

That gave me a twinge of panic. The over-center lock was a steel sleeve that slid down over the pivot arm once the gear was down, preventing it from folding again. If it wasn't in place, there was nothing to stop the gear from coming back up once it touched the ground.

As though we were in a coffee shop, Jacobo started jabbering casually about how he had known all along that flying out to the island was a bad idea and how even before we had taken off he doubted I was a real pilot and felt confident we would all crash and die. He talked about dying as though it were just one more entry in his ledger, rambling on without fear or concern in his voice. The truly weird thing was how explicit he was, imagining not just our deaths but our deaths in a violent, fiery, dismembering fashion whose description would have done Dante proud. I would have stopped him but he was using adjectives I'd never heard before in Spanish, words like *sangriento, destripado,* and *espeluznante* that I made a mental note to remember and try to use in conversation again, should a conversation about horrible accidents ever come up. Oblivious to their effect, he talked on, his every word spiraling his son further into hysteria. The shrieking from the back seat grew epic. Even Tio, drunk as he was, stirred in response.

Accepting that life is a circus and somehow I was in the presence of freaks from the sideshow, I tried to ignore my passengers. This gear thing was a new one to me and I needed time to think. Sadly, the only thought that came to mind was, Are these the people I want to die with? Can't I do better? I would hate to show up at the pearly gates in the company of these two yahoos.

But I stayed calm. I'd had problems with landing gear before and it had always come down eventually. The bad thing here was that I could think of only a couple of things left to do that we hadn't tried yet. And my passengers weren't going to like either one of them.

"Give us a few minutes, Harry. I'm going to g- up the plane and see if I can get it to come down the rest of the way. And by the way, who's the guy in the grass wearing the red shirt?"

"That's Theo," Harry answered. *"Teodoro. He owns the Plaza Paitilla. A good guy to know."*

"In that case tell him the crocodile is about ten feet to his right."

The radio went silent but not before I heard Harry yelling at the top of his voice.

G'ing up the plane meant changing the flight vector quickly so that centrifugal force increased. It would increase on every component of the plane – and on us inside the cabin – but maybe it would force the right wheel down, too.

"Um, don't be afraid about what I'm about to do," I explained to Jacobo and Lincoln. "We just have to maneuver the plane a little to see if we can fix the gear."

The warning was wasted. As soon as I went into a shallow dive and then pulled up sharply, both passengers clutched their hearts and let me know in their individual ways that cardiac arrest can be measured in decibels. I tried that three times, each time going steeper and pulling up harder. Jacobo let out a soprano *wooooo-wooooo-wooooo* and then chanted something unintelligible. Lincoln wailed like a sack full of cats on the way to the river before collapsing between the seats. Even Tio came to momentarily. As we dove, his chin rose from his chest and his eyes opened long enough to gaze unfocused at the scene. Then I would pull back on the stick and his head would fall again. After the third time of doing that he grabbed one of the airsick bags that Lincoln so far had ignored and puked into it. Then he passed out again.

We flew back over the runway where Harry pronounced the effort unsuccessful.

That was it. Time for the last trick. I flew around the pattern and leveled out on final approach, advising Harry to keep his friends clear. Keeping the power in, I made an otherwise normal approach and bounced the plane down on the left main gear. Jacobo clutched at the controls in his panic so that I had to swat him back with my right hand. The bounce threw us back in the air and we ballooned, rising six feet above the runway and floating a moment before sinking back down. I added a touch of power to keep us from hitting too hard the second time. With that technique we bounced four times on the sole main gear – Jacobo flailing each time, me hitting him in response, his son screaming in my ear. Then we climbed out and flew over Harry again.

"*Nope,*" he pronounced. "*Good flying, though. I should practice that.*"

"*Well, Harry, I don't know what else to do,*" I admitted.

"*You could land gear up,*" he suggested.

"*And we would get the plane back to Panama how, exactly?*"

He thought about that. For several minutes we sat on either end of the radio wondering how to get out of this situation. Finally, he called me back.

"*Land,*" he said.

"*What?*"

"*Land. Just land the thing.*"

"*What if the gear collapses?*"

"*What if it does? Stay on the good side as long as you can then let the wing down slow. Even if it digs in you probably won't cartwheel.*"

"*What do you mean, I 'probably' won't cartwheel?*"

"*I mean, you probably won't. Look at it this way,*" he argued, "*if you go back to Paitilla the same thing could happen. It's concrete back there. Which would you rather crash on, a concrete runway or a sand strip? We have scotch.*"

His logic was lacking in every respect.

"*They have fire trucks back there,*" I protested.

Raucous laughter came through the static.

"*PANAMANIAN fire trucks!*"

"*Look, if I lock the handle down, will the hydraulic pressure keep the gear from collapsing?*"

"*Absolutely. Maybe. Who knows?*"

I didn't know what to do.

"*Well, should I try it?*"

Harry's shrug was audible. "*Unusual times call for unusual measures, my friend.*"

That was the attitude that had gotten me into this situation. However, what made up my mind was the realization that by flying back to Paitilla airport not only would I have to suffer the company of Jacobo and Lincoln on the way but that once back over the city I would have to go through the agony of explaining my predicament to a Panamanian control tower and whatever Keystone Kops emergency response team they would field to deal with it. Crashing on an island beach seemed not so bad by comparison.

"*Okay,*" I called into the mike. *"We'll land. But no matter what happens, Harry, don't let me be eaten by a crocodile. Otherwise I'll come back and haunt you forever."*

With that, I flew over the submarine one more time and entered a box pattern. On final I jammed the handle of the manual gear lever under a brace on my seat so it couldn't go anywhere and possibly release pressure from the gear. Jacobo buried his face in his notebook. Lincoln curled into a fetal position on the back seat and sobbed. We won't crash, I vowed to myself. *I refuse to die with people like this.*

But no one died. After all my worrying the landing was uneventful. The left gear touched first and I held the right off as long as I could while friction slowed us down. When airflow over the wing slowed so much that the ailerons lost their effectiveness, I lowered the right wing gently until the wheel on that side touched sand.

I held my breath.

The gear didn't collapse. It compressed, then compressed further, but didn't collapse. It certainly didn't feel right taxing with the front windscreen canted at a crazy angle to the horizon but the strut stayed extended. It was only when we stopped close to the crowd of cheering businessmen that the manual lever snapped free and pressure from the extension system escaped, making us lean further and further to the right as the gear began to fold.

Harry ran to the plane even before we stopped. He saw immediately what was happening. As I killed the engine he grabbed the wingtip and yelled for the other guys to help him.

They rushed forward with the enthusiasm of men normally confined to offices, suddenly thrilled to have a mission in the outside world. Together they grabbed the right wing strut and held us up before the wing could hit the ground. Harry then seized a rock the size of his head and with two great blows on the strut that only a certified airplane mechanic could feel comfortable with, he straightened the scissor arm and knocked the over-center lock into place.

The men cheered. That felt good. Giverson could kiss my ass.

"You'll have to explain that dent to Jorge the Elder," Harry said. He held my door open for me but I refused to get out.

"It'll be easier than explaining why I flew to San Telmo and came back in a boat," I replied.

Jacobo climbed out onto the sand and greeted his friends as though nothing had happened. Lincoln staggered out, too, vomit clinging to his shirt and pants. Alfredo took one look at him and said, "You're swimming to the boat."

Lincoln replied that he didn't like swimming but no one paid any attention.

They unloaded the bags. Tio woke up, said hello as though he had just dozed off a moment before, and climbed down to the ground on his own. Rubbing his eyes, he looked around and set off without a word toward the water.

The businessmen grabbed their bags and followed him. Several made jokes about the grisly smell from the cabin but no one offered to do anything about it. After checking for giant lizards in the vicinity I broke down and hopped out to clean the cabin myself, throwing sand at anything that looked suspicious and then scraping it out the door. The smell lingered all the same.

Harry clapped me on the back before rejoining his friends.

"Alright, Mikey! Good job. Thanks for backing me up on this one."

"Good job? That's all you can say? I just kept a plane from crashing, Harry!"

"Yeah, but you didn't bring any ice. And obviously you upset the passengers because your rental now smells like a hospital."

"Harry, damn it! You didn't tell me about the extra guy, you didn't tell me about all the bags... This had better not become a habit! That every time we do something together you withhold information that threatens to kill me."

"Oh, Mikey. It was just the gear! And you should be grateful. If it weren't for me you would have been bored up there, flying around looking at scenery all the time."

I started to snap back at him and then thought about it. He was right. And why was I flying that Cessna in the first place?

"Alright," I mumbled, adding weakly, "but some of the scenery is nice." Before he could respond I pointed a finger in his chest. "Okay, I'm flying back to the city now. If my engine quits and I ditch in the ocean, DON'T come and get me. You'll probably toss me a life preserver and forget to mention that there's a piano attached to it."

Harry laughed and made a sweeping motion with his arms to indicate the runway was all mine.

"Fly safe, Mikey. I'll drink a scotch for you."

"You do that. And don't get eaten by crocodiles."

He scoffed. "There's only one here and we scared the daylights out of him already. He won't come back down to the beach for weeks."

I took off to the south and made a left turn over the bay, flying high over the pair of yachts and returning waves to the men in the dinghy as they paddled themselves out to their boats. Harry and a few others – including Lincoln – had stripped down to their underwear and were swimming. The water they were in was so clear I could see to the bottom of the bay with its rippled sand curving in parallel lines toward the beach. The reflection from the sky turned the surface turquoise, with bands of green and purple near the coral that flanked the entrance to the cove. The surface was smooth enough that the small wake thrown up by the dinghy rolled in soft waves all the way to the golden sand on the empty beach and the runway that lay beyond.

And in the grass beside the runway the crocodile reappeared. He crawled into sight near the midpoint of the runway then moved ponderously out onto the strip exactly where he had been before when the airplane was parked, where now there lay a pile of mixed-up sand and whatever Lincoln had had for breakfast. And this time he wasn't alone. Four more crocs appeared like logs in the grass, widely separated and moving in parallel toward the airstrip, each as big as the first, as though a bell had sounded and it was time for them to gather in the sun. There would be no landing now.

I keyed the radio to tell Harry then changed my mind. I would tell him when we met again in the city.

19. Snakes

Once I passed my check ride I was a pilot, meaning I was an aircraft commander. Technically that meant I didn't need to fly with an instructor and could command missions on my own from the left seat. However, that was really only true on paper.

In reality, once I passed my check ride I was still a co-pilot. The squadron had a policy that new guys – no matter how much flight experience they had before coming to Panama – had to operate as a copilot and fly from the right seat until they gained a hundred hours of experience in the plane. Getting a hundred hours could take months so even though I was checked out as a pilot it was going to be a while before I was in charge.

While I was waiting, Jem upgraded from copilot to aircraft commander. He didn't want to: he liked being a copilot where he could fly all he wanted but not have to make decisions. Being in charge made him nervous.

But the commander didn't ask for Jem's opinion. At one point when Flutie was grounded for one of his many illnesses, Lt Col Rasmussen needed another pilot and tapped Jem to upgrade. Jem did as he was told, of course, and went through the upgrade training with no problem. But for his first mission in the left seat he wanted an easy mission, something that was boring, predictable, and devoid of any adventure. A chance for him to warm up to the responsibility. He didn't want to go to Colombia, he didn't want to go to Peru: he wanted something close and familiar to minimize the chance that he might do something dumb, different, or dangerous.

Walt met him partway. Walt was the C-27 scheduler and for Jem's cherry flight Walt sent him to the Darien, a remote section of Panama that held the thickest jungle north of the Colombian border. It was close so that was good. But the airstrip was also new to Jem and so were the people he was supposed to collect there. That was different.

His task was to land in a place called Yaviza and pick up a bunch of biologists doing a species count for the Barro Colorado research station. The biologists were a motley group, a youngish crowd from the States who believed that research is enhanced if it's conducted in flip-flops and shorts and while wearing a goatee. For all their knowledge of bugs and reptiles, though, they had a laissez-faire approach to transporting their collections. Jem's first wrong decision as pilot in charge was to allow them to load onto the plane carrying hand-tied shoe boxes and milk crates filled with all manner of creepy crawly things. That was dumb.

Ignoring the obvious risk, he next let the scientists talk him into flying gently and as low as possible so that none of the "samples" froze in the C-27's notoriously cold cabin, or died of hypoxia. "We need to keep them alive," they urged him. Jem, anxious to please, accommodated them. After takeoff he stayed low to keep the temperature up and flew slow enough that they could open the doors and get sunlight inside. That kept all the animals alive. It also kept them alert. That was dangerous.

Eventually, due to turbulence or a packing deficiency some of the critters got loose.

Junior Flats was the loadmaster. Mild-mannered and bookish, he stayed calm at first. He even helped the scientists corral the wayward specimens. Most just skittered across the floor, anyway, looking for a dark place to hide. Those were easy to pick up. Others were more of a challenge, hopping or running or occasionally taking wing. Junior shuffled around with the flip-floppers, finding humor in the situation as some of the bugs made them look like kids going after a greased pig. He collected grasshoppers, beetles, and even a turtle with no problem.

But when someone handed him a supposedly-empty canvas bag and the snake inside it struck and bit him on the hand, the humor stopped. Junior lost all self-control. The snake was a sabanera and not poisonous but Junior didn't know that. The only thing that registered was that a four-foot-long creature of the jungle had just sunk fangs into his flesh. We had all heard stories about two-steppers and Junior's active imagination gave him only moments to live.

In the ensuing chaos two more crates overturned. Reptiles and spiders and even butterflies went in all directions. Already angry, now Junior panicked. He wrapped his hand and grabbed a broom and shouted for the scientists to stay clear. Then he began smashing and swatting anything that moved. Rare or not, if it was within reach he killed it or trapped it and swept it out the troop doors into the ocean below. He thought he was a goner anyway so in the few minutes he had remaining he wanted to get revenge on as many of the little bastards as he could.

The biologists went ballistic. That was six months of hard work that Junior was pushing into the slipstream. When he wouldn't stop they rebelled and rushed him en masse, causing an extended struggle that even JC, the copilot, couldn't break up. People only let go of each other and snapped out of their rage when Jem sounded the ditching horn and pulled a 3G turn, causing everyone to grab for handholds to keep from going out the door themselves. By then over half the specimens had performed a free-fall to oblivion.

The scientists were apoplectic. It's a wonder they didn't throw Junior into the ocean himself. For his part Junior cursed the biologists in terms so colorful you'd have thought he spent his college years working on a dock rather than attending class. In time he reflected on the incident and apologized. But not all of us blamed him for over-reacting. As he explained, "That snake freaked me out."

The story didn't end there. By the time the plane landed the biologists could no longer account for their collection. Nobody knew how many specimens went out the door so nobody knew how many were supposed to be in the boxes. All the scientists could do was gather up what they could, search the cabin for strays, and go home. Nobody considered that they might have missed one.

That they did in fact miss one became obvious two weeks later when Flutie and Kevin Berne used the same plane to fly an instrument sortie around the local area. During the flight a patoca slithered into the cockpit. A patoca is a pit viper, easily one of the Top Ten most dangerous snakes within a thousand miles of my downtown apartment. They had just leveled off at two thousand feet over Taboga Island and headed toward the international airport when Kevin saw the black-and-red reptile writhe around the center panel and head for his boots.

"Aughh!" he yelled and sucked his feet away from the rudder pedals. The snake coiled and struck. It missed Kevin's leg but hit the control column hard enough to make it hum. Kevin jumped even further and hopped up onto his seat. From there he leaped over the snake and down into the cabin.

Flutie was left saying, "What the...?" but when he too saw the snake he followed Kevin in a flash. From then on the patoca was in control of the airplane.

It took them a while to figure that one out. They could stand by the cockpit steps and peer out the front window so they knew they weren't going to hit anything but meanwhile the plane wasn't going anywhere but straight ahead. Even their headsets lay on the floor up front. Through them they could hear the incredulous controller calling them again and again demanding, "Shark 21, where are you going?" as they buzzed the airport and then the eastern suburbs of the city.

The patoca coiled below the radar display and showed no sign of leaving. Occasionally it made forays under the center panel but always stayed in the cockpit so Flutie and Kevin were left to play rock-paper-scissors over who should try to regain his seat first.

Somewhere over Portobelo they worked out a solution. It was messy and involved a cargo strap, the water cooler, and most of the contents of a fire extinguisher but before their fuel got too low they were able to take back the plane.

Back on the ground our mechanics needed five days to dismantle the aircraft from inside out and resolve that no more residents of the wild kingdom lurked there. It was Dale's plane and he was meticulous, removing each panel in turn while Tyrel stood by with a heavy blanket and a can of pepper spray. No more animals were found.

Nevertheless after that no one felt comfortable flying that particular C-27. For a long time it was standard procedure whenever we had it for a trip to climb to 20,000 feet as quickly as possible, put on the oxygen masks, and then depressurize for ten minutes. We hoped the thin air would kill or at least knock unconscious whatever product of our nightmares still hid beneath the floorboards plotting another hijacking.

Of course, nobody liked snakes – in the air or on the ground. We saw them on the ground a lot. They were all over the air base because the jungle was all over and the jungle was their home. With frightening regularity they appeared where people least expected them and either bit somebody, scared the hell out of them, or caused chaos and panic.

Where you lived on base determined which species of snake you feared most. In the housing areas it was boa constrictors that kept folks up at night. There were also fer de lances and bushmasters and coral snakes among the duplexes on Commissary Hill but they usually kept to themselves – boas, on the other hand, wandered with abandon. Since they could grow up to a dozen feet long kids routinely ran panic-stricken into their house yelling that there was a "monster snake" in the yard.

Day or night, boas cruised through neighborhoods like burglars scoping out targets. Mostly they were harmless. They even did the residents a favor by keeping the rodent population down. But the fact that the trains ran on time didn't keep Mussolini popular and boas had a similar image problem, especially when every now and then they snacked on a family pet. People were supposed to bring their dogs and cats indoors at night to keep them from getting in the way of the base police but every so often someone left Princess tied on a leash outside the maid's quarters. In the morning when Princess was gone and in its place was a somnolent snake the thickness of a blanket roll, horror stories spread anew.

Some of the stories weren't exaggerated. One day I stopped by Declan's for a beer and on my way back down the hill encountered a constrictor that stretched the width of the road. It lay there on the concrete, the picture of relaxation, thinking whatever snakes think and not at all worried about wide-eyed bystanders. Since there was no way to pass without rolling over it I stopped my car and waited. I would have gotten out for a better look but lacked the nerve.

Another car stopped from the other direction. The other driver waited with me for the boa to move.

After a while it did. Paying no attention to either of us, it made its way slowly into the jungle that bordered the pavement, slithering in a lazy S that looked more concerned with style than forward movement. The most unsettling thing was that it disappeared the instant it left the road. It truly disappeared, vanishing into choked foliage that had lain undisturbed since Balboa lost his head. We stared at the high grass where the tail dropped from sight, the innocent, lightly-waving grass that gave no hint of anything sinister behind its screen. We wondered what else lay down there, what else lurked only five feet from the road, camouflaged in terrain yet capable of swallowing the spare tire on my truck. We also traded horrified guesses of how much a ten-foot-long reptile ate to keep up its strength.

By the stables and the elementary school people tended to encounter bushmasters. More than one horse was bitten in the stalls or just outside. Riders watched the ground carefully whenever they mucked the place clean. On a jog past the stables one day I saw a dozen people scatter from the building as though a fire drill was in progress. Someone had seen the black saddle-like design moving in the hay so everyone ran like hell.

On the flight line neither boas nor bushmasters were a problem. We weren't sure why unless it was the fact that the terrain there was lower and therefore wetter and maybe not to their liking. The base proper and the runway sat on the wide bottom of a basin that stretched from Commissary Hill to Cerro Verde and the land south of Arraiján. The low elevation drew water to it. Twice a day every day when the skies soaked the earth water collected on the plain before running to the ocean.

The acres of concrete we all worked on didn't help distribute the moisture. When rain poured down the flight line became a reflecting pool. Currents formed at cross-purposes and rushed across the pavement, finally escaping via the drainage ditches at the perimeter fence. From one to two each afternoon, those filled up: the culvert outside our squadron, for example, ran as swift and deep as a mountain stream. All that water left the airfield and poured into the jungle on its way to the beach. The result was that the land around the runway was never dry. Fer de lances and coral snakes loved it that way.

At the north end of Runway 36 was a dip into marshland and then a quick climb into trees and the hills behind the school. On the ramp nearby was where we parked the C-27s. That was where we encountered fer de lances, what the locals called the *"equis"* because of the x-marks on the snake's back.

Crew chiefs saw them the most. We parked our planes toward the grass which meant we had to back out every time we left the chocks. To marshal us out, the crew chiefs would stand thirty feet off the nose in the grass and close to the tree line. More than once I watched one of our guys stroll nonchalantly onto the lawn and raise his arms to signal that he was ready for us to reverse the props – then suddenly leap like a ballerina and dash for the tarmac in great curving hops.

Fer de lances could be long, up to nine feet, but in our area they never got that big. Most were no more than a foot. It was hard to see them even when the lawn was mowed. Guys could be on top of them before they knew it. The terror that encounter inspired made even big men move like gazelles. Nobody needed to be reminded that fer de lances were the deadliest snake in the jungle, or that they struck so fast that even a mongoose (which bests cobras without breaking a sweat) stood only a fifty-fifty chance of getting away unscathed. In all the time I was in Panama only Bob Harcourt was actually bitten by one but that didn't slow down anyone else.

At the south end of the runway was the swamp leading to Veracruz Beach. That was coral snake country. The Army guys vouched for that because they worked at that end of the ramp and often encountered the creatures. Mostly it was the maintainers again, the helicopter mechanics who spent all day out on the ramp, but on at least one occasion one of the Huey pilots got up close and personal with the second-deadliest two-stepper in the country.

It happened because the Huey had a small air scoop low on the chin bubble that ventilated the cockpit. The scoop had a grill over it but the grills fell off and weren't considered important enough to replace. One day a coral snake saw the hole and thought it would be a good place to explore.

Walt and I were in a plane on Taxiway Delta that morning. As we waited to take off we watched a pair of Huey pilots trot out to their birds. They hopped into their choppers, started engines, and hovered over to the runway. But suddenly the second helo dropped to the ramp so hard it bounced on its skids. With the rotor still turning at full speed, the pilot leaped from the cockpit and fled across the concrete without looking back. His aircraft trembled and wavered behind him, light on its skids. Once, catching rotor wash from its wingman, it even lifted several inches and held a not-bad hover over the grass.

Knowing they had to do something, mechanics gathered around the helicopter in a wide perimeter and tried to hem it in. They couldn't, of course, so instead they weaved and dodged in unison with the plane as it twisted unpredictably on the ramp. Walt got on the radio and called out a play-by-play to our guys back at the ops desk: "Oh, one of them's making a move...he's on his feet but no! The helicopter saw him coming and spun around!...He's falling back...falling back...*rejected!!*...Now they're giving ground...collapsing on the left but feinting on the right... this is a close one, ladies and gentlemen...I think the helo's got the upper hand..."

The soldiers danced for a while but didn't move in because no one could figure out what to do or how to approach the Huey. They looked like reluctant Indians circling a wary buffalo. Finally the first pilot parked his own helicopter and ran over to help. Avoiding the tail, he peered through the window to learn the snake's whereabouts and then killed the throttle using the co-pilot's collective. Then even he backed off. When we started our takeoff roll the whole group of them was still at a safe distance, sitting on the ramp observing the empty chopper and pointing occasionally at where they thought the snake might be. Wisely, they awaited someone with more knowledge of reptiles and a very long stick.

20. Flutie

I COULDN'T DECIDE whether to like Flutie or not. He was too quiet and shy, with movements that would try a sloth's patience and a personality as vapid as the de-humidifying pellets we all put in our closets. So quiet he could finish a crew brief before you knew he'd started. So dry that if you needed motivation to face a flight you had best find religion fast because it wouldn't be coming from him. On his best days he resembled an idiot-savant who had left the savant at home. On his worst days no one was sure he was conscious. The saying goes that it's better to stay silent and let people think you're a fool than to open your mouth and confirm it, but in Flutie's case the home truth didn't work in his favor.

It didn't work in his favor, either, that he had bad luck, at least with regard to staying healthy. A week after coming to Panama he walked through a spider web in the hangar and received a bite on the cheek from its owner. Within minutes his face swelled and went numb. The numbness faded but the side that was bitten remained paralyzed. He looked and talked and drooled like a stroke victim chewing antacids. The doctors shrugged. Wait it out, they said. So Flutie did, and we did, too, patiently waiting for his super powers to develop and hounding him to crawl up a wall. "Come on, give it a try," we would urge. Mystic Pete, the commander's exec, was less subtle. Whenever Flutie walked into the orderly room Pete would launch from his desk and drag himself across the carpet, growling "*I am NOT an animal!!*" For a month although he stayed on flight status we kept Flutie as far from the teams and from passengers as we could. It's one thing, after all, to think your pilot is a drooling idiot: it's another for him to hop down from the cockpit and prove it.

The venom wasn't gone a week before Jem suggested a fishing trip to Lago Gatún to catch peacock bass. Flutie dug out his fishing tackle for an inventory. As he strung out lines and hooks and leaders the Pinheads' rental agent, Dixie, arrived with her Jack Russell terrier, Jack Russell. The dog tore into the house and plowed through Flutie's fishing line, sending tackle flying. One leader whipped around and snagged Flutie in the butt. He yelped, scaring the dog who moved even faster and thus tore a chunk from Flutie's behind. Consistent with his previous wound, this one became infected. The same doctors who shrugged before went for surgery on this round, carving out a biblical pound of flesh and leaving Flutie with a bandage the size of an adult diaper. The diaper was Flutie's distinguishing characteristic for a long time. That and yoghurt. His first prescription of antibiotics was filled incorrectly and he ended up taking more than he should have. The medicine killed all the bacteria in his body (including the good kind) so to replenish his supply the doctors made him eat plain yoghurt for weeks. We got used to seeing him waddle through the squadron in oversized pants, clutching a white plastic container with some French label on the front and dribbling yoghurt as he re-learned how to eat with both sides of his mouth. It's a wonder he survived. After he fought a bout of dengue fever and took bird strikes on three successive flights, we decided the man was a menace to himself.

But in one regard fortune smiled on Flutie. The man made money. He had a knack for falling into wise investments and business opportunities and was on his way to being a millionaire before he was thirty. The worst part was he didn't even try. He started out by selling his '77 El Camino upon arrival in Panama after a dock worker told him it would be destroyed on the roads or stolen. He took the money and bought a beater, then on a whim dumped the excess into a Guatemalan savings account when the banks there were offering 60% monthly interest rates in an attempt to beat inflation. Other people lost their accounts to corruption and the exchange rate but somehow Flutie skated by and doubled his money in a matter of weeks. He then loaned it to Vince, who embarked on the short-lived but blindingly successful venture of the Ho-Boat, a floating brothel that serviced container ships waiting to transit the Canal. For two months Vince pulled in money faster than he could count it, putting so many El Chorillo prostitutes on one 40-foot Bayliner that when it pulled away from the Yacht Club you would have thought it would sink as soon as the ropes were untied. He and Flutie and the handful of other investors pulled stakes before the authorities shut the business down – not for breaking any laws but because their bribes weren't high enough – and Flutie moved on. This time he put all his money into the stock of a little-known startup company called Dell Computer – which would have been a brilliant feat of prescience except that he had been trying to buy Tell Commuter, a tiny Canadian company developing electric cars that went bankrupt before the end of the year. But since Flutie's wallet had the luck of half the Irish Republic, his father's geriatric stockbroker misunderstood him over the phone and bought Dell instead. It seemed everything he touched turned to gold...if it didn't put him in the hospital.

But despite his quirks – or perhaps because of them – he was a good pilot. He'd been in the second aircraft when Brad Giverson's formation accidentally raided a working coca lab in Putumayu province and provoked a shoot-out that lasted six hours. Giverson took off and left his team on the ground but Flutie went in and got them back out before too much damage was done. Jerry Miner, the loadmaster on that mission, said Flutie panicked at first and mentally departed the fix for a while but still did some "balls-on flying." Asked what he meant by "mentally departed the fix," Jerry muttered something equally revelatory about "cloud cuckoo land" and twirled his finger by his head. Well, that wasn't news. We knew Flutie was weird. Even in the cockpit he would say oddball things like how he preferred the artificial horizon to the real one because "you never know what the real one is going to do." The good thing to hear was that he could be weird and fly at the same time. Only half of being a pilot is knowing how to fly the plane, after all. The other half is being able to do it when things go wrong, "being able to keep your head when all about you are losing theirs." Charlie Manson thought Flutie was a dolt and believed that the reason he could operate during emergencies was because his brain only processed information on half-hour cycles. Charlie maintained that "If you keep your head when all about you are losing theirs, there's a good chance you haven't grasped the situation." Maybe so, but I still found that preferable to the explosiveness of a Fetterman or the irrational exuberance of a Walt.

My first flight with Flutie was when we flew into Bagua in Peru, early in my tour when the government there was just beginning to act on its touchiness over U.S. involvement in the drug wars. I'd already flown to Colombia twice with Walt and once with Josh so had some idea of what it meant to fly in the Amazon. Peru was new, though, and I looked forward to seeing the country.

As usual, the friction with the government wasn't personal. On the ground we almost never encountered hostility from the locals in any of the countries we flew into. This was especially true in Peru.

But on the ground we were people: in the air we were American military. Put us in an airplane and the friendliness turned to distrust, suspicion, and hair-trigger insecurity that everything we did had a hidden purpose and every flight we made was a spy mission rather than simple cargo hauling. We couldn't blame them. Hell, back in the States a tour of AM radio on any given night showed that many Americans think the military has captured space aliens and flies black helicopters around the countryside to eavesdrop on citizens and mutilate cattle. The same military that supposedly "bumbled" its way through Vietnam, Grenada, and Panama somehow is smart enough and disciplined enough to cover up world-class conspiracies in its own back yard. With that kind of culture back home we could hardly think poorly of Peru.

Factions in the Lima government fed the insecurity. Factions in the Peruvian military did, too. Different airspace sector commanders gave their troops different instructions on how to deal with us, resulting in a roll of the dice every time we went somewhere. It was always a dilemma for us whether to be open and above-board on our flight plans and on the radios and simply tell the truth about where we were going, or withhold information that we thought might be a problem. The dilemma was that if we told the truth, some commander somewhere might deny us clearance and we would end up returning to Panama or to Lima with our cargo or passengers, where we would get chewed out by the Air Operations Center for having wasted gas and time and for delaying some operation at the radar sites. If we "left out" pertinent information in order to get a clearance, sometimes we would surprise the local commanders by landing at airfields in their region or, worse, fly in and out again and be back in Panama City before they even learned about the sortie, if they learned about it at all. Depending on the commander his reaction might be to laugh away the incident. Or it might be to suck up the current humiliation and plan a reaction to the next "incursion." It was a stupid game of conflicting policies and personalities in a country with no central control. We knew it was just a matter of time before the misunderstandings caused a problem.

The danger increased when Alberto Fujimori took control of the country. He instituted a shoot-on-sight policy for unidentified aircraft flying through Peruvian airspace. It was a policy that made sense in a narrow way: throughout the 1980's and early '90s so many drug runners made flights through that part of the Amazon basin that some mornings parts of eastern Peru looked like an Oshkosh fly-in. But the policy was loopy in a broader sense because it demanded that honest flyers adhere to a system that didn't exist. If a pilot filed a flight plan in Lima for a trip to Iquitos, for example, he had to fly through eight sectors of airspace to get there – and there was no guarantee that his flight information would be sent to any of them. Once he took off it was anybody's guess if the Peruvian Air Force (FAP) would know he was coming.

Shooting down unidentified planes made the politicians feel good but it didn't address why most of the planes were unidentified in the first place, which was because the air control system was so disorganized. Between my arrival in Panama in the summer of 1990 and the following February, the FAP shot down 17 light aircraft that we knew about. Most were probably smugglers. Since they usually crashed into the jungle and were never recovered it was hard to be sure. At least one was a missionary and his family whose float plane was shot into the Huallaga River and then strafed. Another was a politician from Cochabamba on his way to a wedding.

The FAP trumpeted its successes and blamed mistakes on people who refused to follow the rules. Since the rules were confusing and few people knew them that was easy to do. Drug flights decreased a little, lending credence to their claims. However, since the basin was so huge and dangerous already most smugglers just took the FAP as another risk to be dealt with. They varied their routes, flew lower and faster, and painted their planes to blend in with the canopy.

For us in the U.S. Air Force that risk was supposed to be mitigated through close cooperation with our Peruvian allies. But we knew tragedy could happen whether we followed the rules or not. So with only vague guidance from the AOC every crew who flew into Peru used its own best judgment as to how to act.

Flutie never seemed aware that a threat existed.

Bagua was in northern Peru, east of the Rio Marañon in the Utcubamba Valley. It wasn't a big town. It wasn't a town at all, just a village on the edge of the jungle with a tortuous dirt road that doubled as a runway for its last quarter-mile into the main street. There was no reason to go there and no reason to end up there: in fact, it was hard to end up there since even the local buses only went to the next town fifteen miles up the road. But someone looking at a map saw the hollow blue circle that marked a sometime-in-the-past runway and thought it might be a good jumping-off place for a nearby radar site so they sent a squad of SEALs down to nose around and get the local color. That in itself was stupid, a poor use of assets like the SEALs even if they were only the guys from Team 8 and nobody special. They had gotten in there by commercial plane, boat, bus, and a good deal of walking; now the AOC wanted to get them out by C-27.

The trouble started in Panama. Garb Taylor, our clearance expert, figured that since Bagua was in northern Peru there was no reason for us to fly past it down to Lima, one of the three official "ports of entry," just to turn around and fly back north. Equally, there was no reason to fly as far east as Iquitos, another port of entry, when we had no reason to go there. (The third port of entry, Arequipa, was down near Chile and out of the question.) So he tried to make arrangements for us to fly into Quito, refuel, and then go direct to Bagua.

It says something about Garb's stunning lack of judgment that he came up with this plan at all. Fly an American military plane – which most Peruvians didn't want in their airspace, anyway – into the capital of Peru's sworn enemy – Ecuador – and then take it directly to an uncontrolled field in the Peruvian hinterlands where it would be obscured from any official Peruvian oversight? Not likely. It was like approving a Russian flight from Havana direct to Elko, Nevada during the Cold War.

But it says something also about Garb's ability to work the system that initially he got us clearance. At least, he got us clearance in the sense that all the papers that needed to be signed had signatures and all the phone calls that needed to be made were made. In other words, on paper we were legal. Unfortunately, the inescapable fact of Peruvian bureaucracy was that nobody was ever sure who was in charge of something. Even if you had clearance from one person there was no assurance that another official might not send an Army patrol to arrest you or launch a MiG-23 to intercept your plane.

On this occasion Garb's plan made it as far as Major Byron's desk. Major Lloyd Byron was our squadron assistant director of operations or ADO, Lt Col Rasmussen's #3 man. He'd come to Panama two months after me. Rasmussen didn't like him but that didn't mean they weren't able to mesh professionally. It just meant that Byron's days were numbered. Everybody knew it, including him.

Byron came out of black operations just as Rasmussen had. None of us at the foot soldier level knew what that meant and nobody enquired. He never elaborated, either. In fact he seemed to have blotted that part of his life from memory, preferring instead to dwell on his time in AC-130 gunships where he spent most of his career.

Gunship guys love to reminisce about their days making things explode and Byron was no exception. He had gun camera video tapes from the invasion that he kept in his office and would show to anyone who asked. Sometimes he would show them to you even if you didn't ask: I was walking by his office one day when he jumped out and grabbed me, saying, "Here, Bleriot, you've got to see this. A 30mm round right through the engine block – then look: we cut this guy in half as he's running away!" He was unique in our squadron in that he didn't view flying as an end in itself: he saw it as a means by which he could shoot something. He was also rare in that he was one of only a few of us who cared about medals. Dale Kweasey and Big Bud were the others. Dale wanted medals because they could speed his promotion; Big Bud liked them because they were round; and Byron craved them because he figured if he accumulated enough he would be a hero and thus have the clout to move back to an assignment he enjoyed – like flying something that killed people and blew things up.

In a nutshell Byron was friendly, flew alright, and seemed to know how to keep a squadron running without making a lot of fuss. His only quirk other than a penchant for carnage was that he was quiet. Not quiet the way Bob Harcourt or Story Earnhardt were quiet, but odd quiet, quiet at the wrong times like when you asked him a question and instead of answering he would just turn and walk away. Your girlfriend does that; people in charge of military units aren't supposed to. He was also apt to make peculiar observations or jokes at inappropriate times. There was the day a bunch of us lieutenants were sitting around the scheduling desk, talking about how ugly Evan's new girlfriend was and listening to Major Harmon defend her with the comment that "Beauty is only a light switch away." All of a sudden Major Byron appeared out of nowhere. "And death is only a 105mm howitzer round away," he whispered to a suddenly-hushed room, then darted out the door. We were left wondering if he was a sociopath or just had a poor sense of timing.

If the former, he was a sociopath with an eye for detail. He recognized that while the Peruvian right hand might say it was alright to fly into an uncontrolled airfield from Quito, the Peruvian left hand would freak out and start grabbing weapons once we did. So he had Garb re-submit a clearance request to route us through Iquitos with no stop in Ecuador first.

I didn't mind going to Iquitos. Though it added hours to our flight time I operated with the belief that the worst time in the air is better than the best time on the ground. Ozzie Oswald was our loadmaster, #91-0103 was our plane, and the weather was good enough that even with two gas stops we should have no trouble getting down and back in one day.

We took off at daybreak and by nine in the morning were overhead Quito.

"Hey!" said Flutie, looking down at the city from 20,000 feet and speaking his first words in two hours, "you know what we should do? We should go land there anyway, just to make the point." He looked up at me wide-eyed, like a child who's just suggested we celebrate Christmas early but keep it a secret from everyone else.

I didn't know him that well and wasn't sure what point he was talking about, so I just stared back and waited for him to continue. He didn't and forgot about the idea in a few minutes. We flew on to Peru.

The trouble that started with Garb germinated in Iquitos. On the ground we were able to get fuel but when we tried to submit a flight plan to Bagua the airfield manager balked.

"*No se puede ir a Bagua,*" he argued. "*No hay torre.*"

"But that's where we're going," Flutie countered.

"But you cannot go to Bagua," the controller said again. "There is no tower there."

"But that's where we're going," Flutie repeated, as though he'd just thought of it for the first time.

The conversation went on like that. About the fourth round I broke in. Flutie's Spanish was good but limited. That and his natural lethargy kept him from adopting a new tack. I pulled out our flight plan from Panama, the one that had Garb's diplomatic clearance number on it.

"Sir," I said. "We have a diplomatic clearance number. We have clearance from Lima to go to Bagua."

The controller took the flight plan and studied it. He picked up the phone, called someone, and explained to the person on the other end what our flight plan said. When he finished, the other person spoke at length. Our controller nodded and said "ahhh" several times as he listened. Then he hung up.

"*No se puede ir a Bagua,*" he concluded. "*No hay torre.*"

The problem was with the flight plan he wanted us to fill out. It was a Peruvian military flight plan. It mirrored the standard civilian form, the one used by the International Civil Aviation Organization, or ICAO, and also had the same information that our U.S. Military Form 1801 had, except that in the block where we had to supply the ICAO identifier for our destination airfield he wouldn't accept "XXXX." The problem was that Bagua wasn't – as the controller kept telling us – an actual airfield. It was just a road masquerading as a runway. The ICAO didn't give identifiers to roads. So Bagua didn't have one. For us it wasn't a problem. Whenever we intended to land somewhere without an identifier we just put "XXXX" on the 1801 and then explained in the Remarks field at the bottom of the page what that stood for. The controller shook his head. Not good enough. If what we put in the box didn't match something on the chart on his desk, we couldn't go there.

"How about Bagua Grande?" I asked. Bagua Grande was just down the road from Bagua – which meant a good two hours by four-wheel-drive – but it had an airstrip that showed up on the map.

The controller looked at his own map, thought about it, then shook his head.

"*No se puede ir a Bagua, no hay torre,*" we all repeated together.

"Okay," Flutie shrugged. "What would you like us to put there? *Qué quiere Ud.?*"

The man was confused.

"We'll put whatever you want. *Qué quiere?*"

The man shrugged. He didn't want anything.

"Dude, what are you doing?"

"Well, he just needs something in the box. Let's just put something. Here..."

He jotted some letters down and then slid the flight plan back to the controller.

"There. Problem solved."

The controller looked at the identifier Flutie had scribbled. B-G-U-A. He scratched his head and, clearly frustrated, said "*No, no.*"

"I don't think it's that simple," I suggested.

Flutie gave me his kid-on-Christmas face again. "Why not?"

He took the flight plan back, erased B-G-U-A, and wrote F-L-U-T instead.

"There. Is that better?"

The controller consulted his list of identifiers. When he winced, I looked over his shoulder.

"Dude, that's somewhere in South Africa."

"Really? Cool!"

"No, see...I think he needs more than just some letters," I said. "He needs to show that we're going somewhere he recognizes. He doesn't recognize Bagua as a field so we can't go there. And we're obviously not going to Pretoria. We need to enter another field's identifier – preferably one that starts with an "S-P" – that he knows. Otherwise, we can't take off."

It took a while but slowly Flutie's eyes focused.

"So...the – only – way..."

"That we can leave..." I prompted.

"Is to tell him we're going somewhere else!"

"Right."

"Hmm. How about SPQT?"

"That's Iquitos. We're already here."

"Oh. Well, we could tell him we're just going to fly around for a while and then come back."

My face told him what I thought of that idea.

"Okay, okay."

I pulled the low chart from my pocket and started scanning for airfields.

"How about Pucallpa?"

"Great! Uh, where is it? South, right?"

I avoided looking at the controller, feeling guilty that we were conspiring to lie right in front of him and getting away with it only because he didn't speak English.

"Yeah, south."

"S-P-C-L," Flutie wrote carefully in the blocks on the flight plan.

"Of course," I added belatedly, "that might have its own set of problems."

"You mean because when we don't show up in Pucallpa they'll get worried?"

"Or mad."

Flutie considered that. He was in charge so ultimate responsibility for any international incident lay with him. Then he shrugged and giggled.

"Ahhh. We can always call them airborne after the pick-up and tell them we changed our minds," he suggested.

I was doubtful but agreed.

"Okay!" Flutie was happy now, relieved not to have to think about it anymore. Giving the controller a reassuring wink, he slid the flight plan back across the desk.

The controller studied it.

"*Pucallpa*?" he asked suspiciously. "*Uds. van a Pucallpa*?"

"*Sí!*" Flutie chirped. "There's a tower there!"

Once airborne we forgot all about flight plans. There was too much to look at out the window. The sky was blue, the clouds were white, and scattered thunderstorms with their verga stretching almost to the jungle floor stood like wickets on a lawn for us to fly between as we cruised west toward the Rio Marañon.

We had plenty of gas and made the trip at 5,000 feet, dropping lower when clouds got in the way and climbing back up when it got hot inside the cockpit. When the Marañon came in sight we flew north of Lagunas, sitting on the east bank of the Huallaga River below where it fed the Marañon, then split the V of the two rivers and headed out over more virgin forest in a straight line to Bagua. Out here there was no way to have turnpoints that meant anything. We flew solely off our map: we knew we had to go west, and if we hit another big river (it could only be the Marañon again) we would turn left and look for landmarks. Lindbergh would have been right at home.

About mid-afternoon Ozzie spoke up. Finally. He'd been in a bad mood all day, sulking in the cabin, his silence adding to the lack of conversation that marked our entire flight.

At least what was bothering him wasn't anything Flutie or I had said. Instead, he'd had his ego bruised by a civilian. The previous afternoon he had stopped at the Burger King on base and gotten to the counter at the same time as a contract crew from Evergreen Air. Evergreen was a commercial cargo hauler that flew a lot of contracts for the U.S. government. People who didn't know any better whispered that Evergreen was a "CIA front operation." It flew stretch C-130s around the theater and at least one plane came through Howard every week. The crews were invariably retired military, career cargo haulers, with decades of experience behind them. It wasn't unusual to encounter a pilot or loadmaster with upwards of 20,000 hours of flying time, which was something since most guys could be on active-duty for twenty years and be lucky to have a quarter of that. Depending on your point of view, 20,000 hours was either something to be proud of or just the opposite. It might mean you were an experienced flyer but since you could only get that much time by flying cargo – which usually means on autopilot high up – a lot of us took the view that it meant you were well-rested.

I never liked the hours contest. In the Air Force, cargo guys flaunted their time airborne by sewing it to the top of the command patch they wore velcroed to their flight suit. Thus, it was common to see guys walk around with "3000" or "4000" or whatever stuck above the MAC patch. When I was in C-5s it was a permanent nightmare of mine that I might stick around long enough to get that many hours. In rebellion I made a patch that said "57" on top of it. It took all of two days before a colonel saw it and chewed my ass.

Because they spent so much time at altitude eating box lunches and sleeping in their seats, Evergreen fliers were almost always slouching, seedy, walking advertisements for Weight Watchers. The day before, as Ozzie started to order his lunch a huge Evergreen loadmaster with a gut so big his flight suit wouldn't zip all the way up moved to the counter next to him.

"Hey!" he barked at the teenager by the register. "Gimme two whoppers, two large fries, one of them apple thingies, and a super Coke. To go." Then he looked down at Ozzie, noticing him for the first time. "Hey, there, Air Force! How goes the war?" he shouted, and peered around to see Ozzie's name tag and command patch. Ozzie had been in C-141s before coming to the Chuck and proudly wore a 2000-hour tag above his TAC patch.

The Evergreen load exploded in laughter. "*2000 hours*? Hell, son! I've got more time than that on the shitter!"

So Ozzie was in a bad mood today. He spent the whole morning sulking in the cabin, staring out the window and thinking of comebacks he should have made. But just past Lagunas he called out traffic.

Flutie was flying. Instinctively he nosed us over toward the trees.

"Where?"

"10 o'clock low, going to nine. Maybe five miles."

Flutie craned his neck to see as we descended through 3,000 feet. All our planes were painted the dark green-and-black camouflage that worked beautifully against trees but made us stand out like a fly on the ceiling against tropical sky. It was always good to be low.

"Oh," he said calmly, slowing our descent. "It's only an Antonov. *Grupo Ocho*."

"Who?" I asked.

"*Grupo Ocho*. Group 8. Military. The People's Express of the Amazon Basin. They fly civilians around the boonies for cheap."

"They fly into Lagunas?"

"It qualifies." He leveled us at 2,000 feet. "It should head off to the south."

"It's banking this way," Ozzie disagreed.

"It shouldn't," I answered. "There are no towns this way."

We continued at 2,000.

"It's an Antonov 26," Flutie said as though it mattered. "Good airplane. A Russian knockoff of the C-130. The Herc-ski." He giggled.

I leaned forward to see around him. The gray silhouette of the twin-engine transport was just below the horizon about three miles distant. It was banking again, angling toward us but falling behind.

"We're this way," I suggested.

"Yeah," Ozzie added. "He might be checking us out."

Which was no big deal. When you flew around the middle of nowhere it was always comforting to see another plane in the sky. Pilots, being pilots, would be curious to know who their company was. Except that inherent to my tentativeness was guilt again. We were supposed to be flying south, not west, and now we had been spotted.

After a minute or two, during which it became obvious the Antonov couldn't keep pace with us and wouldn't get any closer than three miles unless we turned around – which we weren't going to do – the other pilots banked away and continued on their journey.

"You suppose they'll call anybody?" I asked Flutie.

He looked at me wordlessly, then turned his attention back to the sky out front which he stared at for a long time with his mouth hanging open. It was his thoughtful pose.

"Un-hnn-unh," he replied eventually.

I scanned the low chart. "We should have picked a field west instead of south. One far away, to give us more time. If he lands and calls the controllers in Lima, they might start looking for us."

Ozzie came up front.

"Hey, are we talking to anybody?"

"No, why?"

"Just wondered. I don't like the Peruvian Air Force checking us out."

"He was just curious."

"Yeah, well. Maj Harmon says they aren't too happy with us these days. Not us C-27s, us Americans. He says they've been intercepting the photo planes more often lately – and those guys have more clout than we do."

"He didn't intercept us. He's a commuter on his way to drop off another shipment of pigs and goats."

Ozzie shrugged. "I'm not worried if you're not. I just figured he might have buds who fly MiGs."

We flew west for another hour, nothing below us but trees and nothing in the air save the occasional hawk. It wasn't until the terrain started to climb slowly from the south, anticipating the Andes rising up ahead, that Flutie spoke again.

"You suppose they'll call anybody?" he asked.

The rising terrain was in an area called Jumbilla, named after the regional prefecture. The town itself was on the northern end of a ridge off of which ran rivers in all directions, dropping into the jungle and sooner or later circling around to the north to feed the Marañon. One of those rivers was the Utcubamba. It fell away to the northwest, carving out a valley and leading to the town we were looking for.

We went around Jumbilla to the north, staying over the jungle. When Flutie hit the Rio Marañon we turned left, cruised south over the old Peru-Ecuador border at the foothills of the Condor Mountains, then hung another left when we saw the Chinchipe River. The Chinchipe fed the Marañon and the Utcubamba, forming a perfect four-way intersection that we couldn't have missed if we tried. Bagua was another five miles on.

"Gear down," Flutie called.

Bagua was as big in real life as it was on the map, which is to say it was quite small, a crescent of homes facing a common yard. With no more than a dozen structures it looked like a retreat for outcasts. Even the river avoided the town, swinging south around the ridge.

Two bridges crossed arroyos west of the village. To the east the lone road ran in a straight line between the river and the jungle. It was narrow and rocky and from overhead seemed canted left to right, sloping toward the river. I wondered what kind of planes ever landed on it.

The river basin was low and locked in the sun's rays. The whole scene shimmered with heat.

"Can you see anybody?" Ozzie asked over the intercom.

"A naked kid," I replied. "No, two."

"I meant SEALs. How about the guys we're here to pick up?"

Flutie and I strained to pick out figures as we flew over the village. The houses were nice in the sense that they were sturdy. Wood, clay, and plaster went a long way toward keeping the shantytown label at arm's length. The roofs were thatch with the occasional sheet of corrugated tin. Small pens alongside each building held either a garden or a goat. When we passed over the village the naked kids waved.

"No, no gringos."

"No panel, either."

The signal that we were safe to land was supposed to be a VS-17 panel, a bright orange strip of plastic routinely used to mark landing and drop zones. The closest this village came was some hanging laundry.

We circled and passed over again. More people came out of the houses to stare at us. None were American.

Flutie leveled out and stared out front again.

"That sucks," he sighed.

"Maybe they got the pick-up time mixed-up," Ozzie suggested. "Maybe they don't know it's today."

They're SEALs, I thought. Not likely. Besides, looking down at the sun-baked valley with nothing but a muddy village and jungle, whoever I was if I knew my ride was coming I would damned sure be on time to meet it.

"Well, I wasn't going to mention this earlier," I announced, "since it didn't seem to matter, but I grabbed a map off the desk at Iquitos and it's not the same as ours. Our map shows a dirt strip at Bagua and nothing at Bagua Grande, but the Peruvian map shows the reverse."

"Huh?"

"It shows nothing here, but a strip at Grande. Fifteen miles that way," I pointed.

Flutie's mouth hung open again. I really began to wonder how he'd gotten through pilot training.

"You think they got mixed up?"

"They did or we did. Either way, they're not here."

"We've got gas," Ozzie pointed out.

Flutie picked out his favorite spot on the windscreen and gave it some more attention.

"Okay," he shrugged, and pointed us up the valley. I waved good-bye to the kids.

The road we had planned to land on turned from a jeep trail to a hiking path and then to a proving course for mountain goats as it snaked along the embankment on the north side of the river. At times it ran along inclines so sheer only the trees kept it from washing away. Eventually it curved down into the valley again where it crossed several feeder streams until Bagua Grande came into sight.

"That's the town?" Ozzie asked.

"That's it."

A collection of houses appeared in the bottom of the valley. It was only slightly bigger than Bagua but apparently that was enough to merit its name.

"Anybody see anything? Anybody? Bueller? Bueller?"

"I see the airstrip," Ozzie pointed. On the south side of the river a second trail widened before reaching the town. It wasn't much of a runway but someone had cut back the brush within the last month. It paralleled the water and came down the valley from the direction of Jumbilla.

Flutie straightened in his seat. "Oh, yeah. That'll do."

"And there are our boys!"

Most of the SEALs were clustered in the shade of a tree midway up the strip. They had the VS-17 panel stretched across the ground in front of them. That alone would have been enough to identify them but as an added measure two members of the group were stripped to their shorts and laid out comfortably on the ground, sunbathing. Locals didn't do that. They certainly didn't do it wearing Ray-Bans.

We landed to the west and rolled to the end of the strip where Flutie spun us in a one-eighty. The only excitement was that the strip had swells in it that we hadn't seen from the air – they bounced us like a carnival ride as we slowed.

Ozzie moved to the ramp holding his stomach. "These guys owe us beer," he muttered.

Flutie limited his comments to, "Whoa." He always looked like he couldn't believe he had just survived his latest maneuver – which inspired no confidence in me at all.

As the dust settled we made out a half-dozen townspeople who came to the edge of the airstrip to watch us land. They were in a white Mazda pick-up, most piled into the bed. After parking, one guy balanced a small boom-box radio on the roof and they all started dancing.

His radio made me think of something. I pulled out the button for our HF radio, listened to some chatter on 11176, then flipped through the frequencies for Lima Control until I got to 10285 and heard voices. Most of it was soup-can quality, like we had string eight hundred miles long connecting us to the capital. But after a while I heard someone calling for Shark 21.

"Damn."

"Huh?"

"Lima's calling for us."

"Huh?"

I stared at him. "Does your brain operate at a different speed than the rest of ours?"

He giggled. "Why?"

"Because sometimes I'm not sure you're all there. I said, Lima Control is calling us on the HF radio."

"Oh."

"I feel bad about not answering him," I pressed.

Flutie considered that. "So answer."

"What do you want me to tell him?"

"Um, tell him we're at Bagua Grande?"

I wasn't going to do that. The cardinal rule in any airspace lacking radar was never to tell anybody where you were unless you could get something out of it.

"How about if we call him as we're crossing the border?"

Flutie shrugged.

But soon the chatter through the ionosphere told us that wouldn't work. The controller in Lima had determined we weren't at Pucallpa. He apparently called Iquitos, where our buddy behind the counter must have mentioned that we had been interested in Bagua. Then, lo and behold, someone somewhere heard from the Antonov that we had been heading that way. Their system was better than we thought.

"I think he knows we're in Bagua," I said, concentrating hard to make out what the controller was saying. His Spanish, already faint on the frequency, rose and fell with the sci-fi squeals of short wave transmissions. But who was he talking to? He sounded like he was giving someone directions.

The SEALs piled on like we were the hotel courtesy bus taking them to the beach. One of them put on the headset Ozzie offered him. In exchange he handed Ozzie a case of Cuzqueña.

"Hey, pilot, this is the team leader. Thanks for picking us up!"

"No sweat," said Flutie.

"We were a little worried. The chief couldn't remember who told him it was this town, especially after we saw this runway. It doesn't look very level."

Flutie giggled. "Yeah."

The controller was talking to someone on the ground, that much was clear. Someone in Chiclayo, a city on the coast 200 miles away. That didn't make sense to me since we hadn't put Chiclayo on any flight plan. But then I assumed it was just because Chiclayo was the biggest town around. Maybe they had a regional air control center there.

"Hey, they brought us beer!" Ozzie called from the back.

"Yeah, it's the least we could do," the team leader said. "Sorry it's warm. And there's a couple missing. We drank all our own and dipped into yours. Good thing you showed up when you did or you'd be out of luck!"

"In the hell-hole it goes," said Ozzie. "It'll be cold by Ecuador. Hey, sir. You want me to do a walk-around? See if we have any leaks or anything?"

"Sure."

"Load's off-comm, going off the ramp."

"Pilot, how long is the flight?" the team leader asked.

"An hour 'til gas, then three hours after that. We'll be home around nine."

"...noreste ciento ochenta kilómetros...veinte minutos...tenemos cuatro..."

There was a long burst of static and the sound of squelch breaking repeatedly. Another voice.

"...ya han despegado...están al aire..."

Who had already taken off? It could have been us except he mentioned four aircraft.

There followed a long exchange about some kind of authorization. Chiclayo was having trouble receiving Lima and I was having trouble hearing either one of them. Thinking we were causing some kind of rescue operation to kick off, I decided to break in.

"Lima control, Lima control. Este es Shark Veinte-Uno en uno-cero-dos-ocho-cinco."

There was a pause, then... *"Shark 21, dónde está? Cuál es su posición?"*

I thought about lying but figured it was too late, particularly if they were launching search-and-rescue aircraft.

"Señor, estámos en Bagua Grande en este momento."

"Bagua Grande? Bagua Grande? Qué hace en Bagua Grande?" Another pause. *"No tiene autorización aterizar en Bagua Grande! Su plan de vuelo..."*

The rest of his transmission cut in and out but the gist was clear. He was angry. So that's what they were saying about authorization, I decided. Well, we could claim it was a mix-up with the Iquitos controller. The AOC had given us the dip clearance number, after all.

I tried calling Lima back to explain and mollify the controller if it was possible. He didn't respond. Not to me, anyway. He went back to talking to the ground controller in Chiclayo and the two of them became very animated. It was impossible to make out just what they were talking about and frustrating that neither would acknowledge my calls. We still had mountains between us so while they had relatively clear transmissions up and down the coast, our radio was only picking up about every third word, especially from the Chiclayo station. Chiclayo told Lima something about us arriving in fifteen minutes, which made no sense. And he continued to ask about authorization. Why wouldn't they accept that we had authorization? We had our dip clearance number.

And then in three words, it all became clear.

"...autorización a tirar..."

I had been reading off the wrong sheet of music. Hell, I'd been reading from the wrong book entirely.

"You know," the team leader was saying. "This Cuzquena's even better than Cristal. A lot of local beers..."

"Hey!" I interrupted. "Shut up! Pilot, they're sending interceptors!"

Flutie looked at me like I'd grown a second nose.

"What?"

"That guy on the radio. He's talking to Chiclayo. They're really pissed, and Chiclayo's sending interceptors. He just gave them authorization to shoot!"

Flutie's eyes nearly bugged out of his head.

"You're shittin' me."

"You speak Spanish. Listen to this guy!"

Flutie pulled up the button on his radio. Lima was still broken and Chiclayo was worse, but the Chiclayo operator's words were clear. He told his partner in Lima that one aircraft had turned back, but three more were ten minutes away from us.

And he confirmed that the pilots knew they had authorization to shoot.

"Okay, okay, okay. Calm down," Flutie said, as much to himself as anyone else. He held his hands out to emphasize his calmness. "No big deal. It's a big jungle. They don't even know where we are. Nothing to worry about."

"Actually, they know where we are," I said.

"How?"

"Well, I kind of just told them we were here..."

"You *what*?"

"Well, he asked," I replied weakly.

Flutie's mouth dropped open again.

"Hey, you guys are messing around, right?" the team leader asked. He poked his head up into the cockpit with a grin on his face, obviously remembering how his guys had hopped onto a plane in Salinas one night to find the entire crew stark naked. He was a Navy lieutenant named Dave with sandy hair, a deep tan, and a jade turtle hanging from a string around his neck. I had met him at language school and knew he was one step removed from Spicoli in *Fast Times at Ridgemont High*. Give him a surf board and he would look at home on a San Diego beach.

But Flutie finally snapped out of his coma.

"Sit down! *Ozzie!*"

He rapped hard on his side window, where Ozzie was just about to crawl under the nose to check out the landing gear doors. The loadmaster looked up unconcerned.

"Get the fuck on board!" Flutie yelled.

We started to roll while Ozzie was still closing the cargo door. Flutie aimed us along the edge of the strip where the dips and crests weren't as severe. I managed the controls while he steered. We bounced twice. On the third launch the C-27 stayed airborne.

"Ohhhhhhhhhhh..." he moaned from the left seat.

"North?" I asked.

He scrabbled for the map.

"Northwest! Turn around!"

I twisted us into a right-180 and flew back down the valley toward the Marañon. Flutie's plan was simple. The border with Ecuador was closest in that direction. We had to get out of Peru.

As we crossed the Marañon, Ozzie – read into the situation with only a minimum of screaming – spotted approaching aircraft from the southwest.

"Where?" the SEALs shouted, fighting with each other for space at the portholes on the left side.

"How far, Ozzie?"

"Uhhh, five miles? Maybe four. They're just coming over that hill at nine o'clock."

"MiGs? Are they MiGs?" Flutie barked, as serious as I'd ever seen him. He started mumbling to himself with his finger still triggering the intercom: *"...I hope they're MiGs...I hope they're MiGs..."*

"Why the hell do you hope they're MiGs?" I demanded in disbelief.

If the Peruvian aircraft were MiGs they were either MiG-21s or MiG-23s, more likely the former. Either aircraft was a formidable hunter especially to someone flying a cumbersome cargo plane. Much as I loved the C-27, it was no match for something that could pull 7Gs and break the sound barrier.

Flutie twisted his head around as far as he could to see back to our eight o'clock. He didn't answer right away but jabbed his finger straight ahead to encourage me to go faster. I steered us up the Chinchipe Valley at 100 feet above the ground. There was a dirt road on the left side of the valley: a lone man in a donkey-drawn cart looked up in surprise as we passed.

"'Cuz MiGs are *fighters*," he said, his voice panicky but with enough inflection to tell me how little he thought of jet jockeys. "And fighter guys suck." I looked unconvinced so he added, "They hate getting close to the ground."

I wondered if that wasn't wishful thinking. However, Flutie had been to a couple of Red Flags and to the tactical course at St. Joe so he knew what he was talking about.

The town of San Ignacio was up ahead. I couldn't see it yet but knew it was on the left side of the valley so slipped to the right.

"Hey! Bank the other way!" Ozzie called.

"I don't want to go the other way!"

"Well, I can't see! How can I tell you if they saw us if I can't see?"

"Look out the right side!"

"Oh."

I gave him time to move across the cabin. The SEALs reacted faster and were hogging all the windows there so there was a brief scuffle. Propelled by adrenalin Ozzie shoved two of the Navy's finest out of the way. I entered a shallow bank right.

"Oh, shit!" told us all we needed to know.

"How far, Ozzie? Give us something that helps."

"Okay." Our loadmaster collected himself. "They're not MiGs," he said carefully. "Smaller. They look like those trainers."

"Which trainers?" I asked.

"*Our* trainers. The ones that used to come into Altus to do patterns. You know, from Vance?"

Vance was a pilot training base in Oklahoma. My first thought was that the pursuers were F-5s, which looked a lot like the T-38s. Looking at Flutie I could see he was confused as well. Then, simultaneously, our brains clicked.

"Super Tweets!"

Super Tweets were an attack version of the T-37. They had T-38 engines without the afterburner and could carry a formidable array of small bombs and rockets, not to mention nose-mounted 7.62mm Gatling-style machine guns. They didn't stand up well to disciplined anti-aircraft artillery but fortunately most of their targets in the Third World were villages and encampments that lacked real AAA. They were the perfect resistance-quelling platform. And they flew well at low altitudes.

"Crap!" Flutie yelled, banging his head against the seat back while he pounded the map on his leg. "Crap, crap, crap, crap, crap!"

"I can't see them anymore," Ozzie advised, his panic growing. "They went to our six o'clock. If you lower the ramp I can keep them in sight."

"If I lower the ramp we'll slow down," I disagreed, imagining the swirling parasite drag that would develop.

"Oh, right. Never mind. Hey, you guys have guns?" The last question was directed to the team. They must have said no because Ozzie's next comment was a bitter, "What kind of SEALs are you?"

"Where we going, pilot?" I asked, reaching over to slap him on the shoulder.

Flutie stopped banging his head and looked out front. We had a long way to go to the border but the terrain was rising. Our barometric altimeter passed three thousand feet. The mountains were good in one sense: more terrain to fly around and slip over. The problem was we had to climb. That slowed us down.

"Right turn!" he said, staring straight ahead. I banked but he wanted more. "Break right!"

I tipped the wings to ninety degrees and pulled. Our airspeed plummeted but the nose came around. Flutie was pointing us into a ravine that spilled down toward the Chinchipe. It rose but not as steeply as the hills to the northwest. I could see the crest of the pass already.

"*Whooahh!* Found 'em!" Ozzie yelled.

I looked right. The first Tweet was half a mile away, slightly higher and in a dramatic jink upward to compensate for our sudden turn. He now had too much overtake and wasn't going to be able to hold the five o'clock position he'd chosen. The other two were higher and a mile back. As the lead Tweet broke off his approach, the second one banked to roll in on us.

"Lead's going away," I told Flutie. "Two's four o-clock high and rolling in."

But the second fighter's approach was interrupted by us flying into the ravine. Now he had to roll around the right wall himself, which left him with a shortened firing pass as his nose pointed down, arced right, and then came up to keep from hitting the ground. He fired, though, not wanting to miss the opportunity. Flutie and I knew it the instant he did. The bullets tore chunks of rock from a slide on the right slope.

"*Mother f-....!*" Flutie yelled, and followed that up with a torrent of obscenities that he must have been saving up for months. He grabbed the controls and pulled hard. Our nose shot toward the sky. The airspeed bled off to nothing, the needle dropping below 40 and then bouncing around, confused. I had no idea what he was doing. Before we could stall I shoved forward again. Flutie didn't protest – by then he was pushing over himself. We topped an imaginary rise like the lead car on a roller coaster before it makes its big plunge.

The Tweet pilot must have been terrified. He fired then pulled up to keep from hitting the ground, only to see the C-27 suddenly climb toward him and fill his windscreen. He broke hard right still trying to climb, shot past us, and barely missed a tree jutting from the ravine wall as his plane wobbled on the edge of a stall. Lucky for him, we had almost reached the pass. He cleared it with twenty feet to spare and disappeared on the other side. Whatever seat cushion he had must have been sucked so far up his rectum it would take him an hour to pull it out.

We followed the Tweet, not having any choice. Pushing over reduced our drag and we accelerated again, dropping over the pass to see the jet curving down over the trees and then climbing high to the right. At that moment I had no idea where the other two planes were.

"He shot at us!" I exclaimed, then repeated it because I couldn't believe it.

"Yeah."

"They're actually trying to kill us? Why?"

Flutie fluttered his hand over the center panel, wildly pointing at the map on his leg.

"Because *you* told them we were going to Pucallpa!"

I started to protest and then remembered the fighters.

"Where now?"

"Keep the mountains on the left."

"Isn't the border closer to the west?" I argued.

Flutie nodded but overcome by excitement could only mime his response. He waved his arms to signify we had to climb, then did it again.

"Dude, I don't know what that means."

He spluttered his words.

"Up there we have to climb, get slow. Accelerate...better than them...down here. My controls."

He tossed me the map.

Flutie had a point. The whole reason for turboprop engines is to combine the advantages of jet engines with propellers. Jet engines are efficient at high altitudes but props bite into the thicker air down low and allow for better pick-up. Although the AT-37s could maneuver with us and fly faster, we could accelerate quicker. Each time we threw them off with a move they weren't expecting they would overshoot or – second-best – have to pull their nose up and re-compute a firing solution. As long as we could stay fast and unpredictable we would have a chance.

So we hoped.

"Fast, fast, fast, fast,..." Flutie urged our plane on. "Fast, fast, fast, fast, *SLOW...*"

Without warning he chopped the power and jinked hard left. He must have been telepathic because seconds later there was a roar and whine above the sound of our own engines as one of the jets passed us high and right. I never saw any bullets but had to assume the Peruvian had started shooting.

"The terrain climbs again," I warned, breaking away from the window to check the map.

"Low!" Flutie shouted. He bunted again, pulling the nose up so that we climbed 100 feet then instantly pushing over. Back in the cabin we heard someone hit the ceiling. Right after that he pulled up again – and that same someone hit the floor. This time Flutie stood the plane on its right wing as we whiffer-dilled down toward the hills below us. Walt would have been proud.

"Low!" he shouted again.

"You want low ground?"

"Low, low, low, low, low!" He'd lost the ability to form complete sentences.

"Um, okay. Go back to the left."

"I got one!" Ozzie yelled. "No, two! One's wide right for a mile, going away. One's closer...BREAK RIGHT! BREAK RIGHT!"

We didn't have the speed yet for a decent break but the 14-foot propellers clawed the air and dragged us around. The wings shuddered. As they did I caught sight of the Tweet through my overhead window. The pilot had tried to come at us at a forty-five degree angle off the tail, perfect for a slashing shot. By calling a turn, Ozzie was trying to get us nose-to-nose with him before he was ready to shoot. It worked. The pilot pulled the trigger but panicked as he did so, the closure rate too high on an aircraft that was three times larger than his own. I could see the black BBs of his bullets etch a perfect line over my window frame, missing us by perhaps fifty feet. Straight, perfectly spaced, as though someone had packaged the world and stitched a "Tear Here" line across the sky to open it.

"I think there's one behind us!" Ozzie called out. "One guy's hanging back, staying out of the fight. The other one's swinging wide like he's making room."

A line of bullets off the nose answered his question. So much of this dogfight was taking place out of my range of vision I started punching my leg in frustration. Apparently one of the Tweets had tried climbing high and diving straight down on us. Either he'd started shooting too high or scared himself by putting that much ground in his windscreen or was just a plain bad shot. I didn't see him until he roared in front of us in a swooping bottoming-out of his dive. Flutie broke left and accelerated.

The other Tweet still maneuvering for passes tried the same thing. He climbed high and dove but this time we were ready. The instant we saw him climbing above us Flutie turned to chase his companion. He managed to get us close enough that the second Tweet broke off, frustrated, and descended again.

"Bandit, four o'clock!" a SEAL yelled.

Flutie chuckled.

"I leave the office at three-thirty!" he chirped, then shoved the nose over. Out my window, for a moment all three Tweets were in sight lined up one behind the other. Flutie saw them and started to sing.

"Iiiiiiii love a parade!" he wailed. "A handful of vets, a line of cadets, or any brigaaaaaade..."

We dropped into a river gorge perpendicular to the Cenepa valley. There Flutie really started to get weird. When one of the Tweets got in front of us and turned around to play a game of chicken, Flutie held position until the Peruvian broke upward only a quarter-mile away. Flutie broke downward at the same time and then took both hands off the controls to flip off the other pilot as he shot past. Every few seconds he screamed as though someone had delivered an electric shock to his nipples. Then he would be silent, intent, 'in the zone,' eyes burning up the terrain outside, hands locked to the yoke, concentrating on his *mano-a-mano* combat. But just when I thought he'd morphed into Chuck Yeager he would start screaming again. Apparently his zone was more complex than most. Or maybe he knew Chuck Yeager better than I did.

"#3's rolling in again!"

"*Fuuuuuuuuuuuccccccccckkkkkkkkkk*!"

"Where's he coming from?"

"Uh, wait...I think...I don't know! I lost him! No, three o'clock!"

"*Aaaaaauuuuuuuggggghhhhh*!"

Flutie went back to having a conniption. He was flying perfectly, giving a flawless tutorial in 1-v-3 fighter counter-tactics, but now he started doing it while imitating a child's tantrum. He shook his head from side-to-side, pounded on the dashboard, kicked his feet, and in addition to the screams erupted sporadically with verbless, nounless, babbling rants.

"Wickin'-frickin'-goddamn-what'd they-not, not, not, not...who the hell?!"

"I got one on the left side!" one of the SEALs shouted. "He's high on the ridge...he's turning in toward us!"

"Gargitonnniii...jiwessh...crudingafon..."

"Can't see the other two..."

"Aaaahhhhhhh! Stupid, stupid, stupid, stupid! Get low, low, low, low...shiiiiiiiiiiiitt!"

"He's coming right at us! Nine o'clock high!"

Sudden calm. Flutie looked over his shoulder and eyed the fighter with contempt. He stopped yelling and held the wings level this time. We were flying across a series of ridges that stretched down from the Condor mountains, steep-sided hills that plunged sheer from their summits until halfway down where they flared like the skirt of a Victorian dress. Each time we crossed such a ridge Flutie broke down into it to fly what was called the "military crest," parallel to the hill about a third of the distance below the top. Because of the flare in the lower part of the mountain the fighters couldn't come at us from below. Flutie bet they wouldn't come down at us effectively from above, either. To get their guns on line they would have to be staring at ground through the descent, something scary for pilots who flew only a few hours a month. It took faith – flying a straight line while the Tweet plunged off its perch. In fact it was uncomfortable as hell. I prayed Flutie was right.

He was right. The Tweet on the left never even fired its guns, the pilot unwilling to nose over enough to get us in his sights. He flew overhead two hundred feet up and cut around to maneuver into a more promising position behind us.

I was sweating up a storm, adrenalin making my hands shake. Everything I said turned into a shout, every movement I made a jerky release of energy. I stopped pounding my leg but only because I'd given myself a charlie-horse. I'd never been so close to dying for so long. When would it end? When would these idiots finally get us in their sights or change their minds and go home?

"There! Jungle!" I yelled. "Right, one o'clock low!"

We reached the last ridgeline and now had a choice of climbing left into the mountains or diving right to snuggle up close to the trees of the Amazon where they climbed into the foothills of the Andes. Flutie faked left, then broke right.

"Where are we?" Ozzie queried from the cabin.

"South America!" Flutie yelled back, then cackled happily.

Ozzie and the SEALs were indispensable keeping up on the position of the Tweets. Every few seconds Flutie jinked right or left, trying to keep our six o'clock clear and giving the guys in back an opportunity to see if it worked. Once he pulled a completely new one on me: chopping the throttles and kicking in as much right rudder as the C-27 would allow, making it look from above as though we had started a turn when in fact we hadn't. The airframe didn't like it – I could practically feel rivets popping all over the fuselage – but seconds later a frustrated Tweet curved by off our right wing so it might have worked. Since we couldn't always tell when the Peruvians were starting their attacks we just didn't know. It was all we could do just to know *that* the Tweets were attacking much less figure out how to respond. The two things working in our favor were first, the ruggedness of the C-27; and second, the fact that the Peruvians weren't that good.

"Jesus, these guys suck," one of the SEALs announced after the third attack in a row had wobbled in, fired, then broken off the instant we changed speed.

"Farkkle...frickin'...navy...flying....bullsh..."

"Yeah," Ozzie translated. "Don't jinx us, ground-pounder. *One high and right!* Dammit, now I've lost the other two!"

We fought our way into the foothills above the jungle, dipping behind one after another to make the Tweets follow and then popping over the top again the instant they did. For poor precision flyers they deserved credit for persistence. High up, they fired short, careful bursts from every position, sometimes while on our tail, sometimes from the forty-five – one pilot even tried to get below us as we popped over a ridge, hoping to highlight us against the sky so he would have a clearer target. But flying low was our strength. Flutie brushed treetops every time we crossed a ridge. When he banked around terrain he started early so that it looked like we would hit the ground rather than curve around it. The Peruvians weren't confident enough to be that reckless. The closer we got to the trees the more they lagged behind, and distance threw off their aim and their discipline. Once they lost the benefit of altitude they fired with abandon, taking 'hip-shots' and hoping to get lucky. Flutie fought them every step of the way, never relinquishing the controls, never giving them a reliable angle, talking to himself the whole time.

The basic tactic for cargo planes against fast-movers is to turn inside them, close the distance, and never let them stay on your tail, hoping the jets burn so much fuel they get tired and decide you aren't worth the trouble. We hadn't been able to do that because we had three attackers so what finally saved us was that we kept getting farther away from the Super Tweets' base. As Flutie said in one of his lucid moments, "They have to turn around sometime." Abeam the Cangaza Basin they did.

But first they formed up for a strange attack, this time all three jets together in an arrowhead formation. For once they got a good angle on us to start with, starting high at our five o'clock so that none of our spotters saw them until it was too late. Unfortunately for the Peruvians the formation made no sense. They weren't good enough pilots to fly close together, with the result that the bullets from the right jet cut the air a hundred yards off our nose while the left jet spat his into our slipstream. The lead Tweet saved their honor. He shot high but corrected at the last second to score their only hit. Two rounds slammed into our left wing just outside the engine, punching through the flimsy metal skin over the gas tanks and leaving jagged holes where they exited the bottom. We felt the strike clearly inside. Everyone fell silent, anticipating that the next microsecond would bring a catastrophic explosion as the left wing blew up and departed the aircraft.

The Tweets turned around.

"No change on the gauges," I said carefully, afraid the observation itself would provoke a disaster.

Flutie's mouth hung open.

"No," he agreed, so softly I barely heard him. The tantrums stopped. So did the aimless staring out front. He was no longer quiet because he was odd. Now he was quiet because he was drained of energy. We all were. The SEALs re-opened the case of Cuzqueña and passed it around.

We went to Lago Agrio for gas. We weren't leaking fuel and nothing was on fire but none of us knew if the rounds had done structural damage to the wing – and nobody wanted to climb to altitude in steep terrain before we found out. Lago Agrio was down low. It was in Ecuador, in the jungle, and had a long runway that didn't require an assault landing. Best of all, because it was a radar site it had Americans.

We landed and shut down. Flutie and Ozzie checked out the wing while I found the site liaison officer. He was Ecuadorian so my task was to suck up and apologize profusely for landing at an unscheduled field and to make up a non-bullet-strike reason why we hadn't been able to go to Quito. He listened and shrugged, agreeable to whatever I said and not noticing that my voice still shook. The Ecuadorians were more relaxed than their neighbors down south.

"Uhhh, I don't see anything," Ozzie was saying when I came back to the plane. He peered into the holes up top. His voice echoed in the chamber of the wing.

A small crowd from inside the sandbag labyrinth gathered to watch, a surprise visit from anyone being a welcome break. A couple of NCOs in BDU pants and sweaty t-shirts pointed at the punctured metal on the bottom of the wing.

"Hail," I explained.

"No kidding?"

"Uh, yeah. See those clouds up there?" I pointed to the peaks in the direction of Quito. "They don't look bad from here but up close they spit ice like shrapnel."

"Wow."

Ozzie got a flashlight and did everything but pull up panels. Flutie examined the damage from below. Eventually they agreed that the bullets had gone through the narrow partition between the main and aux fuel tanks, hitting neither and not rupturing any lines. Which was good. Some planes had pressurized nitrogen in the empty spaces of a wing to keep sparks from forming. Some planes had a fire-suppressant foam. We had...nothing at all. It was a weak point of the Chuck that we thought about a lot.

For a while Flutie stood off by himself staring at the ground and aimlessly kicking gravel. I knew he was thinking about calling home. What should he tell the AOC? Did they already know? The Ecuadorians didn't, obviously, and I for one was inclined to leave their territory as soon as possible not only to keep from involving them but to keep any diplomatic firestorm from stranding us in an Ecuadorian courtroom. Or jail. It was bad to take advantage of their hospitality but not as bad as languishing for years in an Andean prison.

Eventually he called Panama but not the AOC. He got a line directly to Lt Col Rasmussen. Rasmussen listened while Flutie did the unimaginable and talked for three minutes non-stop. When he was done there was a pause. Then he said, "Yes, sir" twice and hung up the phone.

We flew home.

On the diplomatic front the firestorm was fierce. Flutie, Ozzie, and I were grounded for three weeks while the Air Force, SOUTHCOM, the State Department, and anybody else who wanted to get in on the act investigated, questioned, probed, accused, de-briefed, and dissected the incident in full. The Peruvians blamed us for everything although the U.S. Embassy in Lima learned that neither the government nor the Peruvian Chief of Staff had approved firing on American planes. Fortunately for us, President Fujimori soon slapped down another piece of his shock-tactic economic austerity program and the Peruvians turned their attention to that. The Ecuadorians were cool the whole time. Even though I'd lied to them they appreciated anything that made the Peruvians look bad. The station chief in Quito called to say we had an open invitation to use Ecuadorian bases whenever we wished – and oh, by the way, if we could brief them on some of our counter-air tactics they wouldn't mind that, either.

The AOC was mad, of course. Garb Taylor was embarrassed. Brigadier General Heidl didn't know whether to have us court-martialed or awarded medals. Eventually he did neither. Lt Col Rasmussen dragged all of us into his office and made us stand at attention while he glared, fumed, started to say something then stopped, glared some more, then finally kicked us back out into the hangar without saying a word. Later the Group Commander yelled at us. Then his deputy did, too, afraid to be left out. We stayed grounded for almost a month. During that time I had to work with Garb Taylor up in Current Ops, shuffling paper and updating grease boards. It was worse than getting shot at.

The SEALs thought the whole thing a hoot. A week after we landed in Panama they invited the three of us to their hooch at Rodman, duct-taped us to gurneys, and poured beer over us while Panamanian hookers fed us tequila. After which they pronounced us honorary commandos.

A year later, Peruvian MiG-21s intercepted a C-130 photo-reconnaissance plane out of Howard. It was flying over international waters off Chiclayo at 15,000 feet and had just concluded a scheduled, Lima-approved flight searching for drug traffickers. The MiGs shot it down.

21. Billie

A FEW MONTHS after getting to Panama I found myself trapped in Major Byron's office watching gory footage of his gunships killing people and blowing things up during the invasion. He commented that his flights during that first night were all fun but that at one point there were so many aircraft in the air trying to get their missions done that he almost collided with a C-141.

"Scared the crap out of the whole crew," he remembered. "We broke right to avoid triple-A and found ourselves nose-to-nose with a Starlifter climbing out of a drop at Rio Hato. Missed him by 50 feet. First time I ever thought we wouldn't make it. When I got back to the States I went and did something I'd never done before: I wrote up a will, just in case the next one was for real."

That got me to thinking about times I had been scared doing what I did. I didn't have much to leave anyone but figured maybe having a will wasn't a bad idea. So I called the Legal Office. "Come over after lunch," they said. "Lieutenant Maris will write one up."

The Legal Office was on the second floor of Building 238, a two-story white stucco across the street from the flightline and only fifty yards from my office. Without knowing it I had been parking my car in the lawyers' lot for months.

I left the Jimmy there because that's where it got washed. Every weekday a Panamanian man and his teenage daughter lingered in the shade of a storage building across the street, waiting with buckets to see if they could talk any service people into a car wash. They usually could since a huge mango tree stood nearby and hosted scores of parakeets for several hours each afternoon. They were always friendly and always hard-working and would seal a contract for a wash with a simple exchange of nods when you drove up. Most of us were happy to oblige them at least twice a week, partly out of respect for their ambition but partly because they buffed our hard-ridden vehicles' dents and scratches to a high gloss for fifty cents. An extra dime would get them to do it after the parakeets had gone.

A steel staircase that looked like a fire escape led up the outside of the legal building. I climbed it to find an unmarked door that opened to a hallway covered in thin blue carpet. At the end of the hall was the receptionist.

"Take a seat, sir. Lt Maris is with someone right now but can help you in just a minute."

The seats were right behind me. I only had to pivot to sit down. No one else was in the room but even with just the receptionist and me the office was so small it seemed crowded. There was room enough for a counter, her desk, two chairs for customers, and a faux van Eyck on the opposite wall that hogged space just by having a two-inch-thick frame. I had thought my squadron worked in cramped areas. Compared to the lawyers we lived in style.

Two doorways led off the room. One went to the hall by which I had entered and the other – closed –led to the lawyers' offices.

The second door swung open.

"Sorry for the hassle, ma'am," a master sergeant drawled as he came into the office. His tone was plaintive, confused. "I didn't think it would be that big a deal."

A petite female lieutenant in crisp BDUs followed him. She smiled sweetly. It was a pretty smile, one that reached to her eyes, but it wasn't the kind that meant to share in someone's good fortune. It was more the told-you-so kind, the kind of pleasantness that a proper Southern lady showed an escaped Yankee prisoner as her maid hurried away to warn the colonel.

"Oh, it's a big deal, sergeant," she chirped. "You'll lose a lot of money over this and there's nothing we can do to help you. Not any more. You should have followed my advice six months ago, or three months ago, or even last month. Next time do what I tell you to, when I tell you to do it."

"But I think the shipper needs to look at this situation a little closer."

"Thank you, sergeant. We're all refreshed and challenged by your unique point of view."

"Well, yes, ma'am. But I don't understand why we can't all just step back a minute and start all over."

The lieutenant's smile never wavered.

"It's called a contract, sergeant. Take it up with your commander. If he has questions, have him give me a call. Thank you!" She practically sang her gratitude.

The sergeant looked around the room but found no support. Certainly not from me – I made a point of staring at the still-life and pretending not to listen in. Not from the receptionist, either, who shuffled papers on her desk with the practiced weariness of a woman who has witnessed more than one trip to the gallows.

Shaking his head and posing rhetorical questions to himself about delays and misunderstandings and the advantages of talking things over, the sergeant wandered down the hallway to the exit. When the door closed behind him and we heard his boots clump down the metal stairs, the lieutenant spun on her heel.

"Alice, DO NOT schedule another meeting for him with anyone in this office," she ordered the receptionist, her sweetness gone like a passing breeze, the chirp replaced by the audio equivalent of a heat-seeking missile. "It's a waste of time. I'm tired of that Southern-boy crap. He wants the world to stop and back up five months so he can get another crack at NOT violating the contract that he had all the time in the world to fulfill."

"But..." the receptionist started to say.

"But nothing," the lieutenant cut her off and banged her fist on the desk. "He knew better! He knew better and he was too damned lazy to make his arrangements before he left the States. This time the movers are in the right – if it costs him seven thousand dollars that's unfortunate but I'm sorry, he's a senior noncommissioned officer in the United States Air Force. If it takes an incident like this to teach him responsibility then so be it. This is the fourth time he's been here: DO NOT let him waste our time again. Definitely, don't let him waste *my* time again or I will be one unhappy bitch with a law degree."

I stayed quiet. When she walked through the door I recognized the lieutenant. Or at least I had seen her before. Soon after arriving at the squadron I'd had to do my annual re-qualification at the rifle range. Lt Maris was in the class, too. I remembered thinking she was cute, sexy, and entirely too excited about getting to shoot guns. Still, I wanted to impress her – and didn't. Despite being an expert shot, that day I couldn't hit the bullseye unless I walked up and punched it. She saw my target – the only "Good" among a class of "Excellents" – and gave me a pitying smile. When I saw her mow down a row of mannequins with a full clip on automatic, I tried to comfort myself that she wasn't really my type.

Yet I couldn't ignore her. The week before I'd run into her in the snack bar above the BX. She was sitting with another female lieutenant while I went through the line at the counter. Once she looked my way with a bit of a smirk that I took as flirtation. My heart skipped a beat. Flashing a smile in return, I tried to play it cool and acted as studly as one can while ordering a tuna sandwich. It was only as I was paying that I noticed the string of paper napkins stuck to my boot – they had latched on somewhere near the soda machine, which meant just inside the door, which meant I had been dragging them around ever since. By the time I kicked them clear and looked up, Maris was on her way outside.

So my record with her so far was 0-2.

"Hi!" her voice chirped again, interrupting my reverie.

I looked up into clear brown eyes. The smile was back, lighting a face framed by short blonde hair. Those were two very fast mood changes, I couldn't help thinking.

"Hi."

"You must be Lt Bleriot."

"Yes," I said, at a loss for words. "Hi."

"Hi, again. You thinking of dying anytime soon?"

"I beg your pardon?"

"You want a will, right?"

"Oh. Yes. Yes, I do."

"Well, follow me, then. My office is back here. On the way you can say 'hi' again to Alice if you want."

Her office was down a narrow hallway. There were four rooms back there, all belonging to judge advocates general or JAGs as the lawyers liked to be called. I followed Maris into one the size of a pantry.

"I know, it's a small office," she said before I could make the same observation. "You don't have to tell me. I hate it, I hate it, I hate it, and if there were anything I could do to make it better I would."

"It's efficient," I agreed, regaining my capacity for words.

"No, it's small," she snapped. "And it's not even an office. It's more like hell with fluorescent lighting."

"Why is the ceiling sloped?"

She looked up. The walls were white-washed plaster that had been done in a hurry. The ceiling was white, too, and sloped from eight feet at one end to five at the other. I had to crouch like a hunchback while she found me a chair. Even the lieutenant had to duck just to get around her desk. She pointed to the wall on her right.

"I'm under the stairs," she said in a tone that suggested no response from me would be wise.

I nodded. Around attractive women I had a tendency to ramble when I opened my mouth so I made a conscious effort now to stay quiet.

It didn't last. After several minutes of her shuffling paper around her desk and not saying anything I couldn't take the silence.

"We met once before," I offered.

"Oh?"

"At the gun range. I didn't realize you were a lawyer."

"Yes, I'm an agent of Satan," she said absently without looking up. "But don't worry, my duties are largely ceremonial."

"You're not going to yell at me, are you?" I said, trying to smile.

She stopped writing. "What?"

"Like that sergeant. I don't know if I can screw up a will but I'm sure I'll try. I just don't want you to tell your receptionist never to let me in here again."

She stared at me, trying to figure out what in the world I was talking about. Then realizing I was trying to be funny she opened her eyes wide and spoke like a teacher clarifying something to the class.

"I didn't yell at him."

"Yes, you did."

"No, I didn't. I was polite."

"Yes, but you spoke with that firm tone that women use when they're telling somebody off and they don't want to hear any argument. That's the same as yelling."

Now I got the you're-a-weirdo look. Damn it. Why couldn't I just stay quiet?

Getting the will was easy. Maris moved fast and talked faster. She had me fill out a worksheet listing the things I would leave behind in the event of my untimely demise. It was embarrassing. Answering the questions made me realize I didn't have much in the way of earthly possessions. I wanted to explain to her that Major Byron had suggested I get the will, that it wasn't my idea, that I was doing it as a matter of course rather than because I actually thought my life was worth enough to quantify on a spreadsheet, but she didn't seem to care. I should have realized that she did dozens of wills for people every month and mine was just one more. Instead I watched her dash around and whip pieces of paper one way or another and figured she was in a hurry to get me out of the office so she could move on to more important duties.

"Alice!"

The receptionist appeared in the doorway.

"Alice, go grab Sergeant Dumfries, will you? I need the two of you as witnesses."

That was really embarrassing. Two strangers signing my will as witnesses that I didn't own a damned thing.

"Well, that's it," Maris announced twenty minutes after I had entered the building. "Make a copy and keep it in a safe place. I recommend putting one in your freezer."

"Excuse me?"

"In your freezer. Put it in plastic and slide it under the frozen chicken. In house fires the stuff in freezers rarely gets damaged."

"Oh."

Her blonde hair was cut short so that it curled around the back of her neck to point forward. She looked at me straight on, eyes fixed on mine as though someone had once told her that was the best way to show confidence. It worked. But her confidence didn't impress me nearly as much as her pale skin. I loved her face.

I tried to delay. I had spoken all of five sentences since meeting her and now I was being ushered out the door. I tried to come up with something to spark conversation but her face changed to the same bright-eyed look of disinterest that she had thrown at the sergeant. I couldn't think of anything. Even if I could have it would have come out in a stammer. I didn't want to look stupid so...so I just nodded and looked stupid.

"Thanks," I said.

Her eyes faltered, regarding me now with confusion as well as pity.

"You're welcome."

She preceded me down the hall.

"Bye," she said.

I tried to think of something witty but she turned away, so I just nodded.

"Bye."

22. Billie 2

A LOT OF things happen on a military base because of wives. That's both good and bad. Most people in the military are men and therefore most spouses are women, so despite a movement in the 1990s to change the Officers Wives Club to the Officers Spouses Club the fact remained that if there was a spouse organization on base it was comprised wholly of women. That was the case on Howard.

The OWC met several times a month. Not having a wife I had no idea what they talked about. The only time their efforts affected my life was when they collected money to buy someone a going-away gift or sponsored a burger burn to raise cash for the Christmas party. The club came up in conversation among us pilots only when there was a controversy.

The biggest I remember had to do with JC Crystal's wife, Elaine. Elaine and JC married after he'd been given orders to Panama, which meant the Air Force paid for *him* to move there, not her: she was 'un-sponsored.' Usually when that happens a guy leaves his wife back in the States because otherwise they have to foot the bill themselves for transportation, a place to rent, living expenses, etc. But JC said to hell with that. He wasn't going to miss his wife for two years just because it would be expensive to bring her to Panama. So she came to Panama and they rented an apartment downtown, the only married couple I knew who did that.

Elaine was a doctor. She had an education and a career, and she and JC had no children. So Elaine worked out an arrangement with a local clinic and ended up working full-time for the length of JC's tour. That was unusual. Usually Panama was a tough place for foreigners to get jobs but in this case demand trumped supply and she was able to get what few other spouses in the country could. Working full time she thus had no time to get involved in OWC activities.

At first some OWC members didn't want Elaine in the club, anyway – she was 'un-sponsored,' so some felt she didn't deserve to be there. But when they found out Elaine didn't even *want* to join, they began to poison the water against her, accusing her of being aloof. JC sighed and ignored the dustup. Elaine did the same.

But the spat over Elaine's non-involvement in OWC activities pointed up a trait of the club that a sociologist could write a thesis on. It was that many wives adopted the rank of their active-duty husbands. They believed that if Elaine didn't participate in the OWC she wasn't participating in her "squadron duties." Elaine would respond that she didn't have any squadron duties since she wasn't in the Air Force. But many wives felt they were, even to the point of socializing only with wives whose husbands were equal to or higher in rank than their own.

Some did it more than others. Lt Col Rasmussen's wife, Helen, was laid back but Major Byron's wife, Denise, made a point of introducing herself to junior officers' spouses by saying "you can call me 'Ma'am' if it'll make you more comfortable." Colonel Buncheman's wife insisted that the gate guards salute her when she drove onto base even when it was clear the colonel wasn't in the car. She also parked in the "O-6 and above" parking spot at the commissary when she picked up groceries. General Heidl's wife, too, was well-known for brow-beating other spouses into engaging in base activities. For a while she even insisted that people salute her until the general told her to knock it off. When the general's household goods were shipped down from their house at Langley, somehow she got hold of Big Bud's phone number at the Mobility office and ordered him to supervise their delivery to her new house on base. Bud being a nice guy – and thinking at first that he had no choice – complied as best he could. But then some items – the general's winter flight jacket, for one – turned up missing from the shipping boxes. Heidl's wife chewed him out, yelling at him from the porch of the general's house up by the O'Club until Bud felt so bad he went home to dig his own flight jacket out of the closet to offer it as a replacement. Fortunately Major Byron ran across him at the tailor shop and tempered his enthusiasm before he inadvertently made himself the woman dictator's personal manservant.

Lieutenant Maris knew Joy Heidl. Elaine told me they hung out together sometimes because Heidl's wife liked to shop as much as Maris did. Elaine acknowledged that the general's wife was a pain but apparently she could also spot bargains downtown.

The rank-adoption depended a lot on personality. It was also a tradition, an atmosphere passed down from generation to generation that was hard to overcome. The behavior of the wives paralleled my observation about pilots that everyone needed someone to look down on. For that reason I avoided contact with the OWC whenever possible. After all, they never hosted a lingerie night at the officers club so as far as I was concerned, what was the point? But every now and then they did some good.

For whatever reason, Joy Heidl liked the TV show 'China Beach.' It was a romanticized baby-boomer vision of the Vietnam War and as realistic as a daytime soap but she considered it a documentary. She also liked M*A*S*H. So shortly after I met Lieutenant Maris, Lt Col Rasmussen called me and Rolo into his office for a talk.

"We're having a party," he said with all the enthusiasm of a homeowner discovering termites in the walls.

"Great, sir. What's the occasion?"

"The occasion is that the general's wife wants a party."

"Oh." Rolo thought for a moment. "Is that good?"

Rasmussen eyed him dourly.

"It's good if you don't have a flying hour program to worry about. It's good if you're not trying to train pilots. It's good if you don't have missions to fly across two continents. It's good if you don't have anything else to do with 75 people who otherwise could be gainfully employed."

Rolo grinned. "Well, then it's good!"

Rasmussen nodded, knowing Rolo well enough to understand that while he wasn't the brightest bulb in the chandelier my roommate didn't have a mean bone in his body, either.

"Well, lieutenant, I'm happy to hear you're enthusiastic about it because I'm not. If the general's for it then of course I think it's a great idea but between you two guys and me, I can't stand his wife. She's 150 pounds of menopause in a floral dress and I get the willies just being around her."

I bit my tongue to keep from laughing.

"She wants a party so he wants a party. He wants a party so damn it, I guess *I* want a party. The OWC is organizing it but I need you two to go coordinate with Merrill and make the hangar safe so the women can hang decorations."

"We're having the party in the hangar, sir?" I asked. In addition to the hangar having two airplanes parked in it, it was full of tools, support equipment, and vehicles, not to mention pallets of supplies headed downrange to the radar sites.

"That's right," Rasmussen affirmed. "So you've got your work cut out for you."

The work turned out to be hot and sweaty but straightforward. All Rolo and I had to do was get rid of the "bad" stuff, things that were sharp, mobile, explosive, or otherwise dangerous. The planes went out on the flightline, the guns went to the armory, and everything else went into Hangar 2. Once I learned how to drive a forklift we shuttled everything across the ramp as fast as possible. Done.

Captain Perry Trapazzano, the airfield manager, got stuck with the task of supplying all the "good" stuff, the "authentic China Beach" equipment the members of the OWC wanted.

The tough part came when the women themselves showed up to decorate.

"Okay, lieutenant. Those are going to have to go," a woman whose husband worked in the Group told me. "They don't look military."

She pointed at a row of camo-green conexes we had lined up against the hangar wall.

"Those are conexes," I said. "They're storage lockers for equipment. They're issued by the Pentagon."

"Well, they don't look military. I've seen China Beach and I've never seen those."

Rolo interrupted. He'd spent four hours moving pallets and breathing hangar dust.

"Lady, that show is filmed in California on some studio lot. Maybe the non-military producers just didn't have any military equipment to store in any military lockers. But this is a military base and we military people do. Those lockers are as military issue as I am."

"But they don't *look* military," the woman protested. Others from the club gathered behind her to shake their heads in disapproval. "We only want things that look military out here on the floor."

Rolo was taken aback.

"Lady, *I* don't look military and I'm here. The conexes stay. Update your show."

Soon we were called back to the commander's office.

"Guys,' Lt Col Rasmussen said, making an effort to be calm. "Let me revise my instructions. Make every reasonable effort to accommodate the women's requests. No, check that: make *every* effort to accommodate them, reasonable or not. Okay?" He leaned forward to look right at Rolo. "I don't want any more calls from the colonel, Lieutenant Metzger. Understand?"

Rolo shrugged.

"Yes, sir."

"Lieutenant?" the Group commander's wife asked Rolo the next morning. "Could you find us some more stringy stuff to put over that car?"

Rolo looked around. We had already spread camouflage netting around half the hangar because that's what the wives wanted. An acre of building now looked like the web of a giant green spider.

"Stringy stuff? You mean netting?"

"Of course, netting. That car doesn't look right."

"Car? Are you talking about the Humvee?"

"Yes. It looks out of place. Could you find some netting to cover it?"

"It's a Humvee," he explained. "It's a military vehicle. It's *the* military vehicle now. We have about fifty thousand of them in the Air Force alone."

The woman put her hands on her hips and Rolo quickly surrendered.

"Never mind," he said. "I know, it wasn't on TV. I'll get the stringy stuff and hide the car."

By the night of the party the hangar looked good. We borrowed a Huey helicopter from the Army (thank god *that* was on the show) and also squeezed a C-130 up close to the dance floor. Tiki torches flanked the open hangar doors. We had so many sandbags and so much camo netting that they formed corridors for people to get to the food tables. Everything was lighted by the colored lanterns that from listening to the wives' club tell it must have formed an integral part of every Vietnam campaign. The Pinheads supplied a still reminiscent of the one Hawkeye used on M*A*S*H. They had discovered a way to make alcohol out of yucca – it was strong and clear and mixed well with anything, giving just a hint of stagnant jungle rainwater as an aftertaste. As the *pièce de résistance*, there was a USO-style stage decked in red-white-and-blue. The DJ, an enlisted guy from the Public Affairs office, set up his stereo on the stage and spent most of the night playing '60s rock-and-roll and shouting "Good morning, Vietnam!" into the microphone.

Then there were the costumes.

"I'm not wearing a freaking costume," Rolo vowed when he heard that everyone was encouraged to come dressed in theme.

He felt that way until Friday afternoon, hours before the party, when Major Byron came through the squadron to remind everyone that the general (read: the general's wife) wanted to remind everyone that it was a costume party.

"Are you wearing one, sir?" I asked.

Byron looked off into the distance, perhaps going to his happy place where he could circle targets in his gunship and blast them into a million bits.

"Yeah," he said without enthusiasm.

"What is it?"

He thought some more.

"My wife hasn't told me yet."

In the end Byron got lucky. His wife – like almost all of the women who showed up – dressed as a nurse from China Beach. They thought it a hoot that they got to wear BDU pants and a brown t-shirt and run around with dog tags dangling from their neck. The fact that every woman who served in the military still could dress that way didn't faze them – it was new to them and they thought it was great. Byron copped out and did the same thing. His wife claimed he was some studly helicopter pilot from the show. To us he looked like Major Byron.

Most of the men who showed up came as someone from M*A*S*H. There were a bunch of Colonel Potters, even more Hawkeyes, and quite a few Radar O'Reilly's. To show what we thought of the party most of us in the 155th came as Corporal Klinger.

"I never thought I'd be caught dead wearing a dress," Rolo muttered as we tottered across the hangar floor in high heels. He wore a red dress with poofed shoulders and a blue sash around his waist. He'd bought it after work at the Thrift Shop and was still smarting over the snickers from the clerks.

"You look great," I said, stopping to lean against a non-military-looking conex while I adjusted my own evening gown and tightened a shoe strap. "Like a drag queen from San Francisco, but still great."

"Glad you like it. But these shoes are putting pressure on my ass and that sucks because it still hurts like hell."

His ass hurt for the same reason mine did. After being out of anti-malarial serum for months the immunization clinic had received a fresh batch of gamma-globulin that morning and everyone in the squadron had had to troop up to the hospital to get a shot. It was the least popular shot because it felt like a golf ball had been injected into your ass when the needle was removed. "Rub the affected area," the docs advised, so we did, usually for days afterwards. Rubbing didn't make the pain go away but it made us feel like we were doing something. Now as we came into the hangar it was easy to tell who belonged to our squadron – there was a score of men in dresses all rubbing their own butts.

Lowell came as a woman, too. In theory he was another Corporal Klinger wannabe but in reality he looked more like a juvenile cross-dressing groupie of The Cure. He was accompanied by Declan – in heavy lipstick and with two balloons crammed beneath a tight sweater – who proudly proclaimed himself Lowell's bull-dike companion. They pushed the lesbian theme all night until Colonel Buncheman's wife couldn't take it any longer and showed them the door. Buncheman's wife also didn't believe why they were rubbing their butts. She thought it was some code.

"What's with all the dresses?" Charlie Manson demanded, working on his third beer and giving me the heavy-lidded sideways glance that announced he wouldn't be surprised by any answer I gave him. He still wore his flight suit and had a look that told everyone he was at the party under duress. His wife, Myra, was at his side. She was Panamanian and a sweet lady – how Charlie and his sarcasm won her over no one knew.

"M*A*S*H," I replied. "Corporal Klinger. Remember?"

He watched Evan, already drunk and in a skirt that highlighted his thick, hairy legs, try to lean against the stage, miss, and fall to the floor.

"Really. I thought maybe you were all indulging some inner child."

"I don't have an inner child. I'm just a lesbian trapped in a man's body."

"Well, you're an ugly lesbian."

Myra slapped him on the shoulder.

"Oh, no, Charlie! He is cute! You are a very pretty lady, Miguel," she assured me.

"Really?"

"*Claro.* If I liked women, I would find you very attractive."

So there, my look said to her husband. Charlie went for another beer.

The decision to hold the party in the hangar was a good one. By eight-thirty it was pitch black outside and lightning over the ocean told us a storm was rolling in. The temperature dropped to the low 80s. The air became so thick it sparkled in the party lights.

"My dress is getting clammy," a voice next to me complained.

I turned to see Manny, the Air Force poster boy, decked out in an electric-blue gown and with enough eye-liner to re-paint the nose of a C-27. One hand held a beer while the other rubbed methodically across his ass.

"Manny?"

"Hi. Nice stilettos. I should have worn those."

"You're in a dress!" was all I could think to say.

"I know. My wife picked it out."

"But you're in a dress!" I repeated.

"So?"

"That's not like you. You're so...I mean, you're always so..."

"Anal?" he guessed.

"Well, yeah. I mean, I was going to say 'conservative.' Or 'straight-laced.'. You're not the dress-wearing type."

He shrugged and took a pull from his beer. "I have my moments."

Someone tapped the DJ's microphone.

"Ladies and gentlemen? Ladies and gentlemen? May I have your attention?"

It was Captain John Cargill, the general's aide. Tonight he was dressed like a chaplain which was a good choice since he looked exactly like Father Mulcahy.

"We're going to have our costume contest now. Could we all please...ladies and gentlemen, could we...hello? Hello? Is this thing on?"

The contest took a while since almost all of the people at the party were dressed up enough to compete. Cargill tried to welcome everyone on stage with a cheerful comment on their attire. Then the flyers from the 155th strutted their stuff: quickly Cargill was overwhelmed by the number of men in drag.

"He looks uncomfortable," Lt Col Rasmussen observed.

"He looks like a real chaplain," Major Byron agreed. "I don't think he's used to being around this many men in dresses. Not like us."

We wondered what Byron meant by that.

"He doesn't swear," Walt commented. As usual, he lurked in the background waiting for the right moment to instigate trouble. Tonight he was attired in a prim sun dress with polka-dots. His wife accompanied him. She had chosen to disguise herself as Henry Blake, complete with fishing lures festooning her hat.

"There's nothing wrong with not swearing," she reminded him.

"Damned right, there is," Walt assured us. "And he doesn't do it, ever. He doesn't drink, either. Or smoke, or tell dirty jokes, or cavort with lascivious women."

"Cavort?" Rolo asked. "Lascivious?"

"He's pure as the driven snow," Walt lamented. "We should feel sorry for him. The man is probably very uncomfortable up there. He could use some backup."

"Well, son, I can do something about that," Jem blurted. He set down two of his three beers and hiked up his short skirt. "Watch this!"

Jem ran up the trailer steps. "Helloooooooo!" he minced to the crowd.

Some people responded with cheers. Most clapped nervously. Men wearing dresses are funny. Men who are enthusiastic about wearing dresses cause crowds to clap nervously.

Jem pranced his way over to Cargill like a stripper looking for a tip. Cargill gave an uncertain laugh. Jem hugged the captain. Cargill pushed him away. Jem kissed the captain. Cargill retreated behind the cardboard cutout of Bob Hope. Jem followed him and then got behind him to wrap his hands around and rub the man's chest.

"Heh-heh. Okay, folks, I guess that..."

Jem tousled Cargill's hair, then spun around to the front and gave him another big hug and kiss. That was good but even better was that he managed to moon the audience at the same time. Half the audience cheered. The other half quickly looked away and tried to find something else to pay attention to. Cargill turned red and couldn't speak for a while. The contest was delayed twenty minutes.

"Chaos, panic, and disorder," Walt observed proudly. "My work here is done."

Jem might have had to leave the party except that nature chose that moment to intervene. The storm that was flaunting its power over the ocean chose to come ashore. Rain pounded the roof of the hangar. Wind blew through the open doors, snuffing the tiki torches. The lanterns strung overhead whipped high in the air. A tiny microburst tried to carry away the "authentic China Beach tents."

"The door!" Trapazzano yelled from behind the still. "Close the door!"

The hangar doors were forty feet tall. If you used the hand crank to open and close them they moved about twenty feet per minute. If you manhandled them they moved faster than that.

"The doors!" went the cry. Everyone in the 155th – it was our hangar, after all – sprinted to close the doors.

In retrospect it must have been a sight. Thirty men in drag running full speed across a hangar, trying to keep their dresses from being blown off and simultaneously rubbing their butts, to close a door the size of a windmill.

We got the door closed but not before a current of wind snaked through the opening and upended the mess tent.

"Whoooh!" I exclaimed when Rolo and I got back to our beer. "That was work. I've changed my mind about wearing dresses. They might look good but they're impractical as hell. And these shoes are history."

I kicked off my high heels and felt blood rush back to my feet. Rolo sent his skidding across the floor until they disappeared under some wall lockers.

"Now you see what we women go through," a voice said. "All just to pick up men."

Lieutenant Maris walked up with a glass of punch in one hand and a beer in the other. Rolo said, "bye!" and handed me his cup. He made a quick exit, ducking under the camouflage netting that draped like tapestries around us.

"Where's he going?" she asked.

"He likes pretending to be a woman," I explained, "but the real thing scares him."

"Too bad. You guys looked good running across the hangar. Nice legs. Hairy, but nice."

She had a bright smile that almost but not quite hid the fact that she was buzzed. Either the alcohol or her own amusement made her stare at my feet where the too-small shoes had worn lines into the skin.

"You weren't watching, were you?"

"Of course, I was. I've been looking for you all evening and didn't see you until you tripped going to the door."

"I'm not used to wearing heels."

"I'm glad to hear that."

"You women wear them and other torture devices just to attract men?" I asked.

"And skirts and bras and flimsy dresses," she added.

"We're not worth it."

"Oh, I know," she agreed quickly. "Believe me, I know. My ex-Army-boyfriend reminded me of that."

"Your ex-Army-boyfriend? Is he no longer in the Army or no longer your boyfriend?"

"He may not be in the Army anymore – I don't know and I don't care. But he's definitely not my boyfriend."

"Oh. Sorry."

"Why are you sorry?"

"I thought it was the right thing to say."

She stared at me long enough to suggest I should say something. As soon as I tried she broke in.

"Sometimes I wish I were attracted to women just so I could avoid you guys. But then I remember what women are like – we're worse."

"Really?"

"A lot worse."

"What are you talking about?" The four beers in me made conversation easier than it had been at the Legal Office. "You guys are all soft and bumpy and you smell good. Men don't do any of those things."

"But all we talk about is shopping, make-up, and men," she pointed out. "For me those are good topics for about ten minutes. Then I want to talk about something else so unfortunately that means I have to deal with men. I also like sex," she added, "and for that I definitely need a man."

That made me drop Rolo's beer. The plastic cup hit the floor and sprayed beer over her feet and mine. Maris barely lifted an eyebrow.

"Did I say something wrong?" she asked.

"Um, yeah. You mentioned sex and I lost control of my limbs. Be grateful I didn't fall down."

For the first time I saw her laugh. It was a real laugh and made me realize that most of the time she hid behind a facade of professional disinterest. Lieutenant Maris wasn't as secure as she wanted everyone to believe.

"I'm Mike," I introduced myself.

"I know," she said. "I wrote your will. I'm Lieutenant Maris." She paused long enough to see my disappointment. "But you can call me Billie."

"Billie?"

"Yes."

"That's a guy's name."

"No, it isn't. It's a girl's."

"Billy Williams, Billy the Kid, Billy Carter," I ticked off the names on my fingers.

"Billie Holliday," she replied.

"Good point."

"Billie Jean King."

"She's a lesbian."

"Don't go there."

"Is it short for anything?"

She sipped her beer while considering whether to answer. "It's short for Wilhelmina," she said finally.

"Wilhelmina? You're kidding."

"No, I'm not. My family's German by way of Atlanta, Georgia, and my name is just the tip of the iceberg for their weirdness. So call me Billie and don't mention Wilhelmina again. If you do I'll re-write your will and see that you need it in the near future."

A shout went up from the buffet tables. For an hour people had lined up at the Huey to get their picture taken sitting in the cockpit. Now the line was gone but one couple had stayed behind to enjoy a quiet moment. Perry Trapazzano had just discovered them *in flagrante delicto* and was busy trying to haul the half-naked man into the open. A crowd formed to help him. I hoped it was someone from the Group.

"What are you doing down here?"

"I'm a lawyer."

"I know that. But why in Panama?"

"The Air Force sent me here, same as you."

"Why are you a lawyer?"

"Why are you a pilot?"

"Because I like to fly."

"Well, I like to....litigate."

"Litigate? What does that mean?"

"It means to conduct legal...what is this, twenty questions?" she demanded.

"Yes. I'm trying to find out what you do and you have to tell me in three words or less."

"Why?"

"Because all good jobs can be explained in three words or less."

"Who says?"

"I do."

"And what do you do in three words or less?"

"I fly planes."

"Well, I...do law."

"*Do* law?"

She shook her head. "I litigate. I prepare cases. I present evidence in a format consistent with the Uniform Code of Military Justice. I work with..."

"You get three words."

She stomped on my foot.

"I can't explain what I do in just three words! It's more complex than that."

"No, it isn't."

"It is, too. It's more complicated than just flying a plane."

"Oh?"

"Yes. Wipe that smile off your face. Not everyone's world is as simple as a pilot's."

"Too bad for you."

She frowned and held her beer up to her forehead. Over at the Huey the crowd extricated the romantic couple and was disappointed to find out they were part of the catering staff.

"I'm sorry. Did I just insult you?" she asked.

"Not at all."

"I did, didn't I?"

"No, you just observed that my job and my world are simple and uncomplicated."

"Are they?"

"Not as much as I'd like."

"I'm sorry," she said again.

"Never mind. You didn't say how you ended up in Panama..."

"I asked to go overseas," she said. "And they sent me overseas. Of course, when I said that I meant Germany or Italy..."

"You don't like it down here?"

"It's too hot."

"It's the tropics," I pointed out.

"I don't care. It's too hot. I have fair skin..."

"I noticed."

"...and it doesn't like the sun. And I don't like to sweat."

She finished her beer and looked around for somewhere to toss the bottle. I took it from her before she did – she had a look that suggested she was drunk enough to hurl it into the crowd by the dance floor.

"How much have you had to drink?" I asked.

"Just that one beer," she replied. "Why?"

"You look a little feisty. Like you wouldn't mind getting into a fight. Anything I should know about?"

She sipped her punch and eyed the beer I was holding, enough that I got the hint and handed it over.

"I don't drink very often," she explained.

"I gathered that."

"Actually, I don't usually drink at all."

"Ever?"

"Not unless it's wine in a really nice restaurant. Or beer if I have to."

"If you have to?"

"I can drink a lot of beer if I want to. Sometimes it impresses guys, sometimes it scares them off."

"And tonight? Are you impressing or scaring tonight?"

"Neither. Tonight is mandatory fun. That calls for a drink or four all by itself. And I think this party is stupid."

I looked around the hangar. The party started at six o'clock. It was now after nine and the crowd was as big as ever. Nobody was leaving in part because the weather outside was so nasty. The band played 60's hits and enough people had lost their inhibitions that the dance floor – now that the Huey excitement was over – was full. Another crowd lingered at the buffet tables in front of the barbecue pits. A third formed in front of the conexes where everyone gathered around an open space. Something in the middle of the space brought cheers.

"It's not stupid," I disagreed.

"We were all ordered to be here," she reminded me.

"That makes it sad, maybe, but not stupid. Why don't you mingle?"

"Do I look like a fucking people person to you?"

"I don't know. How about those people? What's that crowd over there doing?"

Billie smiled and swayed on her feet. "They're playing Twister."

I considered that. "Okay, maybe it is a little stupid."

She gulped her second beer. I went to the keg and poured two more, one of which she immediately grabbed.

"It's not stupid because of Twister, flyboy. Get drunk enough and even that's fun. It's stupid because look at all these bored married women getting drunk and dancing around and flirting with every guy in sight. They're hitting on each other's husbands which is bad enough, but they're even hitting on the single guys which they ought to be thrown out for. This is all they have to do on this base! It's pathetic."

"It's a party," I insisted. "Yeah, they're bored but that's why they're here. Be grateful they're not swapping house keys."

"I wouldn't be surprised if they were," she muttered. "And it would be better if they did that than hit on the single guys."

"Do I detect a theme here?"

She glared at the crowd.

"My ex-boyfriend was busted for sleeping with somebody's wife," she said. She squeezed her beer hard enough that she crushed the cup and splashed lager over her hand.

"Ah." I didn't know what to say to that. Now the guy probably was both her ex-boyfriend *and* ex-Army. "But you're not hitting on me just because you're mad at him, are you?"

"No, I'm over him. I still hate him and hope he caught a nasty venereal disease from that whore but I'm over him."

"Good."

"And I'm not hitting on you," she added.

"Yes, you are."

"I am not! God, what egos you pilots have."

I laughed. "You've been looking for me all night. No woman goes looking for a man in a dress unless she wants to hit on him. So you're hitting on me."

"I'm not hitting on you. Okay, maybe I am. I thought of something to make my office more livable."

"Oh, what's that?"

She held out her beer.

"Hold this for me. I have to go to the bathroom."

I took it. She ducked under the camo netting and ran to the door at the side of the hangar that normally said 'Restrooms' but tonight had a wooden sign hanging over it that read 'Latrines.' She got there just as Josh came out. He held the door for Billie and then walked over to me with his usual disgusted look.

"Sheesh," he muttered. "All this fantasy military stuff makes me sick."

"You're telling me," I replied. "I had to help decorate the hangar. I want to know what we're going to do with all this camo netting when the party's over. I don't even remember who we stole most of it from."

He looked at my dress. Josh had stuck with wearing BDUs and thought even that was going too far.

"I see you've set aside some special time to humiliate yourself in public," he commented.

"What do you mean?"

"You really go in for these morale boosters, don't you?"

"No, I just like wearing women's clothing."

"At least you're honest. What are you doing hiding over here?"

"I'm waiting for Lt Maris. She asked me to hold her beer."

"The chick from the Legal Office?"

"Yup."

He thought for a minute, trying to picture her, then put two and two together and matched her with the woman he'd just seen.

"She's not Jewish, is she?" he asked.

"Not as far as I know. Why?"

"Just wondering."

We heard the door to the restrooms close. Josh turned to go.

"I'll leave so as not to interfere with your intimate moment. Find out if she has any Jewish girlfriends."

"I'll get right on it."

He disappeared around a wall of netting just as Billie came back.

"You'll get right on what?"

"Having sex with you," I said.

She shrugged. "You can't rape the willing. Where were we?"

It took me a minute to get over that comment.

"You were saying that this party is dumb," I reminded her.

"I don't like stupid women," she muttered.

"Who does? Anyway, don't be mad at this group. They're bored. They're just letting off steam."

"If they want to party, okay," she replied. "But look how they're acting."

She had a point. It took only a glance around the hangar to spot at least half a dozen wives who had let themselves go further than they would care to remember the next morning. Lucy Povenich, my flight commander's wife who in a few short months would be arrested for mailing marijuana to her sister in the States, was dancing on a table to Brown Eyed Girl. That by itself was fine. That her top had come undone and was working its way to the floor probably wasn't. That the tattooed 19-year-old wife of an Army private at Fort Kobbe was on the table with Lucy and kissing her neck while pulling off her own top almost certainly wasn't. Six other women were doing the macarena out on the hangar floor – the macarena wasn't playing but they danced the moves anyway, exaggerating the motions into something even their husbands didn't want to watch.

"Who is that woman?" Billie asked, pointing to a brunette at the beer keg wearing the requisite brown t-shirt and dog tags.

"Uh, that's Colonel Buncheman's wife."

"She's not wearing a *bra*," Billie said in disgust. "I can see that from here."

We could all see it since the colonel's wife had apparently had some kind of accident with the keg and drenched the front of her t-shirt. That and the cold air from the rainstorm made her lack of a bra hard to miss.

"She's got to be fifty years old!" Billie exclaimed. "What is she thinking?"

"Maybe she's trying to hook up," I suggested.

"Ugghh," was all Billie could answer. "And who's that? Please tell me she's not married to someone in your squadron."

I looked where she pointed. "Oh, actually that one's *in* our squadron. He's a pilot."

"That's a guy?!"

Lowell had snuck back into the party. At the moment he was lounging by the punchbowl and hitting on Colonel Hunley's daughter who was in town on a college break. It wasn't clear that Hunley's daughter knew that Lowell was hitting on her or even that Lowell was male. Under Declan's prompting (Declan stayed out of sight behind the potted palms) it appeared Lowell was trying to befriend the girl first and then at some point in the future bring up the fact that he had a penis. Lowell was famously shy around women but to see him chatting up a storm now it appeared his costume gave him courage he had heretofore lacked.

Billie took another look, tilting her head as she tried to see beyond the rouge and eye-shadow.

"He scares me," was all she said.

"Us, too," I agreed. "But he flies alright."

The Twister crowd grew. It took a while but soon the pilots figured out it was an opportunity to contort their bodies around any women foolish enough to get on the mat.

"Want to join them?" I asked when Billie finished our last beer. Her eyes were growing heavy.

"Why do you ask?"

"You look the Twister type," I said carefully.

"What does that mean?"

"It means that deep down inside there's a little lawyer who – if we give her enough alcohol – would love to get completely uninhibited and engage in a little 1970s suburban middle-class fun."

"You mean by rolling around on the floor with people I work with?"

"In your socks," I nodded.

"What makes you think I'm inhibited?"

"You seem a little uptight."

"Uptight?"

Retreat, retreat, a little voice in my head recommended.

"No, I mean, well, you work in a weird-shaped office all day. It probably makes you just want to get out and do something wild and crazy every now and then. You know, like, play Twister."

She struggled to focus. "You know," she said. "I came here tonight to meet you."

"Me?"

"Yes."

"Why?"

"Because you didn't hit on me at my office and I want to know why."

I tried to think of a reason that didn't involve being a coward and couldn't come up with anything.

"You didn't hit on me out at the gun range, either," she added.

"You had a gun."

"So?"

"So you were shooting everything in sight. It made me nervous."

"You're a wimp. You could have introduced yourself."

"I could have but I looked pretty stupid with my lousy shooting that day," I pointed out.

"You are a bad shot," she agreed.

"I've shot expert three years in a row!" I insisted.

"So why not his year?" She smiled. "And you looked awfully cute dragging a bunch of napkins around the snack bar," she pointed out.

"You had to notice."

"Hard to miss. But you still could have hit on me while I did your will."

"You didn't seem interested," I explained weakly.

She spread her palms in disgust. "Wha...? What was I supposed to do? I took, like, five times longer than was necessary to write your stupid will, just waiting for you to say something. You didn't even have anything to leave to anybody – you think it was easy stalling over nothing?"

"Well,...I thought you were just making sure everything was in order."

"What everything? You don't have anything. 'And to my loving family I leave my clothes?' It's a good thing the Air Force gives you life insurance or the government would just bury you by leaning you up against a tree."

"You could have said something."

"Like what?"

"Like something to help me."

"Like what?" she repeated.

"Like, um, I don't know... How about, 'Hey, I'm single. Would you like to go out sometime?'"

She jabbed a finger into my chest. "That's your job, mister!" she barked.

Rolo reappeared. His dress was torn and the sash around his waist was gone.

"Oh, hey," he greeted us, looking behind him to check if he was being followed.

"What happened to you?"

"I played Twister. Don't do that," he recommended. He dropped to his hands and knees and looked for his shoes underneath the locker. "All the colonels' wives are over there and they're drunk."

"Is that how your dress got ripped?" I asked.

"Yeah. Heidl's wife groped me. And then that major from Finance – you know, the one who yells at us to submit more and more copies of our travel voucher every time we come back from a trip? The one with the eyebrows drawn on so she always looks surprised? She decided she liked my sash and tried to take it."

"You fight back?"

"Hell, yeah, I did. I paid for this thing. Left foot on green, my ass – I hip-threw that bitch."

"How did you lose your sleeve?"

"That was Colonel Hunley's wife. She's looking for their daughter and thought I was one of the guys hitting on her so she tried to search me for my ID. That's what she said she was doing, anyway. Women are as bad as men. They're animals." He looked up at Billie and added, "Present company excepted."

"Not really," she replied. "You want to sue?"

"No, I just want to get out of here. Where are my shoes? Are you guys done?"

"Done what?" I asked.

"Making out, or whatever you were doing over here."

"We were just talking!" I stammered.

"Of course we were," Billie added. "Your friend is clueless." She tried to roll her eyes but it made her lose her balance and stagger into me, so instead she rolled her head around her eyes in an attempt to get the same effect. "It took him a whole appointment not to ask me out so it'll probably take him another month to kiss me."

Before I could answer, Rolo found his shoes. He sat on the floor and struggled to put them on, hiking up his skirt far enough that both Billie and I turned away to avoid the view.

"Good," he said. "I'm out of here. We're going to the Strac Club."

"Do you have a box lunch?" I asked.

"I'll pick up something on the way. Aw, the hell with these."

He slid the shoes back under the conexes. When he left Panama two years later they were still there.

"You leaving in bare feet?" I asked.

"It'll be faster."

"You're not driving, are you?"

"No. Flutie's giving me a ride."

"Flutie? I didn't know he was here."

"He's here. Lt Col Rasmussen made him sit by the keg."

"Why?"

"He's wearing a bikini. Rasmussen figured that would keep people from drinking too much. Do you need a ride? We've got room in the car."

Billie grabbed my hand. "No, he doesn't."

"I don't?"

"He doesn't?"

"No," she said, the beer giving that one syllable several lilts. "We have plans."

"Oh?" said Rolo. "Another party?"

"Kind of. We're going to my office to have sex. You're not invited."

"Fine," he said, nonplussed. "I would probably just ruin the rest of my dress."

"I can't have sex with you," I interrupted.

She turned and stared at me. "Why not?"

"Yeah, why not?" Rolo wanted to know.

I let go of her hand and crossed my arms. "Because you're drunk," I explained. "I can't have sex with drunk women."

"Why not?" she repeated.

"Yeah, why not?" Rolo echoed her again. "Drunk women are the best ones *to* have sex with. That's what alcohol's for."

"It's not right," I stated matter-of-factly.

Billie gave me the same look she'd given me in the Legal Office, the one that suggested she didn't know why she wasted her time on some guys. She tried to think of something convincing to say and then – like any good lawyer – decided that a picture was worth a thousand words. She picked up an empty beer bottle off the floor.

"Okay," she said. "I'm not going to argue. You won't have sex with me if I'm drunk?"

"That's right."

"I will," Rolo offered.

"But will you have sex with me if I'm *not* drunk?" she wanted to know.

"Uh, sure."

"Okay. Then can a drunk person do this?"

She stood on one foot and held both hands out to her sides. She closed her eyes, then with the empty hand she reached in and touched her nose with her index finger. With her other hand she balanced the beer bottle by the neck on the back of her hand. She stood like that for fifteen seconds.

"Bravo!" Rolo exclaimed, clapping his hands. "I couldn't do that sober!"

Billie opened her eyes and put the bottle down. She looked at me and put her hands on her hips.

"So, what do you say, Mr. I-don't-hit-on-girls-until-they-hit-on-me-first?"

I held my hands out in submission. "That's good enough for me."

She grabbed my arm and hustled me toward the door.

"Nice to meet you!" she called to Rolo over her shoulder. "Don't wait up!"

23. The Importance of Being Ernest

Some people have bad luck. Others create their own bad luck for themselves. Jake was special in that he did both.

He also had a lot of names. Ernest was Jake's first name so of course no one called him that. He didn't like 'Brad,' either, which was his middle name because he said it sounded too much like a California beachcomber or a New England yuppie. Somewhere along the line he had picked up 'Jake,' which was innocuous and curt and appealed to his inner child, the kind of child who was forever saying "Hey, everybody, watch this!" and then being hauled before the principal for disciplinary action he never understood. Jake was also called 'Lucy' or 'Link" from time to time. That was a carryover from his college days when frat buddies discovered he had body hair thicker than what's on most people's head. 'Lucy,' as in Leakey's 2 million-year-old archeological discovery, and 'Link," as in The Missing One.

I met Jake in California where he flew C-141s on the same base where I flew C-5s. At the time he was a friend of a friend of a friend. We would run into each other in bars or at parties. He was invariably the one dancing on the bar or chasing some girl with a dollar clutched in his teeth, usually with a bouncer in hot pursuit. The personification of happy-go-lucky, fun only became fun for him when at least three people in the crowd were warning, "Dude, I don't think that's such a good idea." His buddies could depend on him to seek out a good time regardless of the consequences, like the time he led a roof-stomping raid on his squadron commander's house and put his foot through a skylight, or the time in UPT when he tried to crawl from the front seat to the back seat of a T-38 during a solo ride – while airborne – just to confuse the tower. He almost had to eject.

He was absolutely without shame, not even grasping the concept. His favorite gag in a restaurant was to see how loud he could say 'penis' before someone noticed. When my roommates and I threw a toga party, Jake showed up drunk and dropped an entire pizza upside down on the carpet. No problem: he picked the whole thing up, drove back to the pizza parlor in his toga, and chewed out the management for selling him food with hair in it. He went to the Sacramento Convention Center looking for an auto show and stumbled on a National Organization for Women rally instead. Eyes wide shut he blithely wandered the room telling jokes like, "What do you tell a woman with two black eyes? Nothing, you already told her twice," or "Why can't Helen Keller drive? Because she's a woman!" We marveled that he was still alive.

When you are subject to disciplinary action in the military it's called "getting to meet people." At Travis Air Force Base Jake's first chance to "meet people" came quickly. He drove a rented Winnebago full of partyers to the Burning Man in Nevada. When they ran out of money he traded the motor home for beer and a solar-powered car which didn't work. Nevertheless he packed eight people into the car and prayed for high winds, meaning they were still stranded in the desert during an alert notification of his squadron. But people loved him, sometimes even his commanders who found it necessary time and again to punish him as an example. The example worked – for everyone but Jake. By the time he was promoted to first lieutenant there was so much paperwork in his file that he didn't stand a chance of making it past major but he never let that stop him. Though consequences flowed to him the way mudslides look for impoverished villages he followed his instincts no matter how many times they got him in trouble. They say bad luck is better than no luck at all and Jake ran with what he had. Always. It was this consistency that made him popular. His buddies knew they would always be safe in the background when the fallout came around.

I wasn't one of Jake's buddies. When I met him I thought he was an ass. In fact, the real reason I knew him at all was that he hauled me into court.

At a party on the Sacramento River one Memorial Day I tried to impress a civilian nurse with my skills on a jet ski. It was difficult to do since I had never ridden a jet ski before and the one I'd borrowed was the Yugo of watercraft. It was underpowered and the engine kept stalling, stranding us in the middle of the river. Even when the engine worked the machine labored to move its own weight.

So there I was trying to hook up and not doing well, coaxing a half-swamped craft across the river while my passenger rolled her eyes in disgust, when all of a sudden Jake appeared to make me look even worse. With a super-powered Wave Runner and a nurse of his own he proceeded to ride circles around us, whooping and hollering and spraying water in every direction. His girl screamed in delighted terror; mine got drenched. The jet ski we were on dipped and rolled. My nurse fell off and clung to the side, wiping wet hair from her eyes and yelling for me to do something. The engine quit again. Not that it mattered, the gulf in horsepower being insurmountable even when it ran. Jake would plow past us on his river rocket, spin around, and then leap his machine's own wake mere feet away, cutting left then right sharply to catch us with a wall of water. It was all I could do to keep us upright.

Then the police stepped in.

Specifically, it was two state troopers in a police boat. They were spending their holiday weekend trolling the river for BUI's – Boaters Under the Influence. This was California, after all, and to two straight-laced law enforcers missing out on barbecues of their own Jake must have looked like the poster child for river craft mishaps.

Jake was incredulous. He protested, he groveled, he rolled his eyes and pleaded. He cited his constitutional rights as they towed him to shore: had Adam pulled off the same performance even God might have felt bad for not adequately explaining the rules. But God didn't work for the state police. Though they couldn't get him for being drunk as Jake hadn't been drinking, they slapped him with a $500 fine for reckless endangerment.

So we went to court.

Often during the court proceedings I wondered what I was doing there. By all rights I should have been a witness for the prosecution, happy to see the showboater shown up since I was being made to look like the skinny dude on the beach having sand kicked in his face. But for two weeks after the party Jake called me at home, he pestered me at the squadron, he dropped by the house with beer as an enticement: such was his tenacity and such were his powers of persuasion that by the time I finished listening he had convinced me that the government had done him a grievous wrong.

The courtroom agreed with us. A roomful of traffic miscreants with scores of their own to settle nodded and murmured in approval as Jake produced pictures, graphs, scale models of the crime scene, and operating manuals for both models of jet ski to show he could not possibly have done the things the police claimed he had. He paced before the bench, waving his finger in the air to punctuate a lecture on civil liberties. He quoted Jefferson, Madison, the California penal code, and ESPN. He had irrelevant books stacked so high on the evidence table that the state prosecutor asked that they be moved so he could see the judge. With each statement the judge squinted her eyes in confusion, obviously wondering how much she should tolerate and whether she had already lost control of the room. I squirmed in my seat.

"You took pictures of the river?" I asked him on the way to court, glancing in the back seat of his Mustang at all the poster boards and photographs.

"*And* the jet skis, *and* the restaurant!" he said confidently.

"The restaurant? The restaurant had nothing to do with it."

"Yeah, but I needed more pictures."

The judge herself clearly found Jake more amusing than informative. Nevertheless, she let him continue – in part, I believe, because she had the hots for him. For their part, the arresting officers couldn't have cared less. One of them fell asleep.

The coup de grace was when Jake called me to the stand.

"Mr. Bleriot, what do you do for a living?"

"I fly jets."

"For the military?"

"For the Air Force."

"Have you ever flown them in formation – I mean," he added, with an elaborate gesture to the courtroom to show he was rephrasing the question for their benefit. "Have you ever flown your plane close to another plane?"

Most of the courtroom looked like repeat offenders, welfare rats and trailer trash who were as familiar with city court as they were with the K-Mart lunch counter. All of them enjoyed this three-penny opera version of Perry Mason. Half nodded knowingly to show they knew about formations when Jake brought them into his confidence. In the back, the cop who was awake looked at his watch. I felt a bit guilty. Had the fine been less than it was I might have bolted.

"Why, yes, I have."

By the time I finished explaining fingertip formation at four hundred knots, using my hands to simulate the planes like a socially-challenged fighter pilot in a bar, we had won the courtroom over. As stupid as we thought it was, these were people raised to think Top Gun was a documentary. How could an *Air Force pilot* be recklessly endangered on a jet ski? The idea was ludicrous. So was the argument but by then even the judge had had enough. Her gavel came down.

"That's enough, Mr. Hanover. We all thank you for your presentation."

She delayed her verdict for a week and then let Jake off the hook. When she showed up at the toga party with him later in the year I gathered she was still individually thanking him for his efforts.

Jake showed up in Panama not to fly but to fill a flight commander's slot in the Air Operations Center. The AOC's job was to keep track of all U.S. flights in the SOUTHCOM Area of Responsibility. Since the AOR extended from the Texas-Mexico border to Tierra del Fuego, on paper at least it was a mammoth task. In reality, if you excepted our squadron's flights out of Howard and a few around Honduras, everything was so scheduled and programmed that it was like monitoring the departure and arrival screens at a small Midwestern airport. The fact was, there simply weren't that many flights to keep track of. I mean, there *were* – twenty to thirty a day, perhaps. But when you put that into perspective by realizing it was a continent-and-a-half of airspace you were talking about, twenty to thirty flights was nothing. Half of those were commercial airliners or embassy shuttles taking off from the States: they simply flew overhead at forty thousand feet and never needed to talk to anybody, at least not anybody in Panama. The rest were spy planes, tankers, fighters on maneuvers, and the occasional AWACS to coordinate it all.

You got an idea of the AOC's world by its size. It occupied half of a sub-basement below the wing intel shop, a garage-sized structure behind the base exchange whose tiled roof bristled with antennae. Next to the stucco'ed building were several satellite dishes and a two-story array of more antennae with enough guy-wires going in every direction to make you think that flying a kite in the area could crash our communications for all of Central America.

To visit the AOC was to visit a cave. The air conditioning worked too well. It lent a chill stability to the air that kept any breeze from wafting by to suggest that something interesting might be happening somewhere else. Gray cubicles clustered like stalagmites. The walls had neither windows nor pictures and the ceiling was lower than on the floors above, enough so that a tall person instinctively hunched when walking down the corridor. The whole place reeked claustrophobia.

The AOC wasn't supposed to be a bad job. It just acquired that reputation through circumstance and from a few bad apples that passed through. But the Air Force inadvertently confirmed the rumors by making the positions into six-month tours, meaning they were only temporary assignments and that commanders everywhere could use them to cull their ranks. This the commanders did. So it was safe to assume that of the two dozen people in the AOC at any given time only a few really wanted to be there. The rest were in detention, bad boys and girls crowded into the principal's office. Bad boys and girls who had no intention of rehabilitating. On the door to the AOC was a cartoon showing a dozen people running screaming in every direction: the caption read, "Too many freaks, not enough circuses." The room wore its dank air of insouciance like a badge of honor.

The focal point in the AOC was the radio desk. Two people sat there twenty-four hours a day monitoring long-range radios, both SATCOM and HF. The satellite position monitored, among other things, calls from the radar sites scattered around the north half of the South American continent. The High Frequency position monitored short-wave frequencies unique to the AOC but that were accessible to anybody with a ten-watt transmitter and a voice. That was Jake's job. He was there for 180 days to work the night shift listening to distant voices warble through space, bouncing off the ionosphere and around the globe, coming through his headset to transmit either nonsense or information. Ninety-nine times out of a hundred it was nonsense. Every now and then it was important. His commander at Travis volunteered him for the job.

"Yeah, it sucks," Jake admitted in a tired, why-me voice the first time I saw him on base. We hadn't seen each other in months but when he heard he was coming to Howard he looked me up. He hadn't changed. Stocky, sleepy-eyed, always needing a shave: whenever reality floored him with consequences he shook his head and looked skyward as though pleading for help. For someone as active as he was, he was the laziest-looking person I had ever met.

"So what do you do in there?"

Head shake. Eyes skyward.

"In the AOC? 'The Pit' as we call it? You won't believe it. I listen to the radio."

"All night?"

"All freakin' night."

"What do you listen to?"

"I don't know! Outer-freaking-space! Nobody tells me what I'm supposed to listen for so I hear everything. I'm a professional eavesdropper," he pronounced the word with distaste. "But we've got three frequencies and they all channel into these same speakers so unless somebody tells me what frequency they're on I haven't a clue where they're coming from. And they come from all over. I pick up people from the Caribbean, the Pacific, Argentina – you name it. I get Ascension Island, the Azores – the other night I picked up Thule."

"Isn't that in Greenland?"

"*Yeeesss*. And most of the time I don't understand a word of it."

"What, you mean it's in Spanish?"

"Yeah, maybe, I don't know. No, most of the time it's just a bad signal. Static and echoes and waves so warped by the atmosphere it's like a bad recording of some fifties sci-fi flick. 'Ooo-WHEEE-ooo! WHA-WHA-WHA! Oy-ee-oy-ee-oy-ee! Click-click-click!' Dude, my brain is fried after twelve hours of that stuff. Aliens could be sending me messages in all that white noise and I wouldn't know. It's like watching a test pattern on TV and trying to see shapes. I can't believe I've got six months of this bull."

I had to feel sorry for him. Not only was it a bad job but he was persuasive in translating the misery. When Jake was slapped down he could get depressed. When he got depressed he would see the dark side of things so well that once he got started you felt better about yourself just knowing you weren't him.

Yet he could bounce back quickly.

"Hey! But it could be worse. You know what happened two nights ago, my first night on the job?"

"What?"

"I'm sitting there with Ferd, the guy on the satellite freqs, when this call comes in on my speakers. *'Help! Help! They're shooting at me!'* I put my headset on – it takes me five minutes to figure out what freq the guy is calling on because he doesn't think to tell me. Finally I find him and say, you know, very official-like: '*Station calling on One-Four-Decimal-Three-Five-Five upper, this is the United States Air Force Southern Command Air Operations Center. Go ahead.*' The guy comes back, *'They're shooting at me! What do I do?!'* I say, *'Station calling, identify yourself and your location.'* He comes back, '*They're shooting at me! Jesus Christ, what do I do?!*' I finally get some details out of him – oh, and by the way, this goes on for over half an hour. Turns out this guy is sailing somewhere in the Caribbean. He's a hundred miles southwest of Haiti when these two other boats show up and fire on him."

"What, naval boats?"

"No! That's just the thing. Pirates."

"Pirates? *Pirates?* You're kidding, right?"

"Nope. Goes on all the time. I mean, I didn't know it myself but after Monday night I called around and did a little research. Something like three dozen private boats – yachts, sailboats, catamarans – go missing every year. And even more freighters. Freighters like oil tankers and steel haulers and stuff. They just disappear and nobody ever hears what happens to them."

"Good god! So what did you do with this guy?"

"What could I do? I mean, one of our jobs is to serve as a kind of rescue coordination center for the area, but that's only because we have the radios, not the assets. I mean, I never got a chance to find out who this guy was or if he was even an American citizen. He sounded like a Brit."

"Did he get away?"

"Well, while I was talking to him he was still trying to. I guess whatever boats the bad guys had weren't all that fast so this dude was trying to escape. He said he'd already been shot once, in the leg, and was bleeding. He was frantic, man. He kept screaming into the radio, 'What do I do? What do I do? They're getting closer!'"

"So what did you do?"

"We called the coast guard in Haiti and told them about it."

"The Haitian Coast Guard? That's it?"

"What were we going to do? Launch an F-16 – which wouldn't have the legs, by the way, even from Puerto Rico – to go strafe a couple of civilian boats based on a radio call?"

"Yeah, but jeez... Don't we have any way to...?" My voice trailed off.

"No. The fact is, we don't. There are a lot of places in this world where nobody can help you, even if you have a radio."

I thought about some of the places we flew. Jake was reading my mind.

"I know what you're thinking," he said with an enthusiastic nod. "Keep it in mind next time you're down over Santa Middle de Nowhere that nobody will be looking after you but you."

"That's comforting. So how'd things turn out the other night?"

"All I could tell this guy was, 'Go faster, dude' and wish him good luck. After half an hour we stopped hearing from him."

"Wow. You think he got away?"

"I don't know. I kind of doubt it. And I don't think we'll ever know."

I thought for a minute, trying to imagine the loneliness, the desperation the boater must have felt out on the open seas. Trying to run, praying for wind, seeing gunmen on power boats closing in...

Months later Declan and I were sitting around in the hangar daydreaming about how we would each like to sail around the world. Just grab a boat and a girl and head for the horizon. Declan was the sort who flitted from one enthusiasm to the next and yachting was his latest passion. He subscribed to magazines that promised freedom and luxury and adventures on far shores at the helm of some expensive craft. Those same magazines were probably responsible for more wistful dreams than Playboy but I was still willing to discuss the activity in abstract if Declan wished.

The subject of pirates came up. Declan mused out loud how he would be sure to carry an M-16 along on his voyages for protection. Just as he said that, Vince, the dark lord of the mechanic world, happened to walk by.

"Forget the M-16, guys!" he interrupted. "That's not going to scare anybody away."

"Alright, an M-60 then."

Vince grabbed a milk crate and squatted between us.

"You want *real* firepower to protect your domain, dude. And your woman. You don't want no Indonesian thugs crawling over the side to cut your throat and rape your lady, do you?"

Declan recoiled at the image. "No! So what do I need?"

Vince looked around and lowered his voice.

"You need a TOW missile! Just one. Guaranteed, you see a pair of speed boats coming at you and you blow one out of the water – *kaboom!* – from a thousand yards you won't need to bring another one on deck. Maybe a couple of RPGs, though, for good measure. I can get you those, too."

We stared at him. The man was serious.

"A TOW missile, Vince?"

"Tube-launched, Optically-tracked, Wire-guided," he assured us. "The big M-220. You don't even need to hit them. They see a missile go across their bow – guaranteed they'll turn around."

"Isn't that overkill?"

"No such thing as overkill when you're protecting your family, dude. Picture some skinny in the Indian Ocean crawling over the side while you're asleep,..."

"I got it, I got it," Declan stopped him.

"But if the TOW's too big for you my second choice would be a .50-caliber sniper rifle," Vince offered. "That'll go through an engine block like it's butter. Cut a guy in half, too. I can get you that but I've only got two so you'll want to get your bid in early."

"How about grenades?" Declan joked.

Vince scoffed.

"Those are easy. You can get 'em by the dozen. But that's close-in stuff – you want to keep the bad guys at a distance so I'd stick with the TOW."

He stood up to go and patted me on the shoulder.

"You boys ever start looking into that trip, give me a call. I'll hook you up."

At the time we thought Vince was crazy. Now I wondered if he was. The fellow in the Caribbean probably wouldn't have hesitated to use a TOW if he'd had one, judging from his panic. Running, calling for help, waiting for the pirates to come over the side...

I shook the image away.

"And that was just your first night," I said to Jake.

"Yeah," he agreed with a laugh. "Where the hell could it go from there?" He wasn't depressed anymore.

It wasn't in Jake's nature to stay down for long, which made it difficult for anyone to stay mad at him. Like a spaniel that's been bopped on the nose with a newspaper, Jake would sink to the depths of despair and then rise right back with such voluble enthusiasm for a new idea that it would ignite his listeners and draw people into whatever new scheme he was setting in motion. Which meant, of course, that he never learned from experience.

To channel his enthusiasm, Jake did things. While other guys talked, Jake moved. The Air Force simply wasn't all there was to his life, certainly not in Panama. He skied, he boated, he kayaked, he traveled; he bought a motorcycle so he could learn how to ride one; he went hang-gliding on a dare; he could party all night and drink like ten Indians on payday; he always showed up at events with a different beautiful woman on his arm – local women, even though he spoke almost no Spanish; and within ten days of being in Panama he had visited more of the country than most of the guys in my squadron. He called me from a pay phone on the Costa Rican border – right *on* the border – to see if I knew where he was. When I said no, he started shouting, "I'm in Panama! No, I'm in Costa Rica! No, wait, I'm in Panama!" as he hopped from one side of the line to the other. If his commander in California had thought to punish Jake by sending him to a boring job in Panama he failed. Jake was the color that the monochromatic AOC needed and he soon found there was all sorts of trouble to be gotten into down south.

Including trouble with guns.

I arrived at the squadron early one morning to find a message from Jake waiting for me. When I got him on the phone he didn't sound happy.

"Hey, can I come over?"

"Sure. Just show your ID to the guard."

By the time he showed up I was already hard at work behind the scheduling desk trying to figure out how to keep Walt from flying at all during the next week. As always, Walt was ahead of everybody on the 30-60-90-day hours list and had already tweaked the second half of April somehow so that he would stay in the lead. He was the lead scheduler and worked for Major Harmon while I was the junior scheduler and technically worked for him, but I pointed and clicked on the computer until his name disappeared from all but two flights.

"Bucking for promotion?" Jake asked when he saw me. He was in uniform but characteristically disheveled, like someone had found him passed out in the laundromat and thrown him into a spin cycle. The hang-dog look was back.

"To captain?" I replied. "If I keep breathing, I've got that covered. What's up?"

He sighed. "I think I might be in trouble."

I sat back in my chair.

"Jake, you saying you might be in trouble is like the captain of the Titanic saying he might have a leak."

"I'm not that bad."

"Earthquakes aren't that bad, Jake. Plagues of locusts aren't that bad. You're firmly in the bad category."

"Dude, they're after me again. Are you still doing that lawyer chick?"

"Um," I considered, trying to make sense of those sentences as a pair, "*Who* is after you? And I was never doing that lawyer chick, if you're talking about Billie, that is."

"Billie, that's her name? Dude, you're not railing her yet? How long have you been going out?"

It was Monday morning. What had I done to deserve this?

"Hey, there's more to a relationship than just sex."

"No, there isn't. Get moving and close the deal. Anyway, look. Can she help me? I may need her help. I'm back in the doghouse."

"You're in the doghouse so much it's a wonder you don't bark. What is it this time?"

The operations area was empty except for us and Tech Sergeant Laurette, an administrative troop. His desk was on the far side of the room in the corner by the back exit, hidden behind the cubicle walls we had all fought to keep from getting.

In his fourth year in Panama, Joey Laurette was short and plump and so black that if the light dimmed all you saw were eyes and teeth. A native of the Dominican Republic, he became a naturalized U.S. citizen and was now a career man trying to extend his assignment at Howard.

He peeked over the partition as Jake talked. When he realized who Jake was his eyes lit up. With a big grin he made a gun of his thumb and forefinger, pointed it at us, and pulled the trigger.

"Way to go, sir!" he laughed, and gave us a big thumbs-up.

Jake grimaced.

"What's that all about?" I asked.

"You don't know?" he said, surprised.

"Know what? I live downtown, remember? Some excitement here over the weekend that I missed out on?"

Jake threw up his arms and fell into a chair behind the scheduling counter.

"Uh, yeah, you could say that. But they're making a bigger deal out of it than it was," he insisted.

On the other side of the room Laurette snorted.

"Come on, let's hear it," I motioned to Jake. "Give me the Jake Hanover 'this-really-was-nothing' version. It's Monday. I could use a laugh."

Jake sighed. He started to speak, then reconsidered, then huffed and hesitated and wound himself up to tell the story with the innocent disbelief that I remembered from the Sacramento River.

"Okay, you know Sam Povenich's house up above the commissary, back by the Officers' Club? He's on leave in the States with his crazy wife so I've been watching it for him."

"Somebody trusted you with their house?"

"Yeah, can you believe it?"

"I seem to remember Paulie did that in Davis and you filled it with hookers."

"They weren't hookers. It was a sorority."

"Guys were paying them for sex."

"It was a fundraiser. *Anyway*, Saturday night, about twelve-thirty, we're sleeping upstairs – "

"Stop already. Who's 'we'?"

"Ah. Me and Joanie. You know her. The girl from the Yacht Club."

"Joanie the Zonie? You're banging her?"

Another cackle from Laurette.

"Sgt Laurette, you're not eavesdropping, are you?" I called.

"No, sir. Not at all. I'm just monitoring your conversation for quality control purposes."

"Dude, we've been going out for a couple of weeks," Jake answered indignantly. "Where've you been?"

"Downtown trying to keep track of all the other women you've been dating at the same time. What happened to the realtor, the one who was helping you find an apartment? She figure out it wasn't an apartment you were after?"

"No, she was cool with that. I met her family, though. Dude, I think they were all into drug running or something – a big compound downtown, the expensive cars, bodyguards, the whole nine yards."

"And that bothered you?"

"No, that didn't. Her sister did, though. She had a hottie little sister who kept coming on to me. When I did what any man naturally would..."

"Explain to her that you were taken?" I prompted.

"No, I banged her. Then all of a sudden I'm persona non grata at the compound. People seem awfully conservative down here – I meant to ask you about that."

"Never mind, one crisis at a time. Go ahead with the first story. So you and the colonial mistress are going at it on Sam's bed..."

"No, no, we're asleep. We'd already gone at it, now we're asleep. Then Joanie hears something and wakes up..."

"What'd she hear?"

"She hears a breaking sound. Then some voices. She shakes me and says, 'Jake! Jake! Someone's breaking in downstairs!' So I get up to see."

The family housing on Howard Air Base was a standard design. Each house was a duplex, three stories of beige stucco and red trim divided down the center. On each side was a yard, a driveway with a carpark, and outside stairs that led to the living quarters on the second floor.

Since all houses were the same design it was hard for any family to go wrong when they were assigned to one. Most buildings backed up to the jungle, too. With a lawn on three sides and year-round tropical foliage looming over the back, each unit was like living in a garden.

The houses shared a similar interior as well. The ground floor was taken up by a car park, a storage room, and a room that everyone called "the maid's quarters," although having a live-in maid was a practice slowly dying out. On the second floor was the living area, a dining room, and the kitchen. At the top of the house were the bedrooms. It wasn't a lot of space but it was efficient.

The only problem was security.

There were no fences around Howard Air Base. When the base was built in the 1930's a fence was unnecessary since the Bridge of the Americas didn't exist yet. Traffic and the local presence around the base were minimal. Also, at that time the Canal Zone was strictly enforced. Local people needed a pass to be within the buffer area around the canal and Howard lay within that protective perimeter. Furthermore, the jungle itself served as a barrier. Few people, even thieves and spies, were willing to brave the dense forest and swamps that surrounded the base.

In the 1960's that changed. In reaction to an anti-American element growing in the city, base engineers erected fences around the more vulnerable borders of the base. The instant they did, though, Yankee security met Panamanian economic reality: locals stole the fences. So the engineers built stronger fences with intertwined concertina wire – those were stolen, too. They built higher, stronger fences, stretching electric strands along the chain-link and sinking the poles in concrete bases – the strands were sabotaged and the fence disappeared, concrete and all. There was no way to maintain a reliable artificial barrier in terrain where it couldn't be watched, not in a land so poor that even security devices were seen as easy money. Panamanian culture might be lazy but it makes exceptions for theft. After ten years of trying, the fence proposals were dropped. The jungle reverted to its status as the primary – and the only – buffer against intruders.

And it continued to do a good job for a while. Without the incentive of free fencing on the outskirts of the base, thieves were now forced to commit to penetrating the jungle to reach the gold that lay inside – base housing – and many shrugged off the attempt. But over the years others still came, and came, and came. By the time I arrived eight months after the invasion the base was averaging ten robbery attempts per week. Career looters established permanent trails through the undergrowth. Every night they used them to reach the ornamental gardens and neatly-trimmed lawns spread along the hills overlooking the runway, picking different streets each night, pin-pricking the base like larcenous ants assaulting a picnic, knowing there was no way any security force could stop all of them, or even some of them, all the time.

But the Security Police tried. The cops on Howard had decades of experience to draw on and were well-equipped to deal with low-tech intruders. Howard had the only horse-patrol in the Air Force. There was a dog patrol as well. According to Billie, who viewed the police 'rap-sheet' each morning, the German shepherds were the most effective deterrent. They were also the preferred means of apprehending a fleeing looter, even more so than the teams of SPs who monitored the trails using night-vision goggles. Though no deliberate attacks against the police from looters ever occurred, the jungle and the housing area itself was dark, dark, dark at night and no SP with a zest for life wanted to charge around the area at full speed if he could help it. It was easier to release the dogs.

So the base fought back. The reality, though, was the thieves' overwhelming numbers. Someone always got through. Every morning some family on base woke up to find tools or recreational gear or boxes of personal belongings missing. Sometimes cars would be broken into but the preferred targets of the robbers were the storage room and the maid's quarters. Those often held a smorgasbord of American consumer excess. If a family was lucky, some things would be found scattered through the brush just inside the treeline, dropped as thieves lightened their load. Most goods, however, were never recovered, even if boxes taken contained only books, family albums, or heirlooms. Once an item left the base, it was gone. Frustration ran high for the victims.

It also ran high for the police. Common sense, Air Force regulations, and the notion of proportional response limited their options. They couldn't just shoot the invaders for stealing a kid's bike. They couldn't harm them in any way, in fact, though the dogs were encouraged to take a few extra bites. And the Panamanians knew that. Any Panamanian who was caught learned quickly that there were no consequences. The Status of Forces Agreement prevented the U.S. from detaining or punishing trespassers in any way other than to hand them over to local authorities. And everyone knew the local authorities did nothing. Billie fumed over how the Panamanian police released anyone they received from the Americans, unwilling to go to the trouble of prosecuting them. She believed they received kickbacks as well. Stealing from the base was a game, one which the gringos always lost.

"So I get up," Jake continued, "listen for a minute, and sure enough, there's this sound downstairs, like somebody's trying to pry open a window. And I think, 'Sons of bitches, they're breaking into the place!'"

"Could you see them out the window?"

"Wait. So I grab my nine-mil – "

"Your what?"

"My 9mm pistol. It's a Ruger I picked up when I was living in Fairfield."

"I know what a nine-mil is," I said. "What were you doing with it on base?"

It may be surprising to a civilian but gun control is fanatical on a military base. Bases may *have* a lot of guns but they don't get handed around. Personal weapons of any kind are strictly controlled. Nobody can keep a weapon anyplace within the perimeter of a base except at the base armory where the SPs keep them under lock and key, register them, and monitor when they are checked out and for what purpose. A lot of us didn't like it but the fact is that the military defends democracy, it doesn't practice it.

"Well, yeah, I know," Jake squirmed in his seat. "And that may be part of the problem. I mean, I brought it down here and intended to take it to the armory but..."

"But you decided you could get into a lot more trouble by hanging onto it. Okay, I follow you. Go on."

He sighed. I wasn't the sympathetic audience he had hoped for.

"So...I grab the nine-mil and head downstairs. I get to the living room and sure as all hell I can hear them outside. There's this breaking sound. And I get pissed. I mean, I was actually scared coming down the stairs. I'm in my underwear, holding a gun, creeping around in the dark looking for guys who're breaking into my house. Well, not *my* house but the house I'm staying in. But now I get pissed."

Oh, god. I began to wonder if he had killed somebody.

"But I've also got a problem. Sam's front door sticks and the doorknob is loose. It makes this clanking sound and a big screech. I'd tried to fix it all week but there's no quiet way to open it. The only thing you can do is twist and yank hard and that makes noise."

"So the second you open it they're going to know you're there."

"Exactly. And I want to catch them in the act. So I'm trying to figure out a way to do it when all of a sudden I hear glass breaking. And I think, now they're breaking into my car!"

"*Yesssss,*" I prompted.

"So I just went for it," he said. "I grab the door, pull it open – and it makes just as much noise as I knew it would – and jump out on the top of the steps. Sure enough, there they are: four of 'em. Four lazy-ass, gringo-hating, stuff-stealing bastard Panas."

"Don't hold back. Tell me how you really feel."

"Oh, like you don't feel the same way."

"Not at all."

"Bullshit."

"So what did you do?" I feared the answer.

"I jump out on the landing. They're at the bottom of the steps, four of them. One's got a crowbar that he's been going to town with on the door to the storage room. The door's open now and another guy is down on the ground by a box he just pulled out. The glass that broke was from a picture frame that fell out of the box, not from my car. So they all stop what they're doing and look up at me, the one guy with the crowbar kind of raised. And I yell, '*Helado*, motherfuckers!'"

"'*Helado?*' That's ice cream."

"No, it's not. It's 'freeze.'"

"No, it's ice cream. Take my word for it. It can also mean 'frozen' but either way it doesn't make sense when a hairy guy in his underwear yells it while pointing a gun at you. What did they do?"

Jake looked perplexed. "Damn," he said. "That's what I said? No wonder they didn't freeze."

"What did they do?"

"They took off! Fast. Like their clothes were on fire or somebody told them they had to get a job. I mean, they just dropped everything – box, crowbar, everything – and tore ass across the grass toward the treeline. One guy plowed right through the garbage can, fell flat on his face, then got up and kept running."

"So you didn't shoot anyone?"

"No, hell no, you think I'm stupid?"

I waffled. "So why are you in trouble, then?"

"Well,...they take off and they're all running but I'm still really pissed. And scared. How often do I point a gun at somebody? I'm not going to shoot them but I'm still mad. So I point the gun down at the grass and squeeze off a few rounds."

Sgt Laurette started cheering.

"Oh, boy!" I hopped off the counter. "Oh, boy! You shot at them!"

"No, no!' Jake protested. "Nowhere near them. Straight down into the grass."

"Yeah, but you shot the gun! You shot the gun!"

"So?"

"So? You don't shoot a gun on base!"

"Hey, now I know, alright? You want to hear what happened or not?"

Sgt Laurette appeared from his desk and did a victory strut in the middle of the room like a wide receiver who has just scored a touchdown. "*Boo-yah! Boo-yah!*" he celebrated, waving his arms. *"Shoot the man! Shoot the man!"*

I barked at him to be quiet. He stopped whooping and leaned over the scheduling counter with a big grin. The story was better than he'd thought.

"Holy cow, you think they were running fast to begin with? When I fired off those bullets they went to light speed! One guy ran right over the dude ahead of him. Right over him and kept on going. They all went into the trees so fast none of them could have known where they were going. Even with my ears ringing I heard them running into stuff left and right."

Laurette slapped the desk and whooped again. He lived on base.

"That's superb, that is just superb!" he shouted to the empty room. "Mo-fo sons of bitches, breaking into your house. *This is MY house, bitch! Get the hell out!* Whoo-hoo! I would have *paid* to see them run. Paid to see it!" He high-fived Jake, who returned the gesture with somewhat less enthusiasm. "Of course," he added, calming down, "I would have been running just from seeing you in your underwear, sir."

"Then what?" I asked.

"Then the whole neighborhood woke up. It's funny, I pull the trigger and within seconds there are lights going on all down the street."

"Imagine that."

"Boom, boom, boom, one place after the other. I never even had to call the cops. Ten people did it for me. Mick Connor lives in the next place over and he was the first one outside, yelling 'Hey, Jake, what the hell's going on?'"

I could easily imagine Connor shouting that in his Boston accent. He always sounded mad but no doubt in the middle of the night he was in peak form.

"Joanie comes down and she's all upset because she thinks I've killed someone."

"Wonder why she thought that?"

"Then the cops show up. I'm out there already and people are gathering around so I tell them what happened, show them the break-in and where I fired the bullets. The shell casings were right there and you could see the holes in the dirt so it was obvious what happened."

"They weren't mad?"

"Hell, no! They were like this guy," he said, pointing at Laurette. "They thought it was funny. I had to give 'em my gun but I'd planned to do that anyway so it was no big deal. They were joking how that would be the safest street to live on for weeks."

I was incredulous. "That's it? They didn't haul you in and lock you up?"

"Nope," Jake said smugly. "They didn't have a problem with it at all. They *did* call the lawyer on duty, a Captain Smalls, to ask him what he thought. He told them to leave it until the morning and let my commander handle it."

"Wow," I shrugged. "I'm surprised. I thought it was a bigger deal than that."

Jake sagged in his seat. "Oh, it is," he corrected me. "At least, it is *now.*"

"What do you mean?"

"General Heidl found out about it first thing yesterday morning and raised holy hell that I hadn't been arrested. He wants a court-martial. Can you believe it? A fricking *court-martial*? I didn't even have a chance to call Colonel Martin – he called me yesterday right after Heidl called *him.*"

"Martin's your boss over at the AOC?"

"Yup."

"And what did he have to say?"

"Well, you have to understand Martin has been kind of ticked with me lately."

"Why's that?"

"He's still mad about the condom gag a few weeks ago. You know, where we left them on his desk the day his wife came over?"

I held up my hand.

Jake took a deep breath. "Anyway, first he chewed my ass. He's probably going to do it again when I see him in twenty minutes – that's why I'm here early. But I'll give him credit: when he finished yelling he calmed down and asked my side of the story. I told him and then he mellowed a bit. He said he would try to talk the general down from a court-martial but didn't hold out much hope he would be successful. Apparently the general already made some comment about "He that liveth by the sword shall perish by it."

"What does that mean? He's going to put you before a firing squad of 9mm pistols?"

"I think it means that there'll be some kind of action no matter who vouches for me."

"He'll back you up, Martin will," Laurette promised. "If he's a good commander he will. A good commander looks out for his troops."

"Well, yeah," I countered, "but it depends on what his troops give him to work with."

Jake waved that off. "Martin likes me."

"How do you know that?"

"He said he did. He said, 'Jake, I like you and know you try hard. It's just that sometimes you shit too close to the house.'"

"I would call that a qualified endorsement."

"You would probably court-martial me, too," he accused. "It's a good thing I don't work for you."

"No," I corrected. "If you worked for me, first I would counsel you to have a silencer on your pistol so you could have plugged the bastards with nobody knowing. Then, since you didn't do that, I would give you a Letter of Reprimand for keeping the gun in your place and pile you up with extra work around the squadron for about a month."

"An LOR?" he considered. "Not even an Article 15?"

"Call me Santa Claus. An Article 15 would be too much. I would settle for an LOR."

An Article 15 in an officer's file killed his career. Letters of Reprimand a guy could recover from and still be promoted. But then, I didn't like Panas much, either.

"But even if Martin vouches for me I'm thinking I should talk to somebody at the legal office," Jake continued, still worried. "Just in case it gets ugly."

I reached for the phone. "Let's give her a call. Be advised, though, that she's a legal nazi. If she had been on duty Saturday night instead of Smalls she would have arrested you on the spot. Come to think of it, she might have had them court-martial you on the spot."

"You're kidding. She looks so nice."

"Oh, no, my friend. Beware the lawyer within."

Billie, though she hadn't slept with me since that night in her office, had given me a number to call where I wouldn't have to go through her secretary to speak to her. Every time I used it I reminded myself that the trade-off was lacking.

She answered on the first ring.

"Hey, your ears must have been burning."

"If you were talking about me I hope you were saying good things," she responded coyly. She sounded as good as she looked.

"I didn't know there were any bad things one could say about you. I certainly don't know any."

She laughed. "Maybe one day, pilot-boy. Maybe one day."

"I won't hold my breath. You sleeping better?"

Billie had been living in bachelor's quarters on Albrook until she met me. Then, persuaded that it was important to experience local culture, she moved into an apartment outside the back gate. It was a nice place but right away she had trouble with her upstairs neighbor. The woman was a secretary by day but a hooker at night. Five nights a week with every customer she stripped and screwed to the tunes of "Hotel California." It was driving Billie crazy. The sound of squeaking springs was bad enough but now she had gotten to the point where she couldn't bear any song by the Eagles.

"The earplugs are helping. I really pray for weekends, though."

"Hmm. Well, hey, this call is professional. I have a legal dilemma to ask you about."

"Sure, go ahead. You revising your will?"

"No, even better. A guy I know had a little incident with the SPs Saturday night. It might not be much but it might be a lot so he wants to touch base with you lawyers. Can I pass him the phone?"

The laughing stopped. "Is this the shooter?" she asked curtly.

"Is that what we're calling him?"

"If it's him don't pass him the phone. I don't want to speak one word with him. I don't even want to know who he is."

"Whoa," I said. "That's a little extreme, isn't it? So he fired a gun on base – I thought you guys were there to serve all our legal needs."

"Mike," she said patiently, then paused and started again. "First of all, he's lucky I wasn't on duty Saturday night." I threw an I-told-you-so glance at Jake. "Whatever Darren Smalls was thinking he was wrong. They should have arrested your friend on the spot."

"Why?"

"Why? *Why?* Well, if for nothing else they should have thrown him in jail for being stupid. For god's sake, Mike, he violated all four of the fundamental rules of criminal activity: admit nothing, deny everything, make counter-accusations, and flee the scene. Your friend's an idiot!"

"Or innocent."

"Whatever. Second, I'm a *prosecutor,* Mike. A JAG. If there's a court-martial – and off the record it's looking that way – someone in this office is going to prosecute him. For all I know it'll be me. He doesn't want to talk to me and I don't want to talk to him. Jeez, you pilots don't know anything except flying, do you?"

"Should we?"

"Yes, Mike. It's a big Air Force."

"That's why I hang out with you, Billie. To keep me honest. So who does he talk to?"

"Do you have a pen? Take down this number: 424-1180. Her name's Emma, she's the ADC."

"What's an ADC?"

"Oh, god. You guys *are* hermits. The Area Defense Counsel, Mike. The defending lawyer for the base. She's the only one he should talk to. Period."

"Huh," I said. "I didn't know you guys divided yourselves up like that."

I heard her suck in her breath. She must have counted to ten because it was a while before she replied.

"That's why you guys need to get off the flightline once in a while," she exhaled, knowing I hated this speech. "To see how the rest of the Air Force works."

"I didn't know there was more to the Air Force than flying," I countered, knowing she hated that reply. Point, counter-point. "But speaking of getting out, how about dinner on Thursday? I keep hearing about Las Bovedas but the word is I need a beautiful woman to accompany me or I'll get all kinds of looks."

She softened a little. "You'll get fewer looks if you take a beautiful *local* woman, not me. Not many Americans go there."

"What can I say? I have no taste."

"How romantic."

"Look, you know if you say no I'm just going to keep asking so why not avoid having your phone tied up all day?"

"I could unplug it."

"I'll camp out in your parking space."

"I don't have one. They don't deem me that important," she replied, but I could tell she was going to say yes. "Let's see, Thursday?" There was the sound of pages flipping in her organizer. "Sure, I'd love to. Las Bovedas is a formal place, you know. You'll have to wear a tie. Do you own a tie?"

"I'll cut something from the drapes."

"And we'll need reservations."

"I'll have my people call their people."

"I can hardly wait."

"Great. Let's say around eight. I'm sure we'll talk before then."

"As long as it's not about your friend."

"Wouldn't think of it. I'll have him call, who is it again? Emma?"

"You do that."

I hung up the phone. Jake looked at me in disbelief.

"I'm glad your social life is settled," he exclaimed. "I'm going to prison and you're trying to get a date."

"Not just trying. Succeeding. I knew she would want to go. Las Bovedas is as elegant as the Panas get. No woman passes up a chance to get dressed up."

"Wonderful. Glad to hear it. By the way, did you happen to pick up anything relevant to me, the guy who's going to be sitting in a jail cell while you're eating crab cakes?"

I held up the number.

I had met Emma before. I just didn't know it.

Earlier in the month I had gone on a double-date with Josh to an Indian restaurant off Tumba Muerto. Anyway it was supposed to be a double-date. His girlfriend of the week was setting me up with a friend of hers who called in sick at the last minute. Rather than let me bow out quietly Josh insisted I come to dinner with the two of them. I obliged, feeling very much the odd man out.

While we waited to be seated a whirlwind blew by. Medium-height, ample figure, deep brown eyes, long black hair coiled atop her head like an explosion waiting to happen, Emma entered the foyer from the dining room and instantly dominated the scene. She was talking, loudly, about something to her date, who she gripped tightly at the elbow and hustled along the way the Secret Service leads the President from a hostile crowd.

What I noticed first about Emma were her breasts. I couldn't help it. Fashion designers would call her voluptuous. My mother would describe her politely as big-boned. All I could picture was the king in that Monty Python movie saying, "She's got *HUUUGE* tracts of land!" And Emma knew it for she was dressed in a Goth outfit of black-on-black with a plunging neckline that revealed at least a five-inch line of surging ghostly-white cleavage. I had to look away before I lost my balance and fell in. Her mascara was dark, her eyebrows like pitch, and her nightborne hosiery climbed from stiletto heels. A whip would not have been out of place as an accessory. She conquered the room before she had taken three steps. In her wake was a trail of exhausted wait staff.

We stepped back to let the two of them pass but if Emma noticed us she gave no sign, engrossed in her own words and tugging her date the way a storm carries along a small boat. He was American and clean-cut, obviously military and obviously in over his head. I wondered if he had aimed for the cleavage initially and now was terrified he might get what he'd asked for. He had the submissive look of a dog afraid to be beaten.

As they passed, the guy caught sight of Josh. He lunged for him with his one free arm, grasping for a lifeline.

"Josh! Josh Breitling! Hey, Emma, this is Josh Breitling! How's it going, guy?"

He couldn't quite pull himself free but he managed to stop her before us. His eyes were pleading. Help me, they said. *Help me.* It was pathetic. And amusing. But while sympathy came easy, I wasn't going to help him. She looked hungry. Who would she go after if he managed to get away?

"Hey, Art," said Josh carefully, the wary look on his face impossible to miss. "How's it going? How's the Navy treating you?"

"Good, good." Art just managed to get his feet steady against the anchor pull of his date. "Hey, have you met Emma Llanbedr – Capt Llanbedr? She's a legal eagle for you guys."

We heard an encouraging chuckle that went nowhere as he turned to present her and met the gaze of a praying mantis about to feed.

"Hello, so pleased to meet you," she said warmly. Her voice was liquid. It flowed from curving ruby lips that enunciated each syllable with the precision of a diction coach. Her eyelids batted so much as she spoke I wasn't sure she even saw us. No matter. She returned immediately to looking at her man.

An awkward pause. Josh's date didn't speak English and I was sure he was thinking the same thing I was: 'It's been nice knowing you, Art.'

"So,..." Art struggled.

"Yes, anyway, we're just out for dinner," Josh said at the same time. "Pretty good food, is it?"

But that was as far as it went. Emma, impatient, re-established her grip and practically whipped her sailor around in a hip throw.

"It's excellent, excellent," she said sweetly over her shoulder as she muscled him out the door. "Sorry, but Arthur and I have to rush. Bye."

The last we heard from Art was a distant, "Heh-heh, maybe we could join them..."

Josh and I looked at each other.

His date said innocently, "*Esa fue una mujer formidable.*"

The trial never happened, though not for lack of trying on the JAG office's part. That is, on Billie's part.

It was thrown into Billie's lap after Captain Smalls was counseled for – well, even he wasn't sure what he was counseled for except failing to predict the politically-correct course the wing commander would follow. I used to see him around the base and was happy that the wrist-slap affected him not at all. Smalls came to the Air Force from private practice, unlike Billie who enlisted out of law school. He had money and experience, two things that give one confidence regardless of profession. He was relaxed enough that if the higher-ups wanted to play with the rules he would state his case and then roll with the punches. I often wondered how he and Billie got along working in the same office.

The irony of her taking the case was that she and Emma were great friends. The Area Defense Counsel on any base is a position removed from the normal legal goings-on so as not to create a conflict of interest. On Howard the removal was physical: the ADC's office wasn't even on base, it was across the highway on Rodman Naval Station. The ADC reports directly to the wing commander and runs his own show with only the interest of the client as a guide, steering clear of what the Air Force wants done or what the base wants done or of any point that a particular commander is trying to make. It's a remarkable amount of latitude given how the military usually operates. Consequently, lawyers of all kinds want the job. Good lawyers with experience behind them usually get it. Billie aspired to be an ADC one day after a couple of tours as a prosecutor. I wondered if that would suit her. Her aggressiveness and enthusiasm for prosecution made me wonder if defending people could bring her the same satisfaction as sending people to the electric chair. Pit bulls, after all, are rarely lauded for saving small children.

Which is why it was strange to me that she and Emma were such pals. But pals they were, as I found out after Jake plunged himself into the complex mix of base politics, legal maneuvering, and intricate behind-the-scenes dealing that was the military justice system. Before his troubles I never even knew the Area Defense Counsel existed. After it I saw Emma everywhere. As it turned out, she and Billie did everything together: trips, dinners, drinking, dancing, shopping. Shopping. Lots of shopping. I realized after a while that one reason Billie kept going out with me was because she always had something new to wear. She and Emma were regulars at the finest clothiers and dress-makers in the city: Madame Jeannette's, La Perla, La Casa de Viviana on Transistmica. They were also regulars at the discount stores on Central, even the shops on the fringes of the Chorillo labyrinth where poorer Panamanians sifted through mounds of castoffs piled high on the floor. One night much later, after the case had been thrown out, Billie and I stopped by Emma's apartment near the Plaza Porras. In the course of the mandatory whirlwind tour of every square foot I learned she had two side bedrooms (two entire *rooms*) converted into extra closets. Billie never got that bad but even in her place I could never find a hangar for my flight suit.

But while I saw Emma a lot we never became close. Which was just as well since she seemed to have only two relationships with men: cold professionalism and sex toy. As for the former we had nothing in common to begin with. As for the latter, maybe, thank god, I just wasn't her type. The only time she ever looked at me with other than detached amusement was after Billie and I finally got around to sleeping together on a regular basis. Until then she'd seen me as pathetic; afterwards she appraised me differently, as though perhaps she had underestimated me and now maybe might be interested in exploring my abilities on her own. But that died quickly after a double date where she tried to make conversation by asking me if I liked cats. "Depends on the sauce," I replied. It was meant as a joke but Emma adored the feline species and didn't take kindly to such humor.

But Emma liked Billie and Billie liked me, so Emma tolerated me. And that was enough.

Jake wasn't so lucky.

During her first year in Panama Emma had gone through an ugly divorce. Her husband was a fourth-generation Zonie and had been around during that time, afterwards moving to the States and leaving her at an assignment he'd had a large part in pointing her toward in the first place. She felt abandoned in more ways than one. The anger and frustration of the experience fed a natural aggressiveness that she now directed toward whatever she was working on. That included men. In her first year she had been angry. Now in her second year she was vulnerable. Vulnerable and needy. Very needy. It got to the point that whenever I saw her look at a guy it was always with the eyes of a hunter viewing prey. With some women I might have fantasized about just that situation. With Emma I felt scared and weak, like a gimpy calf in a running herd. Whether it was anger or the lack of companionship, the shift in her emotional life abetted an already voracious desire for sex. Not just any sex. Primal sex, Discovery Channel sex, Ron Jeremy sex. Wild, crazy, throw-things-around-the-room-and-rock-the-chandeliers-below get-out-of-my-way-I'm-coming-through sex.

With his usual timing, Jake showed up at just the wrong moment.

The last I saw of Jake before the AOC transferred him back to the States was when he practically crawled into my office and fell into a chair like a blood donor who'd stayed on the gurney too long.

"Congratulations!" I said. "I hear the whole case was thrown out."

"Yeah," he muttered.

"No admissible evidence: no gun, no bullets, no shell casings – obviously, no Panas. The cops were so busy laughing they never read you your rights."

"Yeah," another whisper.

"They couldn't even use your confession since you told them right off the bat what you'd done."

"Yeah."

"Billie says Emma tossed that in her face and left her nothing to work with. You know, Billie loves to win. *Has* to win, most of the time. But Emma did such good work even Billie couldn't be mad. She's kind of happy for you."

At the mention of Emma's name Jake shifted uncomfortably. He looked around as though expecting her to walk through the door. He always looked rumpled but now he was just plain worn out, his flight suit hanging loosely on his frame, bags forming beneath his eyes, his tousled black hair more than usual out of whack with gravity and the comb.

"Dude," he mumbled like an old man straining to get last words on his will, "you've got to help me."

I snapped shut the flight manual I was reading.

"You've got to be kidding," I said. "I've already found you a lawyer. What more do you need?"

He winced. "That's just it. She's gonna *kill* me, dude! I've never met a woman like her. Hell, I've never heard of a woman like her."

My worst suspicions were confirmed.

"That bad?"

He nodded and squirmed. His legs seemed to be giving him trouble.

"It started out good. It started out great! The first day I met her she was all over me. She said she would help me out, they didn't have a case, she would make the general eat his words... Remember how worried I was? Dude, I felt so much better after talking to her."

"Well, she knows what she's doing..."

"Shut up. Then within, like, two days, she's like, 'Hey, let's have dinner.' Okay, Joanie's out of town and this chick's my lawyer – I figure, what's the downside? Before I know it we're in the sack and she's throwing down like a fifty-cent hooker on dollar night. She's amazing! She's incredible! You don't even want to get me started."

"No, I don't."

"Have you seen her *boobies*? She's built like a Picasso and screws like a rabbit with a one-day kitchen pass."

"Jake, I really don't..."

"It was great at first. I stayed at her place until I realized I wasn't getting any sleep. So I went back to my hotel but then she would come there just to shag. Then she would drop by before breakfast. Then she started meeting me for lunch except we wouldn't eat lunch..."

"You know, *I* just had lunch..."

He yawned, still talking. "It doesn't stop. In – out, in – out,..."

"Oh, come on!"

"She's like the fricking Energizer bunny with the same reproductive instincts. We've had sex on the roof, sex on the floor, sex on the beach. She even came down to the AOC the other night and we had sex on the short wave radio. Ooo-WHEEE-ooo, WHA-WHA-WHA...I thought I still had my headphones on and then I realized it was her making all that noise. Dude, you don't know what I'm going through."

"No, but thanks to you I've now got a nasty image. You know, Jake, I don't understand what you're complaining about. A lot of guys dream of being in your position. She's hot, she's got big boobs, and she loves sex. And she kept you out of jail."

"You don't understand what I'm complaining about?!" he cried. He tried to lean forward in his chair to pound on my desk but didn't have the strength to do it so he contented himself with punching the side panels like an angry child in a tantrum. "I can barely walk, you unfeeling bastard! My pecker's about to fall off! I'm keeping him on duty with popsicle sticks and masking tape but one of these days you're going to get a call from me saying, 'I've fallen and I can't get it up.' She's killing me, dude! She's a maneater and she's draining the life right out of me!"

"And what a horrible way to go," I said with no sympathy whatsoever. I threw the manual on the desk. "Hey, dude, I'd love to help you – oh, wait a minute, actually I wouldn't because I've already done that. Twice now, I believe, and your biggest problem is you're getting laid too much as a result of it. Hmm, too bad, so sad, but if you think you're getting any pity from me you are oh-so-wrong."

"Oh, dude, no. No. I'm sorry. I really am. I'm sorry if your girl is more of the repressed type but you don't *understand.* I've got to get away from her!" His eyes lit up as he had an idea. "Hey! What do you say we swap for a while, hmm? You could leave your cloister and go pound Emma to your heart's content while I hang out with Marion the Legal Librarian for a while and get some rest. Come on, what do you say?"

"Not a chance."

"I'm begging you!"

I leaped away as he lunged for my collar.

"Jake, give it up. You could crawl across the isthmus on your knees and I would still say no. Are you kidding? Swap Billie for her? Volunteer to be the Horn of Plenty for a woman who's a deranged cross between the Queen of Sheba and a black widow spider? You're out of your mind."

He slid off his chair onto the floor, on the edge of tears.

"*Miiike,* she could walk through this door any second and take off her clothes. I'd be done for!"

"Now that would be interesting. Hey, I think I hear her now in the hall..."

He actually started to panic.

"Alright, look," I said. "You're getting short here, anyway. I hear the AOC is packing you up to get you out of the general's line-of-fire in case he thinks of something else. When does your plane leave?"

"Thursday. The Freedom Bird."

I checked my watch.

"Forty-eight hours."

"Ohhhhh..."

"Jake, forty-eight hours is nothing."

"OHHHHHHH..." he groaned again, giving me an incredulous stare.

For the first time I started to feel pity for him. Then I had an image of being swamped in the Sacramento River. My pity melted away.

"Yup," I sighed. "Forty-eight hours of non-stop teeth-rattling, bed-shaking, car-rocking, pelvis-grinding pleasure are all that stands between you and escape to a recuperative, self-imposed celibacy up north. Think you can hang or – sorry – think you can *stand* it that long?"

When he stumbled out of my office I had my doubts.

The Freedom Bird took off from Howard Thursday afternoon. I don't know if it was Jake but I heard reports they had to carry somebody on board. Maybe even his bad luck had finally run out.

24. Christmas

Living at the Tamanaco got old after a while. Not having a phone was a major inconvenience. Worse, the electric company must have hired somebody with a work ethic because after the first month our power started going out with regularity every two or three days. No matter how many trips we made downtown, no matter how many times we complained to Señor Cabal, we were asking the impossible to have normal utility service. We stopped paying rent in an effort to apply pressure. All that got us was elaborately formal letters from Señor Cabal's lawyers. *Muy Señores nuestros, lamentamos la actitud que Uds. tienen...* We never understood how both our landlord and the power company could be so punctual about telling us to pay but completely unable to read their own terms of the contract.

The situation came to a head in November. We came home one afternoon to find that a four-foot section of the railing on one of the balconies had fallen off. Just blown off in the wind. We couldn't even see where it landed in the lot twenty-three floors below. The concrete on the balcony itself started to crumble from the outside in. On that same night the stove burned another of Rolo's dinners and a pipe broke inside the wall of my bathroom, sending a jet of water through the plaster and across the toilet. Some of the water found its way to various cracks that had developed in the hallway floor, cracks that apparently were structural in nature because our downstairs neighbors came up to complain about being rained on. Until then we had seen the cracks as a nuisance – now we noticed they were appearing in the floors of other rooms as well. So in addition to intermittent power, we were without water and our apartment was physically falling apart around us. We sent an emergency letter to Señor Cabal. It produced no result.

A few nights later my beeper went off and I had to make the wee-hour trek down the street to a pay phone. While I was gone Rolo woke up and smelled smoke. He determined it was coming from the apartment below and tried to run downstairs to warn the residents. The power was out again, though. Not being able to see, Rolo ran into his own coffee table and banged his shin. In pain, wanting to kill someone, he instead hobbled downstairs and pulled the fire alarm for the entire building. Nobody evacuated – they don't do that in Panama – and the fire department never came, either. But the noise did wake a number of residents. As I stood out in the street hearing the alarm but seeing nothing happen other than lights come on all over the building, an idea occurred to me. Every night thereafter at two or three in the morning we would get up and pull the fire alarm from a different part of the building. The residents complained, the management got frustrated, and we quietly hinted it might be an electrical problem caused by the power company messing with our box. The management complained to the company, who complained to Señor Cabal, who sent his lawyers over to yell at us. We asked for power, they demanded money. We asked for water, they told us to get lost. We showed them the contract with their client's name on it, they threatened to kill us. Murder trumping a lawsuit, we decided to move.

Josh told us of an opening in the Torres Bahia Vista, where he lived. That was only four blocks away so we gathered up our belongings before the lawyers could go home to collect their guns. In the end we left Señor Cabal, his crumbling apartment, and a bill for December's rent. Not a good start to our stay in-country but – we were confident – it could only get better.

Our new apartment was in the tower next to Josh's. Everything about it gleamed. Unlike the Tamanaco with its drab paint and air of abandonment, the Bahia Vista was all post-modern shine. There were mirrors, marble, and polished metal at every turn. The elevators were fast and silent. The security guards were polite. And the apartment...

"We can play football in here!" Rolo exclaimed.

The main room was cavernous, an expanse of white ceramic tile and black trim that culminated on the east side with picture windows overlooking the city. The kitchen had long counters, the laundry room was clean, and the three bedrooms each could have been termed "master." The apartment took up half of the 14th floor. It was entirely more space than we needed but the price was right and the location was better. We signed on.

The holidays approached. We decided to have another party. Part of me wanted just to sit in the corner and enjoy a comfortable apartment for the first time in eight months but that would have to wait. Most of our friends were staying in Panama for Christmas and in true overseas-assignment fashion we all shared the homesickness together. Any chance to get together was met with enthusiasm. Even those who had braved a visit to the Tamanaco decided to give us the benefit of the doubt on our new pad.

Rolo, of course, would cook. He was in heaven in the new kitchen. Though the Chinese appliances were smaller than we were used to he made the best of the situation. No one could get in his way. Turkey, ham, roast-beef, Italian sausage – all were on the menu and fifty pounds of additional meat was stocked in the freezer just in case. I decorated the apartment and stocked the bar. I even found a CD of salsa tunes with a Christmas theme. Harmony, good cheer, and friendship were all on tap for this, our second housewarming party.

"I'll bring the dessert," Josh insisted, cornering me in the squadron one day in December.

"I think Rolo was going to make something," I replied, thinking Josh felt obligated.

"No, no! He's making the *dinner.* I'll bring the dessert. It'll be the best thing you ever tasted."

"Beer?"

"No, you idiot. A *tres leches*! Remember the *tres leches*?"

It sounded like a rock band. When I couldn't place it, Josh was incredulous.

"Guatemala, remember? The Camino Real hotel? That brunch we had the morning after those girls wanted to have group sex?"

"I remember the brunch," I admitted. "I don't remember group sex."

"Well, maybe not sex in a group. But as a group they all wanted to have sex with us. Anyway, *the tres leches*: it's that white cake that's soaked in cream. It's half liquid, half cake, and all heaven. Mmmmm...." He smacked his lips at the memory.

"You're going to make a cake?" I asked. It was my turn to be incredulous.

Josh was taken aback as though I had suggested he would scrub his own floor.

"No! I don't bake. But I know the best bakery in the city. It's in Punta Paitilla. Kosher, too."

"Very important for a Christmas party," I agreed. Josh was a party animal but he had begun taking an interest in his Jewish heritage and liked to throw out bits of it from time to time.

"I'll put in the order tomorrow," he said. "You'll love it. Everyone will love it. It's heaven on a plate, I promise. And the chick who makes it is a hottie. Don't think you'll be eating anything else."

"Okay," I said, having trouble believing that someone could get so excited about a dessert.

"No, seriously. I've got dessert covered. Tell Rolo. I won't take no for an answer."

I told Rolo. He said, "Fine."

There was one tiny hitch at the Bahia Vista Towers. Unlike at the Tamanaco where we'd had to drive round-and-round up seven stories of parking garage to get to our reserved slots, the Bahia Vista had a basement complex. Our spots were right by the entrance so we pulled in, parked, and walked to the door as conveniently as if we owned the penthouse suite. But a week after move-in I got to my car one morning to find that someone had stolen the stereo speakers from the trunk of the Jimmy.

I didn't care that much. The soldier who owned the truck before me built a custom box-frame into the trunk to hold enormous ghetto-blasters for his listening pleasure. Me, being a geek I listened to local radio and instructional Spanish tapes. I didn't need huge speakers. Still, they were mine and were worth good money so I complained to the apartment manager. She in turn brought the issue up with Wackenhut, the company that provided security for the building. Wackenhut investigated the burglary. In the end a couple of guards were fired, I was reimbursed $400, and the matter was resolved quickly and quietly. For Panama, that was a first.

The problem arose as a result of the theft report I filed with Wackenhut. As part of the investigation, a guard came to our apartment one day and sat down with me to write out the details of the theft. What brand of speakers were they, where was the car parked, when did I last see them, and so forth.

The guard's name was Elena. She was tall and thin with an attractive face and a sawed-off shotgun looped over her shoulder. She was friendly, professional, and we got along great. From then on whenever I saw her in the lobby we talked. After a while she flirted openly with me and I did the same with her. We seemed perfect for each other. There were only two things about her that gave me second thoughts: first, she carried a gun. That has never been a trait I've sought out in women. Second, she always greeted me with an unusual welcome.

"Guapo, guapo, sea mi sapo," she would say as I came up to the door.

It was a cutesy thing that was sexy at first, even though literally translated it meant something along the lines of, "Hey, handsome. Be my little toad." I chose not to translate it, accepting it as one of those phrases that sounds better in its native language, the same way "Cut me some slack" or "Pussy Galore" would confuse anyone in literal Russian. It was just something Elena liked to say. Since Billie treated me like a convenience and I wasn't dating anyone else it was hard to get hung up on details. Eventually I took her out to dinner.

On that first date I realized we had absolutely nothing in common. I realized also that I had made a huge tactical error. I was out with a woman who not only carried a gun, but who by the time we finished dessert had decided that marriage was just a matter of time. When I took her home that night I explained as tactfully as I could that we weren't meant for each other and should just remain friends. She countered by taking off her clothes and insisting we have sex in the car.

I hated situations like that, partly because a little voice in my head always woke up around then and started saying things like, "You know, she has a point. Just screw her," but mostly because they never involved the women I wished they did. Billie, for example, never disrobed and insisted I have my way with her on the spot. Well, okay, she did it that once but she hadn't done it lately. If she had, I never would have found myself in compromising situations with Wackenhut security guards. Since she didn't, here I was on the east side of Panama City in a poorly-lit neighborhood of crumbling tenements trying to talk a desperate woman into putting her clothes back on.

Elena didn't take no for an answer. She didn't take "Hell, no," either, nor did she accept "Get out of my car, you're scaring me you crazy bitch." I reasoned, I pleaded, I gave her a stern lecture, but no matter what I did she wouldn't get out of the car, demanding we have sex because after all we were a couple now. If we didn't have sex, she threatened, she might even start screaming. That worried me the most: one second she was coy and soft-spoken, the next she was threatening to accuse me of rape. Both faces of Eve were in my front seat. I had a psycho on my hands.

In the end a tiny parking space saved me. Amongst the mass of local vehicles jammed onto her street the only place to squeeze in my car was too narrow to open both doors. As sincerely as I could, I told Elena that I would have sex with her but wanted to do it in her bed rather than my beat-up old car. But first she had to get out because otherwise she wouldn't be able to open the door. Excited, she gathered up her clothes and hopped out – and I drove away as fast as I could. Lying was a horrible thing to do but not nearly as horrible as it would have been to sleep with her and then try to leave the next morning. I felt safer, too, when halfway back to the Bahia Vista I found her .45-caliber pistol where it had fallen between the seats.

"You dumped off a woman who carries a shotgun for a living?" Rolo asked me the next day. "You do live dangerously, don't you?"

"I have her pistol."

"Great, you guys can have a shootout in the lobby. Why didn't you just sleep with her?"

"She's psycho."

"They're all psycho. You should have slept with her."

"Why don't *you* sleep with her?"

"She doesn't want me."

"She might now. After I'm dead, that is."

"You should have just slept with her. All she wanted was sex. It would have calmed her down and you wouldn't have anything to worry about now."

"What?"

"Calmed her down. The sex. That's how it works."

"Maybe that's how things work on Planet Rolo," I told him, "but here on earth it's pretty much the opposite. She has dreams of going to the Land of the Big Department Store up north. I was the vehicle to get her there. One game of hide-the-salami wasn't going to change her mind."

"Maybe, maybe not. Maybe she really loves you."

"You keep saying stuff like that and I'll use this gun on you."

"Don't get mad at me because you're a player."

"I am not a player!"

"You're a player."

"I wanted dinner! I wanted a date! Billie juggles me like a dentist appointment so I just wanted to go out once and have a normal evening. Does that mean I have to marry the woman and take her home to mom and dad?"

Rolo squinted carefully through the peephole before going out the front door.

"Okay. I'm just saying, you played with the girl's heart and now it's coming back to haunt you. Shame on you, Mike. Shame, shame, shame."

To hide, I parked the Jimmy at the Pinheads and stayed in our apartment through a three-day weekend. A couple of times the doorbell rang but I stayed quiet and didn't answer, crouched behind the coffee table with the .45 in my hand. Elena was a woman so it wasn't out of the question that she would blast the hinges off the door and burst in screaming, snakes growing out of her head, a leash at the ready. I had seen Fatal Attraction. The first night Rolo came home and as a joke yelled, "Run! Run! She's right on my tail!" but he stopped that when he saw me barricaded by the television with the gun cocked.

Afraid that eventually he would be caught in the crossfire, Rolo brokered a compromise. He had to because I couldn't. When I finally ventured from the apartment I did try to talk to Elena but the effort fizzled. She kept growling and eyeing the shotgun in her kiosk.

Instead I learned her work schedule. With great difficulty I arranged my comings and goings around her shifts. Rolo refused to do that so he kept running into her. She was hostile to him at first, then realized she needed her pistol back before the company found out it was missing. So she became nice. For Rolo that was more disconcerting. Worse, she started flirting with him which made Rolo realize he had to do something fast or we would both be hiding behind the TV. He played hardball, telling Elena he would inform Wackenhut of her behavior (and her missing weapon) unless she backed off. Further, she would get the gun back (minus bullets) only if she transferred to another building.

The response was predictable. Elena freaked out. She berated Rolo with a stream of Spanish invective that would have made a Mexican border guard blush. Rolo, his command of Spanish as weak as ever, ignored it. His stoicism turned Elena on. She became coquettish then, smitten with a man who could fake incomprehension so well. She became convinced that he was using the situation to get to know her and agreed to all his terms.

The week before the Christmas party, Rolo came home one night exhausted.

"I'm going to kill you," he growled, dropping his flight gear on the floor.

"Get in line," I told him.

"I'm serious."

"So am I. The C-130 guys want me dead because I slept through their alert cancellation again and never called them, meaning they showed up for work at 4:30 am for nothing. The commander wants my head on a plate because I took the annual flying hours up to the Group but left the report on the exec's desk and didn't realize Cargill was on leave, meaning the Group Commander never saw our numbers. Walt has arranged a hit on me because I scammed his trip to Honduras. And the chick downstairs wants to pump me full of lead because I kicked her psycho butt to the curb. You want to kill me? It's an eclectic fraternity, my friend. Get in line."

"Speaking of the chick downstairs," he interrupted, "the good news is, you haven't seen Elena in a week, right? Because she transferred to another building, right? One in Punta Paitilla? And that was all because of me, right? I saved your bacon."

"You did and I bought you a ton of beer to say thanks. You're the best roommate a guy could have."

"So now she's in love with me, you idiot!" he yelled. "She cornered me this morning on my way out. She wants me to come to a party!"

"Are you going to go?"

"And get stuck having sex with her in the front seat of my car? Not on your life."

"Why not?" I sneered. "It might just calm her down."

He glared at me. "Very funny. Thanks to you I wouldn't even be able to pull that 'parking spot is too small' trick. And what's with that *Guapo, guapo, sea mi sapo* stuff? She keeps saying that – it's creeping me out."

"I don't know. It has something to do with toads. She says it whenever she's turned on."

"Well, turn her off. She's your psycho, not mine. Tonight I had to walk up fourteen flights of stairs because she's camped out by the elevators waiting for me to come home. You've given your Glenn Close to me!"

I considered that and, not able to stop myself, chuckled with satisfaction. He tackled me.

Rolo was a wrestler in college so it didn't take long for me to be on the losing end of the fight. He was just about to break my neck in a half-nelson when a voice from the doorway said, "Do you guys always get along like this?"

It was Josh, standing in the doorway with the disgusted look he reserved for anyone low enough to engage in male-to-male contact. Rolo released me, not because Josh was there but because he suddenly realized he had left the door half-open. Elena could have gotten in, in which case we would both be dead.

"He started it," Rolo explained. "He gave me a psycho woman."

"They're all psycho," Josh replied. "Oh, that security guard chick? Oh, yeah. She really is nuts."

"Thanks for noticing. Well, he's pawned her off on me, the bastard."

Josh nodded in appreciation. "Good move, Mike. I wouldn't have thought you capable of that. Well, listen. I didn't come over to help you losers with your woman problem. I came over to look at your fridge."

"You looking for a new one?"

"No, no. I just have to see how big it is. For the cake."

"Ah, yes," Rolo nodded, "the *tres leches*."

Josh eyed him, sensing a challenge. "What's that supposed to mean?" he demanded.

"What does what mean?"

"The way you said that."

"The way I said what? *Tres leches*? It's your cake, I didn't mean anything."

Josh relaxed – somewhat. "It's a great cake," he maintained. "Everyone'll love it." He went into the kitchen.

"He's very excited about the cake," I whispered to Rolo. "Don't rain on his parade."

"It's a cake!" he growled. "And it's not like he's making it himself. It's store-bought!"

"What's wrong with that?"

Rolo recoiled like a dairy farmer offered a slice of Velveeta.

"Store-bought? Are you kidding? You don't eat *store-bought* cake!"

"Well, he likes it for some reason so be nice."

"I'll be nice. I'll dump it on his head."

"Be nice."

Through the kitchen door Josh pronounced his verdict.

"What the hell is this, an Easy-Bake Oven? And Jesus, look at this fridge. It's tiny!"

Rolo and I hung our heads, with me at least reflecting on what stage of life we must have achieved to be ashamed of the size of a kitchen appliance. But we had no choice. Our landlord was Chinese, a merchant up in the Free Trade Zone of Colón, and he had outfitted the apartment with Chinese appliances. The Hanjin water heater was mounted on the wall above a Sintek washer and dryer, with a Huan refrigerator keeping them company. All came with the apartment. Until now Rolo and I had seen no reason to spend money to replace them.

"Yeah, they're a little small," Rolo apologized.

Josh studied the refrigerator. "Small? I had something bigger than this in college. Where's your real refrigerator?"

"That's it."

"That can't be it. No." He searched around the kitchen.

"That's it."

He returned to the refrigerator again and examined it with disgust. His reservoir of the emotion was bottomless. The top of the appliance barely came to the level of his nose but he exaggerated his contempt by crouching to look inside.

"At least tell me you didn't buy this thing."

"No, they came with the apartment."

"Well, that's something. Wait a minute – they?"

We pointed him to the laundry room where he could view the washer-dryer. Josh crept around the corner as though expecting an attack. At first he didn't say anything, inspecting both machines and the wall-mounted water heater like a Russian scientist trying to figure out how to reverse-engineer them. Finally he burst out laughing. He laughed so hard he had trouble being sarcastic.

"You...I can't believe...who would ever...it's *Chinese*! You have a Chinese washing machine! Did you get egg rolls with it?"

"Look, the owner..."

"What do you do when you want to wash *two* pairs of pants at the same time?" he wailed. "Empty the pockets? Does the little guy inside have to pedal faster?"

"It's not so small," Rolo argued, going back to the refrigerator. He grew defensive but despite himself he, too, had to view the shelves inside from a crouch. Now that Josh mentioned it, it did look tiny.

Josh laughed himself out of breath. He wiped tears from his eyes.

"Ohhh, you guys," he repeated several times.

"You still want to leave your cake with us?"

Josh put a hand on the wall to catch his breath.

"No, no. No, no, no. Not now. Whoo-boy, I don't think so. You've answered my question, which was do you have enough room to store it here? Hell, you don't have enough room to store the frosting, let alone the whole cake. I'll just keep it at my place." He found his way down the hall toward the door. "I'll walk it over when it's time for dessert," he sighed, making a visible effort to get his words out.

"It gets clothes really clean," I blurted, grasping for anything to regain self-respect. "And it's quiet. It makes hardly any noise on the spin cycle!"

Josh had a come-back ready but since my comment convulsed him in giggles he couldn't share it with us. He hunched by the door, holding his stomach until the spell subsided.

"Ooooh, Ninja washers!" he tittered. "Oh, boy. Oh, boy, you guys crack me up. But don't worry, my cake will save the day."

Christmas in the tropics is a strange thing. It is, after all, a Christian holiday slapped onto European winter solstice celebrations with bits of Germanic pagan festivals and American commercialism to adorn it. Everything about it suggests cold and snow yet in Panama those elements were as foreign as the money Panas spent in their stores.

Still, marketing prevailed. Businesses downtown announced Christmas sales in breathless red letters on their windows. Churches erected mangers in their front yards. The city strung bunting and silver bells along the streetlights of Via España. A large sign even hung across Calle 50 that said *Feliz Navidad* in gold block letters until a rainstorm knocked out all the letters except for Feli...N...i. Declan thought that was perfect, given that Christmas with palm trees had a distinct Fellini-esque feel to it that the Italian movie director would appreciate.

All the military bases tried to capture some of the spirit from home. On Howard, different squadrons painted Christmas greetings on large plywood signs that were then stood in the grass along the main road. Ours was drawn up by Lucy Povenich, Sam's wife.

Sam was a good guy: solemn, stoic, clean-cut, a touch on the serious side but not so much that he was a chore to fly with. He came to us from flying B-52s up in South Dakota. He was a careful professional who did all his work with such precision that many of us believed he was sucking up to somebody in order to get promoted. Except that Sam didn't care much about promotion. Or if he did, he didn't make a big deal about it. He just liked doing his job well. If the Air Force needed him in Panama, that was good enough for him.

Sam's wife, on the other hand, was a handful. Lucy was lovely and educated but she felt trapped by military life. Bored out of her skull in Panama, each day was a challenge. Early in the new year she would be arrested when somebody at the post office discovered she was mailing pot to her sister in the States. Now, though, she was known mostly for getting high whenever Sam was out of the country and wandering the streets of the base housing area late at night in an expensive and carelessly tied nightgown. Other wives rallied around her and tried to rein her in – the Officers' Wives Club tapped her to put paint to plywood and come up with a squadron holiday greeting. That Lucy did but the result only raised more questions about her. She painted a bizarre Christmas scene that showed a C-130 being pulled through the starry sky by eight reindeer and a tiny *chiva* bus. The *chiva* bus was plowing through a crowd of Panas. Out of the back of the -130 jumped Santa Claus in a parachute, one hand held to his nose in a manner that suggested he was either clearing one nostril like a farmer or inhaling like a Hollywood producer. As he floated through the air Santa spilled the contents of his bag of gifts. They turned out to be little C-27s, C-21s, and T-43s, all falling in a flurry of snowflakes. We assumed they were snowflakes. Merry Christmas to All His Little People, the sign proclaimed, leaving us to wonder among other things who were all the little people, what had Lucy been snorting when she painted the picture, and had Lt Col Rasmussen known about the sign before it went up?

Flying tapered off as the holidays approached. Rasmussen was torn about that: he wanted to give people time off but at the same time felt that if we stopped making runs to the jungle the troops at the radar sites would feel they had been abandoned. To avoid that impression he requested through the Group that the 155th be allowed to make "morale runs" to all the sites in the days leading up to December 25th. "Morale runs" would be out-and-back visits where instead of carrying gas and pallets of MREs we took wrapped presents or something unusual that the troops didn't normally see. The colonel was thinking of fresh food and maybe beer – whatever SOUTHCOM would approve. The Group thought it was a great idea but ordered up a different cargo than what Rasmussen had in mind: 700 fruitcakes wrapped to survive into the new millennium.

"Fruitcakes?" Rasmussen fumed, hefting one like a football and tossing it in a perfect spiral across the tarmac. It bounced and rolled and came to rest undamaged in the hot sun. "They don't want fruitcakes!"

Still, in addition to being timeless the cakes had red ribbons and therefore a Christmas theme. So we loaded them up, added several dozen cases of beer, and started making the rounds.

Major Harmon and Walt thought they would have every location covered by the 22nd and still be able to give the aircrews a couple of days off before the holiday. But weather and diplomatic clearances fouled his plan. On the 23rd he asked me and Rolo to make one more run the next day. Of course I said yes. I'd made my first trip as an aircraft commander earlier in the month and was anxious to get more hours as the guy in charge. Rolo was less happy about the tasking. An ideal wife, he was worried about having his dinner all ready to go for the Christmas party. But he signed on, knocking on wood all the way to the airplane and praying we wouldn't break somewhere downrange. Staff Sergeant Clunk Andrews volunteered to be our loadmaster.

Our trip was simple, an out-and-back to two radar sites in the jungle. Lago Agrio was in north-central Ecuador. Puerto Leguizamo was further east in the Putumayo region of Colombia. Lago Agrio was quiet but it gave easy access to a vast section of jungle where drug flights were known to cross. Leguizamo was also quiet where the base itself sat but the region its soldiers patrolled was a hornet's nest of FARC activity. The favorite pastime of the rebels there was to intercept and burn vehicles that crossed the border from Ecuador.

Neither airfield was a tremendous challenge to reach since they were both in flat terrain. Lago Agrio even had an NDB approach in case the weather was bad. An NDB wasn't much better than homing in on a talk radio station but for the middle of the jungle it was high technology. At least I thought so.

"If the weather's bad, I'm not risking my life for fruitcakes," Rolo informed us shortly after takeoff on Christmas Eve morning.

"What are you saying?" Clunk asked.

"Just what I said. I'm not risking my life for fruitcakes. I know my roommate here has a strong sense of mission-hackedness and would be willing to poke his nose into the weather or land during a civil uprising just to get this crap delivered. I'm not so motivated. So I'm just informing you guys now. I want to get there and back as fast as possible."

"In other words your devotion to duty doesn't extend to serving your fellow man who's serving his country in a lonely tent in the jungle?"

"My devotion to duty," Rolo sniffed, "extends to the dinner party I'm hosting tomorrow night. The last I heard, Sergeant, you were invited, so you'd better make sure my country-serving butt is back in time to put the oven on."

We flew to Puerto Leguizamo first. The weather there was clear with a view all the way to the mountains along the border. The only hazard was of the olfactory kind: someone had set fire to a pile of trash half a mile from the runway and smoke from the fire drifted across our approach. There must have been dead animals in the pile. Dead animals and old tires and last year's onion crop. The smell was horrific. It got inside the plane and wouldn't leave. When we landed and opened the cargo doors the soldiers meeting us thought at first their fruitcakes were the source of the odor and refused to board. Only when we showed them the beer did they offload the pallets.

When we tried to take off there was another delay. Cattle from a nearby pasture broke through a fence and wandered onto the runway. We thought at first they were going somewhere but then realized they were just trying to escape from the smell of the fire. The cloud which crossed our approach hung over the pasture as well so the cattle, rather than smell the burning carcasses of their brethren, escaped upwind. That meant onto the airstrip. A hundred of them now blocked our path, milling about the runway and pulling grass from the center berm.

"You've got to be kidding," Rolo groaned, checking his watch. Even if everything on the flight went like clockwork he still wouldn't get home until evening.

Colombians from the battalion jumped into jeeps and tried to herd the cattle back where they came from. Soldiers make bad cowboys, though; whenever they got one part of the herd moving in the right direction another part wandered the opposite way. It was like watching someone chase the bulge on a water bed. We helped for a while but when Clunk was charged by a startled cow we retreated to the safety of the cockpit.

After an hour and a half of fruitless work the Colombians lost their patience. They herded as many cows downhill as they could and opened fire on the rest. As we took off we rolled past bleeding carcasses lying in the high grass.

At Lago Agrio the weather was also good but thundershowers dotted the region like enormous jellyfish, their tentacles long rain shafts that stretched to the ground. We had no problem flying between them and finding the field but lightning that arced between the clouds made things interesting.

On the ground the radar troops were in good spirits. Months earlier someone had tossed two grenades over the perimeter fence in a failed effort to destroy the installation's radar. The explosions caused damage but nothing serious – the radar was repaired and moved farther from the public road. Now this month someone had upped the ante by creeping inside the fence and firing an RPG at the radar's base. The projectile struck the sandbag barrier instead of the dish so again the radar was spared. This time, however, the assailant was caught. His confession at the hands of the Ecuadorian army yielded intelligence that led to a roundup of FARC sympathizers hiding out in the nearby town. For the moment the bad guys had been kicked out of the area. Troops at the site were jubilant.

"Haven't had a shooting in two weeks," the major in charge bragged. "With the new fabric along the perimeter fence we even let guys walk around without body armor during the day."

"Oh, goody," Rolo offered, wiping sweat from his brow.

The major smiled. "It's the little things."

Their mood was so good the troops insisted we join them for lunch inside their sandbag labyrinth. Clunk was amenable but Rolo was against the idea, anxious to get on our way. On his behalf I declined but the major and his staff insisted. We went back and forth with me making polite excuses and the troops rejecting every one. It got to the point that refusing risked causing bad blood – the assembled faces began to suggest we thought we were too good to hang out with ground-pounders. So, reluctantly, I laughed it all off and accepted their offer.

The lunch stretched on. First we mingled, then we ate, then there was a roast of some sort where the major and others made speeches and handed out awards like "Warrant Officer Most Likely to Move to Ecuador after Retirement" and "Radar Repairman Most Likely to Catch an STD from a Local." The troops included us in their revelry and that in itself was unusual.

They just didn't want us to leave, seeing us as their link in this holiday season to someplace closer to home. Still, Rolo fidgeted.

"Dude, we have got to get out of here!" he hissed. "I have stuffing to make. I have a leg of lamb in a marinade. Carrots don't peel themselves, you know!"

Finally, we made our excuses and retreated to the plane. The troops were heartbroken to see us go. Some followed, making awkward conversation as though believing that if they just kept talking the link to home would stay unbroken. A number slipped us last-minute Christmas cards to drop in the mail at Howard.

"For God's sake, start her up," Rolo pleaded as we climbed into the cockpit.

"No kidding," Clunk agreed over the intercom from outside where he monitored the engines. "This place is starting to resemble the Hotel California. 'You can enter anytime you like but you can never leave.'"

But then we had one more delay. When I pushed the button on the #1 engine the Start light didn't illuminate. There was a sequence of events to every start and each step was important. The Start light had to come on to tell us the valve had opened, the Ng had to rise to tell us the engine was turning, the exhaust temperature had to climb once fuel was pushed to the engine, and so on. The light not coming on was meaningful because if it didn't come on we couldn't know that it had later gone off; i.e. we wouldn't know if the start valve had closed when the starter was no longer needed. If the start valve didn't close it was possible that bleed air would continue to the starter and cause it to overspeed, possibly flying apart in a hundred pieces and sending shrapnel through the engine. It was one of those situations where a pilot has to decide "Is this nothing, or am I about to cause a million dollars worth of damage?"

"That's not right," I said, aborting the start.

"Why isn't it coming on?" Rolo demanded.

"Damned if I know. Let's try again."

The second time was just like the first. We aborted the start.

"I have my Swiss army knife," Clunk offered.

"Use it. Open the cowling."

I hopped out of the seat and grabbed the stepladder from the cabin. Clunk crawled up to the engine and looked inside. It was a desperate hope: none of us were qualified to perform other than basic maintenance on the engines. Even if we were, we didn't have spare parts on board. It wasn't like we carried a replacement starter valve just for the heck of it.

"Anything?" I called up.

"Nothing," Clunk replied. "No fan belt's unbuckled. The ben-wobbly shaft appears to be in good order. Even the flux capacitor appears to be working."

"In other words, you have no clue what you're looking at. There's a reason you're a loadmaster."

"Because I was too smart to be a pilot," Clunk scoffed, undeterred. "Besides, it's not like you could do any better up here."

He was right about that.

"Anyway, I don't see any leaks or scorching or anything. Everything looks normal. Clean as a whistle."

"Well, do something," Rolo called from the window. "I have a dinner to make."

Clunk climbed down the ladder and shuffled his feet in the dirt.

"I can dance," he said. "That's about all you're going to get from me. If the light's out, it's out."

We consulted the aircraft manual. It told us to get a mechanic if the Start light didn't come on. We looked at each other.

"Any of you see a mechanic?" I asked.

Rolo pointed out the window. "Seven hundred miles that way."

For a while nobody spoke.

"If we continue the start," I asked finally. "What's the worst that could happen?"

The worst was that the starter would fly apart. The most likely was that the engine would start normally and we would be able to monitor it by looking at all the other gauges. How willing were we to roll the dice?

"Do you want to miss your dinner party?" Clunk asked.

"Do you want to spend Christmas in Lago Agrio?" Rolo demanded.

"Do we all want to lose our wings?" I replied.

But in the end we decided that if everything else looked normal during the start then the light itself was probably the only thing malfunctioning. So we pushed the button again.

"Looking good," Rolo muttered as the gauges spun up. "Looking good..."

My hands hovered over the controls, ready to yank everything to shutoff if the slightest hiccup occurred. But nothing unusual happened. When the engine spun up we saw a drop in bleed air pressure that told us the start valve had closed. My heart rate returned to normal.

Rolo checked his watch for the fiftieth time that day. He groaned.

"Please let's get out of here," he begged. "I'm four hours behind schedule. Make the nightmare end."

We took off but Rolo's bad dream wasn't over yet. The sun set before we left Ecuador's airspace. By the time we cleared Colombian waters the stars were out. That made everyone sit straighter in their seats. Though we flew at night all the time, it was never routine: pilots get nervous when they can't see outside. Every noise from the plane convinces them that something is about to go wrong. Droning at night is like staying up late in a big house reading a scary book – you hear sounds that you never notice during the day.

An hour out from Panama City, Rolo claimed to hear one of those sounds. It was a scraping coming from the right side. Neither Clunk nor I could hear it but Rolo swore it was there. We cross-checked the instruments and saw that the #2 engine was burning twenty degrees hotter than #1. While we tried to figure out why, red blips popped up all over the radar screen.

"Did the weather guy talk about storms tonight?" I asked no one in particular.

"Isolated stuff," Rolo replied.

"That looks more than isolated."

We maneuvered around the blips but that got harder to do as we neared the isthmus. Then the rain started. Driving rain hit us even when we stayed in the dark areas on the radar. It fell so hard that water pouring over the nosecone distorted the radar picture. Vertical lines appeared that washed out colors.

"Great," Rolo muttered. "How are we supposed to avoid the storms now?"

For an answer I got on the radio. First I dialed up the ATIS frequency and listened to a scratchy recorded voice tell us recent weather conditions at Howard. They weren't good. It had been raining for over an hour and the ceilings went down to 500 feet. Ignoring the Panamanian controllers, I then called directly to the Howard Approach controller. He was surprised to hear from us, yet another sign that nobody ever read our flight plans. He also sounded anxious.

"Shark 14, this is Howard Approach. Someone's actually flying tonight? I've got you weak but readable. Go ahead."

"Roger, Howard. Shark 14 is seventy miles south at flight level two-zero-zero. We're inbound to land. Request weather at the field. Also, we know there are storms in the area but we're in heavy rain right now and can't see the cells on our radar. Can you vector us around the worst ones?"

The reply was immediate and frantic.

"Sir, there are cells all around you!"

We looked at each other.

"Why's he getting hysterical?" Rolo asked angrily. "We're the ones in the weather. I don't need him making my ulcer worse."

"Uh, roger, Howard," I radioed back. *"Can you do your best, please?"*

Rain in Panama was as common as petty theft. Hard rain that lasted for hours and threatened to close all the airports was less so. The controller gave us updates that made me wonder if we would be able to land at all. When he told us the storms weren't moving, I considered diverting to Davíd. The plane rocked in turbulence.

"I can't see out the windows," Clunk spoke up, poking his head into the cockpit. "How bad is it out there?"

"Apparently, it's bad enough that you can't see out the window," I replied. "It's ugly. The big question will be when we get to the bottom of the approach. If we break out, we're fine. If not, we don't have the gas to try again. We'll have to head west to Davíd."

Rolo threw up his hands up in frustration.

"Perfect!" he yelled. "Fricking perfect! I knew this would happen. I knew it! If I had more rank I would kick Harmon's ass. 'A simple out-&-back,' he said. *'A simple out-&-back!'* There's nothing simple about it. This party is a disaster and it hasn't even started yet."

"Dude, relax. I know you have a dinner to make but if the weather's junk, that's it. We'll make one try but that's all. I'm not going to risk crashing a plane just because you have a soufflé to get to."

"Oh, I know, I know," he insisted. "I don't want to crash, either. I'm just saying that I predicted this. I predicted it!"

"Shark 14, come left to a heading of 330 degrees. There's a monster cell off your nose that I'll try to take you around."

"That's awfully kind of him."

"No kidding. Why did he have to tell us it was a *monster* cell? We didn't need to know that."

The controller vectored us to within thirty miles of the field. He offered to take us the long way around the pattern, to the north out over Lago Gatún, but I declined. The storms thinned out that way but it meant we would have to fly an extra fifteen minutes. Also, the approach to Runway 18 was over steep terrain. We would have to circle to land at the bottom of it and that meant we couldn't go as low on final. If we only had one approach to make I wanted it to be the most precise one available.

The controller was disappointed at my refusal – we could almost hear him shrug with resignation. A short while later he told us he couldn't take responsibility for any more vectors. We were cleared for the ILS.

"Good luck, sir," he called with a tone of finality that none of us liked.

"You want to fly it?" I asked Rolo.

He brushed water off his sleeve from where it had dripped inside the window.

"No. If we don't break out I want to be able to blame you."

But in the end the approach wasn't that bad. At least, all the way down to five hundred feet it wasn't that bad. The clouds stayed impenetrable, the rain never lessened, and the lightning flickered every few seconds just to up the tension, but the instruments never wavered. I stayed on-course and on-glide-slope better than I ever did in clear conditions, since clear conditions never give the same motivation as bad weather. As Manny liked to say, a bad storm when you're low on gas is quite the "focusing experience."

My focus sharpened even more at five hundred feet. It was there as I was glued to the instruments and Rolo was peering through the rain-streaked glass to make out the runway that the number two engine coughed and seized.

"What the...!"

"Leave it! Leave it!"

The plane yawed right. I stomped on the left pedal and banked to keep us level. The glide slope indicator on the HSI climbed, meaning my move caused us to descend and now we were too low. I increased power to catch the glide slope. That increased the yaw. I banked more, thinking for just a second that I was about to face one of the worst nightmares of any pilot: performing a go-around in bad weather on one engine with low fuel.

Then at four hundred feet the rabbit lights broke through the clouds. The pole-mounted beacons that I saw regularly on my runs cut through the rain outside and danced across the swamps abeam Veracruz Beach to point us toward the runway.

"There! Come left!" Rolo pointed.

At three hundred feet – one hundred feet above our minimums – the threshold lights came into view, the most beautiful sight in the world. Right behind them was the concrete.

We landed in pouring rain, our lights illuminating drops that hit so hard they bounced back up and made it look like a second storm coming up from the earth.

On Alpha ramp we shut down the remaining engine. Clunk wasn't thrilled about going outside to position the chocks. Neither was I and neither was Rolo. Anyway, Rolo was about to come un-glued from the strains of his day so he stayed in the copilot's seat and beat on the armrests. In the dark, in the rain, we sat inside the plane and waited for the bus from Base Operations to arrive, trying to resolve how a simple day of pure motives and holiday cheer had turned into a Texas-sized roundup of stress. The noise from the torrent hitting the roof was deafening.

Billie smiled at me. She had done that before but it was always at my expense, not the way she looked at me now. Her smile was one of sympathy.

"Wow," she said. "So how long was your day?"

"Nineteen hours," I counted. "By the time we got home last night it was midnight. It sucked."

"And it sounds like nothing went right?"

We stood by the Christmas tree in my apartment. It wasn't a real tree. Neither Rolo nor I had had the time or desire to buy an over-priced shrub on the local market so at the last minute I fashioned an electric facsimile from thirty strands of Christmas lights strung from the ceiling fan in our living room. The strands stretched from the fan to the floor where they were taped down so as to hold a flared, teepee shape. It worked. The bulbs flickered randomly, throwing colored glows across the apartment to accent the reds and greens that half our squadron wore to the party. The "tree' was a fragile creation—transparent, shaky, and dangerous if any of the wires developed a short – but in that sense it was a perfect metaphor for Panama.

"Well, the guys down south got their fruitcakes," I reflected. "And the beer. They were happy to see us so that's something. In fact, that's everything since the whole reason was to bring them a little Christmas cheer. It was just so painful. And scary. I've never lost an engine in weather."

"No kidding. In a storm like that you could have crashed."

"Maybe," I admitted. "But mostly it just made for a long day."

She smiled again and put her hand on my arm.

"If only the taxpayers knew," she said brightly and leaned up to kiss me on the cheek. "I'll say thank you on their behalf."

I didn't know what to say. Finally, in her eyes I had done something right.

"Is that why your roommate is a little short-tempered?" she asked, changing the subject. She gestured with her glass across the apartment to where Rolo was lighting candles under serving dishes on the buffet table. He wore an apron with the grinch on it and had a dish towel over one shoulder.

"Short-tempered?" I asked, surprised. "Did he say something to you?"

Walt leaned between us to pluck the cherry from my egg nog.

"Rolo's not short-tempered," he explained to Billie. "He's just strained from the pressures of throwing a party. You know how women get during the holidays. Mike's wife is one very busy lady."

Billie took the cherry from his fingers and put it back in my drink.

"I'd like to see you call him Mike's wife to his face," she dared him. "We'll see how you enjoy New Year's from a hospital ward."

"I offered to help," Declan's wife Sue joined the conversation. "He gave me a flat No."

"So did I," T.J. offered. "I can watch an oven, at least. He would hardly talk to me. He's all one-word answers tonight."

"Give him a break, folks," I pleaded. "He had a long day yesterday, too. We got home late and he was in the kitchen until four. You know how he is – the man wants to be a chef so everything has to be perfect. The best thing you can do for him is eat a lot, drink a lot, and tell him everything is delicious."

"That I can do," T.J. agreed.

Josh sauntered by with a margarita in hand. He caught the end of the discussion.

"And if the food is a little off," he suggested, "don't worry. I've got a dessert later on that'll make you forget all about it."

"Josh..."

"Don't worry, Mike. I'm serious. They delivered it this afternoon. I took half the shelves out of my refrigerator to make room for it. It's perfect. It even *looks* perfect. I couldn't bring myself to taste even the frosting for fear of ruining the presentation. You'll love it."

He was interrupted by a roar from the middle of the room.

"Dinner is served!" Rolo bellowed. "It's the best I could do."

He motioned us toward the table and then walked head-down back to the kitchen.

Of course, he had no reason to be dissatisfied. Every chef may desire perfection but if so they forget that those of us on the eating side of the equation usually settle for a lot less. In fact, wasting perfection on the people in our squadron was foolish. Watching T.J. wade into the buffet table, I considered that Rolo could have done just as well by heating up fifty TV dinners.

"Oh, this is fantastic!" the big man swooned, surveying the array before him. "Birds of the air, beasts of the field – come to papa!"

So the dinner was fine. It was better than fine, it was excellent. Everyone said so and they didn't exaggerate.

As people chowed down, Rolo relaxed. Christmas music wafted from the stereo, good conversation flowed from our friends, and most of all, he finally took time to have a beer. The stress of the last thirty-six hours faded into memory. He mingled with his guests and eventually ended up by my elbow.

"Hey," he said, holding out a fresh Soberania. "Sorry I've been such a jerk the last few days."

"Don't worry about it," I said, and took the beer.

"No, I mean it. I totally mis-prioritized. All day yesterday I was worrying about getting home. That left you to take care of the flying by yourself. I shouldn't have done that."

"Everything worked out," I shrugged. "The important thing is it's Christmas. Everybody's together and they're enjoying a great meal. So, cheers."

He was glad I wasn't angry. So glad that he wanted to share the good vibe. When Josh came by a little later to announce he was running next door to pick up the dessert, Rolo offered to help him.

"You want to help?" Josh repeated, amazed.

"Yeah, why not?"

"I thought you were jealous of my cake."

Rolo waved away the very idea.

"Hey, it's Christmas. If my roommate can put up with me sulking all the way to Ecuador and back, I can be a big enough man to recognize you've got a killer dessert."

Josh was flabbergasted.

"Well, okay, then!" he babbled. "Thanks! Yeah, it's killer. It's also big," he laughed. "You're not kidding, I'll need somebody's help to carry it over."

The two of them left to catch the elevator downstairs.

Lowell put down his plate and made gagging noises.

"I think I'm going to be sick," he complained. "All this fricking good cheer is ruining my dinner."

T.J. offered to finish it for him.

Charlie Manson corralled me to talk about the engine failure. He made me tell him the day's whole story and then adopted his evaluator-serious tone.

"Dale and the boys tore it apart. Nothing wrong with the engine. Had to be the rain. A gust and too much water. Nothing to do with the Start light. That was electrical. Pure coincidence."

I sipped my beer and nodded. "I thought so."

He snorted. "But you didn't know, did you?"

"No."

"So why didn't you stay in Lago Agrio?"

"Would you?"

He laughed. The serious tone disappeared.

"No, but expect some questions from Giverson on Monday," he warned. "Rasmussen knows the deal and has no problem but Giverson will still want to do his jerk-from-the-Group routine."

"I'll be on my best behavior," I promised.

He headed for the kitchen and another margarita. "I wouldn't. I would tell him to go to hell. But that's up to you."

I went to look for Billie in the crowd. She found me first.

"What is it with you guys?" she demanded, her earlier smile gone.

"You guys, who? I'm alone."

"You pilots," she said. "I started talking to that guy there..." she pointed to Declan, "and he – did you know that's his wife?"

"Yeah, sure," I nodded. "Her name's Sue."

"Well, apparently he's trying to talk *Sue* into piercing her nipples so for some reason he dragged me into the discussion and wanted my help convincing her."

"What did you say?"

"I didn't say anything! I hardly know them!"

"Well, Declan's a little..."

"So then I left them and went over to those two," she continued, nodding toward Lowell who had crawled inside the electric Christmas tree and was talking through the strands to Mick Connor. "That guy sitting down is bragging about how his girlfriend – he's dating the general's daughter, I take it – wants to be a virgin until she's married."

"So what's wrong with that?" I asked.

She jabbed a finger into my chest.

"So they only engage in anal sex!" she hissed. "Now why would he tell that to a perfect stranger?"

"I don't know. Pride?"

"And then I finally thought I'd escaped by talking to those two," she said, waving her drink in the direction of Jem and Evan, "because they were talking about telescopes and geometry and I thought, okay, at least there are a couple of geeks in the crowd. But it turns out the only astronomy they know involves pointing a telescope at some girl's window and the only geometry they know involves triangles. As in threesomes. They asked me to have sex with them. Both of them. At once!"

"What did you say?"

She sucked in her breath and wound up to hit me.

"Look," I proposed, dodging out of the way, "we don't get out much. You have to remember, you see things differently than we do."

"I beg your pardon?"

"It's Panama, remember? You're attractive, white, single, and an officer – one of what, three on the base? You're surrounded by ten thousand guys on this side of the isthmus alone. You have your pick. You can get a date or sex whenever you want. Not so for us. If we hit on you or your two hottie friends, you laugh and call us desperate. If we ignore you and go downtown, you call us sleaze for picking up the local women. We lose either way. Not that that justifies them being crude in front of you," I hastened to add. "But remember, we're men. It's on our minds a lot."

"What are you talking about?"

"You asked what the deal was with pilots. I'm trying to explain why we're so single-minded."

"Is it the same with you? Is sex all you think about?"

"Yes. I mean, no."

"And are you a sleaze?" she demanded. "Have you been sleeping with local women?"

"No, of course not! Why do you think I keep bugging you?"

That was a good answer. She calmed down.

"Okay, then," she said.

"And just for the record, we pilots are not single-minded. If you give us a chance we also talk about flying and money. In fact, once Josh gets back, if you're interested he'll fill your head with more than you ever wanted to know about the stock market."

On cue, there came a yell from the hall.

"YOU DID IT ON PURPOSE!"

Rolo stormed into the room followed closely by Josh. Josh held a huge white cardboard cake box that was crushed on one side and wet along the top.

"I did not! It was an accident!"

"You didn't want my cake to ruin your dinner so you dropped it on purpose!"

"She had a gun! She scared me and I dropped it. I'm sorry!"

Josh set the box on the table like someone laying down an injured child. Then he turned toward Rolo, fists raised.

"Whoa, whoa, whoa! Guys, calm down," I rushed to intervene. Manny also stepped between Josh and my roommate. That was a good thing – nobody could hit Manny, he was such a nice guy. But then, Josh's face was flushed purple. I'd never seen him so angry.

"What happened?"

"He threw my cake into the street!" Josh yelled.

Rolo threw up his hands.

"I did not! I threw it on the sidewalk...I mean, I dropped it on the sidewalk. It's not completely ruined..."

Gingerly, Manny lifted the lid on the crumpled box. Half the cake came with it, stuck to the top as it was from being dropped upside down. Rolo was right – the cake wasn't completely ruined, it was just 99% ruined. It looked like it had been run over by a chiva bus.

I glared at my roommate.

"Mike!" he protested. "I didn't do it on purpose! Elena's down there!"

"What! Elena?!"

Instinctively I ducked and looked toward the door, then the TV stand – my favorite hiding spot.

"We were carrying the cake over from next door," he explained while Josh fumed. "It's big – look, even smashed it's big. Neither one of us wanted to carry it alone so we each had an end. We get outside, cross the driveway, I'm just coming over the curb to the door, when BAM! Out of nowhere, I hear this husky voice say, '*Guapo, guapo, sea mi sapo.*' Then she jumps out from behind the pillar. I freaked!"

"You're damned right, you freaked!" Josh exclaimed. "You threw my cake eight feet in the air!"

"She's a psycho!" Rolo yelled back.

"Who's *she*?" Billie asked. "Who are you talking about?"

"Mike's psycho girlfriend."

"Your *what*?" Billie demanded. Faster than the eye could follow she put her glass down and adopted the angry-woman pose, hands on hips, eyes afire.

"She's not my girlfriend!" I insisted. "She's just mad because I wouldn't have sex with her!"

That turned out to be a poor defense. Every face in the room, male and female, found the excuse hard to swallow. Jem perked up his ears.

"Can I meet her?" he asked.

"No!"

"You have a girlfriend?" Billie repeated.

"No!"

"Then why did Rolo say you did?"

"It's *his* girlfriend!" I insisted. "I gave her to him a long time ago."

Rolo shook his head and waved his arms. "Mike's seen her naked," he said by way of defense.

"Could we just get back to the cake?" I pleaded.

"Yes, *my* cake," Josh wailed. "The one he trashed!" He pointed an accusing finger at my roommate.

"I'm sorry," Rolo repeated.

Josh was so distraught he couldn't hear the apology. He leaned over the *tres leches,* overcome with emotion. "This was my dessert. I just wanted to bring dessert. It's Christmas. You've taken my Christmas..."

"Come on, Josh," Manny urged. "There, there...

"Yeah, dude," Lowell called from the back of the crowd, "It's not like he ran over Tiny Tim."

Josh's head snapped up.

"...and it cost me seventy-five dollars!" he yelled back.

He rushed at Rolo and once again Manny and I had our hands full keeping them apart. With help we got them separated but then I was left figuring how to repair the evening. What was there to say?

Walt's wife filled the breach. Sarah was a health nut who lived on tofu, wheat germ, and herbs she grew in her kitchen. It was common knowledge that she wouldn't touch sugar even if the Pillsbury Doughboy held a gun to her head. Her body was a temple. But now she walked over to the cake box and lifted the lid.

We watched as she took a knife and carefully scraped the top half of the *tres leches* back into place. Then she carved the box itself so the crumpled pieces wouldn't interfere with serving. With deft movements we never expected from someone who ate alfalfa sprouts, she reformed the original oval shape of the cake so that the crushed parts almost looked like part of the design. Loose crumbs were molded into the center. Pools of cream she scooped back into the cracks. Nobody said a word. Josh's fists began to unclench.

There was no way to recover the mashed words *Feliz Navidad* but Sarah painstakingly rehabilitated the frosting around the crown of the top layer well enough to get *liz vida.* Then she stabilized the cave-in at the bottom where the cake hit the street. Surprised – and caught up in the good will of her efforts – we stood quietly and watched her work. When she was finished you could have stood five feet from the table and never known anything had happened.

Finally she cut a small piece of cake from the most dented side and put it on a paper plate. Milk oozed from the frosting under pressure from the knife. Then she cut a much larger piece and handed that one to T.J. Together they took forks and held the plates out for all to see.

"Merry Christmas, T.J.," she said.

"Back at you, lady," he replied, eagerly eyeing his gift.

Simultaneously they tasted Josh's masterpiece. Everyone held their breath.

"Delicious," she pronounced.

"Damn, that's good," T.J. agreed.

A sigh escaped from the crowd. The tension in the air evaporated.

"Then let's eat," Kurt advised, pushing his way to the table. "After all it's been through let's put this thing out of its misery."

"Yeah," someone agreed. "And we want to do it before that chick gets up here and kills Mike."

Everyone surged forward to have dessert. Everyone except for Billie who grabbed my arm and spun me around.

"I'm waiting," she warned. "For an explanation."

"You won't believe me," I told her. "Talk to Rolo."

"No. I want to hear it from you. Then I'll talk to your roommate. You're right, I won't believe you but this way if you perjure yourself I'll castrate you with that cake knife."

I took her into the kitchen and told her the whole story. She listened quietly, keeping her arms crossed and watching my face carefully for any of the sweating, twitching, or wandering eyes that were my tell-tale signs of lying. When I finished she left the kitchen and buttonholed Rolo for his version.

"Hey," said Evan, coming through the swinging door. "So what's with this security guard?"

"Forget it, Evan," I cautioned. "You don't want any part of her. She carries a gun and she's nuts. Didn't you hear what Rolo said?"

Evan sniggered. "Why do you think we're interested?"

"We?"

Jem popped up behind him. "Yeah, we! Us!"

"She's psycho," I repeated.

"But will she do a threesome?" Evan wanted to know.

"And," Jem added, "does she take it in the can?"

"I don't know!"

They turned and high-fived each other.

"Well, we are going to find out!"

They performed a white-boy-overbite dance with each other, anticipating their conquest.

"Go armed," I suggested and left the room. At the dinner table Walt handed me a beer. He stood against the wall with an instamatic camera.

"Merry Panamanian Christmas," he said.

"Back at you."

"You know, Mike," he said. "You're fitting right into this crazy country."

"I wouldn't say that."

"No, you are. I was worried about you when you showed up but you've taken to the mayhem down here like a fish to water." He paused to snap a shot of Tommy Goode with his arm around Charlie Manson's wife. Because Tommy's girlfriend was insanely jealous, Walt could trade the photo later for a flight.

"I almost crashed my plane yesterday, this is my fifth home in six months, and a local woman is trying to kill me," I pointed out.

"That's what I mean. You're blending right in. Which reminds me: Harry mentioned the other day that he's looking for a pilot. You know Harry, right? He needs somebody who can fly in bad weather. I gave him your name."

"What does he need a pilot for?" I asked. "To go back out to San Telmo?"

Walt sipped his beer and readied his camera as he watched Evan and Jem try to talk Billie into drinking a beer while they held her upside down. "No. He said something about stealing a plane."

"*Stealing* a plane?" I waited for the punch line but none came. Walt acknowledged my silence with a confident nod.

"Don't complain, Mike. It's been a whole day since you last almost killed yourself. By the time New Year's rolls around you'll be looking for a new adventure just to keep from being bored."

Skinny Steve shouted from the window just then. Looking down at the street below he watched a Panamanian in a Land Cruiser back into his Pathfinder, then park and walk away without so much as leaving a note. With a whoop of excitement, Steve dashed for the elevator. As the music on the stereo switched from salsa to a Spanish version of *Silent Night*, the rest of us heard the sound of sheet metal crumpling as Steve put his truck in four-wheel drive and floored it into the offender.

I surveyed the room, filled with all those people who I would not soon forget. It was a Panamanian Christmas alright, and for all that Walt was right. I couldn't complain.

ABOUT THE AUTHOR

Michael Bleriot is a military and civilian pilot. He has flown over 4,000 hours in two dozen aircraft, including over a thousand hours in the C-27.

Made in the USA
Charleston, SC
08 June 2012